Stories from a Siberian Village

Northern

Illinois

University

Press

DeKalb

1996

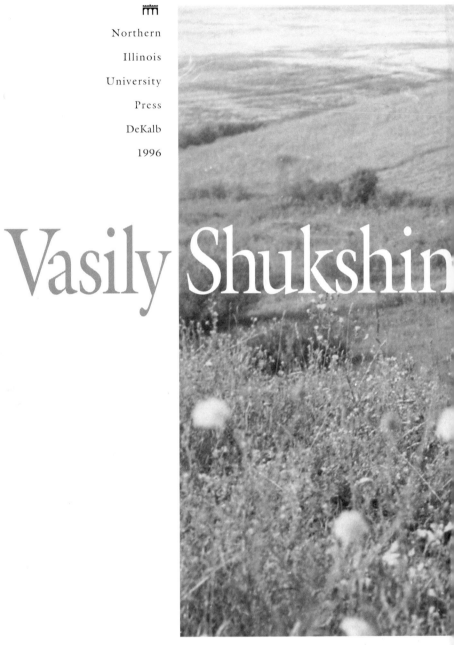

Vasily Shukshin

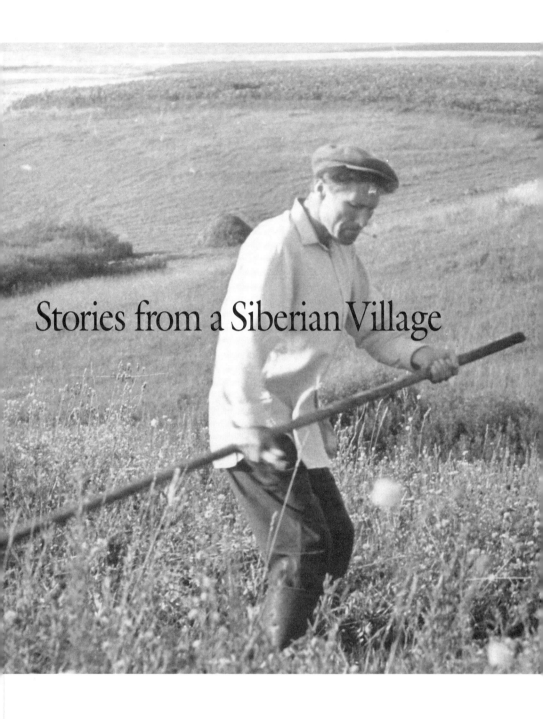

Stories from a Siberian Village

Translated by Laura Michael and John Givens

Foreword by Kathleen Parthé

© 1996

by Northern Illinois University Press

Published by the Northern Illinois

University Press, DeKalb, Illinois   60115

Manufactured in the United States

using acid-free paper

Design by Julia Fauci

∞

Library of Congress

Cataloging-in-Publication Data

Shukshin, Vasiliĭ

[Short stories. English. Selections]

Stories from a Siberian village /

Vasily Shukshin ; translated by Laura Michael

and John Givens ;

preface by Kathleen Parthé.

p.   cm.

ISBN 0-87580-211-7 (cloth—alk. paper).—

ISBN 0-87580-572-8 (pbk.—alk. paper)

1. Shukshin, Vasiliĭ Makarovich—

Translations into English.

I. Givens, John. II. Michael, Laura. III. Title.

PG3487.U5A26   1996

891.73'44—dc20

95-46643

CIP

The cover and title page photographs of

Vasily Shukshin were selected and provided

by Mark Volotsky, Director of the Gorky

Flim Studio Museum in Moscow.

Dedicated to our parents

Sandra Michael,

Gary Michael,

Marian and Calvin Schwenk,

and the memory of Rex D. Givens

Contents

Shukshin at Large

Kathleen Parthé

When I began my own work on Russian Village Prose, I expected to give a prominent place in my research to stories by the ever popular Vasily Shukshin. But the more I fine-tuned my characterization of this literary movement, the more elusive a figure Shukshin proved to be. Try as I would, my list of parameters—based on the works of dozens of rural writers—never allowed me to hold on to Shukshin for very long. I finally gave up and contented myself with a caveat in the preface, warning readers not to be shocked by Shukshin's virtual absence from the book that followed.[1] They were shocked anyway, because Shukshin would seem at first glance to be a charter member of the *derevenshchiki* (writers of Village Prose).

Shukshin and his characters do indeed come from the Russian village and often return there to live (some never left in the first place, except, perhaps, for military service). They are not ashamed of their country background and are hurt by the dismissive attitude of city folk toward them, and they worry about whether their children will be lured away to a life in the city. But Shukshin provides many more points of contrast than resemblance to post-Stalinist rural literature. For instance, while he favors as his protagonists adult males who work as truck drivers or in some other nonagricultural occupation, and who live for their leisure hours, for their personal *prazdnik* (holiday, in an emotional sense), Village Prose focuses on old women and children and on the dignity of agricultural labor. While Shukshin's characters live for the nights and weekends, the inhabitants of Village Prose are much more oriented toward the daily routine (what Russians call *byt*). The setting in Shukshin is a village, settlement, or town, but rarely the specific native region *(malaya rodina)* of the derevenshchiki, which is nearly always marked as being in a particular section of central or northern Russia, or Siberia, and whose political, cultural, and ethnographic history is often given in great detail.

Another significant contrast is the fact that Village Prose stakes a great deal on traditional Russian ideas of group behavior, not so much the *sobornost* (conciliar spirit) of Russian Orthodoxy, but a more domestic village collectivity in which the combined efforts of villagers is what ensures survival. A single peasant is a member of many groups: of the living family, of the *rod* (everyone you are related to, past, present, future), and of the village. The idea of collective behavior covers not only work but also leisure time. Holidays are meant to be group celebrations, and in general, individual initiative is not particularly encouraged. In *Harmony,* Vasily Belov's ethnography of the village, the author stresses that no one really admired a peasant-Stakhanovite, because peasants had to conserve their strength during slack periods to get through the several very busy times of the year.[2]

In story after story, Shukshin's characters prove themselves to be loners by choice. Their ideal is to get away from everyone else, to spend their spare time luxuriating alone in the *banya* (bathhouse) all day Saturday, or to gather together with just a few friends to drink and talk, and their conversations can take a very serious, philosophical turn. They are peasants with the nervous systems of intellectuals. Rather than bowing to accepted wisdom, Shukshin's people challenge it at every turn, if only to prove that they are truly alive (not unlike Dostoevsky's "underground man" who recognized the human need to occasionally declare that $2 \times 2 = 5$, just to preserve one's psychological freedom). In a Shukshin story, the main character is more than likely to be a bit of an oddball. In this and many other senses, Geoffrey Hosking's subtle characterization of Shukshin as standing "rather to one side of the 'village prose' school" works for the characters as well as for their creator.[3]

Shukshin views the village and its inhabitants with an affection that has a very ironic resonance; he is more interested in cranks and eccentrics than in the "righteous ones" so dear to writers of Village Prose, and a good *skandal* is more to his taste than lamentations over the end of traditional village harmony.[4] It was the ironic stance of Shukshin's narrators that brought him to the attention of leading Russian critics like Marietta Chudakova, who saw in this stance Shukshin's resemblance to "youth prose" writers of the 1960s (e.g., Vasily Aksyonov and Vladimir Voinovich).[5]

It was only in 1985, eleven years after Shukshin's death, and after Village Prose as a movement had faded, that erstwhile derevenshchiki began to sound more like Shukshin. Valentin Rasputin's "The Fire" ("Pozhar," 1985) and Viktor Astafiev's "The Sad Detective" ("Pechal'nyi detektiv," 1986) and "Liudochka" (1989), as well as other stories from this period, left the past-oriented village for the starkly realistic present and a more urban setting.[6] Their characters, like Shukshin's of the 1960s and 1970s, were caught between city and village, awkward, unhappy, and nowhere completely at home, with little solace for their aching souls. But Shukshin's gentle irony was replaced in these newer works by something sharper and humorless, virtually free of any possibility of redemption, save by means so drastic as to be untenable to most readers. The glasnost-era stories had a definite agenda, something that is missing in Shukshin, whose works lobbied only for *volya* (personal, rather than political, freedom) and for more time for the spirit to rest from life's exigencies.

Shukshin for the most part successfully negotiated the traps set for independently minded writers in Russian literature; he was able to play—and be—both the clever peasant and a remarkably quick study of urban literary and cinematic mores. What he could not foresee were the dangers his reputation might face after he died, not immediately, but in the turbulent years since 1985. The writer and his literary legacy have been misread in at least three different—and mutually exclusive—ways: (1) as survival-at-a-price; (2) as an example of the no longer relevant nonconformity of the 1960s; and (3) as a Russian martyrdom at the hands of *chuzhie* (people alien to Russian culture).

The initial period of euphoria at the onset of glasnost soon gave way to a rereading of the literary past, which often took the form of an analysis of behavior and a settling of scores. Because of the stark contrast between the power crudely wielded by members of the Writers' Union hierarchy, and the enormous suffering inflicted on some of Russia's most talented literary figures, an equation was established in some quarters between success and compromise. There was a tendency to collapse all works published in the Soviet Union into one canon of compromise and evasion. The words of poet Osip Mandelstam—one of Stalinism's most poignant victims—resonated in posttotalitarian Russia: "I divide all works of world literature into those written with and without permission. The first are trash, the second—stolen air."[7] As a writer who published officially rather than in the samizdat underground, who made films in state-run studios (the only way to make films in those days), and who joined the Party in 1955, Shukshin by default was included in the group of slightly tarnished survivors whose willingness to make adjustments in order to reach a wide audience stood in stark contrast to those who refused—often at a very high price—to participate in a government- and Party-regulated culture. The question was raised whether Shukshin ought to be remembered as a craven opportunist or as a somewhat less culpable "permitted anomaly."[8]

To the stigma of survival was added the onus of sudden irrelevance, mainly at the hands of younger critics and writers who began around 1990 to stake out their own territory in Russian literature by adapting a remarkably nihilistic attitude toward the literature of the Soviet period. Writers who were published in the Soviet Union during the "period of stagnation" (1964–1984) were collapsed into one tacitly (or openly) opportunistic group, and in a similar maneuver, those who were *not* published widely in Russia until after 1985 were reduced to a category of political dissidents, for whom aesthetics is always a secondary consideration. Shukshin loses either way, whether one emphasizes how much he was able to publish, or how much of his work was censored or held back. By leveling the landscape, critics and writers are able to find a place for themselves as having, in retrospect, been "in opposition not only to Soviet power but to dissidents as well."[9]

The final danger Shukshin has faced is of being turned into another Boris and Gleb (the earliest Russian martyrs) by contemporary right-wing nationalists.[10] The tendency in Russian culture since the death of Pushkin in 1837 has been to invest writers who died early and/or tragically with the same crown of martyrdom for Russia formerly reserved for religious figures or tsars. In the years after 1985, this tactic was increasingly used by the nationalist right in its campaign to prove that Russia had long been under a virtually genocidal attack by sinister forces, and that one of the most effective strategies of these cultural "wreckers" (to use a Stalinist term) was to destroy the nation's leading writers. Writers who died in duels (Pushkin, Lermontov) are depicted as victims of "cosmopolitan plots," while those who committed suicide (Esenin, Mayakovsky) or died of illness (Blok, Gorky) are said to have been murdered. At first, Shukshin's death was simply attributed to stress caused by the enemies of "genuine" Russian literature, but at least in some quarters, the murder theory has gained credence, and was presented by some of his Moscow acquaintances as an undisputed—if little known—fact at a celebration in July 1994 of what would have been the writer's sixty-fifth birthday, in his Siberian home town of Srostki.[11]

While the reader of the present volume might not be obsessed with the question of where Shukshin fits or does not fit in Russian literary history, it was only in accepting that he is not primarily a derevenshchik, that I was able to realize that his is an utterly distinctive voice that defies all efforts to place it in any context other than its own. As I read through these stories once more, I was reminded at times of Pushkin, Turgenev, Dostoevsky, Tolstoy, and Chekhov, as well as a number of twentieth-century writers, both rural and urban. But one rarely gets the feeling that Shukshin is seriously imitating another writer's style or borrowing a plot, if for no other reason than that he was not as avid a reader of the Russian classics as one might expect. His sources were generally more popular, for example, Russian folklore and the narratives and conversations he heard not through the mediation of literature, but firsthand. This gives Shukshin's work a much rougher—and often fresher—feel than one might be accustomed to. Sometimes his stories are tightly structured, and sometimes they just sort of wander off at the end, like a storyteller who forgets the point of what he is saying and decides to stop without really resolving anything.

The more distinctive an author's style, the harder it is to preserve both meaning and atmosphere in translation, but a gifted translator enables a literary work to move to another linguistic and cultural setting without the constant and awkward feeling of foreignness. The English versions that John Givens and Laura Michael have crafted are truly impressive because through them Shukshin's stories *live*—we can hear the characters laugh, cry, whine, moan, and complain about their aching souls and, in numerous other ways, make themselves heard. While the Russianness of these characters is in no way diminished, they are now so at home in English that their inherent universality comes across very strongly. They remind me of colorful people I have met or heard about over the years, especially one fellow, lovingly remembered as "Black Jack" Lustgarten, who understood perfectly the Shukshinian need of a holiday for the soul. When not at work, Jack might be found enjoying himself at a neighborhood bar while his five-year-old grandson, perched high on a bar stool, thoughtfully sipped a root beer. On Sundays, Jack delighted in having the entire extended family sitting around the dinner table telling stories that were valued much more for their color than for their accuracy. But if someone cut him off while driving, Jack was capable of chasing the guy all the way from Brooklyn to New Jersey, and he liked those people who annoyed him to think that he owned a gun. Like Shukshin's heroes, he knew his own worth, and, like Shukshin, he died too soon, leaving a lot of great stories untold. Most readers of this book will find themselves supplementing Shukshin's gallery with their own memorable people, which makes reading these stories an even more enjoyable—and moving—experience.

Shukshin has been too long absent from the body of Russian literature easily available in English. While the relatively few earlier translations were good, these versions are even better, and many of the stories are translated for the first time. Framed by John Givens's lively and very informative introduction—a hint of what his forthcoming book on Vasily Shukshin will cover—this is a volume that I have read with pleasure and recommend with enthusiasm.

Notes

1. Kathleen Parthé, *Russian Village Prose: The Radiant Past* (Princeton: Princeton University Press, 1992).

2. Vasilii Belov, *Lad: Ocherki o narodnoi estetike* (Moscow: Molodaia gvardiia, 1982); this book has been reprinted in an expanded form since 1985 (Moscow: Molodaia guardiia, 1989).

3. Geoffrey Hosking, "The Twentieth Century: In Search of New Ways, 1933–80," in *The Cambridge History of Russian Literature,* ed. Charles Moser (Cambridge: Cambridge University Press, 1989), 565–66.

4. Hosking defines *skandal* as "a conflict which brings to the surface deep and wounding feelings," ibid., 565.

5. Marietta Chudakova, "Notes on the Language of Contemporary Prose," [no translator listed], *Soviet Studies in Literature* 9, no. 1 (Winter 1972–1973): 37–112. The article originally appeared in *Novyi mir* 1972, no. 1: 212–45.

6. Rasputin's story has been translated by Gerald Mikkelson and Margaret Winchell and appears in their collection of Rasputin stories called *Siberia on Fire* (DeKalb, Ill.: Northern Illinois University Press, 1989).

7. Osip Mandelstam, "The Fourth Prose" (written 1928–1930), in *The Noise of Time,* trans. Clarence Brown (San Francisco: North Point Press, 1986), 181. For a more extended discussion of the politics of literary survival, see Kathleen Parthé, "What *Was* Soviet Literature?" the concluding piece of a forum called "Russian Literature in the Soviet Period: On the Margins of Literary History," *Slavic and East European Journal* 38, no. 2 (Summer 1994): 290–301.

8. Russian structuralists, in reference to pre-Petrine literature, spoke of a "cultural canon" and a "zone of permitted anomalies, exceptions to the rules." Jurij Lotman and Boris Uspenskij, "New Aspects of Early Russian Literature," trans. N. F. C. Owen, in *The Semiotics of Russian Culture,* ed. Ann Shukman, Michigan Slavic Contributions, no. 11 (Ann Arbor: Department of Slavic Languages and Literatures, University of Michigan, 1984), 38. What they said of this earlier period is true of the Soviet era as well, especially the post-Stalinist years.

9. Writer Dmitrii Prigov, as quoted by David Remnick, in "Letter from Moscow. Exit the Saints," *New Yorker* 70, no. 21 (18 July 1994): 57.

10. For an analysis of this phenomenon, see Kathleen Parthé, "The Empire Strikes Back: How Right-Wing Nationalists Tried to Recapture Russian Literature," *Nationalities Papers* (forthcoming).

11. I am indebted to John Givens for sharing with me a letter written to him and Laura Michael from a leading Shukshin scholar, Svetlana Mikhailovna Kozlova, describing the absurd and depressing aspects of this event.

Vasily Shukshin
A Storyteller's Story

JOHN GIVENS

Legend

Vasily Shukshin's three-thousand-mile journey from a Siberian backwater all the way to Moscow—where he became a phenomenally successful writer, movie director, and actor—stands as the central motif of his life. It has become part of the writer's legend, one told even before Shukshin's premature death at the age of forty-five. The legend—with its appropriately folkloric overtones—goes something like this. Once upon a time, an ambitious Siberian peasant decides to make a name for himself in the distant capital of his country. His poor, long-suffering, twice-widowed mother bursts into tears over the prospect of losing her only son. She begs him to stay and work the land like the other peasant boys do, but he is adamant. She eventually gives in to his wishes, sells the family cow, gives her son the money, blesses him, and sends him on his way. After a long journey, and with only military fatigues for clothes, the peasant lad appears on the threshold of one of the most prestigious schools in the capital. Raising eyebrows by his appearance in the palatial halls of the school, enduring the taunts of the sons of the local nobility, the peasant lad successfully passes a variety of tests and wins the right to appear before a tribunal of elders who will decide his ultimate fate. Hoping to trick him into a disqualifying answer, the tribunal asks him provocative questions about his peasant heritage. Our hero, however, understands their game and plays the role of the sly peasant, delighting the one elder sympathetic to his cause and winning the day.

As in many legends, success and fortune follow. The only thing that is missing from the fairy tale is a long life and happiness. In this respect, Vasily Shukshin's biography is as sad as any Russian play. A legend, of course, can be understood in two ways: as a folk story about a real person, or as a key or a map to a person's life and art. In Shukshin's case, the folktale itself suggests a key to unlocking the important issues of his biography and works. This key is the distance—geographic, cultural, and political—that lies between Shukshin's early life in the Altai region of western Siberia and Moscow, where he came into fame and spent most of his adult life.

The legend related above had its origins in the ecstatic reviews of his first film, *Zhivet takoi paren'* (*There Lives This Guy*, 1964), in which Shukshin's successful debut as a director was seen as the outcome of the unlikely path he had traveled to become a filmmaker. Shukshin was praised as a self-made man: an ordinary Siberian of peasant descent and a latecomer to the world of art who had overcome all obstacles through sheer dint of will and originality.[1] Shukshin's friend and fellow Siberian writer Yury Skop later expanded on this common perception of Shukshin in a well-known article in *Literaturnaia gazeta* in 1968. Claiming to be quoting Shukshin, Skop recounts the peasant lad's now legendary appearance in 1954 before the entrance committee at the All-Union State Institute of Cinematography (*Vsesoiuznyi gosudarstvennyi institut kinematografii*, better known by its acronym, VGIK). According to Skop, Shukshin, of necessity wearing his military fatigues at the examination, stood out from his rivals. His strange clothes and his rural accent—all the trappings of an ignorant Siberian hick—supposedly inclined the committee toward treating him less than seriously. Instead of the usual queries, Shukshin was allegedly asked a series of patronizing, mocking questions. One committee member, for instance, asked him to show how a peasant behaves in bitter cold. Shukshin stomped his feet, patted himself, and shivered, but forgot, as his interrogator pointed out, to make his nostrils stick together from the cold. Another committee member supposedly asked Shukshin whether he knew where the nineteenth-century Russian literary critic Vissarion Belinsky was currently living, to which Shukshin allegedly answered: "You mean, the critic? Ain't he already kicked the bucket or something?"[2]

In Nicholas Galichenko's account of the examination, Shukshin was ignorant of Tolstoy's works. When the committee next asked Shukshin whether he had ever heard of the famous nineteenth-century civic poet Nikolai Nekrasov, Shukshin supposedly answered in a rage: "I had a few drinks with him. He was a personal acquaintance."[3] Soviet director Alexander Mitta adds in his reminiscences that Mikhail Romm, the well-known Soviet filmmaker who led the VGIK studio where Shukshin eventually studied, asked the applicant during the committee's examination whether he had ever read *War and Peace*. "No," Shukshin is said to have answered with a pun, "it's a very thick *[tolstaya]* book."[4] In all of these accounts, Shukshin's nerve and ability to play along with the patronizing provocation of the committee were enough to carry the day.

Nearly everyone who mentions some variant of this legend implies that it helps us to understand the personality or the works of the writer. Critic Lev Anninsky was the first to view Shukshin's appearance before the entrance committee as an exercise in mutual provocation and improvisation.[5] Those who repeat one or another version of this tale, however, have rarely commented on the implications that this "creation myth" holds for Shukshin and his art, nor has anyone been too careful as to which particular account is privileged. Other factors that may have played a role in Shukshin's acceptance into VGIK—such as the quota guaranteeing a place to a certain number of applicants of rural or proletarian origin,[6] or Shukshin's candidate membership in the Communist Party[7]—are ignored as they lie outside the parameters of the legend. Few mention the written and oral examinations Shukshin had to pass before being allowed to appear for his final interview with the selection committee. Instead, a narrative suggesting the sly peasant winning over his cultured city antagonists by exaggerating the liabilities of his rural background is the version preferred by friends, biographers, and critics.

Even Shukshin's own version of this event, first published in 1969, encourages such an interpretation:

> [The committee] was stunned by whom Mikhail Ilich [Romm] had recruited. After all, I noticeably stuck out from the others around me by my Neanderthal backwardness and uncouthness. The chair of the committee asked ironically:
> "Have you heard of Belinsky?"
> "Yes," I said.
> "Where does he live?"
> Everyone in the committee fell silent.
> "Vissarion Grigorievich? He kicked the bucket," I said and began to prove with unruly fervor how Belinsky had "kicked the bucket."[8]

Despite the hyperbole that has accompanied the VGIK episode, this part of his biographical legend nevertheless does seem to contain some essential truths about Shukshin the writer and about the cultural-social environment he sought to enter. At that time in Russia, VGIK was second only to the Gorky Institute of World Literature in its reputation as a center of the Soviet intellectual and social elite.[9] Shukshin, with his odd attire, rural accent, spotty education, and Siberian peasant heritage, must have felt woefully out of his element. VGIK students "represented the cream of Soviet society" and were often "the progeny of highly placed bureaucrats and established cultural figures."[10] In letters home dating from his institute years, Shukshin spoke about his fellow classmates as the children of "writers, actors, executives."[11] Shukshin, on the other hand, was born and raised in a muddy Siberian village, the son of "an enemy of the people." His father was executed during the rural purges in 1933, either for "sabotage in the kolkhoz" or for "inciting an uprising."[12] These facts changed Shukshin's life and engendered an identity crisis that the writer would never quite overcome, a crisis made all the more acute by his mother Maria Sergeevna's decision to renounce, for the sake of her family, her husband's name, taking her maiden name, Popova, after her husband's arrest. Thus, until he turned sixteen and applied for his internal passport, Shukshin was Vasily Makarovich Popov. The name appears conspicuously in an autobiographical cycle of stories (included in this collection) on which the writer worked from 1968 until his death six years later. In "From the Childhood Years of Ivan Popov," the first-person narrator refers to himself and his sister as *vrazhenyata* (children of the enemy). Thus, it is likely that the inferiority complex that marked Shukshin's entrance into the world of letters was not only a result of the physical, cultural, and social distance between Siberia and Moscow; it was also a corollary of the pall of illegitimacy under which Shukshin grew up and lived as the son of an "enemy of the people." Although Shukshin's father was posthumously rehabilitated in 1956, the marginalization the writer experienced during the first twenty-seven years of his life continued to find expression in his short stories and novels. Makar Shukshin makes his shadowy appearance among fathers who rebel against the new Soviet order (in Book One of Shukshin's novel, *The Lyubavin Family),* among fathers who leave for the camps and certain death (in Book Two of *The Lyubavin Family),* and among fathers who return from the camps (in Shukshin's story "Priezzhii" [The new arrival]). He can also be seen in the seventeenth-century Cossack father and rebellious champion of the peasantry, Stepan Razin (from Shukshin's story "Stenka Razin," and in Shukshin's novel, *Ia prishel dat' vam voliu* [I have come to give you freedom]). The "father" theme—part of the broader polemic between center and periphery that informs Shukshin's life and works—has yet to be seriously mined for its obvious contribution to the Shukshin legend.

Shukshin's realization of the great distance separating him from the other VGIK students can be detected even in a paper he wrote as part of the entrance process. The essay, which Shukshin titled "Whales, or How We Joined the Ranks of Artists,"[13] was supposed to describe the corridors of the institute during exam week. Shukshin chose instead to paint what one critic calls "a rather caustic portrait" of the elitist Muscovite kids who had an "insider's" familiarity with the world of cinema and the institute.[14] In his essay, Shukshin addressed an issue that would resonate throughout his creative career, not only the genuine social dichotomy he observed at VGIK, but also the subtler juxtaposition of cultural values he witnessed around him. What was born in the clash between the heritage of Shukshin's *malaya rodina* (native region) and the background of his urban competitors was more than just a gnawing sense of inferiority and embarrassment. It gave birth to his unique artistic diction as well, which was markedly different from the smooth talk of his fellow VGIK applicants. This idiom had its roots in the folk dialects of the Altai and stood in stark contrast to the "cultured" but affected words that, according to Shukshin's essay, "sprinkled like peas" from the lips of his classmates. Shukshin's recognition of his native artistic diction, however, did not come quickly:

> I was ashamed of my rural dialect, the words I was used to but that no one spoke here. And, in order not to stick out, I even tried for a while to relearn how to speak and to express myself just like all the well-read, educated Moscow kids.
>
> I remember this agonizing period. My own self-ridicule, my own shame that I was mutilating, mangling my thought because I was mangling my words. And when I had gotten through this awful school of speaking in an alien tongue, I hated both myself and others who did the same thing. And for the rest of my life I hated any affected manner of expression.[15]

The differences between the substandard dialect and culture of his Siberian village and the language and culture of the Moscow intellectual and social elite forced upon Shukshin the status of the "other," the outsider, an identity Shukshin would make good use of as an artist but one that would also take its toll on the writer.

Leonid Kuravlyov, a VGIK classmate who later starred in Shukshin's first two films, described Shukshin's early years in the capital in the following way:

> Not too long ago a critic wrote that at first Shukshin felt himself to be a pariah at VGIK, which was true.
>
> It seemed to him that people here were from some other sphere than he, a native of the village of Srostki in the Altai. That, by just his very appearance at VGIK, he had introduced a loud dissonance into some sort of long-established traditions. That he represented an outsider.
>
> He clearly sensed all of this, without a doubt. Hence his shyness—to the point of sickness and tremors, I would say.[16]

This dissonance, however, was encouraged by Romm in his VGIK studio, whose star pupil was the future internationally acclaimed filmmaker Andrei Tarkovsky. Tarkovsky, born into an old intelligentsia family, was one of the bright and talented Moscow dandies (the Russian term is *stilyaga*) who doubtless set Shukshin's teeth on edge at their first meeting in Romm's studio.[17] According to Romm, Tarkovsky and Shukshin were "a direct antithesis to each other and didn't like each other very well," a situation that was, however, "very useful to the studio. . . . Many talented people grouped themselves around them. Not around them, I'll say, but thanks to their presence."[18] As Neya Zorkaya comments, Tarkovsky and Shukshin "presented two sides of the artistic Russian character, two poles of the national talent, one contributing a sophisticated means of expression and the other a geniune folk spirit and close links to the people."[19]

Shukshin's rivalry with Tarkovsky confirms the polemical nature of his development as an artist. The clash between Shukshin's "genuine folk spirit" and the sophisticated artistry of Tarkovsky and other VGIK students became the fire in which Shukshin forged his artistic identity. It was at VGIK that Shukshin came to understand and fully appreciate the rich folk culture he knew from life in the village. His use of simple, dialectal turns of speech belonging to his own Siberian family and neighbors allowed him, in one critic's assessment, "to reintroduce into Russian letters a variety of style unknown since the formulation of the tenets of socialist realism in the early 1930s."[20] The simplicity, unaffectedness, and authenticity of his characters' rural speech was a breath of fresh country air in the capital's literary journals and set Shukshin apart from other writers. Linguistically, Shukshin and his texts remained in the provinces.

This feeling of provinciality and the sense of inferiority and insecurity that accompanied it haunted the writer throughout his brief career. When in 1974 Shukshin looked back on his years at VGIK, he admitted that he had come to the institute "a profoundly provincial person remote from art. It seemed to me," he continued,

> that this was apparent to everyone. I had come too late to the institute—at twenty-five both my learning and my knowledge were relative. I had a hard time studying. Extremely hard. I accumulated knowledge in piecemeal fashion and with gaps. Besides that, I had to find out what everybody else already knew and what I had passed over in life. And after a while I began to hide, I guess, my growing strength. And, strange as it may seem, in some twisted and unexpected way, I would arouse in others the certainty that, yes, they were the ones who should be artists, and not me. But I knew, knew beforehand, that I would lie in wait for the moment when . . . well, when I would turn out to be more solid, and they with their endless pronouncements about art, would turn out to be less so. All the time I concealed within me from the eyes of others an unknown person, some sort of secret warrior, an undeciphered person.

"Just imagine," he concluded, "it's sort of a stupid thing, but it always seems to me that they should refuse me this—my right to be an artist."[21] To realize that Shukshin said this at the height of his popularity as a writer, actor, and director tells us a great deal about the seriousness of his provincial complex.

Although the intellectual circles in which he moved in Moscow refined and educated him to a degree, we can see traces of this complex in the sometimes rough, self-conscious, aggressive tone of Shukshin's stories and essays.

A certain rudeness, impertinence, and audacity seem to lurk just beneath the surface of the writer's personality, a desire to provoke others and to do away with polite fictions. The poet Bella Akhmadulina remembers how unsociable and quiet Shukshin was in the apartments of Moscow intellectuals in the mid-sixties. He would sit "somber and shy, not responding to polite inquiries . . . his untamed, willful gaze flashing from time to time while dirty snow melted in puddles around his boots." These knee-high rural boots, Akhmadulina explains, were not the only footwear he happened to own but rather were "a sign, a confirmation of his moral and geographic allegiance, a declaration of his disdain for other customs and conventions."[22]

Like so many of his characters, Shukshin was in his own right a bit of a village eccentric capable of odd actions and acts of rebellion. It is hardly surprising that the misadventures of the hero of Shukshin's story "Oddball" are largely autobiographical,[23] or that Shukshin should use his own birthday (July 25) as the date of Bronka Pupkov's incredible attempt on Hitler's life ("Mille Pardons, Madame!") as well as the date of Venya Zyablitsky's "incarceration" of his mother-in-law in an outhouse ("My Son-in-Law Stole a Truck Load of Wood!"). Shukshin clearly felt a strong kinship with these elemental village types who are, at their core, deeply creative folk artists and even philosophers unable always to control their emotions. Such was Shukshin himself, from his well-documented drunken brawls with the police[24] to the time he convinced an airport authority to let him and a reporter stand in for no-show flight attendants so that they could make their final connection on a trip back to Siberia.[25]

The Russian title of Shukshin's story "Oddball" *(chudik)* denotes both wonder and strangeness and captures an important aspect of Shukshin's characters and the world they inhabit: they are the quirky inhabitants of an incomprehensible universe, arbitrarily governed but wondrous nonetheless, at once a source of creation and an inspiration for creativity. His heroes—like those of writer Mikhail Zoshchenko, to whom he is sometimes compared—are yesterday's peasants who are still learning to speak and act like people do in the newspapers, radio, and television, in short, like city dwellers. Shukshin's stories—like those of the writer Andrei Platonov—chronicle how this linguistic and cultural transformation (engendered by political changes and the bureaucratization of all spheres of life) can distort human personalities and lead to bitter misunderstandings and explosive clashes. In this context, the geography that informs Shukshin's life and stories is not one tied to ethnically or ecologically specific features. Rather, it is the distance—sometimes great, sometimes very small—that lies between the village and the urban centers. Whether that space must be traversed by plane (such as the terrifying four-hour flight that kept Granny Malanya from visiting her son in Moscow in the story "Country Folk") or by bus (as in "Vanka Teplyashin"), the consequences are equally weighty for the villager making the journey.

Shukshin's negotiation of that distance rightfully stands at the center of the writer's legend and is likely a major source for the writer's talk about an "unknown, undeciphered" alter ego. This "other person" that Shukshin kept buried within appears to be a direct outcome of what one critic claims was Shukshin's desire "to preserve for himself the right to a certain amount of provincial 'autonomy.'"[26] It is precisely this provincial autonomy that emerges as the lesson of the Shukshin myth. A peasant by birthright and the son of a purged kulak, Shukshin was independent and class-conscious to his dying day. High-strung and unpredictable, he presented a disturbing figure to many in the capital. "It seems to me," Tarkovsky states, "that they expected something dangerous, explosive from him. And so when he died, everyone began to thank him for the fact that this explosion never took place."[27]

Life

Shukshin was born on 25 July 1929, in the village of Srostki, some four hundred miles southeast of Novosibirsk in the west Siberian region of Altai. About his Altai ancestors, Shukshin noted:

> I seldom envy anybody, but I do envy my distant ancestors, their persistence, their great strength. . . . I wouldn't know what to do with such strength now, in our day. I can imagine how difficult it was for them to make their way to the Altai—from the north of Russia, from the Volga and from the Don. I only imagine it, but they made it—on foot. And were it not for our modern distrust of pretty speeches, I would permit myself to say that I bow low to their memory, that I thank them with the most precious word that I have managed to keep in my heart; they found and settled—for themselves and for those who will come after us—a beautiful homeland.[28]

The peasants who made the Altai their home were much better off than their central Russian counterparts. Ever since the region was first settled at the beginning of the eighteenth century, Altai peasants enjoyed a better way of life than did those in European Russia. They paid low land taxes and were allowed more mobility. By the mid-nineteenth century, there existed a whole class of well-to-do peasants known as *starozhily*. These starozhily were able to hire less fortunate, landless new arrivals to the region as day laborers.[29] By 1917, over half of the village of Srostki (224 out of 425 families) belonged to the starozhily, including six of the ten families by the name of Shukshin. The four poorer Shukshin families were recent arrivals from the Samara province. Shukshin's properous great-grandfather Pavel Pavlovich Shukshin, also from Samara, included in his household the family of his youngest son Leonty (Shukshin's grandfather) and Leonty's son, Makar (Shukshin's father, then four years old), as well as his eldest sons Ignaty and Mikhail, all of whom were listed in the 1917 census as starozhily.[30] Thus, at least on his father's side, Shukshin could trace his heritage back to one of the older and better-off families in the village. By the time Soviet power reached these remote corners of Siberia, however, this heritage would have dire consequences for the fate of both Shukshin's father and the writer himself.

Unlike peasants in central Russia, starozhily like the Shukshins had nothing to gain from communism, since they already enjoyed a relatively comfortable life. Although tolerated during Lenin's New Economic Policy of limited private ownership and free-market economics (1921–1928), the starozhily were eventually targeted for elimination as a class by Party activists sent from Moscow. Labeled kulaks and accused of exploiting poorer peasants and resisting Soviet efforts to organize agriculture, the starozhily perished during Stalin's policy of collectivization, begun in 1929, the year Vasily Shukshin was born.

The ironic coincidence of Shukshin's birth with the advent of forced collectivization figures prominently in Shukshin's literary biography. The massive destruction of entire villages and the uprooting of families through inclusion in collective farms *(kolkhozy)* or migration to the cities haunt the histories of Shukshin's characters. Four years into collectivization, Makar Shukshin was arrested; he was either executed shortly thereafter or perished in the labor camps. The fact that Makar had broken with his father and married into one of the poorer families in the village did not spare him from the wave of purges meant to liquidate all vestiges of the prerevolutionary way of life in the village. Shukshin's mother was faced with the difficult task of raising her two children alone (Shukshin's sister, Natalya, was born three years after the writer). Like the Shukshins, Maria Sergeevna's father, Sergei Fyodorovich Popov, and his family had emigrated to the Altai from the Samara province, but they were much later arrivals (they came in 1897) and much poorer.[31] Collectivization may have actually improved the Popovs' lot, but not that of their daughter. Maria Sergeevna was faced with an entirely new and different difficulty, one unknown before the arrival of communist power: that of being the widow of an "enemy of the people."

Nadezhda Alekseevna Yadykina—a contemporary of the writer whose own father disappeared in the same rural purges—relates in her reminiscences of Shukshin how the wives of purge victims were labeled by their neighbors *sebulonki* (a neologism meaning wives of Siberian camp inmates).[32] The children of purged peasants—Shukshin and Yadykina included—were called *deti sebulontsev* (children of Siberian camp inmates). The lot of the sebulonki and their children was a harsh one. Not only did the purges deprive them of their husbands and their fathers, not only were they ostracized by their fellow villagers, but they were also the last in line for such things as communal farming implements and horses, making the daily task of survival even more difficult. Yadykina describes how many of the sebulonki (including Maria Sergeevna and her children) formed a tightly knit group, doing such things together as gathering berries and singing songs (mainly prison songs, two of which figure in Shukshin's prose).[33] These songs, Yadykina indicates, were the spiritual mainstay of the sebulonki.[34] It is also clear that they had a significant impact on Shukshin's own themes.

The injustice that took away his father and the lies that justified such an action help to locate one important source of Shukshin's passionate need to tell the truth, which became the guiding principle for his life as an artist. "I can only tell the truth about life," he wrote. "I cannot do more than that. I consider that the sacred duty of the artist."[35] "Consciously not to tell the truth" was the worst sin a writer could commit, according to Shukshin.[36]

In a later recollection of his youth, Shukshin said that in his home and the homes of his relatives "life was built on a rockbed of truth and justice" and that "the feeling of truth and justice was very highly developed indeed. It is only when people have this feeling that they can live in a meaningful way. This vital law—that truth must be observed—gives a person confidence in the value of his presence on earth."[37] These themes permeate Shukshin's works, especially stories such as "Uncle Yermolai," "My Son-in-Law Stole a Truckload of Wood!" and "Critics." They culminate in Shukshin's novel about Stenka Razin, whose intense craving for perfect justice is a trait shared by many of Shukshin's characters.

Despite the hardship and tragedy of his childhood, Shukshin reconstructs his early years as an innocent—even joyous—time. His autobiographical cycle, together with "Uncle Yermolai," dwells primarily on the wonder of childhood, rather than on the grim reality of the adult world of Stalin's Soviet Union. It relates events in the writer's childhood through the age of fifteen, including descriptions of pranks played on the village muzhiks, visits by spell-casting gypsies, attempts by village activists to kick the family out of Srostki, Maria Sergeevna's second marriage, the family's move to Biisk and then back to the village, the outbreak of the war and the death of Shukshin's stepfather at the front, an early passion for books, the harsh Siberian winters, work in the fields, and his first love.

There were normal mishaps and misadventures, such as the night young Shukshin's blanket caught fire when he fell asleep reading under the covers by the light of a hollowed-out potato filled with kerosene. (Maria Sergeevna had forbidden her son to keep the lantern lit after everyone had gone to bed because the kerosene for the lantern was in short supply.)[38] Equally disastrous was Shukshin's attempt, upon finishing his compulsory seven-year schooling in 1943, to apprentice with his uncle Pavel Shukshin as a bookkeeper in Ogundai (Gorno-Altaisk). These trials and tribulations are described in a semiautobiographical story called "The Bookkeeper's Nephew" ("Plemianik glavbukha"). The same story relates how its adolescent protagonist once took out his anger against a neighbor by blinding the neighbor's pig in the left eye so that it would walk around in circles, another supposedly true incident from Shukshin's own childhood.

Shortly thereafter, Shukshin enrolled in the Biisk vocational technical school where, according to his sister, at about the age of sixteen he began to write stories and submit them to a Moscow journal. Presumably, these early submissions were all rejected, although we may never know for sure. The mystery of these submissions would itself make a good subject for a story. According to his sister, Shukshin apparently used their mother's house in Srostki as a return address. Partly because he knew Vasily was away at school, the village postman assumed the bundles addressed "To Vas. Mak. Shukshin" were to be delivered to an illiterate uncle of the writer, a Vasily Mak*simovich* Shukshin, who used the paper (a huge deficit item at the time) to roll cigars without ever trying to find out the contents of the pages. Shukshin's mother, who recognized the handwriting on one of the uncle's cigars, never had the heart to tell her son what had become of his early writing.[39]

Shukshin left the Biisk vocational school two and a half years later, either because he failed engine mechanics or because of an outburst of profanity directed at a teacher.[40] He returned to Srostki, worked for a while on the collective farm, and in 1946 or 1947 at the age of seventeen, left the Altai, eventually making his way to Moscow. The countryside was being exploited to feed cities in the process of rebuilding after the war, and conditions in the Altai were dire. Postwar food demands from Moscow devastated the region, second only to Ukraine in grain production, and even triggered a famine in 1946. Kolkhoz workers were paid next to nothing in wages and foodstuffs. Shukshin's options at the time were limited: either remain with his mother and hope for change, or leave his family for the city. Shukshin chose to leave. The scars this choice left upon the writer would never heal. Indeed, the great migration from the countryside to the cities because of collectivization, war, and postwar rebuilding would become a constant concern in his artistic and publicistic writings. Leaving his mother crying on the ground by the road leading out of the village, and with the proceeds of the sale of the family cow, Shukshin embarked on a journey that would essentially keep him from ever returning home.

In his publicistic writings Shukshin would grapple with the guilt he felt

at abandoning his rural roots, even chiding himself in one essay with his
own suspicions of the real reason for his departure:

> So why did I myself leave the village? Maybe, if I wanted not to be too sly
> about it, I could just up and say: It was like this—when the time came, I
> picked myself up and set off to look for a better lot in life. I forgot the peas-
> ant's "eternal" love of the land, magnificently overcame the "urge to till the
> earth," and shuffled down the street in my dress shoes, dreaming of getting an
> "apartment with its own john." At least that would be honest.

Shukshin, however, refutes his self-accusation a few sentences later: "But
then I came to my senses and thought: hold on, what time are we talking
about? That was 1946! Those times were nothing like today. There was
famine, they didn't give you anything for your work; whoever could leave,
left *involuntarily*." [41]

In a technique also characteristic of his short stories, Shukshin manages
to raise different possibilities in the minds of his readers as to narrative moti-
vation here. Is this a confession? A justification? An accusation? Did Shukshin use the harsh circumstances of the postwar village to conceal his own
ambitions for a better life in the city? Or was he really forced into exile from
his malaya rodina by policies emanating from the capital? If we are to judge
by the account the writer's sister Natalya gives of her brother's departure,
Shukshin might have had good reason for his mock confession. Natalya, after all, implies that her brother left for strictly material reasons.

> . . . [H]e came home to Srostki from his third year at the vocational school
> and says: "Mom, I'm going to Moscow." Mama was very upset. Why? What
> for? We didn't know anyone or have any kinfolk there. And it was such a diffi-
> cult time—the postwar years. . . . How he convinced mother, I'll never know,
> she was impossible when it came to this, but she understood, she felt it in her
> heart: you can't keep a young man at home. [42]

Although this seems to refute Shukshin's justification, the truth must lie
somewhere in the middle. While Shukshin could have stuck it out at home,
his departure was at least partially dictated by the bleak state of the Altai in
the USSR in the late 1940s. There is no doubt, however, about the acute
guilt Shukshin felt over the reasons he and others left the village. This guilt
finds its expression—to a lesser or greater extent—in many of his stories:
narratives in which families are split between the village and the city (in the
present collection, "Country Folk," "All by Themselves," "Oddball"); accounts in which sons who have found a better life in the city visit their
home village ("Ignakha's Come Home" and "Cutting Them Down to

Size"); tales about the great pull of the village ("Styopka" and "Vanka Teplyashin"); and stories that touch upon the relative merits of living in the city as opposed to the village ("Wolves" and "Alyosha at Large").

Whatever the reasons for Shukshin's departure, his venture into the world was no easy one. As one of what Geoffrey Hosking calls the "children of the Soviet Union's whirlwind years of social change," Shukshin joined the migration of people "torn from their moorings by war, urbanization, political oppression and the creation of a modern industry and a collectivized agriculture" who were swept "into factories, building sites, army barracks" and then "pushed back out again into a world ill prepared to receive them."[43] For two or three years Shukshin wandered around central Russia, working odd jobs (metalworker, scaffolder, painter's apprentice, longshoreman)[44] and living in workers' dormitories or sleeping on park benches at industrial sites in and around Moscow. The writer's own transient life during this period was doubtless the initial source for his later narratives about human beings in transition, people who belong neither wholly to their childhood villages nor to the cities of their adult years. They are either moving from the country to the city or adapting to a countryside that is absorbing city culture and values. Although the actual uprooting of millions of Russians and the transformation of the village are not described as such in Shukshin's stories, they form the background against which many of the writer's heroes must be viewed.

This transient atmosphere is often communicated metaphorically or existentially in Shukshin's works, as in the case of Maksim Yarikov from "I Believe!" who vaguely, but aptly, expresses the malady common to many of Shukshin's protagonists: "the soul aches." In seeking the physical roots of this malady or attempting to transcend it spiritually, these characters become itinerant truth seekers who clash with falsehood, complacency, and pettiness. Often their quests are propelled by a combination of naïveté, misdirected passion, restlessness, rootlessness, or impulsiveness, and often they end up in the quintessential Russian *skandal,* defined by Hosking as "a conflict which brings to the surface deep and wounding feelings."[45] Any of a number of stories from this collection could be cited in such a context, including "Critics," "My Son-in-Law Stole a Truckload of Wood!" "The Microscope," "Alyosha at Large," and "I Believe!"

Shukshin was drafted into the Soviet navy in August 1949 but was discharged early due to severe stomach ulcers in February 1953. He returned to Srostki and by the fall of the same year received his high school equivalency diploma, effectively making up for three years of schooling in six months—the impressive result of the intensive work habits that would become routine for Shukshin in his three future professions as actor, movie director, and writer. After a brief stint as the head of a village night school and a short-lived marriage,[46] Shukshin again resolved to leave the Altai. His experiences in Moscow and Leningrad and his time in the navy had instilled in him a strong sense that he could succeed only by educating himself in the capital. The muddy streets of Srostki clearly presented a bleak future to the demobilized sailor. If we are to judge by Shukshin's stories about young Siberian villagers working and studying in big cities,[47] this second departure from the village was no easier on the writer's conscience than the first. On the second occasion, Shukshin's mother sold her *banya* (bathhouse) and some handwoven rugs and gave the money to her son for the trip.[48]

Shukshin arrived in Moscow too late to make the entrance examinations for the Gorky Institute of World Literature, where he had originally hoped to study. Instead, he applied (against the rules) simultaneously to the Historical Archives Institute and to VGIK. The Historical Archives Institute accepted him into its night-degree program; VGIK, as we know, accepted him into its movie director's department. Shukshin, like any good son, telegraphed the positive news to his mother and asked her advice. She suggested he enroll in the day-degree program at VGIK.[49] The rest, as they say, is history.

Art

It was Shukshin's great fortune that he ended up in Mikhail Romm's studio at VGIK, for it would be Romm who would give the twenty-five-year-old student both the freedom he needed to find his own artistic identity and the advice and tutelage needed to develop his considerable, but uneven, talents. Romm was a rarity in those days, a well-known director and teacher at a prestigious school who "encouraged his students to think for themselves, to develop their individual talents, and even to criticize his [Romm's] work"[50] (which included two films on Lenin made in the 1930s). In his studio, Romm created an "unconstrained creative environment, unusual for the normally stodgy and conservative VGIK."[51] Shukshin recalls:

> In Romm's studio we learned more than just directing. Mikhail Ilich also required us to try our hands at writing. He would send us to various objectives—the post office or the train station—and ask us to describe what we saw there. Then, in class, he would read and analyze our sketches. He once advised me: "Don't be in a hurry to send your work to a journal, give it to me first."

Romm would read the stories, make comments, give them back to Shukshin, and order him to keep writing. Finally, toward the beginning of Shukshin's fifth year at VGIK, Romm told the aspiring writer to start sending his compositions to journals.[52]

That same year, 1958, the young VGIK student got his big break as an artist. The journal *Smena* accepted his first short story for publication,[53] and Shukshin was offered the lead role in a film by a young, but established, film director, Marlen Khutsiev. *The Two Fyodors (Dva Fedora)* released in 1959, was a great success and Shukshin attracted praise for his work in the film. Suddenly in demand as a talented new actor, Shukshin appeared in two other films in 1959 and 1960 before finishing his degree work at VGIK.[54] Although his graduation project, *Lebyazhie Calling* (*Iz Lebiazh'ego soobshchaiut,* 1961), suffered by comparison with the more sophisticated, nontraditional senior projects of the new postwar generation of young VGIK alumni (one critic has called it "aesthetically tongue-tied"[55]), the undertaking was distinguished by one factor: its creator's singular investment in it of all sides of his creative talent. Not only did Shukshin write the scenario for the film and direct it, he played the lead role as well—an unprecedented undertaking for a diploma film at VGIK. Shukshin would repeat this feat over a decade later in his best-known films, *Pechki-lavochki* (1973)[56] and *Red Kalina Berry* (*Kalina krasnaia,* 1974). His tripartite creative identity as writer-actor-director, however, had already become his calling card as early as his directorial debut in 1964. By the time *There Lives This Guy* made its triumphant procession across movie screens throughout Russia, Shukshin had behind him an established reputation as an actor (seven films since 1958) and as a writer of a critically acclaimed collection of stories (*Country Folk,* 1963). With the success of his first commercial film as well, Shukshin's name was henceforth invariably preceded by the triple epithet "actor-writer-director."

There is a particular aptness to this epithet for Shukshin because he was sometimes criticized for being a jack-of-all-trades (and, by implication, master of none) due to his refusal to give up any one aspect of his triple creative endeavors. This criticism became particularly acute in posthumous articles expressing regret that Shukshin allowed his acting and directing to interfere with his writing. It is also clear, however, that his art was, at its core, very theatrical and inclined to oral transmission, that his tripartite creative identity was not a happy accident of fate nor the consequence of overarching ambition but a necessary and organic feature of his makeup as an artist. After all, the notion of the artist combining the roles of actor, writer, and director in one person was long familiar to Shukshin and harked back to his native region and childhood days.

In a posthumously published interview given in 1974 (the year he died) Shukshin declared: "I grew up in peasant surroundings, where notions about what art is and why it exists were special. These notions were such as to lead art more toward the song, the fairy tale, the oral tale and even the well-made tall tale, but, I would note, of an entirely creative nature." He adds: "If you want to concretize and seek further the origins of the creative path I have been traveling, they, of course, lie in the art of the oral tale."

Shukshin remembered the stories told him by his mother and the tall tales told by peasant men during breaks from work in the fields. These popular storytellers were the early embodiment of Shukshin's later tripartite creative persona. According to Shukshin:

> The folk storyteller *[narodny rasskazchik]* is *both a playwright and an actor, or, more likely, a whole theater in one person.* He composes the situation, plays the parts of all the characters, and comments on the action. Moreover, even if the narrator takes it into his head to lay out some concrete, real-life happening, then this real fact also is told in a very vivid, rich way, undergoing the most incredible coloring—to the point of hyperbolic acuteness and deft fibbing.[57]

In other words, for Shukshin the story is primarily an orally transmitted genre and involves a teller and a listener, and the writer becomes not so much a *pisatel* (one who writes) but a *rasskazchik* (one who tells). As he states elsewhere, "[I]t is often not understood that a writer (a storyteller) is an ordinary person, the same person who met a friend on the street and wanted to tell him some incident or other from his own life."[58]

Storytelling in this context becomes performative and the storyteller assumes the role of the orchestrator of the performance. Character dialogue—the "live human voices" that Shukshin took as an indicator of successful writing[59]—occupies a central place in the story's poetics, and character type *(kharakter)* becomes the dominant factor of its plot, as Shukshin indicates in a working note. "Plot?" Shukshin asks. "Plot is character type. If you have the same situation but two different people in that situation, you'll get two different stories: one about one thing, another about something else entirely."[60]

Given the informal, oral qualities of the folk narrator's art, it is not surprising that Shukshin's stories—and his films—often contain humorous incidents and mishaps, even in narratives that are essentially tragic. One of the most attractive aspects of his talent, Shukshin's humor can be lightly ironic (as in "Country Folk," "The Microscope," "Oddball," and "Stubborn"), farcical ("Mille Pardons, Madame!," "A Roof Over Your Head," "Let's Conquer the Heart!"), or satiric ("Cutting Them Down to Size" and "My Son-in-Law Stole a Truckload of Wood!") and seems to derive from the prominence of humor in the folk imagination and the organic links between humorous genres and folk art forms. As it turns out, folk humor serves more than just comic ends, especially in Shukshin's works. In his reliance on folk buffoonery *(skomoroshestvo)*, the creative act of laughter *(smekhotvorchestvo)*, and folk satiric constructs *(narodnoe smekhovoe iskusstvo)* aimed not only away from the teller but at him as well, the folk storyteller can interrogate the values and truths of his society by turning those concepts upside down in a humorous fashion. Shukshin's dependence on character types and dialogue is another obvious factor explaining the humorous tone of many of his stories. The sharp exchanges between recognizable types from Shukshin's gallery of characters are often as comic as they are laden with serious content.

Apart from their humorous effects, the centrality of dialogue and character type in Shukshin's poetics has two other important outcomes. First, Shukshin's voice or that of his narrator often becomes but one of several voices in the text and therefore relinquishes monologic narrative control. Second, the oral nature of Shukshin's stories and the conversational and dialectal quality of characters' speech polemicize with the neutral literary style of the state-sponsored artistic doctrine of socialist realism, still dominant in the sixties and seventies. Shukshin's narrative style democratizes the text, so that no single voice—whether narrator or character—and no single level of language is allowed to dominate. The "spontaneity," "immediacy," "informality," and "sound quality" of Shukshin's dialogues demonstrate his inclination toward "the speech of the other."[61] As one critic asserts, "Shukshin addresses his reader, calling on him to take part in the dialogue, and anticipates a direct answer from him."[62] This need for dialogic contact with the "other"—the listener, reader, viewer—is an essential part of both Shukshin's and the folk storyteller's art.

Central to Shukshin's artistic priorities was contact with the reader or listener, "how to get through to him, to touch his heart."[63] "I personally see art not as an experiment," Shukshin stated in an interview, "but primarily as the opportunity for an essential conversation."[64] According to Shukshin, "The artist, when he creates, unconsciously tries to find among his viewers, readers, and listeners people like himself," because if a work of art does not evoke a response it is only "affectation or art for the sake of form" and therefore "is fruitless and artificial."[65] For Shukshin, being artificial was the danger inherent in the attempt to be artful. The value of art, it seemed, lay not only in its formal qualities, but also in its ability to provide the artist and his audience with a pretext for dialogue.[66]

Many of Shukshin's protagonists suffer from just such a need for dialogic contact. It is not surprising that a good number of them are likewise folk storytellers of a sort or folk artists, whose art becomes their medium for contact with others. In this regard, Bronka Pupkov from "Mille Pardons, Madame!" is perhaps the ultimate folk storyteller in the present collection. The outlandish tale of his mission to assassinate Hitler is replete with unbelievable details (such as concrete bunkers with electric light bulbs in the middle of battlefields, Hitler's close proximity to enemy lines, and Bronka's "fluent" German), yet it nevertheless touches and enthralls his listeners and provides its teller with the exquisite transport of artistic intercourse. Other protagonists such as Vanka Teplyashin from the story by the same name and Uncle Yemelyan in "Strangers" are also folk storytellers after a fashion, molding events from their lives into stories for others.

Folk art fulfills a similar function. In "All by Themselves," Antip's balalaika playing inspires a heart-to-heart conversation between Antip and his wife. Kolka's accordion playing in "Meditations" sweetly torments kolkhoz chairman Matvei Ryazantsev with memories of his youth and premonitions of his death. "Oddball" Vasily Knyazev tries to make up with his sister-in-law by painting her baby carriage with folk motifs. Vasyoka in "Stenka Razin" attempts to tell stories with his sculptures, such as the one depicting the betrayal of the famous Cossack leader by his fellow Cossacks.

Certainly, such contact with the audience was crucial to Shukshin himself, who strove in three professions to establish his essential conversations with readers and viewers. Moreover, the scripts for Shukshin's first three films—*There Lives This Guy, Your Son and Brother* (1966), and *Strange People* (1971)—were actually drawn from stories in his first three collections—*Country Folk, There, in the Distance* (1968), and *Men of One Soil* (1970)—as if to emphasize the artist's great need to reach his audience in any medium possible. And Shukshin did not stand on principle when it came to where his works got published. Rather than let a story that had been rejected by the major literary journals go unread, Shukshin often turned to obscure provincial journals, newspapers, and literary weeklies as outlets. He also seemed less concerned with the political allegiances of the journal or newspaper than he was with getting his work out in a form true to his artistic intent. His early publications in the conservative journal *Oktiabr'* gave way to a long association with the liberal *Novyi mir* partly because *Novyi mir* censored his works less stringently than *Oktiabr'*. But even *Novyi mir* limited the amount of dialectal and substandard elements in Shukshin's stories and refused to publish either of the writer's novels.[67] In a similar fashion, Shukshin switched from Gorky Film Studios to Mosfilm in 1973 not so much for political reasons, but because Gorky Studios had failed to approve Shukshin's long-standing request to shoot a film on Stepan Razin.

What in the end was to be gained through this essential conversation, this contact with the "other"? For Shukshin, the answer seems to be connected to the word *volya* (unbounded personal freedom). A similar concept in Shukshin's works is expressed by the equally amorphous notion of a "holiday of the soul" *(prazdnik dushi)*. Identified as a "key word"[68] in Shukshin's lexicon and the "'golden thread' of his entire mature writing,"[69] *volya* figures as a major theme in his works and an important concept in his

life. This word denotes freedom in the sense of nonconstraint, release, liber-
ation. The other Russian word for freedom is *svoboda,* but between the two,
volya is the richer in its evocation of meaningful, expressive associations in
the Russian mind. According to Michel Heller,

> one cannot consider these words fully synonymous in Russian. In Dal''s dic-
> tionary, *Tolkovyi slovar'* (1880–1882), the word *svoboda* occupies less than one
> half of a page, while the word *volya* has two full pages. In Ozhegov's contem-
> porary dictionary, *Slovar' russkogo iazyka,* a note is given for the expression as
> *na voliu* and *na vole* [at liberty]: "colloquial." This should signify that these
> expressions have a "non-literary" character. The word *volya,* which almost dis-
> appeared from the contemporary Russian literary language, returns in the
> works of Shukshin as a symbol of disappearing features of the Russian national
> character. The word *svoboda,* in those cases where it appears, carries signs of
> its urban origin, while the word *volya* [which now has the primary denotation
> of "will"] enters as a rural, Russian word.[70]

Shukshin's choice of the word is a conscious one. With its rich folk associations, colloquial resonance, and expansiveness (Dmitry Likhachev defines
volya as "freedom plus wide expanses"[71]), *volya* is a leitmotif well suited to
the central polemic of Shukshin's life and art. Rural in connotation, substandard or nonliterary in nature, denoting opposition to constraint in any
form (whether imposed by the powers that be, human nature, or the laws of
the universe), volya captures the essence of Shukshin's artistic program. He
threw off literary, especially stylistic, constraints and half-lies promoted by
the standardized and neutered Soviet classics that dominated literature of
the Brezhnev era, a period corresponding to ten years out of Shukshin's fifteen-year literary career. He did so largely through his efforts in the short
story and his use of intimate and familiar styles, aspects belonging to the
province of the folk storyteller and the provinces whence he hailed.

In the broadest sense, volya articulates the peasant muzhik's traditional
dream of freedom and is something of a folk liberty. As such, it is tied to
the peasant's desire to overcome the burdens he has carried from time im-
memorial. Shukshin's protagonists, who come directly from the modern
peasantry, suffer in their own search for volya when their visions of release—
often as vague and boundless as their native Siberian landscapes—are
clouded by petty bureaucrats, antagonistic colleagues, unsympathetic wives,
or by the finality of death. The search for volya in this latter context becomes existential, if not metaphysical, and is reflected in stories such as "I
Believe!" "Alyosha at Large," "Meditations," and "Passing Through." In
other contexts, release is sought by peasant men trying to conquer the mys-
teries of science ("The Microscope" and "Stubborn"), the power of

religious belief ("Tough Guy"), or the mystique of the Ph.D. ("Cutting Them Down to Size").

Not all students of Shukshin agree on what precisely volya represents in the writer's works. Diane Nemec Ignashev asserts that volya is the search for artistic freedom "in a world of censured texts and stories." Heller equates volya with the quest for physical and metaphysical freedom. Hosking describes volya as "something beyond the immediate and empirical, the contingent and imperfect."[72] All three definitions are important for our understanding of volya in Shukshin's stories, but even more important is the figure of Stepan Razin.

The word *volya* appears for the first time in one of Shukshin's earliest stories, "Stenka Razin" (written in 1960 and first published in 1962), and figures most conspicuously in the title of the writer's most important novel, *Ia prishel dat' vam voliu* (I have come to give you freedom). In both cases, the concept of volya is personified by Stepan Razin, the Cossack leader of the 1670 peasant revolt against Tsar Alexei. Shukshin was fascinated by the image of Razin. The historical intercessor for the peasantry and the hero of epic poems and folksongs, Razin was simultaneously a real-life avenger and a fixture of the Russian folk imagination. For Shukshin, he embodied volya as he galloped across the steppe, disdainful of a settled and easy life. Razin vanquished complacency, compromise, resignation and capitulation by taking direct and usually deadly action against anything or anyone standing between him and his goal. His provincial revolt in the name of the people was undoubtedly attractive to the son of a purged Siberian peasant.

Razin was the bearer of the ultimate means toward achieving freedom: rebellion. Volya, too, implies some sort of revolt, an act of willing, an exercise of freedom. The tragic lesson of Shukshin's novel, however, is that rebellion in the name of an ideology—even one which aims to liberate the peasantry—is futile; one must first liberate oneself from the slave within. Volya—as Razin discovers—is more a personal challenge than a condition or right that can be given to another. The ataman's volya-seeking revolt is undermined by his own Cossacks, who eventually betray the rebel leader in return for promises from the tsar of amnesty and increased pay for guarding the empire's southern borders.

During Shukshin's short creative career, Razin was a kind of obsession as the subject of a separate short story, a screenplay, and a novel. Shukshin went so far as to include in his novel on the ataman a sort of autobiographical legend of his own. In the novel, Razin pays a peasant *skomorokh* (a type of Russian medieval jester and folk artist) to impersonate exiled Patriarch Nikon of the Russian Orthodox church, whose "appearance" in Razin's host was designed to increase popular support for the campaign. When

Razin asks the skomorokh about his origins, he finds out that the peasant hails from a little village called Shuksha, whose name, of course, links the skomorokh with Shukshin's distant relatives. The effect is to associate Shukshin and his art with the skomorokh and thus with Razin's cause. Razin's revolt from the provinces in the name of the peasantry becomes the historical and textual reflection of various aspects of Shukshin's own polemic with the center. His polemic may be artistic (the oral art of the folk storyteller versus art according to the plan), historic (Razin's campaign to free the peasants from the consolidation of serfdom in the seventeenth century as a symbolic righting of the wrong of collectivization in the twentieth century), social (the defense of the patriarchal peasantry from usurpation by the [step]fatherland of Stalin's Soviet Union), or personal (Shukshin's vindication of the execution of his father). The "I" of the novel's title (*I Have Come to Give You Freedom*) becomes ambiguous in its reference. While ostensibly coming from the lips of the novel's hero, it is also uttered by and associated with the name on the cover—Vasily Shukshin. Shukshin, like Razin, offered his readers volya through the vehicle of his art. And through his art he sought to achieve some form of self-liberation—from the slave within, from the constraints of his own society, and from the hard lot of his fellow peasants, past and present.

Was Razin, then, Shukshin's "secret warrior," his "undeciphered" alter ego? It seems clear that, to Shukshin, Razin was. This does not mean that all of the writer's stories must be viewed through the prism of peasant revolt. On the contrary, although the Razin theme emerges in various stories, novellas, novels, and films, Shukshin's art is broader and deeper than even the larger than life figure of Razin. Nevertheless, there is a sense of revolt against petty tyranny, unfairness, and falseness common to the individual quests and fates of many of Shukshin's heroes, including those in this collection.

The concept of volya also speaks to the role of the folk storyteller. For all the "wealth of speech, invention, [and] unexpected devices" of his art with its "verbal and thespian decorations," the concerns of the folk storyteller were always channeled toward two things: the meaning of the story and the effect on the listener. "The main thing," Shukshin claimed, was "to say a lot through a little, to touch the reader to the quick as forcefully as possible."[73] The folk storyteller's art was laconic and cathartic. "A work of art," Shukshin wrote, "is when something *happens:* in a nation, to a person, in your fate."[74] Art so heavily invested in stimulating a response in another is by definition closely linked to the goal of stimulating action, loosening bonds, encouraging self-actualization—all concepts directly tied to volya as an artistic and philosophical goal.

It is not surprising, then, that in the last two years of his life Shukshin took an active interest in the theater, a genre he had once considered vastly inferior to the cinema. The theater offered the sort of immediacy and direct contact with his public that Shukshin craved, as an artist; the possibilities for shared catharsis that the theater presented to him were especially well suited for volya-inspired art. Shukshin's play *Energetic People* premiered in May 1974 to positive reviews. He was at work on another play, *And They Woke Up in the Morning,* at the time of his death in October of that year. It was published posthumously in its unfinished state.

Final Projects

The writer's last two collections of short stories—*Types (Kharaktery)* and *Conversations under a Clear Moon (Besedy pri iasnoi lune)*—appeared in 1973 and 1974. These two anthologies offer proof of the depth and maturity of Shukshin's art and mark a phase of his creative life that had run its course. Shukshin alludes to this in interviews dating from these years.[75] He was obviously engaged in a serious reevaluation of his art, and besides his fascination with the theater, he had become increasingly interested in longer prose genres. One result was the long fairy-tale novella, *Until the Cock Crows Thrice (Do tret'ikh petukhov),* in which Shukshin uses poetic and narrative devices and even whole characters from the traditional Russian folk story. The subject matter is telling: Ivan the Fool, from Russian folklore, is sent by the other characters with whom he lives in a Moscow library on a journey in search not of wisdom but of a *certificate* attesting to his wisdom. Ivan's misadventures mirror those of another Ivan, the hero of Shukshin's 1973 film *Pechki-lavochki,* in which an Altai tractor driver travels with his wife to Moscow and then to the Black Sea on vacation. The long train ride between Ivan's Siberian village and the nation's capital is a physical journey as well as an abstract exploration of the social and cultural values of Soviet society. Both works are thinly veiled commentaries on Shukshin's own journey from Siberia to Moscow for just such a "certificate of wisdom."

Shukshin also became interested at this time in cine-novellas *(kinopovesti).* More than just screenplays, these cine-novellas were written in narrative form and intended for separate publication in literary journals and for filming. When one such cine-novella, *Red Kalina Berry,* was brought to Soviet screens in the spring of 1974, it proved to be the greatest success of Shukshin's career and is still recognized as the single work that permanently secured his reputation. Controversial in its themes and almost killed by censorship (Brezhnev himself supposedly gave the film its final approval for wide release),[76] *Red Kalina Berry* created a sensation wherever it was shown throughout the nation. It relates the failed attempt of a repeat offender, the thief Yegor Prokudin, to give up his former gang of urban criminals and to reclaim the folk heritage of his rural childhood. In the story and the film, Yegor endures an agonizing period of self-interrogation and exploration in the quest for his true identity, only to die a tragic death at the hands of members of his former gang.

Shukshin's own sudden death from a heart attack only six months after the film's release augmented the movie's already strong resonance with audiences. As a shocked nation mourned Shukshin's unexpected death, the murder of Yegor Prokudin was reenacted each night on the movie screen. The temptation to view the death of the film's hero as a foreshadowing of Shukshin's own fate was great, and even led to speculation that the writer, actor, and director—like his hero—had been similarly beholden to unsavory types who did him in. According to this theory (another of the legends by which readers and critics have sought to understand Shukshin), these unsavory types, while not members of a gang of criminals, played a similarly shady role within the Soviet cultural establishment. They were the same people who meted out punishments and rewards for artistic orthodoxy and who had the power to determine an artist's fate—the same people (or so the story has it) who almost flunked a young Siberian applicant during his VGIK entrance exams, and who later prevented him from realizing his most cherished creative project: the film on Razin. It was allegedly these people (in one critic's words, the "literary mafia" of the capital) who really killed Shukshin through a system of constraints and compromises that eventually proved too much for him to bear.[77]

This part of Shukshin's legend, of course, can never be fully proved or disproved. It is a fact, however, that *Red Kalina Berry,* more than any single work or event in the writer's life, shaped Shukshin's public biography, especially in the decade following his death, the decade of the so-called "Shukshin boom." The tragedy of Yegor Prokudin became that of Shukshin's premature end. In many ways, this association still affects our critical interpretations of Shukshin, who, like Yegor, seemed doomed to die in that nether region between the city (Moscow) and his long-abandoned rural home.

This perception of a Shukshin torn between Moscow and Siberia was only strengthened by the posthumous publication of interviews done before his death, in which Shukshin expressed his desire to give up the cinema and return to Srostki. Of his three muses, he vowed he was going to pick only one—literature—and dedicate himself to it in his native Siberia. "Srostki has long been luring me back. It's even appeared to me in dreams. . . . I should tell you that there, in my native region, I always write in a kind of frenzy, with inexhaustible strength. . . . A writer, of this I am convinced, can exist and move forward only thanks to the power of those life-giving juices with which his native surroundings nourish him."[78] The peasant lad, it seemed, was finally going to come home.

It seems apparent that one of the writer's ambitions—should he ever have made the move to Srostki—was to master the novel as a genre, and thus finally be granted entrance into the realm of *bolshaya literatura* (literally, big literature, or serious, significant literature). Shukshin had published two novels: his first novel entitled *The Lyubavin Family,* published in 1965, about the arrival of Soviet power to a remote Altai village in the 1920s; and the novel on Razin, whose book version came out late in 1974. Both novels were coolly received and suffered by comparison with his more successful short stories. What made Shukshin an interesting story writer—a laconic, expressive style, a taut narration centered on a single major event, the liveliness of the dialogues—was stretched to the breaking point in his novels, particularly in *The Lyubavin Family,* where such a style and narrative voice seemed to be lost in the expansive medium of the larger form. Shukshin's lively dialogues, when extended to fill the chapters of a novel, became overly cinematic and read like movie scripts.

A third novel, the sequel to *The Lyubavin Family,* is set in the 1950s and treats the fate of the second generation of Lyubavins growing up under Soviet authority, but it also failed to create a stir when it was published in 1987. Part of the reason for the relative lack of interest in the only work he wrote "for the drawer," probably has to do with its appearance at a time when more sensational "delayed prose" (such as Rybakov's *Children of the Arbat*) was seeing the light of day. Book Two of *The Lyubavin Family* reworks several of Shukshin's stories and one novella from the 1960s but focuses more directly on the consequences of Soviet rule in the Altai during and immediately after the Stalin period. This novel is Shukshin's most overtly political work and probably could never have been published before perestroika due to its treatment of the grim legacy of Stalinism and the hypocrisy, cynicism, and corruption of the Party. One of the most important passages in the book is a poignant letter from a father—on his way to Stalin's labor camps—to his son, then an infant, who only reads its contents some twenty years later. In this, and in other scenes in the book, Shukshin is obviously dealing with painful aspects of his own biography. Perhaps more than any other of the writer's works, this sequel reveals the deeper polemic informing Shukshin's art, one that has to do with the debate the writer conducted between himself and society over his place in Soviet life and culture.

We can only guess what novels might have been composed by an older Shukshin and even whether he would have actually made the move back to Siberia. It seems doubtful that the "sly peasant" could really have found peace and happiness by returning home, or that Shukshin could have abandoned two of his three creative careers. One thing seems certain: the later Shukshin whom we never saw would likely have been a different Shukshin, perhaps no longer the writer of short stories about village eccentrics and their scandals, which is how he is usually perceived, especially in the West.

It is equally clear that Shukshin's fame will continue to rest primarily on his short stories, a genre he helped to revitalize in contemporary Russian literature.[79] Though it speaks to only one of the artist's three creative personas, this legacy would doubtless have satisfied Shukshin. In a working note, he writes: "Throughout his life, a storyteller writes one long novel. And he is evaluated later, when the novel is finished and the author has died."[80] Shukshin's stories—taken altogether—are such a novel, as the writer's friend and fellow actor Georgy Burkov pointed out in 1983. Burkov reports that Shukshin advised him to read the collected stories as if they were a unified whole. "I took his advice," Burkov related, "and unexpectedly found I was reading a novel, with many fates, a mass of plot lines, and all of it fantastically constructed. A novel with a variety of the most truthful sketches, genre scenes, and miniatures. Precisely a novel. One enormous canvas, its parts—novellas, stories, scenarios—all lively and versatile."[81] Shukshin's "novel," the one he wrote in his stories and films, was left unfinished at the time of his death, but enough of it was completed to secure him an important place in the history of twentieth-century Russian literature and to suggest that Russia lost a major talent when it lost Vasily Shukshin.

Notes

1. See especially M. Klimakova, "Zhivet takoi paren'," *Moskovskii komsomolets*, 7 June 1964; N. Zhelezniakova, "'Zolotoi lev'—prostomu parniu," *Ogonek* 36 (1964): 29; T. Osipov, "Est' takoi paren'. . . ," *Uchitel'skaia gazeta*, 5 December 1964, 4; Ia. Varshavskii, "Dobro pozhalovat' na komediiu!" *Komsomol'skaia pravda*, 24 June 1964, 4; I. Vasil'iev, "S podkupaiushchei iskrennost'iu," *Volga*, 8 December 1964.

2. Iurii Skop, "V Sibiri dobro—sibirskoe: v gostiakh u Shukshina," *Literaturnaia gazeta*, 3 July 1968, 3.

3. Nicholas Galichenko, *Glasnost: Soviet Cinema Responds* (Austin: University of Texas Press, 1991), 12.

4. Aleksandr Mitta, "Kak o nem napisat'?" *Iskusstvo kino* 1 (1971): 114.

5. Anninskii's comments are from his text for *Vasilii Shukshin*, a brochure published by the Soviet Cinematographers' Union in 1976 (unnumbered).

6. This fact is mentioned in passing by Vladimir Korobov in his book *Vasilii Shukshin* (Moscow: Sovremennik, 1988), 30.

7. Famous Soviet director Sergei Gerasimov mentions Shukshin's Party membership while talking about the latter's entrance into VGIK. See Gennadii Bocharov, "Esli govorit' o Shukshine," *Komsomol'skaia pravda*, 24 November 1974, 4.

8. Vasilii Shukshin, "Mne vezlo na umnykh i dobrykh liudei . . . ," in his *Voprosy samomu sebe* (Moscow: Molodaia gvardiia, 1981), 151–52.

9. Diane Nemec Ignashev, "Song and Confession in the Short Prose of Vasilii Makarovich Shukshin: 1929–1974" (Ph.D. diss., University of Chicago, 1984), 45.

10. Ibid.

11. This quote, taken from a selection of Shukshin's letters to his mother and sister, was published by Boris Iudalevich, "Rodnaia moia . . ." in *Shukshinskie chteniia,* ed. V. Gorn (Barnaul: Altaiskoe knizhnoe izdatel'stvo, 1984), 189. I have translated *otvetstvennye rabotniki* as "executives."

12. This information comes from Shukshin himself. See his "Siberian Pies" in the cycle "From the Childhood Years of Ivan Popov" in this volume.

13. The essay was reprinted in Shukshin's *Voprosy samomu sebe* in the commentary to "Mne vezlo na umnykh i dobrykh liudei . . . ," 152–56.

14. Ignashev, "Song and Confession," 32.

15. Quoted in V. I. Fomin, *Peresechenie parallel'nykh* (Moscow: Iskusstvo, 1976), 295–96.

16. Leonid Kuravlev, "Kak berezy . . . ," in *O Shukshine: ekran i zhizn',* ed. L. N. Fedoseeva-Shukshina and R. D. Chernenko (Moscow: Iskusstvo, 1979), 224.

17. See the biography of Tarkovsky in chapter 1 of Vida T. Johnson and Graham Petrie, *The Films of Andrei Tarkovsky: A Visual Fugue* (Bloomington: Indiana University Press, 1994).

18. Mikhail Romm, *Ustnye rasskazy* (Moscow: Soiuz kinematografistov SSSR, 1991), 14.

19. Neya Zorkaya, *The Illustrated History of Soviet Cinema* (New York: Hippocrene Books, 1989), 275–77.

20. Ignashev, "Song and Confession," 45.

21. Shukshin, "'Eshche raz vyveriaia svoiu zhizn','" in his *Voprosy,* 232–33.

22. Bella Akhmadulina, "Ne zabyt'," in *O Shukshine,* 331.

23. See Shukshin's 1967 essay "'Tol'ko eto ne budet ekonomicheskaia stat'ia . . .'" in his *Voprosy,* 25–31, for details of Shukshin's own mishaps on a trip back to Siberia.

24. See Marlen Khutsiev's "Krupnyi plan" in *O Shukshine,* 321; and Gennadii Bocharov's "Esli govorit' o Shukshine" in his *Nepobuzhdennyi* (Moscow: Molodaia gvardiia, 1978), 133.

25. See Evgenii Sorokin, "'Nesu rodinu v dushe . . . ,'" *Molodaia gvardiia* 7 (1989): 260–61.

26. Gleb Goryshin, *Zhrebii: rasskazy o pisateliakh* (Leningrad: Sovetskii pisatel', 1987), 113.

27. Andrei Tarkovskii, "Dlia menia kino—eto sposob dostich' kakoi-to istiny," *Sovetskaia Rossiia,* 3 April 1988, 4.

28. Shukshin, "Slovo o maloi rodine," in his *Voprosy,* 66; English translation from "The Place Where I Was Born," in Vasily Shukshin, *Articles,* trans. Avril Pyman (Moscow: Raduga, 1986), 218.

29. In the preceding summary of the history of the peasant in the Altai, I have relied on Ignashev's well-documented and expanded treatment of this topic in her "Song and Confession," 1–6.

30. The data pertaining to Shukshin's paternal lineage is discussed in more detail by V. Grishaev, "Vasilii Shukshin: materialy k biografii" in his *Tropoiu pamiati: zapiski kraeveda* (Barnaul: Altaiskoe knizhnoe izdatel'stvo, 1987), 54.

31. Ibid.

32. *Sebulonki* derives from *seblak,* the villager's dialectal distortion of *Siblag— Sibirskii lager'* (Siberian [labor] camp).

33. One of the songs, "V voskresen'e mat'-starukha" ("On Sunday an aged mother") serves as the title to one of Shukshin's stories written in 1967. The other song, "Ne veitesia, chaiki, nad morem," ("Oh gulls, don't wing your way out o'er the sea") is featured in "Odni" ("All by Themselves") written in 1962 and included in this volume. The other prison songs the sebulonki would sing, according to Iadykina, included "A v Barnaule tiur'ma bol'shaia . . ." and "V tom sadu pri do-line" ("In Barnaul the prison is large . . ." and "In that garden by the valley").

34. See N. A. Iadykina's reminiscences in *On pokhozh na svoiu rodinu,* ed. V. I. Ashcheulov and Iu. G. Egorov (Barnaul: Altaiskoe knizhnoe izdatel'stvo, 1989), especially 93–96.

35. Shukshin, "Kommentarii" to "Monolog na lestnitse," in his *Voprosy,* 48–49.

36. Shukshin, "Nravstvennost' est' Pravda," in *Voprosy,* 59.

37. Shukshin, "The Place Where I Was Born," 222; "Slovo o 'maloi rodine'," 68.

38. See the account of Shukshin's mother, Mariia Sergeevna Shukshina-Kuksina, in *On pokhozh na svoiu rodinu,* 15.

39. Natal'ia Zinov'eva's story is related in Grishaev, 65–66.

40. The reader is referred, respectively, to Skop, 3; and Grishaev, 80–81.

41. Shukshin, "'Tol'ko eto ne budet ekonomicheskaia stat'ia . . . ,'" 25–26.

42. See Natal'ia Zinov'eva's reminiscences in *On pokhozh na svoiu rodinu,* 26.

43. Geoffrey Hosking, *Beyond Socialist Realism: Soviet Fiction since Ivan Denisovich* (London: Granada, 1980), 162–63.

44. Shukshin, "Kommentarii" to "Zaviduiu tebe . . . ," in *Voprosy,* 97.

45. Geoffrey Hosking, "The Twentieth Century: In Search of New Ways, 1933–1980," in *The Cambridge History of Russian Literature,* ed. Charles Moser (Cambridge, England: Cambridge University Press, 1989), 565.

46. For more on Shukshin's marriage to Mariia Shumskaia, see the accounts of V. Ia. Riabchikov and A. M. Kalachikov in *On pokhozh na svoiu rodinu,* 55 and 67–68, respectively.

47. I have in mind "Len'ka" (Lyonka), "Voskresnaia toska" (Sunday boredom), "Zmeinyi iad" (Snake poison), and "I razygralis' zhe koni v pole" (Oh, see the horses frolic in the fields).

48. Dar'ia Il'inichna Faleeva, a neighbor of Shukshin's mother, provides this testimony in *On pokhozh na svoiu rodinu,* 105. She mentions as well that Mariia Sergeevna later sold first one half of her home, then the other, in order to send money to Shukshin in his dormitory, purchasing a smaller *izbushechka* (tiny peasant hut) for herself.

49. Natal'ia Zinov'eva, *On pokhozh na svoiu rodinu,* 27.

50. Johnson and Petrie, 21.

51. Ibid.

52. Shukshin, "Mne vezlo na umnykh i dobrykh liudei . . . ," in his *Voprosy,* 152.

53. "Two on a Cart" ("Dvoe na telege") appeared in the number 15 issue of *Smena* for 1958.

54. The films *Zolotoi eshelon* (The golden echelon) and *Prostaia istoriia* (A simple story) are now, according to Ignashev, remembered only for Shukshin's performance in them ("Song and Confession," 49–50).

55. Iurii Tiurin, *Kinematograf Vasiliia Shukshina* (Moscow: Iskusstvo, 1984), 61. See 54–73 for more on Shukshin's first film.

56. "Pechki-lavochki" is an untranslatable expression that literally means "stoves and benches," but whose contemporary significance has to do with trivial domestic worries. The hero of the movie repeats the phrase in a variety of not always appropriate circumstances.

57. V. I. Fomin, *Peresechenie parallel'nykh* (Moscow: Iskusstvo, 1976), 296. My emphasis.

58. Shukshin, "Kak ia ponimaiu rasskaz," in his *Voprosy,* 116.

59. Shukshin, "Iz rabochikh zapisei," in his *Voprosy,* 249.

60. Ibid.

61. L. A. Muratova and L. G. Riabova, "Signaly razgovornosti v khudozhestvennom dialoge i skaze V. M. Shukshina," *Iazyk i stil' prosy V.M. Shukshina,* ed. A. A. Chuvakin (Barnaul: Altaiskii gosudarstvennyi universitet, 1991), 61.

62. G. G. Khisamova, "Dialog v rasskazakh V. M. Shukshina," in *Iazyk i stil' prozy V. M. Shukshina,* 47.

63. Shukshin, quoted in Fomin, 297.

64. Shukshin, "Vozdeistvie pravdoi," in his *Voprosy,* 189.

65. Shukshin, "'Eshche raz vyveriaia svoiu zhizn','" in his *Voprosy,* 222.

66. Shukshin, "Vozdeistvie pravdoi," in his *Voprosy,* 189.

67. See chapter 2 of Ignashev's "Song and Confession" for a detailed treatment of censorship and Shukshin's texts.

68. Michel Heller, "Vasily Shukshin: In Search of Freedom," trans. George Gutsche, in Vasily Shukshin, *"Snowball Berry Red" and Other Stories,* ed. Donald M. Fiene, trans. Donald M. Fiene et al. (Ann Arbor: Ardis, 1979), 215.

69. Ignashev, "Song and Confession," 85.

70. Heller, 215. The bracketed portions of the text are the inserted notes of the article's translator, George Gutsche.

71. Dmitrii Likhachev's Russian is: *"Svoboda, soedinennaia s prostorom."* See his "Zametki o russkom," *Novyi mir* 3 (1980): 12. Ignashev hypothesizes that Likhachev's inclusion in his 1980 article of a section on *volya* was probably prompted by discussion of Shukshin's notion of the term ("Song and Confession," 86).

72. See, respectively, Ignashev, "The Art of Vasilii Shukshin," *Slavic and East European Journal* 32 (Summer 1988): 426; Heller, 213–33; and Hosking, *Beyond Socialist Realism,* 179.

73. Quoted in Fomin, 297.

74. Shukshin, "Iz rabochikh zapisei," 247.

75. See, in particular, "Esli by znat' . . ." in his *Voprosy*, 206–18.

76. See Hedrick Smith, *The Russians* (New York: Ballantine, 1977), 510–11, for more on the story behind the release of Shukshin's film.

77. Grigori Svirski makes this link between Shukshin's fate and that of Yegor Prokudin explicit, identifying conservative establishment writers Anatolii Sofronov and Mikhail Sholokhov as the "bad guys" in Shukshin's personal tragedy:

[Shukshin] was a far-seeing, sensitive and nervous man. The Sofronovs and Sholokhovs killed him with kindness as they corrected the line he took. He himself felt that the vodka-sodden literary Mafia would finish him off eventually. It was no accident that his Mafia killed off the leading character in the film he had made just before his death, *Snowball Berry Red*, which he scripted, directed and acted in. (*A History of Post-War Soviet Writing: The Literature of Moral Opposition*, trans. and ed. Robert Dessaix and Michael Ulman [Ann Arbor: Ardis, 1981], 299).

Writer Viktor Nekrasov echoes these sentiments: "Yegor Prokudin has left us, murdered by evil people. Vasily Makarych—Vasya Shukshin to his friends—has left us, too. Who murdered him is not known, but he was murdered" ("Vzgliad na nechto," *Kontinent* 12, pt. 2 [1977]: 118).

78. Shukshin, "Kommentarii" to "'Esche raz vyveriaia svoiu zhizn' . . . ,'" in his *Voprosy*, 243–44.

79. Evgenii Sidorov, "The Short Story Today," *Soviet Literature* 6 (1986): 4.

80. Shukshin, "Iz rabochikh zapisei," in his *Voprosy*, 249.

81. Georgy Burkov, "'Pri Shukshine vsegda byla tetradochka . . . ,'" *Literaturnaia Rossiia*, 9 September 1983, 17.

Translators' Note

Although Vasily Shukshin was born in Siberia, set most of his stories there, and shot three of his films in the region, he is generally not considered a Siberian writer. This is perhaps because he seems so unlike other Siberian authors of his generation, such as Valentin Rasputin and Viktor Astafiev. While their prose meditates on Siberia as a last repository of moral and ecological purity and seeks to chronicle and preserve the ethnographic heritage of its inhabitants, Shukshin's stories seem far less concerned with Siberia as a region or historic place. The works of Rasputin and Astafiev often incorporate Siberian dialects unfamiliar to many Russians not from those regions, therefore more obviously situating these two writers in Siberia, as compared to Shukshin, whose substandard character speech rarely strays far from what might be heard in the countryside around Moscow. Still, Siberia was a powerful locus for Shukshin, and we ignore at our peril its significance in the writer's life and works. The inhabitants of the Altai in Siberia were Shukshin's self-professed favorite subject matter; it was their lives and fates that he thought came across most precisely in his stories and novellas. Even if he does not always specifically indicate that a given village in a given story is necessarily located in Siberia, Shukshin was adamant that writers write about what they know. He knew village life in the Altai, and that is what he wrote about in the majority of his stories. His desire to return to the Altai shortly before he died only underscores the importance he attached to his Siberian homeland. The universality of the villages and villagers that populate Shukshin's prose is more a tribute to the writer's talent and profundity than a reason for discounting their Siberian inspiration.

Therefore, we chose to limit our collection to stories set in the village, *Shukshin's* village, the one he created out of the many he knew growing up in Siberia. We hope that the twenty-five stories included in this volume will help give the fullest picture of what that village was like and what it meant for Shukshin. Readers who have enjoyed Shukshin's stories will no doubt be able to name a few favorites that did not make our collection. This is unfortunate but also unavoidable; after all, Shukshin wrote some one hundred and thirty stories, and there are even several of our own favorites that we were unable to include. Our goal was to offer the reader stories spanning Shukshin's career, especially since many commentators on the writer tend to overlook the stories he wrote between 1960 and 1964, his supposedly more "sentimental" early period. Six tales from those years were selected for the present volume, including "Stenka Razin," a story that held enormous personal importance for Shukshin. We also chose a number of stories that Shukshin himself later brought to the screen. These include "Styopka" and "Ignakha's Come Home" from Shukshin's 1966 film *Your Son and Brother* and "Oddball," "Mille Pardons, Madame!" "Meditations," and "Stenka Razin" from his *Strange People* (1969). We also thought it appropriate to conclude with Shukshin's autobiographical works—"Strangers," "From the Childhood Years of Ivan Popov," and "Uncle Yermolai"—as a kind of afterword to the preceding stories, allowing Shukshin, as it were, to have the last word on Shukshin. Finally, of the twenty-five stories in our collection, eleven have never appeared before in English in any country, and twenty have never appeared in English translations published in the West.

Difficult as it was to decide which stories ought to be in the collection, translating these stories also presented a challenge. Shukshin's stories have an oral quality to them; they often seem to be written as if they were being told to an audience. Consequently, his sentences have a very conversational tone to them, complete with parenthetical asides and elaborations, colloquial turns of speech, parceling of sentences, use of folk sayings, avoidance of gerunds, almost complete absence of participles, and frequent use of the second person singular. The narrator often shifts between present and past tense (as people do when telling a story), and his voice frequently blends into those of his characters just as his characters' voices sometimes intrude upon the narration. Shukshin's narrator prefers short, uncomplicated sentences and often uses the conjunction "and" to link sentences and provide transitions. Character dialogue is often elliptical, and (appropriately enough for a filmmaker's stories) dialogue, not descriptive narration, propels Shukshin's plots. In his stories, Shukshin makes liberal use of ellipses to mark pauses, and dashes for counterpoint. Where possible, we tried to preserve these stylistic elements in our translation. Inevitably, English syntax and usage occasionally got in the way, forcing us to sacrifice some of the characteristics of Shukshin's style, which we have summarized above, for the sake of a natural-sounding English translation. For instance, we could not always preserve the rich, dialectal flavor of Shukshin's character speech without running the risk of making his protagonists sound too much as though they hailed from certain parts of rural America. We strove, however, to make Shukshin's villagers speak in an authentic, believable idiom.

Our sources for the definitive versions of Shukshin's stories are volumes two and three of his six-volume collected works, *Sobranie sochinenii v shesti tomakh* (Moscow: Molodaia gvardiia, 1992–), compiled by his widow, Lidiia Fedoseeva-Shukshina. Two parts of the cycle "From the Childhood Years of Ivan Popov" were published only posthumously: "The Letter" appeared under the title "Pis'mo" in the newspaper *Sovetskaia Rossiia* on 27

July 1988; "Siberian Pies" was published as "Solnechnye kol'tsa" in the same paper a year later on 12 July 1989. We deviated from these sources on only two occasions: in "Stenka Razin," we added a line, for the sake of clarity, from an earlier version published in Shukshin's first collection, *Sel'skie zhiteli* (1963); and in "First Acquaintance with the City" from his autobiographical cycle, we restored a line that appeared in the story's 1968 publication in the number eleven issue of the journal *Novyi mir*. The line is important because it mentions how Shukshin was a "child of an enemy of the people" because his father had been officially liquidated during the rural purges—facts discussed elsewhere in the cycle as well.

Except in those areas primarily of interest to researchers (Russian titles, notes in the foreword and introduction, as well as the list of Shukshin's works), we employ a transliteration system aimed at approximating the Russian sounds for readers unfamiliar with the language. The stories are not in chronological order. The years that appear at the end of each story indicate composition and publication dates, with the latter in parentheses when they differ. The glossary that follows the stories provides entries for historical personages (Lysenko, Gogol, Voroshilov, and others) as well as explanations of Soviet organizations (the Komsomol, GPU, kolkhoz, and so on) and terms specific to the village (banya, sleeping benches, izba, muzhik, and so on).

The debts we incurred while undertaking this volume are numerous and we would like to acknowledge them here. While we have benefited greatly from the advice of those listed below, we take full responsibility for any infelicities or errors in our translation. Our greatest debt of gratitude goes to Anna Aleksandrovna Maslennikova, professor of English linguistics at the University of St. Petersburg, who painstakingly checked all of our English translations (often late into the night) and provided detailed and invaluable commentary. She was a wonderful and tireless consultant on issues of the Russian language and Russian and Soviet culture. Kathleen Parthé has been an early and important supporter of this undertaking, from suggesting a venue for the project, to making numerous and helpful suggestions on the introduction and translations, to writing the insightful preface to this book. Lev Loseff also read the manuscript in full and provided many valuable comments on matters of translation and culture. Lidiia Fedoseeva-Shukshina has kindly granted us permission to do these translations and offered her complete cooperation from the inception of this volume. Mark Volotsky, the director of the Gorky Film Studio Museum in Moscow, deserves a special thank you for his generous offer of photographs from the museum's archives. Calvin Schwenk gave us important feedback on our stories from the point of view of a nonspecialist. Also very useful was the commentary included in the Russian reader edition of Shukshin's short stories, *Rasskazy*

(Moscow: Russkii iazyk, 1984). Every translator benefits from the efforts of those who have gone before, and we would like to acknowledge as well all of the previous translators of Shukshin's works, whose translations are listed in the bibliography at the end of this volume. Galya Diment, James Rice, Deming Brown, and Svetlana Mikhailovna Kozlova (of the Shukshin Center at Altai State University) have all helped or encouraged us in various ways in our work on Shukshin, and we would like to thank them, too. Finally, we wish to thank the director of Northern Illinois University Press, Mary Lincoln, for her enthusiastic support for this project and the managing editor, Susan Bean, for all of her help.

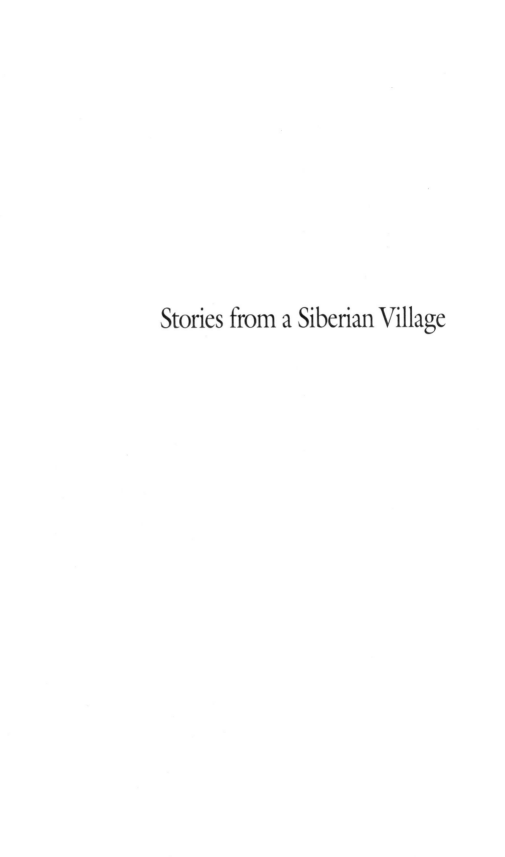

Stories from a Siberian Village

Country Folk

"Well, how about it, Mama? Do what you used to in the good old days—come and see us. You'll see Moscow, it'll really be worth your while. I'll send some money for the trip. Only it's better to get here by plane. It'll be cheaper. And send a telegram right away. So I know when to meet you. The main thing is, don't be scared."

When Granny Malanya'd read this, she pursed her dry lips and became thoughtful.

"It's Pavel invitin' me to come see him," she said to Shurka, glancing at him over the top of her glasses. Shurka was Granny Malanya's grandson, her daughter's son. Her daughter's personal life hadn't panned out (she'd gotten married for the third time), and Granny talked her into handing over Shurka for awhile. She loved her grandson, but kept a tight rein on him.

Shurka was doing homework at the table. At Granny's words he shrugged his shoulders: "Go ahead, if he's invitin' you."

"When's that vacation of yours?" Granny asked sternly.

Shurka pricked up his ears.

"Which one? Winter?"

"Which one do you think, summer?"

"January first. What about it?"

Granny pursed her lips again and became thoughtful. Shurka's heart contracted with anxious joy.

"And what about it?" he asked once more.

"Nothin'. Get back to your homework." Granny hid the letter in the pocket of her apron, put on her coat, and went out of the izba.

Shurka ran over to the window to look where she was headed.

By the gate, Granny Malanya met up with a neighbor and in a loud voice started to tell her all about it.

"It's Pavel invitin' me to stay for a spell in Moscow. I don't rightly know what to do. I just can't make up my mind. 'Come see us, Mama,' he says, 'I've missed you awful bad.'"

The neighbor said something in response, but Shurka couldn't hear what, and Granny replied loudly:

"'Course I could go. I've never once seen the grandkids, just their pictures. But it's awful scary to think about it . . ."

Two more village women stopped next to them, then another one came, and then another . . . Soon a whole lot of folk had gathered around Granny Malanya, and she would tell each new arrival the same story.

"It's Pavel invitin' me to Moscow. I don't rightly know what to do . . ."

It was clear that everybody advised her to go.

Shurka stuck his hands in his pockets and started to pace around the izba. The expression on his face was dreamy and thoughtful, just like his granny's. Overall he took after his granny a lot. He had the same lean build, high cheekbones, and the very same intelligent little eyes. But their natures were not in the least alike. Granny was energetic and wiry, loud-mouthed and very curious. Shurka was also curious, but he was shy to the point of idiocy, modest and thin-skinned.

That evening they composed a telegram for Moscow. Shurka wrote, Granny dictated.

"Dearest Son Pasha, if you really want me to come, then, of course, I can, though in my old age . . ."

"Whoa!" said Shurka. "Who on earth writes telegrams like that?"

"Then how do you think it should be done?"

"Will come. Stop. Or like this: Will come after New Year's. Stop. Signed: Mama. That's it."

Granny actually took offense.

"You're in the sixth grade, Shurka, but you don't get anythin'. It's high time you smartened up!"

Now it was Shurka's turn to take offense.

"Fine," he said. "Do you know how much it'll cost if we write it that way? About twenty rubles in old money."

Granny pursed her lips and became thoughtful.

"Well then, write this: Sonny, I consulted with some folks around here . . ."

Shurka set down his pen.

"I can't do it that way. Who cares if you consulted with some folks around here? They'll make fun of us at the post office."

"Write what you're told!" ordered Granny. "Do you think I'd begrudge my son twenty rubles?"

Shurka picked up the pen and, with a condescending frown, bent over the paper.

"Dearest Son Pasha, I spoke with some neighbors over here—everybody advises me to go. Of course, in my old age I'm a bit scared . . ."

"They'll still redo it at the post office," put in Shurka.

"Just let 'em try!"

"You won't know."

"Keep writin'. I'm, of course, a bit scared, but . . . it's okay. I'll come after New Year's. Stop. With Shurka. He's become quite big now. Anyhow, he's an obedient boy."

Shurka left out the words about him becoming big and obedient.

"I won't be so scared with him. Goodbye for now, Sonny. I miss you all awful bad."

Shurka wrote "terribly" instead.

"At least I'll see your little ones. Stop. Mama."

"Let's count 'em up," Shurka gloated and began to tick off the words with his pen, whispering "one, two, three, four . . ."

Granny looked over his shoulder and waited.

"Fifty-eight, fifty-nine, sixty! Okay. Sixty times thirty is one thousand eight hundred? Right? Divide by one hundred and we get eighteen . . . It'll come to a little over twenty rubles," Shurka announced triumphantly.

Granny snatched up the telegram and hid it in her pocket.

"I'll go to the post office myself or you'll just keep multiplyin' it out, smarty pants."

"Go right ahead. It'll be just the same. Maybe I made a mistake in the kopeks."

Around eleven o'clock their neighbor Yegor Lizunov, the village school custodian, came over. Granny had asked his folks to have him drop by to see her when he got home from work. Yegor had traveled a lot in his time. He had even flown around in planes.

Yegor took off his sheepskin coat and hat, and with his calloused palms smoothed down his graying hair, which was damp with perspiration. He took a seat at the table. The smell of hay and harnesses filled the room.

"So, you wanna fly."

Granny climbed down to the cellar and got a jug of her sweet home-brewed beer.

"Yes, fly, Yegor. Tell us everything in order—all the hows and whats."

"So what's there to tell?" Yegor patiently, even a little condescendingly, watched Granny pour the beer. "Go to town and get on the Biisk-Tomsk train, ride it to Novosibirsk, and ask there where the city Aeroflot agency is. Or you could go straight to the airport . . ."

"Hold it right there! Don't you 'could' me to death, now. Just tell me what I'm s'pposed to do. I don't need to know what I *could* do. And go a little slower, too. Or else you'll make a muddle out of it."

Granny gave Yegor a glass of beer and looked at him sternly.

Yegor touched the glass, stroked it a bit.

"Well, so you get to Novosibirsk and right away ask how to get to the airport. Remember that, Shurka."

"Write it down, Shurka," Granny commanded.

Shurka tore a clean sheet from his notebook and began to take notes.

"When you reach Tolmachovo, ask again where they sell tickets to Moscow. Get the tickets and board the TU-104 and in five hours you'll be in Moscow, the capital of our Motherland."

Granny listened to Yegor mournfully, her head propped up on her dry little fist. The more he talked and the simpler the trip seemed to him, the more anxious her face became.

"In Sverdlovsk, it's true, you'll land . . ."

"What for?"

"You have to. They won't ask you. They just land you and that's that." Yegor decided that now he could finally take a drink. "Well," he said, "here's to an easy trip!"

"Hold it! In Sverdlovsk, do we have to ask 'em ourselves to land us or do they just land everybody?"

Yegor took a drink, grunted with relish, and smoothed down his moustache.

"They just land everybody. Good beer you've got here, Malanya Vasilyevna. How do you make it? I wish you'd teach my old lady."

Granny poured him another glass.

"When you stop bein' so stingy you'll have good beer."

"How's that?" Yegor didn't understand.

"Put more sugar in it. You're always tryin' to get by on the cheap. Put more sugar in those hops and then you'll have beer. It's a cryin' shame to add tobacco to it like you do."

"Ah . . . ," Yegor said thoughtfully. He lifted his glass, glanced first at Granny, then at Shurka, and drained it. "A-ah," he said once more. "There's somethin' to that of course. But in Novosibirsk, when you're there, mind you don't mess up, now."

"What do you mean?"

"Well, you know, anythin' can happen." Yegor took out his tobacco pouch, lit up, and blew an enormous white cloud of smoke out from under his moustache. "The most important thing, of course, is that when you arrive at Tolmachovo, don't mix up the ticket counters. Or else you could end up leavin' for Vladivostok."

Granny became alarmed and poured Yegor his third glass. Yegor drank it right up, grunted, and began to elaborate on his idea.

"Sometimes a person goes up to the eastern ticket counter and says 'Gimme me a ticket.' But he won't ask what that ticket's for. So he ends up flyin' in the exact opposite direction. So, you see, be careful."

Granny poured Yegor a fourth glass. By now Yegor had completely loosened up. He became talkative.

"Yes indeed, if you're gonna fly, you'd better have nerves of steel. For instance, as it's takin' off, the first thing they do is give you a piece of candy . . ."

"Candy?"

"Naturally. That candy means 'Don't think about what's goin' on, don't pay any attention.' But, as a matter of fact, that's the most dangerous moment. Or they say to you 'Fasten your seat belts.' 'What for?' 'Regulations.' Hah! Regulations! They might as well say: 'We're just as likely to flip over and that'd be that.' But no—it's always 'regulations.'"

"Good heavens, good heavens!" said Granny. "So then why do people fly in 'em, if it's like that?"

"Well, if you're afraid of the wolves, don't go into the woods, as they say." Yegor looked over at the jug of beer. "Over all, jets, of course, are more dependable. As for propeller planes, they could break down at the drop of a hat, and there you'd be . . . What's more, they often catch fire, those engines do. One time I was flyin' from Vladivostok . . ." Yegor arranged himself more comfortably in his chair, lit up a new cigarette, and looked at the jug again. Granny didn't budge. "So we're flyin' along, I look out the window: the engine's on fire!"

"God forbid!" Granny gasped. Even Shurka listened with his mouth half open.

"Yes, well of course I start hollerin'. The pilot comes runnin' up. Well basically it wasn't anythin'. He just gave me a good cussin' out. 'What are you doin',' he says, 'causin' a panic? Sure it's on fire. Don't worry about it. Just sit tight.' That's the kind of procedures they follow in those aircraft."

This seemed improbable to Shurka. He had expected that the pilot, upon seeing the flames, would have put them out by speeding up or by making a forced landing. But instead of that he just cussed Yegor out. That seemed odd.

"There's one thing I don't get," Yegor went on, addressing Shurka. "Why don't they give the passengers parachutes?"

Shurka shrugged his shoulders. He didn't know that passengers weren't given parachutes. That, of course, was also strange, if it were really true.

Yegor snuffed out his cigarette in the flower pot, rose halfway in his seat, and helped himself to the jug.

"Some beer you got, Malanya!"

"Don't you lay into it so awful vigorous, now. You'll get drunk."

"This beer is just . . ." Yegor shook his head and took a drink. "Whoo-ee!

But the jets, now, they're dangerous, too. If somethin's broken in one of 'em, the whole thing drops like a rock. It's over in a second . . . And there's nothin' to pick up afterwards. Three hundred grams are all that's left of a person. Clothes and all."

Yegor frowned and fixed his eyes on the jug. Granny picked it up and carried it off to the other room. Yegor sat for a little while longer and then stood up. He was swaying slightly.

"But, on the whole, don't be scared!" he said loudly. "Just take a seat far away from the cabin—in the tail—and you'll be fine. Well, I'll be off."

He walked heavily over to the door and put on his sheepskin coat and hat.

"Give my kind regards to Pavel Sergeyevich. That really is some beer you got there, Malanya! It's simply . . ."

Granny was displeased that Yegor had gotten drunk so quickly. They hadn't gone over everything properly.

"You've become a real lightweight, Yegor."

"It's 'cause I'm tired." Yegor pulled a wisp of straw from the collar of his coat. "I told the bosses, let's haul the hay in the summertime. They'd hear nothin' of it! And now after that blizzard the roads are all covered with snow. All day long we might as well have been crawlin' through it—barely made it out to the nearest haystacks. And then there's that beer of yours . . ." Yegor shook his head and laughed. "Well, I'm on my way. It's all right, don't be timid. Fly. Just take a seat far away from the cabin. Goodbye."

"Goodbye," said Shurka.

Yegor went out. They could hear him carefully step off the high porch, cross the courtyard, open the wicket gate with a creak and, once out on the street, quietly break into song:

"Far and wide the ocean stretched . . ."

And then he fell silent.

Granny gazed thoughtfully and mournfully out the darkened window. Shurka was rereading what he'd written down from Yegor.

"It's terrifyin', Shurka," Granny said.

"People *do* fly, you know."

"Maybe we'd better go by train?"

"By train! We'd spend my whole vacation on the road!"

"Good Lord! Good Lord!" sighed Granny. "Let's write Pavel. And we'll an-nul-li-fy the telegram."

Shurka tore out another sheet from his notebook.

"So we're not flyin'?"

"Where on earth would we fly? It's so awful, saints alive! Three hundred grams, clothes and all . . ."

Shurka became thoughtful.

"Write: Dearest Son Pasha, I consulted with some knowledgeable folk around here . . ."

Shurka bent over the paper.

"They filled us in on what it's like flyin' on those planes. And me and Shurka decided to do this: we'll go in the summertime by train. 'Course we could go now, but Shurka's vacation's awful short."

Shurka paused for a second or two and went on writing.

"And now Uncle Pasha it's me who's writing, on my own. Yegor Lizunov, from the village school (if you remember him), scared Grammy. For instance, he cited this fact: he looked out the window and saw that the engine was on fire. But if that had happened, the pilot would have put out the fire by speeding up, like they usually do. My assumption is that he saw the flame from the exhaust pipe and panicked. Please write Grammy that it's not so terrifying, but don't write about me, that I wrote you. Or else she won't go in the summertime either. It'll be time to work in the garden here, look after the hogs, chickens, and geese. She'd never leave them. 'Cause we're still country folk, you know. And I'm wild about seeing Moscow. We're covering it at school in geography and history, but you yourself know, that isn't the same thing. And in addition our Yegor said, for instance, that passengers aren't given parachutes. That's out and out black-mail! But Grammy believes it. Please, Uncle Pasha, make her ashamed of herself. She really loves you terribly. You should say to her, how can it be, Mama, your own son is a pilot, a Hero of the Soviet Union, with lots of medals, and you're afraid to fly on some stupid civilian plane. And after we've already broken the sound barrier! Put it like that and she'll fly in a second. She's really proud of you. Of course, you deserve it. I personally am proud of you, too. But I'm wild about seeing Moscow. Well, goodbye for now. Yours truly, Alexander."

And meanwhile Granny was dictating:

". . . We'll go closer to autumn. There'll be mushrooms then, maybe I'll have time to make some corned beef and some of my berry jam. You know over there in Moscow you've got to buy everythin' from the store. And they sure don't make things like I do, from scratch. So that's how it is, Sonny. Give our best to your wife and the little ones from me and Shurka. That's all for now. Did you get it all down?"

"Uh-huh."

Granny took the sheet of paper, put it in an envelope, and addressed it herself:

"Moscow, Lenin Avenue, Bld. 78, Apt. 156.

To Hero of the Soviet Union, Lyubavin, Pavel Ignatyevich.

From his mother in Siberia."

She always wrote the address herself. She knew it was more likely to get there that way.

"Well that's that. Don't mope, Shurka. We'll go in the summer."

"I'm not mopin'. But maybe you should start gettin' ready a little bit at a time. You might change your mind and fly."

Granny looked at her grandson and didn't say anything.

During the night Shurka heard her tossing and turning on the stove. She'd sigh quietly and whisper something.

Shurka couldn't sleep either. He was thinking about how many unusual things life promised in the very near future, the likes of which he'd never even dreamed before.

"Shurk!" Granny called.

"Huh?"

"They probably let Pavel into the Kremlin, don't you think?"

"Probably. What about it?"

"It'd be nice to go there once . . . just to take a look."

"They let everybody in nowadays."

Granny was quiet for awhile.

"They don't just let anybody in," she said in disbelief.

"Nikolai Vasilyevich told us."

They were quiet for another minute or so.

"But what about you, Grammy? You can be so brave," Shurka said with displeasure, "and now you're all scared of somethin'. What're you so afraid of?"

"Go to sleep," Granny ordered. "You're a brave soul. You'd be the first one to fill your pants."

"Wanna bet I wouldn't get scared?"

"Go to sleep. Or else I won't be able to get you up for school again tomorrow."

And with that, Shurka quieted down.

1961 (1962)

I Believe!

On Sundays an intense depression would come on in waves. It was a kind of inner, caustic anguish. Maksim could feel it physically, the vile thing. It was as if a slovenly, unwholesome, brazen hussy with bad breath were running her hands all over him, caressing him, trying to kiss him.

"It's come on again!"

"Oh, good God! You jerk! You just wanna be like everybody else! Depression!" mocked Maksim's wife, Lyuda, an unaffectionate working woman. She didn't know what depression was. "What are *you* so depressed about?"

Maksim Yarikov looked at his wife with black, flashing eyes. He clenched his teeth.

"Go ahead—cuss," she egged him on. "Bitch away. Maybe it'll make that depression of yours pass. You're an old hand at bitchin'."

Sometimes Maksim would get a hold of himself and wouldn't fight. He wanted folks to understand him.

"There's no way you'd understand."

"Why wouldn't I understand? Explain it and I will."

"Fine. Say you've got everything—arms, legs, and the other organs. What size they are is another matter, but everything, so to speak, is where it should be. Your foot gets hurt, you feel it. You get hungry, you whip up some dinner. Right?"

"So what?"

Maksim sprang lightly to his feet. (He was a forty-year-old, slightly built muzhik, ill-tempered and rash. Even though he was a hard worker, he never got worn out on the job.) He paced the room and his eyes glittered ferociously.

"But a person's also got something else—a soul! Right here"—Maksim pointed at his chest—"and it aches! I'm not makin' it up! I can actually feel it—it aches!"

"Sure you don't ache somewhere else . . . ?"

"Listen!" Maksim yelped. "If you wanna understand, then listen! Just because you were born a blockhead doesn't mean you can't at least try to understand that there are some people who have souls. I'm not askin' you for a three-spot for vodka. What I really want . . . Oh, you're a fool!"

Maksim completely flew off the handle because he suddenly realized that he could never explain what was happening to him, and his wife Lyuda would never understand him. Never! If he ripped into his chest with a knife, extracted his soul and held it out to her on the palms of his hands, she'd just say, "What a lot of tripe!" And he himself didn't believe that a soul could be like that, a piece of meat. No wonder, then, that all these explanations were just empty words. Why should he get himself all riled up?

"Ask me, when it comes right down to it, who it is I hate most of all on this earth and I'll answer: people who don't have a soul. Or who have a rotten one! Talkin' with people like you is like bangin' your head against the wall."

"What a bunch of crap!"

"Get outta my sight!"

"Then why're you so nasty if you've got a soul?"

"What do you think a soul is, anyway—a spice cake or something? My soul can't understand why I'm draggin' it around like this, so it aches. That's why I'm in a bad mood. My nerves are all on edge."

"Well, go ahead and be nervous, damn you! Normal folks wait for Sunday and relax in a civilized fashion. They go to the movies. But this guy goes and gets a case of the nerves, see. Jerk!"

Maksim would pause by the window and stand there motionless for a long time, looking outside.

A winter landscape. Freezing cold outside. The village would darken the clear, frozen sky with its gray smoke—people were trying to keep themselves warm. If an old woman passed by carrying buckets on a yoke, you could even hear, through the double-paned windows, the crunch of the firmly packed snow under her felt boots. A dog would start barking just for the heck of it and then would quiet down—because of the freezing cold outside. People would stay at home, in the warmth. They'd chat, get dinner together, talk about their neighbors. They'd hit the bottle too, if they had one on hand, but drinking didn't make things any more cheerful.

When Maksim was depressed, he wouldn't philosophize, wouldn't think of asking anybody for anything. He'd feel pain and malice. But he wouldn't direct his malicious anger toward anybody or feel like punching anybody in the face. And he wouldn't feel like hanging himself. He wouldn't feel like anything—that was what was so damn tough to handle. And he wouldn't feel like lying motionless on his back, either. And he wouldn't feel like drinking vodka—he didn't want to be a laughingstock, that was repulsive.

In the past, he'd hit the bottle. And when he was drunk, he'd suddenly start confessing such abominable sins that it would make other people, as well as himself, feel uneasy afterward. Once in the police station, when he was dead drunk, he beat his head against one of the walls all covered with various posters and started howling. This was the story he told that time: He and some other muzhik had together invented a powerful engine the size of a matchbox, and they had handed over the plans to the Americans. Maksim acknowledged that this was vile treason, that he was a traitor, a "Vlasov of science," and he begged to be taken by convoy to the prison camps at Magadan. Moreover, he wanted without fail to walk the whole way barefoot.

"Why on earth did you hand over those plans?" the sergeant tried to find out. "And to whom?"

That Maksim didn't know. He only knew that he was "worse than Vlasov." And he wept bitterly.

On one such agonizing Sunday, Maksim was standing by the window and looking out at the road. Again it was clear and freezing cold and the chimneys were smoking.

"Well, what of it?" Maksim thought angrily. "It was just like this a hundred years ago. So what's new? It'll always be like this. There goes that kid, Vanka Malofeyev's son . . . And I remember Vanka himself, when he'd walk along just like that, and I was the same myself. Some day they'll have kids, too, and so will theirs. Is that all there is? What's the point of it all?"

Maksim felt thoroughly nauseated. Then he remembered that Ilya Lapshin had company, a relative of his wife, and that the relative was a priest. A real live priest with long hair. The priest had something wrong with his lungs—he was ill. He'd come to the village to get well, which he planned to accomplish by consuming badger fat. Ilya would get him the badgers. The priest had a lot of money and he and Ilya often drank hard liquor. The priest drank nothing but hard liquor.

Maksim set off for the Lapshins.

Ilyukha and the priest just happened to be sitting at the table, drinking and chatting. Ilyukha was already plastered. He was nodding drowsily and muttering that next Sunday, not this one, he'd bag twelve badgers in a flash.

"I don't need so many. I need three good and fat ones."

"I'll bring twelve, and you can choose which ones yourself. My job is to bring 'em. And you can choose the best ones yourself. The main thing is for you to get back on your feet. I'll bag 'em for you—twelve of 'em . . ."

The priest was bored with Ilyukha and he was glad when Maksim arrived.

"What can I do for you?" he asked.

"My soul aches," Maksim said. "I came here to find out if the souls of believers ache, too."

"Want a drink?"

"Just don't think that I came over specially for a drink. Of course, I could have a drink, but that wasn't why I came. I'd be curious to know: does your soul ever ache?"

The priest poured some alcohol into the glasses and pushed one over to Maksim along with a decanter of water.

"Dilute it to suit your taste."

The priest was a large sixty-year-old man, with wide shoulders and enormous hands. It was hard to believe that he had something wrong with his lungs. His eyes were lucid and intelligent. They would gaze intently, even impudently at you. He didn't seem like the type to wave some censer around, he was more like a man on the run from his alimony payments. He was not at all beneficent or sanctimonious looking. With a mug like that, he didn't by a long shot fit the description of somebody who could untangle the living, trembling threads of human trials and tribulations. All the same, Maksim immediately felt that things would be interesting with this priest.

"Your soul aches?"

"It does."

"I see." The priest took a drink and wiped his lips on the corner of the starched tablecloth. "Let's approach this from afar. Listen carefully and don't interrupt." The priest settled down against the back of his chair, stroked his beard, and with obvious relish, began to speak.

"The moment the human race appeared, evil appeared, too. The moment evil appeared, so too appeared the desire to fight against it, against evil, that is. Good appeared. So then, good appeared only after evil appeared. In other words, if evil exists, then good exists, if evil does not exist, then good does not exist. Do you follow me?"

"Go on, go on."

"Don't you go-on me—you haven't harnessed me yet!" The priest, it was obvious, adored deliberating like this—in an odd, rambling, irresponsible way. "What is Christ? Christ is the incarnate good, called upon to destroy evil on the earth. For two thousand years he has been present among the people as this idea, a champion against evil."

Ilyukha fell asleep at the table.

The priest poured some more for himself and Maksim. With a nod he invited Maksim to take a drink.

"For two thousand years in the name of Christ we've been trying to destroy evil, but the end of this war is not in sight. Don't smoke please. Or at least go over there to the vent with your noxious fumes."

Maksim snuffed out his home-rolled cigarette on the sole of his boot and continued to listen with interest.

"What's the matter with your lungs?" he inquired out of politeness.

"They ache," the priest explained curtly and reluctantly.

"Does the badger fat help?"

"It does. Let's go on, my pathetic son . . ."

"What did you say?" Maksim was surprised.

"I asked you not to interrupt me."

"I was just askin' about your lungs . . ."

"You asked me 'Why does the soul ache?' I am sketching you a picture of the universe in an easy to understand way, so your soul will find peace. Listen carefully and comprehend. So, then, the idea of Christ sprang out of the desire to overcome evil. Otherwise, what would we need Christ for? Picture this: good has triumphed. Christ has triumphed. But then, what do we need him for now? The need for him passes. So, Christ is not something eternal and abiding, but rather he is a temporary means, like the dictatorship of the proletariat. Whereas *I* want to believe in eternity, in an eternal, vast power and in an eternal order that will come to pass . . ."

"You mean, communism?"

"What about communism?"

"Do you believe in communism?"

"I'm not supposed to. You're interrupting again!"

"That's all. I won't any more. But could you . . . speak a bit more clearly? And don't be in such a hurry."

"I *am* speaking clearly. I said, I want to believe in eternal good, in eternal justice, in an eternal Higher Power that started all this here on earth. I want to get to know this power, and I want to be able to hope that this power will be victorious. Otherwise, what's the purpose of all this? Huh? Where is such a power?" The priest looked inquiringly at Maksim. "Does it exist?"

Maksim shrugged his shoulders.

"I don't know."

"I don't know, either."

"I'll be damned!"

"I'll be twice damned! I don't know such a power. It's possible that it is beyond me as a human being to know this power, to take it in and comprehend it. In that case, I refuse to understand my existence here on earth. This is precisely how I feel about it, and you with your aching soul have come to the right man, for my soul aches, too. Only you came for a ready-made answer, while I myself am trying to bail my way to the bottom. But it's an ocean. And we can't bail it out by the cupful. And when we swallow this vile stuff . . ." The priest downed his alcohol and wiped his lips on the tablecloth. "When we drink this stuff, we are bailing from the ocean in hopes of reaching the bottom. But—by the cupful, the cupful, my son! The circle is closed—we are doomed."

"Forgive me . . . May I make a comment?"

"Fire away!"

"You're some . . . interesting priest. Do priests like you really exist?"

"I am a human being, and nothing human is alien to me. That's how a certain famous atheist put it, and he put it very well.[1] True, it was a little presumptuous on his part—nobody took him for a god in his day, either."

"So, if I've understood you correctly, there is no God?"

"I said, 'There is no God.' Now I say, 'Yes, there is.' Pour me some more, my son, dilute it so it's one part water to three parts alcohol, and give it to me. And pour yourself some, too. Pour away, my guileless son, yes, we may see the bottom, yet!" The priest took a drink. "Now I'll say that God exists. There's a name for him—Life. That's the God I believe in, not the one we've cooked up. What kind of God is that—kind, soft, hornless, wishy-washy: a regular calf! See what we've gone and cooked up! There isn't such a God! There is, however, a severe, mighty God—Life! It offers both good and evil together. This is, strictly speaking, what God is. How come we determined that good must overcome evil? Why? It'd be real interesting to me, for instance, to think that you came to see me not to find out some greater Truth, but to drink alcohol, that you've been sitting there, straining your eyes, only pretending that you're interested in listening."

Maksim stirred in his chair.

"It's no less interesting to me, however, to think that all the same it's not alcohol that you need, but the Truth. And I would be very curious, finally, to ascertain which is really the case? Did your soul bring you here or did the alcohol? You see, I'm using my noggin, instead of just feeling sorry for you, poor lost soul that you are. Therefore, in accordance with this God of mine, I say: your soul aches? Good. Good! You've at least begun to stir, damn you! Or else it'd be impossible to drag you with all of your spiritual inertia off your berth on the stove. Live, my son, weep and kick up your heels. Don't be afraid that you will lick frying pans in the other world,[2] for you'll receive enough of heaven and hell right here in this one."

The priest spoke loudly, his face glowed, he had broken out in a sweat.

"You came to find out what to believe in. You guessed correctly: believers' souls don't ache. But what should we believe in? Believe in Life. How it'll all end up, I don't know. Where everything is bound, I don't know either. But I find it extremely interesting to run there together with everybody else and, if I can, to leave the others behind . . . Evil? Well, evil exists. If somebody in this magnificent race does something underhanded to me like trip me up, I'll get up and give him one in the mug. There'll be no turning the other cheek. Give him one in the mug and call it quits."

"But what if he's got a stronger fist?"

"Then that'll be my lot in life—to run behind him."

"Where are we runnin' to?"

"To never-never land. What difference does it make to you, where? Everybody's going the same direction—the good and the wicked together."

"Somehow I don't feel like I'm headed anywhere," Maksim said.

"That means you're weak in the knees. A paralytic. That means your lot in life is to sit around and whine."

Maksim clenched his teeth. His burning, malevolent gaze bored into the priest.

"And how come I got stuck with such a wretched lot in life?"

"You're weak. Weak as . . . as a boiled rooster. And don't roll your eyes."

"You're a helluva priest! And what if I give you one right here and now upside the head, for instance? What then?"

The priest broke into loud and hearty laughter, sick lungs and all!

"See this?" He showed his own massive paw. "It's never let me down. Survival of the fittest would then take its course."

"And if I bring a gun?"

"They'd shoot you for it. You know that. Therefore, you won't bring a gun, because you're weak."

"What if I stab you with a knife. I'm capable of it."

"You'd get five years. I'd be in pain for a month and heal up. While you'd drag out five years."

"Fine. So then why on earth do you—of all people—have an aching soul?"

"I'm ill, my friend. I've only run half the distance and gone lame . . . Pour some more."

Maksim poured.

"Have you ever flown in a plane?" the priest asked.

"Sure. Lots of times."

"Not me. I flew out here for the first time. It was glorious! When I was boarding, I thought, if this flying barrack should flip over and crash, then that's how it's supposed to be. I won't feel sorry for myself and I won't cower. I felt marvelous the whole way. And when it yanked me off the earth and carried me aloft, I even patted it on its side: well done! I believe in the airplane. Overall, there's a lot of fairness in life. Here they go lamenting that Esenin didn't live long enough. Just about the length of a song. But had that song been longer, it wouldn't have moved us so. There is no such thing as a long song."

"You'd never know by the way they get goin' in those churches of yours . . ."

"That's not a song, that's a moan. No, Esenin's time here on earth was exactly the length of a song. Do you like Esenin?"

"Uh-huh."

"How about singing one of his poems?"

"I can't."

"Then just sing along a bit, and don't throw me off."

And the priest began singing in a deep voice about the ice-covered maple tree, and he sang so sadly and wisely that it's true—it did wring your heart. At the words "Oh, I myself of late have also become unsteady on my feet," the priest pounded the tabletop with his fist, broke into tears, and shook his mane.

"Sweet, sweet Esenin! He loved the peasants! He pitied them! Sweet man! And I love you the same way. Is that just? It is. Is it late in the game? It's late . . ."

Maksim felt that he was also beginning to love the priest.

"Father! Father! Listen here!"

"I don't want to!" the priest wept.

"Listen here, you tub of lard!"

"I don't want to! You're weak in the knees . . ."

"Weak! I'll leave people like you in the dust within the first kilometer! Weak in the knees . . . You TB case!"

"Pray!" The priest stood up. "Repeat after me."

"Go to hell!"

With one hand the priest easily lifted Maksim up by the scruff of the neck and made him stand by his side.

"Repeat after me: I believe!"

"I believe!" said Maksim. He really liked those words.

"Louder! Triumphantly: I be-lieve! Together: I be-lie-e-ve!"

"I be-lie-e-ve!" they wailed out together. The priest led, quickly chanting the following as if reciting mass:

> "In aviation, in the mechanization of agriculture, in the scientific revolu-u-tion! In the cosmos and weightlessness! For they are obje-e-ctive! Together! After me!"

They began roaring.

"I be-lie-eve!"

"I believe that soon everybody will gather in big, stinking cities! I believe that they'll suffocate there and run back to the open fields! I believe!"

"I belie-eve!"

"In badger fat, the horn of the bull, in the erect shaft! In the flesh and blood of the bo-dy!"

. . . When Ilyukha Lapshin forced open his eyes he saw the colossus of a priest vigorously flinging his powerful body around the room, throwing himself impetuously into the dance, squatting and kicking and yelling and slapping his sides and chest:

> I believe, I believe!
> Tah-da, tah-da, tah-da—one!
> I believe, I believe!
> Oom-pah, oom-pah, oom-pah—two!
> I believe, I believe!

And circling the priest, with his hands on his hips, Maksim Yarikov tried to follow in step, chiming loudly in a womanish voice:

> Whoo-ee, whoo-ee, whoo-ee—three!
> I believe, I believe!
> Hey, you! Hey, you! Hey, you—four!

"After me!" the priest exclaimed.

"I believe! I believe!"

Maksim came up behind the priest and they silently danced a circle round the izba. Then the priest threw himself into the dance again, squatting as if over an icehole and flinging out his arms. The floorboards sagged.

> Oh, I believe, I believe!
> Tra-la, tra-la, tra-la—five!
> All those little shafts—man alive!
> I believe! I believe!
> And where there're six, there's sure to be sex!
> I believe! I believe!

Both the priest and Maksim danced with such a fury and in such a frenzy that it didn't seem at all strange that they were dancing. They either had to dance or rend the shirt on their breast and weep and gnash their teeth.

Ilyukha looked and looked at them and then lined up to dance, too. But he could only shout out "Yee-haw! Yee-haw!" once in a while in his thin voice. He didn't know the words.

The priest's shirt was soaked through on his back. Under the shirt, mounds of muscles rippled powerfully. He obviously had never before known the slightest fatigue and his illness had not yet managed to eat away at his taut sinews. They probably weren't that easy to eat through. Before he'd let that happen, he'd gobble up the whole badger population. And if necessary, if so advised, he'd ask them to bring him a nice, plump wolf—he wouldn't go out without a fight.

"After me!" the priest commanded again.

And the three of them, led by the fierce, fiery priest, set off dancing around and around. Then the priest, like a big, heavy beast, pounced again into the middle of the circle, making the floorboards sag. The plates and glasses on the table started clinking.

"Oh, I believe! I believe!"

1971

Cutting
Them Down
to Size

Old Agafya Zhuravlyova's son Konstantin Ivanovich had come home. With his wife and daughter. To have a visit and rest up. Novaya was not a large village, and so when Konstantin Ivanovich actually came rolling up in a taxi, and when everybody in the family took forever dragging suitcase after suitcase out of the trunk, the whole village knew immediately: Agafya's son had come with his family, the middle son Kostya, the rich one, the scholar.

By evening everybody knew all the details: he himself was a Ph.D., his wife was a Ph.D., too, and their daughter was still in school. They'd brought Agafya an electric samovar, a bright flowery robe, and some wooden spoons.

That very evening the muzhiks gathered on Gleb Kapustin's porch. They were waiting for Gleb.

At this point, a few words should be said about Gleb Kapustin so that it's clear why the muzhiks had gathered on his porch and what they were waiting for.

Gleb Kapustin was a fat-lipped, towheaded muzhik, about forty years old, well read, and venomous. Now it had somehow turned out that the village of Novaya, though not large, had produced many notable people: one colonel, two pilots, a physician, and a correspondent . . . And now there was Zhuravlyov the Ph.D. And somehow it had become the custom that when notable people would come to the village on vacation, when folks would crowd into an izba of an evening to see some notable local boy and listen to some wondrous tales or talk about themselves, if the fellow were so inclined—that was the time when Gleb Kapustin would arrive and *cut the notable guest down to size*. Many people were displeased with this, but many others, especially the muzhiks, just waited for Gleb to come and cut the notable down to size. It wasn't really that they even waited—they'd actually go to Gleb's and then all go see the guest together. Just as if they were going to a performance. Last year Gleb had cut the colonel down to size—

brilliantly, beautifully. They'd begun talking about the War of 1812 . . . It became apparent that the colonel didn't know who had ordered the burning of Moscow. That is, he knew that it was some count, but he mixed up the name and said it was Rasputin.[1] Gleb soared high above the colonel like a hawk . . . and cut him down to size. Everybody got excited, the colonel swore. Some of them ran off to the teacher's house to find out the name of the arsonist count. Gleb Kapustin sat still, flushed in anticipation of the moment of truth, just repeating, "Compose yourself, compose yourself, comrade Colonel. After all, we aren't in Fili, are we?"[2] Gleb emerged the victor while the colonel beat his head with his fist, utterly bewildered. He was very upset. For a long time afterward they talked about Gleb in the village, remembering how he'd just repeated, "Compose yourself, compose yourself, comrade Colonel. After all, we aren't in Fili." They were amazed at Gleb. The old men wondered why he'd put it that way.

Gleb would chuckle and narrow his steely eyes somewhat vindictively. In the village all the mothers of notable people disliked Gleb. They were afraid of him.

And now along came Zhuravlyov the Ph.D.

Gleb came home from work (he worked at the lumberyard), washed up, and changed his clothes. He didn't bother to eat supper. He went right out to join the muzhiks on the porch.

They lit up. They talked for a bit about this and that, deliberately avoiding any mention of Zhuravlyov. Then Gleb looked over toward old Agafya Zhuravlyova's izba a couple of times, and finally asked:

"Does old Agafya have guests?"

"Ph.D.'s."

"Ph.D.'s?" Gleb was surprised. "O-oh. Won't be able to lick *them* barehanded."

The muzhiks laughed. Some folks, they said, couldn't—but some could. And they kept looking impatiently at Gleb.

"Well, let's go and pay a little visit to the Ph.D.'s," Gleb suggested unassumingly.

And so off they went.

Gleb walked a little ahead of the rest, calmly, with his hands in his pockets, squinting at old Agafya's izba, where at that moment there were two Ph.D.'s. It generally happened that the muzhiks would escort Gleb in this way. It was just like escorting an experienced village fistfighter when folks find out that a new tough guy has appeared in a rival neighborhood.

They didn't talk much on the way.

"What field are the Ph.D.'s in?" Gleb asked.

"What's their specialization? Damned if I know. Old Agafya just told me they were Ph.D.'s. Both him and his wife."

"There are Ph.D.'s in technical fields and then there are those in general studies—they're big on bullshitology."

"All in all, Kostya was a real whiz in math," someone who'd gone to school with Kostya remembered. "He was a straight-A student."

Gleb Kapustin was originally from a neighboring village and didn't know the local notables very well.

"We shall see what we shall see," Gleb promised vaguely. "There are more Ph.D.'s these days than you can shake a stick at."

"He came in a taxi."

"Well, he's gotta maintain his reputation." Gleb gave a short laugh.

Konstantin Ivanovich, Ph.D., greeted his guests cordially and made a fuss about getting some food on the table. The guests waited unassumingly while old Agafya set everything out. They chatted with the doctor and reminisced about how in childhood they had done this or that together.

"Ah, childhood! Those were the days!" the Ph.D. said. "Well, please take a seat at the table, friends."

Everybody sat down at the table. And Gleb Kapustin sat down, too. For the time being Gleb held his tongue. But it was obvious that he was getting ready to pounce. He smiled and went along with their talk about childhood days, but all the while he kept glancing at the Ph.D., sizing him up.

Around the table the conversation got friendlier, they'd even begun to forget about Gleb Kapustin . . . And then he started in on the doctor.

"What field do you make yourself distinct in?" he asked.

"You mean, where do I work?" The Ph.D. didn't understand.

"Yes."

"The philology department."

"Philosophy?"

"Not exactly . . . Well, I suppose you could call it that."

"It's a necessary thing." Gleb needed it to be philosophy. He became animated. "Well, and what do you make of primacy?"

"What primacy?" Again, the Ph.D. didn't understand. And he looked attentively at Gleb. Everybody looked at Gleb.

"The primacy of spirit and matter." Gleb threw down the gauntlet. Gleb affected a casual pose and waited for the gauntlet to be taken up. The Ph.D. took the gauntlet up.

"As always," he said with a smile, "matter is primary."

"And the spirit?"

"The spirit comes next. What about it?"

"Is that part of your qualifying exams?" Gleb also smiled. "You'll excuse us. We all . . . are a long ways away from any centers of learning. Even if a person in these parts wants to have a good chat, it's impossible to round somebody up—there's just nobody to talk to. So, how does philosophy define the concept of weightlessness these days?"

"As it always has. Why 'these days'?"

"It's just that there's this recently discovered phenomenon." Gleb smiled, looking the Ph.D. straight in the eyes. "That's why I'm asking. Natural philosophy, let's suppose, will define it one way, and strategic philosophy quite another."

"But there is no such thing as strategic philosophy," the doctor got all riled up. "What exactly are you talking about?"

"Precisely. But there is a dialectic of nature." Gleb had everybody's attention as he calmly continued. "And philosophy defines nature. Weightlessness has recently been discovered to be one of the elements of nature. That's why I'm asking. Is there a noticeable sense of confusion among the philosophers?"

The Ph.D. broke into sincere laughter. But he was the only one laughing. And he felt awkward. He called his wife over.

"Valya, come here. We're having . . . the strangest conversation."

Valya came over to the table. But Dr. Konstantin Ivanovich still felt uncomfortable because the muzhiks were looking at him, waiting for him to answer the question.

"Let's ascertain," the Ph.D. began seriously, "just what we're talking about."

"All right. Second question. What's your personal opinion about the problem of shamanism in the autonomous regions of the north."

The Ph.D.'s laughed. Gleb Kapustin also smiled. And waited patiently for the doctors to have their laugh.

"Sure, it's possible, of course, to pretend that such a problem doesn't exist. I'll gladly laugh along with you . . ." Gleb once again smiled magnanimously. He in particular smiled at the doctor's wife, who was also a Ph.D., a Ph.Dame, so to speak. "But even if we do, the problem as such won't just go away. Will it?"

"Are you serious about all this?" Valya asked.

"With your permission." Gleb Kapustin half rose in his seat and bowed with reserve to the Ph.Dame. And he blushed. "The question, of course, is not of global significance, but from the point of view of the likes of us, it'd be interesting to find out."

"Well, what is the question then?" the Ph.D. exclaimed impatiently.

"Your view on the problem of shamanism," Valya prompted, again laughing involuntarily. But she caught herself and said to Gleb, "Sorry."

"That's all right," said Gleb. "I understand that I might have asked a question that's not in your field of specialization."

"But there isn't such a problem!" the doctor blurted out once more, as if delivering a jab straight from the shoulder. This was unfortunate. He shouldn't have done that.

Now it was Gleb who laughed. And he said:

"Well, that makes things easier."

The muzhiks looked at the Ph.D.

"Get the woman off the cart and the horse'll go farther," Gleb added, citing a proverb. "There isn't such a problem, and yet these . . ." (Gleb gestured intricately with his hands) ". . . natives dance and ring their little bells . . . Right? But if we want it . . ." Gleb repeated, "if we w-a-n-t it, it's as if they don't exist. Right? Because if . . . Very well! One more question. What do you think about the fact that the Moon is a man-made object?"

The Ph.D. looked mutely at Gleb. Gleb continued.

"Scientists have hypothesized that the Moon lies in an artificial orbit and it's assumed that intelligent beings live inside it . . ."

"Well?" the Ph.D. asked. "What of it?"

"Where are your calculations of the natural trajectories? Where, if at all, can the cosmic sciences be applied?"

The muzhiks listened attentively to Gleb.

"If we allow that mankind will be visiting more and more often our, shall we say, cosmic neighbor, we can also assume that one fine moment these intelligent beings will no longer be able to restrain themselves and will crawl out to meet us. Are we ready to understand one another?"

"Who are you asking?"

"You, the thinkers . . ."

"And are *you* ready?"

"We aren't thinkers, our salaries aren't that high. But if you're interested, I can share with you in what direction our thoughts are leading us provincials. Let's say an intelligent being has surfaced on the Moon. What would you like us to do? Bark like a dog? Crow like a rooster?"

The muzhiks laughed. They stirred in their seats. And once again fixed their eyes attentively on Gleb.

"But, all the same, we need to understand one another. Isn't that right? How?" Gleb paused inquisitively. He looked at everybody. "I suggest drawing a map of our solar system in the sand and showing him that I'm from Earth, you see. And that, even though I'm in a space suit, I also have a head and that I'm an intelligent being, too. To confirm this, it's possible to show him on the map where he's from by pointing at the Moon and then at him. Isn't that logical? And so we've ascertained in this way that we're neighbors. But that's all we've done! Next, I've got to explain the laws by which I've evolved in order to reach my present stage . . ."

"I see, I see . . ." The Ph.D. stirred in his seat and shot a meaningful look at his wife. "That's very interesting. Exactly what might those laws be?"

This, too, was unfortunate, because his meaningful look was intercepted. Gleb soared upward . . . and from way up there in the heavens he swooped down on the Ph.D. And thus it was that in all of the conversations with notable people from the village the moment would arrive when Gleb would soar up like a bird of prey. It was likely that he always looked forward to this moment, exulted in it, because afterward everything else happened automatically.

"Inviting your wife to laugh?" Gleb asked. He asked serenely, but inside he was probably all aquiver. "That's fine . . . Only, maybe first of all we should at least learn how to read the papers. Huh? What do you think? They say that doesn't hurt Ph.D.'s either . . ."

"Listen here . . ."

"No, we've done our listening! We've had, as they say, the pleasure. Therefore, allow me to point out, Mr. Ph.D., that a doctorate is not just a suit, you know, that you buy once and for all. Even so, a suit has to be cleaned sometimes. But a doctorate—that is, if we've agreed that it's not a suit—needs all the more . . . to be kept up." Gleb spoke quietly, insistently, without pausing for breath. He was on a roll.

It was uncomfortable to look at the Ph.D. He was clearly at a loss, looking now at his wife, now at Gleb, now at the muzhiks. The muzhiks tried not to look at him.

"We can be easily impressed around here. All you have to do is roll up to the house in a taxi and drag five suitcases out of the trunk . . . But you forget that the flow of information moves evenly in all directions. What I mean is that you can also make the wrong impression here. That also happens. You might expect that people around here have never seen Ph.D.'s with their own eyes, but we've seen them, Ph.D.'s and professors and colonels. And we have pleasant memories of them because they are, as a rule, very simple people. So this is my advice to you, comrade Doctor: come down to earth more often. I swear, there's a sound principle behind this. And it's not so risky. It won't hurt so bad when you fall."

"There's a name for this: doing a smear job," said the Ph.D. "What's the matter, did you break loose from your chain? What exactly—"

"I don't know, I don't know," Gleb interrupted him hastily. "I don't know the name for it. I haven't done time nor have I 'broke loose from my chain.' What are you driving at? Around here," Gleb looked at the muzhiks, "nobody's done time either—they won't understand you. And your wife here's gaping at you. And your little daughter over there is going to hear you. She'll hear you and she'll 'do a smear job' on somebody in Moscow. So that slang could . . . end poorly for you, comrade Doctor. Not all means are good, believe me, not all means. After all, when you were taking your qualifying exams, you didn't 'do a smear job' on your professor. Isn't that right?" Gleb rose to his feet. "And you didn't 'use and abuse somebody' to get what you wanted. And you didn't use prison slang. That's because professors are to be respected—your fate depends on them, but it doesn't depend on the likes of us. You can use your prison slang with us. Isn't that how it is? Well, you shouldn't have. We around here also know a thing or two. We also read the papers, and it even happens that we read books from time to time. And we even watch television. And just imagine: we're not in raptures over shows like "The Club of the Jolly and Quick-Witted" or "The Thirteen Chairs Tavern."[3] Why not, you ask? Because it's the very same kind of presumptuousness. That's okay, they say, everybody'll gobble it up. And they do, of course, there's nothing you can do about it. Just don't pretend that all those folks on TV are geniuses. Some of us see right through it. You all should be more modest."

"A typical slandering demagogue," the Ph.D. said, addressing his wife. "All the usual traits are there."

"You're off the mark. I have never, in all my life, written a single denunciation, anonymous or otherwise." Gleb looked at the muzhiks: they knew this to be true. "That's not it, comrade Doctor. Do you want me to explain what makes me tick?"

"Please do."

"I like to take people down a peg or two. Don't stick up so high above the waterline. More modesty, dear comrades."

"But where in the world did you see any immodesty in us?" Valya couldn't hold back any longer. "What's so immodest about us?"

"Think good and hard about it when you're all by yourselves. Think it over and you'll understand." Gleb even gave the Ph.D.'s a look of pity. "No matter how many times you say 'honey' it won't make your mouth any sweeter. You don't have to take a Ph.D. exam to understand that. Do you? No matter how many times you write the words 'the people' in all of your articles, nobody's any smarter for it. So when you venture out among those very people, be a little wiser. More prepared perhaps. Or else you may well make a fool of yourself. Goodbye. Have a nice vacation . . . among the people." Gleb grinned and walked unhurriedly out of the izba. He always left alone like that after meetings with notable people.

He didn't hear the muzhiks later saying, as they went their separate ways from the Ph.D.s' house:

"Sure did a number on him! . . . Clever sonuvabitch. How does he know so much about the Moon?"

"Cut him down to size."

"Where does he get it from?"

And the muzhiks shook their heads in amazement.

"Clever sonuvabitch. He really put poor Konstantin Ivanych through the wringer . . . Eh? . . . Really hung him out to dry. And that Valya, you know, didn't even open her mouth."

"What could you say? Not a damn thing. Kostya, you know, wanted to say something, of course . . . But he couldn't get a word in edgewise."

"Gotta hand it to him! He's a clever sonuvabitch!"

You could almost even hear a little pity or sympathy for the doctors in the muzhiks' voices. Gleb Kapustin, on the other hand, had once again amazed them. He'd astounded them. Even delighted them. But we can't say that they loved it. No, it wasn't a question of loving it. Gleb was cruel, and nobody anywhere has ever yet loved cruelty.

Tomorrow Gleb Kapustin will go to work and ask the muzhiks nonchalantly (it's all an act):

"Well, how's that Ph.D. getting on?"

And he'll grin.

"You cut him down to size," they'll tell Gleb.

"No harm done," Gleb will remark magnanimously. "It's good for him. Let him think things over in his spare time. Or else they all get too big for their britches."

1970

The Microscope

Something like that meant you had to make up your mind once and for all. So he did.

He came home one day not himself, all ashen. Without looking at his wife, he said:

"Um . . . I lost the money." With that, his misshapen nose (it was crooked and hooked) turned from an ashen hue to red. "A hundred and twenty rubles."

His wife's mouth fell open. A pleading, questioning look flashed across her face: could this be a joke? But no, old hooknose never joked. He didn't know how. She asked stupidly:

"Where?"

At that, an annoyed grunt escaped him.

"Now if I knew that, I'd have gone and—"

"Well, now you've done it!!" she roared. "It'll be a long time before you try gruntin' at me again!" And she ran to fetch a frying pan. "How's nine months sound, you creep!"

He snatched up a pillow from the bed—to deflect the blows. (Those ancient warriors just showed off with their fancy shields. A pillow's what you really need!) They began to go round and round the room . . .

"The pillow! You're gettin' the pillow dirty! You're the one who'll have to wash it!"

"I'll wash it all right, you hooknose! But I'll get two of your ribs before I do. They're as good as mine!"

"Hey, watch it! You're gettin' my hands! . . ."

"Handsies-pansies! Little hooked nosies!"

"You're gettin' my hands, dummy! Tomorrow I'll have to go on sick leave! It'll be harder on you."

"Go ahead!"

"It'll be harder on you . . ."

"So what!"

"Ow!"

"Take that!"

"Well, haven't you had enough?"

"No. I'm just gettin' started. Gotta get it all outta my system, you hook-nosed twat! Woodpecker . . ." At this point, she managed to land a painful blow on his head. The thud gave even her a bit of a scare.

He threw down the pillow, grabbed his head, and started groaning. She looked at him searchingly: was he faking or did it really hurt? She decided it really hurt. She put down the frying pan, took a seat on a stool and began wailing. With moan after plaintive moan, she lamented:

"Why oh why is this my lot in li-i-fe? . . . How I kept savin' and savin'! . . . Why oh why, when I never let myself have even one extra piece of white bre-ead! . . . Why, I never bought my dear little kids sweet treats! . . . I scrimped and scrimped, you hook-nosed twa-at! . . . Why oh why? . . . Each kopek I put aside made me happy, 'cause my dear little kids were gonna have nice, warm coats for winter! And they wouldn't hafta go to school shiverin' in nothin' but rags . . ."

"Now when've they ever gone around in rags?" he couldn't hold back.

"Shut up, twat! Shut up! You took the food right out of your very own children's mouths! You ate it up and didn't even choke! You could've at least choked on it—then we'd all feel a little better."

"Thank you for the kind words," he hissed venomously.

"Oh you twat! . . . Where'd you go? Maybe you'll remember? Maybe you forgot the money somewhere at work. Maybe you put it under your workbench and forgot it?"

"How could I have left it at work! I went to the savings bank on the way home from work. As if I could've left it at work . . ."

"Well, maybe you dropped in on somebody, you twat?"

"I didn't drop in on anybody."

"Maybe you stopped somewhere to drink beer with all them other drunks? . . . Try and remember. Maybe you dropped it on the floor. Run and see, they'll still give it back to you."

"But I didn't go anywhere to drink beer."

"Then where on earth could you have lost it, twat?"

"How'm I s'posed to know?"

"This takes the cake! . . . Right now we coulda been takin' the kids, tryin' coats on 'em . . . I already had my eye on which ones to get. And now others'll buy 'em up. Oh, you're a twat, a twat . . ."

"That's enough! You're just like a broken record: twat, twat . . ."

"Isn't that what you are?"

"There's nothin' we can do now."

"You're gonna work double shifts, twat! You're gonna work till you're nothin' but skin and bones . . . There'll be no pint of vodka after the banya now, oh no! It'll be well water for you . . ."

"I don't need my pint. I'll make do without it."

"You're gonna walk to work, too! There'll be no bus ridin' for you."

He was surprised at that.

"I've gotta work double shifts *and* walk there? That's a good one!"

"Yes, walk! You'll walk there and back, twat! And when you hafta, you'll run so's not to be late. You'll pay for this, for that money! You won't forget it for a long time."

"I'm not so sure about a double shift, but I can probably pull off a shift and a half for a month—that's do-able," he said seriously, rubbing his injured spot. "I've already made arrangements with the foreman . . ." He didn't realize at first that he'd let the cat out of the bag. But when she gave him a puzzled look, he corrected himself: "Soon as I saw the money was missin', I went back to work and made arrangements."

"Well, gimme the savings book," she demanded. She looked at it, sighed, and once more said bitterly: "Twat."

For about a week, Andrei Yerin felt lousy. He was a joiner in a small workshop attached to the state grain-purchasing agency (Zagotzerno), located nine kilometers from the village. His wife was always in a bad mood; she kept calling him a twat. He also got angry, but he didn't dare do any name-calling himself, at least out loud.

However, the days went by . . . His wife calmed down. Andrei waited. At last he decided that the time was right.

And so, late one evening (he really was at the grind one and a half shifts a day), he arrived home with a box in his hands, and in the box, you could tell, there was something kind of heavy. Andrei was quietly radiant.

It often happened that he'd bring some kind of work home. Sometimes it was various small wooden things, little boxes wrapped up in paper. So nobody was surprised that he had come home with something. But Andrei was quietly radiant. He stood in the doorway and waited for his family to notice him . . . And, indeed, they did.

"How come you're standin' there all aglow like . . . like a bare ass in the moonlight?"

"Here . . . They gave it to me for shock labor." Andrei walked across the room to the table and took a long time unpacking the box. At last he opened it. And he set out on the table . . . a microscope. "A microscope."

"Whatcha need it for?"

At that Andrei Yerin began to fuss about. But he didn't fuss about guiltily, as he usually did. This time his fussing had a touch of superiority to it.

"We're gonna scrutinize the moon!" And he roared with laughter. His fifth-grade son also burst out laughing: as if you could look at the moon through a microscope of all things!

"What's so funny?" Mother took offense.

Father and son just rolled with laughter.

Mother leveled a stern glance at Andrei. He calmed down.

"Did you know that you're surrounded by microbes at every step? Say you've ladled yourself a mug of water . . . Right?" Andrei ladled himself a mug of water. "Do you think it's water you're drinkin'?"

"Oh, go on."

"No, answer the question."

"It's water I'm drinkin'."

Andrei looked at his son and once again couldn't help roaring with laughter.

"She thinks she's drinkin' water! . . . Well, ain't she a fool?"

"Twat! I'm gonna get the fryin' pan right now."

Andrei sobered up.

"It's microbes you're drinkin', honey, microbes. Along with the water, you'll toss down a coupla million—that's how it is. Just like a little snack!" Once again father and son couldn't keep from laughing. Zoya (his wife) headed for the corner to fetch the frying pan.

"Lookee here!" Andrei shouted. He ran over to the microscope with the mug in his hand, adjusted the instrument for a long time, let a tiny drop of water fall on the glass slide, put his eye to the viewing scope and looked through it, barely daring to breathe for some two long minutes. His son stood behind him—he was dying to have a look, too.

"Dad! . . ."

"There they are, the varmints!" Andrei Yerin whispered. With a kind of ghastly delight he whispered: "Out for a stroll."

"Come on, Dad!"

The father twitched his foot.

"Back and forth, back and forth! . . . The varmints!"

"Daddy!"

"Let the child have a turn!" Mother ordered sternly, also clearly interested.

Andrei reluctantly tore himself away from the eyepiece, and gave up his place to his son. And he eagerly and jealously fixed his eyes on the back of his son's head. He asked impatiently:

"Well?"

His son didn't say anything.

"Well?!"

"There they are!" the little boy roared. "White little things . . ."

Father dragged his son away from the microscope and gave the spot to his wife.

"Take a look! So you think it's water you're drinkin' . . ."

Mother looked for a long time . . . First with one eye, then the other . . .

"Don't see a thing!"

Andrei got all indignant, he became surprisingly bold.

"You must be blind! She can sniff out any kopek in your pocket, and yet she can't make out a single microbe. They're practically leapin' up in your face, you fool! The little white things . . ."

Since she couldn't see any white things, but father and son had, mother didn't get upset.

"Ah, there they are . . ." Maybe she lied. She'd occasionally fib like that. She was capable of stretching the truth.

Andrei firmly pushed his wife away from the microscope and fastened his eye to the viewing scope. And again his voice fell to a whisper.

"Damnation, look at 'em go! Look at 'em go!"

"Are they kinda cloudy?" the mother asked her son from somewhere in back. "Kinda like blobs of fat in soup? Are those them?"

"Qui-et!" Andrei barked, not tearing himself away from the microscope. "Blobs of fat . . . You're the blob of fat. You're a whole hunk of ham." It was strange, but Andrei Yerin was becoming the loud domineering master of the house.

The older son, the fifth-grader, burst out laughing. His mother whacked him on the back of the head. Then she brought the younger kids over to the microscope.

"Okay you, Mr. Ph.D. of sour cabbage soup! Give the children a look. Quit hoggin' it."

Father gave up his place at the microscope and began pacing about the room in agitation. He was thinking about something.

While they ate supper, Andrei kept thinking about something. He'd glance over at the microscope and shake his head. He scooped up a spoonful of soup and held it out to his son:

"How many of 'em in here? Approximately."

His son frowned:

"At least half a million."

Andrei Yerin scowled at his spoon.

"At least. And we—gulp 'em right down!" He swallowed the soup and pounded his chest. "And they're gone. Now the old organism'll kick in and start thrashin' 'em around down there. It'll take care of 'em!"

"If I didn't know better, I'd swear you *asked* for a microscope!" His wife looked at the microscope with mild displeasure. "Maybe they'd have given you a vacuum cleaner instead. 'Cause we don't have anythin' to do the vacuumin' with."

No, when God was creating woman, he went overboard. He got carried away, the Creator did. Like every artist does, however. But, on the other hand, this was no Rodin's Thinker he was making, either.

Twice during the night Andrei got up, turned on the light, looked through the microscope and whispered:

"The lousy varmints! What're they up to? What the heck are they up to? And they don't even sleep!"

"Don't you go crazy now," his wife said. "It wouldn't take much to push you over the deep end."

"Soon I'll start makin' discoveries," Andrei said, crawling back into the warmth of the blankets toward his wife. "Have you ever slept with a scientist?"

"What next!"

"You will." And Andrei Yerin tenderly patted his spouse's soft shoulder. "You will sleep with a scientist, sweetie pie."

For probably about a week, Andrei lived as if in a dream. He'd arrive home from work, carefully wash his hands, and wolf down his supper . . . He'd cast sidelong glances at the microscope.

"The thing is," he'd tell them, "man is s'pposed to live a hundred and fifty years. The question arises, then, why is it that he only lives sixty, seventy tops—and then turns up his toes? Microbes! The bastards cut short a man's time on earth. They worm their way into your organism and the moment you weaken the least little bit, they take over."

He sat with his son at the microscope for hours on end. They were doing research. They examined a drop of water from the well, and from the bucket that held drinking water . . . When it rained, they examined a raindrop. Father also sent his son to take a sample of water from a puddle . . . And there it was just swarming with the little white things.

"Damnation! Look at 'em go! So how on earth can you fight 'em?" Andrei lost heart. "A man steps in a puddle, comes home, and tracks the water into the house. Then along comes a barefooted child and—pow! He picks 'em up. And how's a child's organism gonna fight 'em off?"

"So you should always remember to wipe your feet before you come in," his son remarked. "But you never remember to."

"That's not the point. We've gotta learn how to destroy 'em right there in the puddle. Or you see—I'll wipe my feet, I know all about it now, but take that Senka Marov . . . Just try and prove it to him: he'll go trampin' through everythin' just like he always has, the fool."

They also examined a drop of sweat, for which his little son had to run around outside till he was ready to drop, then his father took a spoon and scraped some moisture off his forehead. They got a drop and bent over the microscope . . .

"They're there, too!" Andrei pounded his knee with his fist in vexation. "You just try and live a hundred and fifty years! They're even in our skin!"

"How 'bout tryin' some blood?" his son suggested.

Father pricked his finger with a needle, squeezed out a dark red berry of blood, and shook it off onto the slide. He bent over the eyepiece and let out a groan.

"We're done for, Son—they've gotten into our blood!" Andrei Yerin straightened up, he looked around him in amazement. "So that's how it is. But those lousy parasites—they've known it all along! They know it better'n me—and they've been keepin' it a secret!"

"Who?" His son didn't understand.

"Scientists. They've got microscopes better'n ours—they can see every-thin'. But they've been keepin' it a secret. They don't want to alarm the population. But why not tell us? Maybe we could all put our heads together and figure out a way to destroy 'em. But no, they've all agreed to keep it a secret. A panic would erupt, they'd say."

Andrei Yerin sat on his stool. He lit up.

"To think people die from such tiny creatures!" Andrei looked crushed.

His son looked through the microscope.

"They're chasin' each other! Those ones are a little different . . . They're kinda round."

"Round, long—they're all the same. Don't tell your mother for now, that we saw 'em in my blood."

"Let's take a look at mine."

Father looked closely at his son . . . Both curiosity and fear were reflected in the elder Yerin's eyes. His hands, hardened and worn by many years of work—large hands, smelling of resin—trembled slightly on his knees.

"No, better not. Maybe the little ones at least . . . It's too much!" Andrei stood up and kicked his stool in anger. "They've learned how to wipe out lice, bedbugs, all sorts of maggots, but here we've got some kinda . . . they're smaller than the tiniest of nits, and you can't do anythin' about 'em! What good are all those doctors' degrees?!"

"You can see a louse, but these . . . How do you get rid of 'em?"

Father thought for a long time.

"Turpentine? . . . Won't work here. Vodka's gotta be stronger, but you see how I drink it and they're still swarmin' in my blood!"

"So vodka goes into the blood, then?"

"Where else? What else makes people tipsy?"

One day Andrei brought what looked like a long thin needle home from work . . . He washed up, winked at his son, and they went into the other room.

"Let's give it a try . . . I sharpened this wire—maybe we'll manage to prick a pair of 'em."

The tip of the wire was ever so slender—no thicker than a hair. For a long time, Andrei poked around in the drop of water with this tip. His breathing became heavy . . . He even broke out in a sweat.

"They keep runnin' away, the bastards . . . No, it's too thick. We won't be able to prick 'em. We need a thinner one, but a thinner one's out of the question—it can't be made. All right, we'll go eat supper now, and then we'll try givin' 'em an electric shock . . . I got a hold of a battery: we'll hook up two wires and we'll short-circuit 'em. Then we'll see how they do."

But just when they were having supper, along came an untimely guest: Sergei Kulikov, who worked with Andrei at Zagotzerno, dropped by. On account of its being Saturday, Sergei was tipsy, which is probably why he wandered on over to Andrei's in the first place—for no special reason.

Of late, Andrei had no time for drinking sprees and it was with surprise that he realized that drunks disgusted him. They always behave like stupid idiots and say all kinds of absurd things.

"Come in and sit down with us," Andrei said reluctantly.

"Don't bother about us. We'll just sit right here . . . What do the likes of us need? We'll be fine here in the corner!"

What's with the hard-luck act, Andrei thought. Fool.

"Whatever," he said.

"How 'bout lettin' me have a look at your microbes?"

Andrei became uneasy.

"What microbes? Go sleep it off, Seryoga . . . I don't have any microbes."

"Whatcha bein' all secretive for? It's not some weapon ya got tucked away, now, is it? It's a matter of science . . . My boy's been dronin' on at me nonstop: Uncle Andrei wants to destroy all the microbes. Andrei!" Sergei pounded his fist on his chest and fastened his fierce gaze on the "scientist." "We'll cast a gold statue in your honor! . . . We'll make you famous throughout the world! And I worked next to you! . . . Andryukha!"

Although Zoya Yerina couldn't stand drunks either, she felt flattered nonetheless that people around the village were calling her husband a scientist. More out of her old habit of grumbling when the opportunity presented itself than out of her true feelings on the matter, she remarked:

"Couldn't they have awarded him somethin' else as a bonus? What're we gonna do with a microscope? My man's gonna go outta his mind—he doesn't sleep nights. Why couldn't they have awarded him somethin' like a vacuum cleaner . . . 'Cause we don't have anythin' to do our vacuumin' with and there's no way we can save up for one now."

"What award?" Sergei didn't understand.

Andrei Yerin broke out in a cold sweat.

"You know, they gave him that bonus . . . that microscope . . ."

Andrei tried desperately with his eyes to tip Sergei off. But it was no use. Sergei was staring at Zoya the way sheep do, dully and fixedly.

"What bonus?"

"The one they gave all of you."

"All of who?"

Zoya looked at her husband, then at Sergei . . .

"Didn't they give you a bonus?"

"You could wait till kingdom come before they'd give you a bonus! Go ahead and try to wait 'em out. I'd like to see the day they'd give out bonuses . . ."

"But Andrei here was given that microscope . . . for his shock labor . . ." Mrs. Yerin's voice dropped ominously—she understood everything.

"Oh sure! They'll give out bonuses all right!" a drunk Sergei kept on ranting from his corner. "Last month I overfulfilled my quota by 30 percent . . . Ain't that so? Andrei here wouldn't let me lie about it . . ."

In one instant everything came crashing down and flew at a terrible speed straight for the abyss.

Andrei stood up . . . He took Sergei by the scruff of the neck and led him out of the izba. Outside, he whacked him once on the back of the head, then asked:

"Do you have a three-spot? Let me have it till pay day . . ."

"Sure . . . What'd you go and hit me for?"

"Let's go buy a drink. You pathetic sonuvabitch! What the hell do you think you're doin' burstin' in on people drunk like that? Now look what you've done . . . A chunk of wood with eyes in it, that's what you are."

Andrei spent the night at Sergei's. They drank themselves senseless. They spent all of their money on vodka and borrowed some more from somebody else till payday.

It was only on the following day, close to dinner time, that Andrei showed up at home . . . His wife wasn't there.

"Where is she?" he asked his son.

"She went to town, to that . . . what's it called? . . . the consignment shop."

Andrei sat down at the table and rested his head in his hands. He sat like that for a long time.

"Cussed me out, did she?"

"No. Well, a little bit. How much did you blow on vodka?"

"Twelve rubles. Oh, Pyetka . . . Sonny . . ." Andrei Yerin, not raising his head, grimaced bitterly, gritted his teeth. "What's that got to do with it anyway?! You wouldn't understand 'cause of you're bein' so young . . . You wouldn't understand . . ."

"I understand: she'll sell it."

"Sure she will. Yep . . . Gotta get those coats. Well, all right—that's fine, winter coats. It doesn't matter . . . Gotta do it: winter'll be here soon. Study hard Pyetka!" Andrei raised his voice. "Get into science even if you hafta crawl into it on all fours—it's a great cause. You don't have any change in that piggy bank of yours, do you?"

"Nope," Pyetka answered. He could have been lying.

"Well, that's all right, too," Andrei agreed. "You study hard. And don't ever drink . . . Now, they don't drink, those scientists don't. Why should they? They've got lots to do without all that."

Andrei sat there a little while longer. He shook his head sadly . . . And he went off to the other room to go to bed.

1969 (1974)

Tough Guy

The third work brigade from the kolkhoz Giant put a new warehouse into operation. From the old warehouse, which had once been a church, they removed some empty, nasty-smelling barrels, bags of cement, sacks full of granulated sugar and salt from the village store, heaps of matting, and harnesses. (The work brigade only had five horses, but there were enough harnesses here for at least fifteen. Now that'd be just fine—can't have too much of a good thing—if it weren't for those damn mice. The harnesses had been treated with tar and sprayed with all sorts of chemicals, but the mice went on gnawing away at them just the same.) There were also brooms, rakes, and shovels . . . And now the little church stood empty, of no use to anybody at all. Even though it wasn't a large church, it had livened up the village (which at one time had been attached to an estate). The church was its focal point and a showpiece that drew people's eyes from far and near.

Foreman Nikolai Sergeyevich Shurygin stood for a while in front of it, thinking . . . He walked up to a wall, chipped away at a bit of the brickwork with a crowbar that happened to be lying nearby, lit a cigarette, and went home.

When he met with the chairman of the kolkhoz two days later, Shurygin said:

"That little church is all emptied out now . . ."

"So."

"So what're you gonna do with it?"

"Close it up and leave it be. What of it?"

"That brick's good stuff. I could put it to use makin' a pigsty, instead of haulin' bricks over from the factory."

"It'd take five men two weeks to pull it down. That's no ordinary pile of bricks—might as well be made of cast iron. Hell if I know how they laid those bricks!"

"I'll tear it down all right."

"How?"

"No sweat. I'll hook three tractors up to it—it'll fly apart like a house of cards."

"Give it a shot."

On Sunday, Shurygin gave it a shot. He called in three powerful tractors . . . Three thick cables were wound around the little church at different levels. Ten logs were placed under the cables—at the corners and in the center of one wall . . .

At first Shurygin gave orders for this job just like he did for any other—with lots of yelling and cussing. But when people started running up, when all around they started gasping and sighing and showing how sad they were about the church, Shurygin suddenly felt like some important official with unlimited powers. He stopped cussing and wouldn't look at people—as if he didn't hear them and didn't see them.

"Nikolai, you followin' orders, or what?" people asked. "You didn't go and think this up yourself, now did you?"

"What'd it ever do to you?"

Mikhailo Belyakov, the tipsy warehouse manager, crawled under the cables to get over to Shurygin.

"Kolka, why you doin' this?"

Shurygin, shaking with anger, was livid:

"Get outta here, you stinkin' drunk!"

Mikhailo backed away from the foreman in astonishment. And everybody all around fell quiet, equally surprised. Shurygin liked to hit the bottle himself, and he'd never called anybody a "stinkin' drunk" before. What was the matter with him?

Meanwhile the logs were reinforced and the cables aligned . . . In a moment the tractors would begin roaring, and something unprecedented would happen in the village—the church would come down. The older folk had all been baptized in it, funeral services for their grandfathers and great-grandfathers had been held in it. They were as used to seeing it there as they were to the sun in the sky each day.

Once again voices began to sound out.

"Nikolai, who ordered it, huh?"

"*He* did! . . . Can't you see how he keeps turnin' his ugly mug away, the devil!"

"Shurygin, stop bein' so pigheaded!"

Shurygin paid absolutely no attention. He just kept on, with the same look of concentration on his face and the same principled severity in his gaze. Shurygin's wife, Klanka, was nudged out from among the ranks . . . Klanka saw that something incomprehensible was going on with her husband. She timidly walked up to him.

"Kol, why do you wanna tear it down?"

"Get outta here!" Shurygin ordered her as well. "Don't butt in!"

Some of the villagers walked over to the tractor drivers to try to buy time, while others ran off to call the district authorities and to fetch the village school teacher. But Shurygin had promised the tractor drivers a bottle of vodka each and extra pay for the job.

The teacher came running up. He was still a young man and was respected in the village.

"Stop that this instant! Who's responsible here? This church is from the seventeenth century! . . ."

"Mind your own business," Shurygin said.

"It *is* my business! It's the people's business!" The teacher was all worked up and couldn't find words powerful and persuasive enough. He turned beet red and kept yelling: "You don't have the right! Barbarian! I'm going to write the authorities!"

Shurygin waved at the tractor drivers . . . The engines roared. The cables began to tighten. The crowd gasped quietly in horror. The teacher tore loose from the crowd, ran up to the side of the church that was to be toppled, and stood under the wall.

"You'll have to answer for murder! You idiot . . ."

The tractor drivers stopped.

"Outta the way!" Shurygin roared. And the thick veins on his neck bulged.

"Don't you dare touch the church! Don't you dare!"

Shurygin ran up to the teacher, grabbed hold of him and carried him away from the church. The puny teacher did his best to break loose, but Shurygin's arms were like iron.

"Let's go!" he shouted to the tractor drivers.

"Everyone! Stand next to the wall!" the teacher shouted at everybody. "Hurry! . . . They won't dare! I'll go to the regional authorities, they'll put an end to this! . . ."

"Let's go, damn it all!" Shurygin yelled at the tractor drivers.

The tractor drivers slipped into their cabs and grabbed hold of the controls.

"Go stand by the wall! Everybody! Stand by the wall!"

But no one stirred. Shurygin's fury had glued them to the spot. Everybody was speechless. They all waited.

The cables strained, squeaked, cracked, rang out . . . One log was crunched. A cable, which had cut into a corner of the church, sang like a balalaika string. It was strange, but you could hear everything so clearly, despite the roar of the tractors as they strained with all their iron strength. The top of the church trembled . . . The wall opposite the one they were trying to knock down suddenly tore open, cracking all along its entire breadth . . . A terrible lacerated fissure, black in its depths, began to open wide on the white wall. The top of the church with its little dome bowed, bowed, and came crashing down. The earth shuddered as if struck by a shell. Everything was lost in a cloud of dust.

Shurygin let go of the teacher, who, without saying a word, walked away from the church.

Two tractors continued clawing the earth with their caterpillar treads. The cable at the middle elevation cut through a corner and was now senselessly crumbling the bricks from two walls, cutting deeper and deeper into them.

Shurygin stopped the tractors. They began to reset the cables.

Folks started going their separate ways. Only the most curious and the kids stayed on.

In three hours, everything was finished. All that was left of the church was a low shell with rough edges. The church lay in a formless heap, in ruins. The tractors drove off.

All sweaty and completely covered with dust and bits of plaster, Shurygin headed for the store to make a phone call to the chairman of the kolkhoz.

"That's it—she bit the dust!" he shouted into the mouthpiece cheerfully.

The chairman, obviously, didn't know who'd bit the dust.

"The church, that's who! She bit the dust, I said. Uh-huh. Everythin's under control. The teacher kicked up a bit of a fuss . . . Yep! He may be a teacher, but he's worse than an old woman. Forget it, everythin's under control. She dropped like a rock! A lot of it crumbled, uh-huh. And they're all stuck together to boot, three or four bricks to a clump. I don't know how we'll pry 'em apart. I tried with a crowbar—that damn church was tough, a real pain in the ass. You were right—it's just like cast iron! Yep. Goodbye. Don't worry about it."

Shurygin hung up. He went up to the shop girl, a woman he'd dragged out of bed during the night on more than one occasion when somebody came from the district center to do a bit of fishing and stayed afterward at the foreman's place late, till the cock crowed twice.

"Did you see us do a number on the church?" Shurygin was smiling; he was satisfied.

"Doesn't take brains to do somethin' stupid," the shop girl said, not hiding her malice.

"Why stupid?" Shurygin stopped smiling.

"What'd it do to you? It was just standin' there."

"Why should it just stand there bein' of no use? At least we'll get some brick from it . . ."

"Poor you! As if you couldn't find some anywhere else! You idiot!"

"Stupid bitch!" Shurygin also became angry. "Keep your mouth shut if you don't know what you're talkin' about."

"Just try and wake me up in the middle of the night again, just try, and we'll see who wakes who! Stupid bitch, huh? I've half a mind to give it to you right in that onion dome of yours—with a five-kilo weight! Then you'll know what a stupid bitch is!"

Shurygin wanted to call that fool of a shop girl a few other names, but just then some of those ever present village women walked up.

"Gimme a bottle of vodka," he snapped.

"Sure—he's gotta wet his whistle," they started in behind him. "It's all dried out."

"Naturally—from all the dust!"

"And itchin' to do the devil's work . . ."

Shurygin turned and looked sternly at the women but there were too many of them, it'd be impossible to shout them down. And their malice toward him was somehow unusual: they really hated him through and through. He picked up the bottle and went out of the store. On the threshold he turned around and said:

"I'll shut your yaps!"

And he beat a hasty retreat.

He walked, fuming with anger. "It's not like they prayed there or somethin', the parasites—but they've got to go and make a stink. Nobody gave a hang as long as it just stood there—and now they're raisin' hell."

Passing by the former church, Shurygin stopped for a long time and watched the kids rummaging around in the bricks. As he watched, he calmed down. "They'll grow up and remember how I tore down the church when they were kids. I sure remember how Vaska Dukhanin took the cross off it when I was a kid. And here the whole thing came crashin' down. 'Course they'll remember. They'll tell their kids: Uncle Kolya Shurygin fastened cables on it and . . ." Shurygin suddenly remembered the shop girl. "It had no business standin' there bein' an eyesore," he thought spitefully and unrepentantly.

At home Shurygin met with open rebellion: his wife had left for the neighbors without fixing supper, and his ailing mother laid into him from her spot on the stove.

"Kolka, you're a cursed heathen, you are! What a sin you've taken on your soul! . . . Didn't say a word to nobody, walked 'round real quiet, you devil . . . If you'd just breathed one word maybe good folk would've talked some sense into that head of yours. And now look. . . Woe and misery be on our house! Can't even show our faces to folks now. They'll curse you, you know, cu-urse you! And you won't know the hour when disaster'll overtake you, could be right here at home, could be some tree'll fall on you somewheres."

"Now why would they go and curse me? Nothin' better to do?"

"'Cause it's a s-i-n!"

"Did they curse Vaska Dukhanin? He took the cross off it. Just the opposite, he became a big shot . . ."

"Them were different times. Who put you up to it, to destroy it, now, of all times? Who? 'Twas the devil made you do it . . . Just you wait, the authorities'll put you on the hot seat yet. That there teacher's writin' letters, so they tell me; he knows where to write, too. You'll see. . . . Little mother church, you stood your ground durin' good times and bad! And now *he* comes along . . . The bug-eyed heathen!"

"Fine. Just lie there and be sick then!"

"Can't show our faces to folks . . ."

"It's not like they went there to pray! It just stood there—nobody even noticed it . . ."

"Who says we didn't notice it? Used to be, wherever you was comin' from, you'd see it. And no matter how tuckered out you was, when you saw it—it was good as bein' home already. It'd boost your strength."

"It'd boost your strength . . . As if anybody goes around on foot these days! This is the atomic age, isn't it, and they're feelin' sorry for a church. There isn't a club in the whole village—and not a single soul gives a hoot. But take away the church and they get all upset. They'll get over it!"

"It's *you* as gots to get over it now! It's *you* as'll shrivel up and die from shame now . . ."

To keep from hearing any more of her grumbling, Shurygin went into the other room, where he sat down at the table, quickly poured himself a full glass of vodka, and downed it. He lit a cigarette. "Not a one of those devils will touch the bricks now," he thought. "Well, to hell with 'em! I'll shovel 'em all into a pile with a bulldozer. Let the nettles grow over 'em."

His wife came home late. Shurygin had already drained the bottle, felt like drinking another, but wasn't up to seeing that nasty shop girl again—it'd be too much. He asked his wife:

"Go get me a bottle."

"Go to the devil! He's a pal of yours now."

"I'm askin' you . . ."

"Folks were askin' you things, too, but did you listen to 'em? So don't go askin' anybody for anythin' now. You idiot."

"Shut your trap. You're just takin' their side."

"Their side! Their side is where all the good folks are! Not your side, you ignorant slob! They asked you, the whole village did, they pleaded with you—but no! You just goggled your eyes at 'em . . ."

"Shut up! Or I'll belt you one!"

"Belt away! Just try and touch me, you shameless slob! Just try and touch me!"

"No, this'll probably go on all night. Everybody's lost their mind," Shurygin thought.

Shurygin went outside and started up his motorcycle . . . It was eighteen kilometers to the district center. They had a store there, the chairman of the kolkhoz was there. He could have a drink and chat for a while. And at the same time tell about the scene folks had made here . . . At least have a few laughs.

As he turned out of the alley, his headlight picked up the ugly pile of bricks in the dark. It smelled musty, like a cellar that had been disturbed.

"From the seventeenth century," Shurygin remembered. "Here it is, here's your seventeenth century! He's gonna write the authorities, see! Go ahead and write!"

Shurygin stepped on the gas . . . and sang loudly, so everybody would know that all those curses had put him in a wonderful mood:

> You're outta, outta, outta line!
> I'm a soldier from company nine.
> From division thirty-one.
> Boop dee boop, tiddle dee dum.

The motorcycle rolled out of the village, pierced the night with its gleaming blade of light, and took off down the dirt road in the direction of the district center. Shurygin liked going fast.

1969 (1970)

Styopka

And spring has come—sweet and muddle-headed, like a girl approaching womanhood.

The village roads are knee-deep in mud. People walk alongside the wattle fences, clinging to the pickets. And if some fellow from the state cattle-purchasing organization (Zagotskot) should grab onto a picket, it's likely to stay right there in his hand, because all the men from Zagotskot are for some reason beefy themselves, and their faces are like rough red cloth. The owners of the gardens give them hell.

"You parasite, you don't wanna get your boots dirty so I hafta fix my fence every spring."

"If you're so worried about your fence, you should've tossed some gravel on the road."

"What about you? Did your arms shrivel up and drop off? *You* go and do it..."

"Then don't go cussin', if you're so smart."

Each night the gray mounds of snow in the fields, having thawed out underneath, sink lower and lower with a melancholy sigh.

In the poplar trees by the river, something breaks and resonates with a quiet exulting sound: kee-yoo!

The ice has floated down the river but there are still isolated ice floes that sparkle in the sun and scrape the rocky shoal with their slippery stomachs. And at the bends in the river, the ice floes stick their blue snouts up on the bank, brush aside the pebbles, swing around, and continue floating on their way—to die downstream.

A damp breeze whirls and makes you lightheaded . . . The smell of manure is strong in the air.

In the evenings, before going to bed, people become kinder.

Large pots of soup are being warmed on trivets outside. Cheery flames dance, damp brushwood crackles. There's a pensive quality to the warm air . . . The day is done. Unhurried, idle conversations are carried on in low voices—tomorrow will be another day and once again there'll be various things to get done. But for now you can rest up, have a smoke, grumble about your lot in life, and think about God knows what: that maybe your life—your fate—could have been better . . . But actually it's not too bad even the way it is—it'll do.

On one such pensive and fine evening, Stepan Voyevodin—bypassing the main road—came home to his native village.

He came in from the side where there are fewer peasant homesteads, sat down on the slope, which was still warm from the sun, and sighed. And he began looking at the village. He'd apparently walked a long way that day and was worn out.

He sat for a long time like that and looked.

Then he got up and went into the village.

Yermolai Voyevodin was still pottering around in his shed—planing a shaft for a wagon. The shed smelled of pine shavings, cheap tobacco, and the odor of the wooden walls as they cooled off. There was already very little light left in the shed. Yermolai squinted and swore gently, out of habit, whenever his plane hit a knot in the wood.

. . . It was at this moment—on the threshold, in the doorway—that his son Stepan suddenly appeared.

"Howdy, Pop."

Yermolai lifted his head and looked for a long time at his son . . . Then he blew out of one of his nostrils, wiped his nose with the bottom of his sateen shirt, like the village women do, and once again looked closely at his son.

"Styopka, is that you?"

"Yep . . . What's the matter, don't you recognize me?"

"Well! . . . I'll be damned . . . And here I thought I was dreamin'."

Stepan dropped his nearly empty knapsack on the step and went over to his father . . . They hugged and kissed each other loudly on the cheek.

"So, you've come home?"

"Yep."

"How come you're early? We were expectin' you in the autumn."

"I worked off my time . . . So they let me out early."

"Well . . . I'll be damned! . . ." The father was happy for his son, happy to see him. He just didn't know what to do next. "That mutt Borzya's still alive," he said.

"Really?" Stepan asked, surprised. He didn't know what to do either. He was also happy to see his father. "Where is he?"

"Runnin' around here somewhere. You know on Saturday all the womenfolk hung their laundry out to dry—he tore everythin' to pieces. He was playin' around, the sonuvabitch, and went and started pullin' 'em down . . ."

"Crazy scamp."

"I'd have shot him, but figured you'd get upset . . ."

They sat down on the workbench and lit up.

"Everybody well?" Stepan asked.

"Not bad, well enough. How was it doin' time?"

"Not bad, it was all right, we worked a lot."

"In the mines, I s'pose?"

"What makes you think that? We felled trees."

"I see." Yermolai nodded. "Did you get some sense knocked into you?"

Stepan scowled. "That's not the point, Pop."

"See here, Styopka," Yermolai shook a crooked, tobacco-stained finger at him. "I hope you know better than to go swingin' your fists where you shouldn't. You all picked a fine time to fight, you and your damn jailbirds . . . We have enough trouble around here without that . . ."

"That's not the point," Stepan said once again.

It was getting dark in the shed. But the smell of wood shavings and cheap tobacco was still just as intoxicating.

Stepan got up off the workbench and ground out his cigarette butt with his foot. He picked up his puny knapsack.

"Let's go into the house and let them know I'm here."

"That deaf girl of ours," Father began as he stood up, "almost went and got herself married." He kept wanting to tell some important piece of news, and somehow nothing would come to mind.

"You don't say?" Stepan was surprised.

"Didn't know if we should laugh or cry."

As they walked away from the shed, his father told him about it.

"One time she comes home from the club and signs to me: I'm gonna bring a suitor home, she says. I tell her: I'll bring you a suitor all right, and when he's done with you, you won't be able to sit down for a week."

"Maybe you shouldn't have."

"Whatcha mean, maybe I shouldn't have? Maybe my ass . . . Some fella decides he's gonna deceive some girl—so he chooses the easiest target. Who the heck would want a girl like that? So I tell her, I'll bring you a suitor all right . . ."

"You should've at least looked him over. It might've been on the level . . ."

At that moment the "bride" herself—a sturdy girl about twenty years old—came out onto the porch. She saw her brother, clasped her hands together, and started mumbling joyfully. She had deep blue eyes, like little flowers, and she looked at you with incredible trustfulness.

"M-emm, mm," she mumbled and waited for her brother to come up to her. She watched him from the top step of the porch. And she was so very happy at that moment that it brought tears to the muzhiks' eyes.

"Here's a 'meh' for you," Father said crossly and dried his eyes with the palm of his hand. "She kept waitin', she marked x's on the wall—for how many days you had left," he explained to Stepan. "She loves everybody, like a fool."

Stepan frowned, went up the steps, awkwardly gave her a light hug, and patted her on the back . . . But she clutched onto him tightly and kissed his cheeks, forehead, and lips.

"All right now," Stepan resisted and tried to free himself from her hearty embraces. He felt embarrassed but happy at being smothered with kisses. He couldn't push his sister away.

"See here," he muttered in confusion. "Well, that'll do, that'll do . . . enough already . . ."

"Oh, let her," his father said and dried his eyes again. "You see how much she missed you."

Stepan finally disentangled himself from his sister's embraces. He looked her up and down happily.

"Well, so how've you been?" he asked.

His sister signed "fine."

"Things is always fine with her," his father said, going up onto the porch. "Let's go and make your mother happy."

At the sight of Styopka, his mother burst into tears and began wailing.

"Lord God, Heavenly Father, you heard my prayers, they winged their way to you . . ."

Everybody felt a little uncomfortable.

"Mother, your happiness sure do look like grievin'," Yermolai noted sternly. "Whatcha snivelin' for? Well, he's come home now. It's time to be happy."

"I *am* happy, d'you think I'm not?"

"Well, then don't bawl."

"Are you well, Sonny?" his mother asked. "Maybe they let you go early 'cause of some ailment?"

"No, everythin's a-okay. I worked off my time and they let me go."

Neighbors and relatives began arriving.

The first to come running over was Nyura Agapova, their neighbor, a robust young woman with a round, kind face. While still in the entrance hall she started talking up a storm, perhaps a little too joyously and disjointedly.

"Here I am a-lookin' out the window: good gracious me, but isn't that Stepan come home?! And it's true—it *is* Stepan . . ."

Stepan smiled at her.

"Howdy, Nyura."

Nyura wrapped her warm arms around her handsome neighbor and planted her half-starved widow's lips on his, which were chapped and smelled of tobacco and the wind from the steppe . . .

"You're throwin' off heat like a stove," Stepan said. "Haven't got another husband, have you?"

"And where are they around here, suitors that is? There's two and a half available muzhiks for the whole village."

"So what's the deal, do you need five?"

"Maybe I was waitin' for you?" Nyura laughed.

"You go to the devil, Nyurka!" His mother got jealous. "You stay outta the way—give other folks a chance to say somethin'. Was it awful hard, Sonny?"

"Not at all," Stepan began telling his story. "It's nice there. For instance, here I see a movie once a month, right? But there—two times a week. If you want, you can go to the recreation and reading room and hear lectures like 'On the Honor and Conscience of the Soviet Man' or 'On the Conditions of the Working Class in Capitalist Countries.'"

"So they hauled you all off just to show you a buncha movies?" Nyura asked merrily.

"What do you mean? . . . There weren't just movies, of course . . ."

"They're educatin' 'em," his father jumped into the conversation. "They're straightenin' them fools out."

"There are lots of interestin' people," Stepan went on. "Brave as eagles, some of 'em . . . And there are educated ones, too. We had two engineers in our work brigade . . ."

"What were they in for?"

"One for some accident at a factory, the other for gettin' in a fight. He also smacked somebody upside the head with a bottle . . ."

"Maybe he was lyin' about bein' an engineer?" His father was doubtful.

"Can't get away with any lies there. Everybody knows everythin' about everybody there."

"Did they feed you all right?" his mother asked.

"Just fine, there was always almost enough. It wasn't bad."

More people arrived. Stepan's buddies came. It got real noisy in the Voyevodins' small izba. Stepan kept having to start his story all over again.

"Not at all, actually, on the whole it's pretty nice there! Do you see films here often? Well, we did twice a week. Do you guys get performers around here? Well, there was a steady stream of 'em comin' to see us. There was plenty of grub, too . . . And one time we had a magician come perform. He picks up a glass of water like this . . ."

Everybody listened to Stepan with interest. They were a little surprised, they'd say "hmmm," "you don't say!" or they'd try to tell their own stories, but others kept asking new questions and Stepan would start talking again. He had become slightly intoxicated from this long-awaited meeting, from the questioning, from his own stories. He even started making up a thing or two on the sly.

"Was security tight?"

"Nothin' doin'! They started takin' us to work at a sovkhoz and left us damn near by ourselves."

"Anybody try to escape?"

"Hardly any. There's not much point to it."

"Now they say that if a guy's done somethin' wrong in prison, they lock him up in a cell you can barely turn around in . . ."

"Solitary confinement. That's rare, that's if he's done somethin' real bad . . . That's for real crooks, we weren't sent there much."

"That must be where they put all the thieves!" exclaimed one simple-minded fellow. "They prob'ly all steal from each other, right?"

Stepan burst out laughing. So did everybody else, but they continued looking expectantly at Stepan.

"They come down real hard on that there," Stepan explained. "There, if a guy's caught red-handed he gets the crap beaten outta him right on the spot . . ."

Meanwhile his mother and deaf sister hurriedly heated up the banya and his father ran to the store for vodka . . . Somebody brought some salted fatback in a cloth, somebody else brought meat pies, leftovers from earlier in the day, and others brought some sweet home-brewed beer in a container made of birch bark—the holiday had come as a surprise, so the hosts didn't have time to prepare for it. By the time they all sat down at the table, it was already starting to get dark.

And little by little the modest celebration warmed up. Everybody talked at once, interrupted each other, laughed . . . Stepan sat at the head of the table. He kept turning to the right and to the left, wanting to tell more stories, but nobody was listening very closely any more. And Stepan himself wasn't trying awfully hard either. He was just happy that folks were having a good time, that he'd given them some pleasure, allowed them the opportunity to get together, talk, laugh . . . And to make sure they were really having a good time, he started singing a touching song that came from the places where he'd just been:

> Mother, forgive me, your daughter, do-oo,
> For all my misdeeds,
> For not listening to yo-ou . . .

For a moment a hush almost fell over them: Stepan was completely carried away by a sense of the good he had wrought and of his love for people. He was noticeably tipsy.

> Oh I tho-ought that prison w-was a joke,
> And now th-this joke has cost my life!

Stepan sang.

The song didn't go over well—folks couldn't appreciate the feelings of the repentant sinner. It left them cold . . .

"It's a prison song!" that very same simple-minded fellow explained enthusiastically. That was the fellow who thought that there were only swindlers and thieves in prison. "Quiet everybody!"

"So how's that, Sonny, are there lots of women doin' time?" his mother asked from the other end of the table.

"A good number."

And a lively debate ensued about how rough it must be for women there.

"And you know, they musta left their kids behind."

"The kids go to an orphanage . . ."

"I wouldn't put women away!" one fairly tipsy man said sternly. "I'd lift their skirts over their head and belt 'em!"

"It won't help," Yermolai started arguing with him. "If you flog 'em, see, they just get meaner. When I was young, I taught my old lady a couple of lessons with the strap, and to spite me she bore me a deaf girl."

Somebody struck up a song. One that was familiar and dear. From their native parts.

> My father ever worked the soil,
> Alongside him I, too, did toil . . .

Others joined in. They sang loudly and not quite together. Then, bit by bit, they started sounding better.

> Three days and nights I did so strive
> To set my sister free-ee . . .

They got carried away by the song—they sang with feeling, frowning as they stared at the table in front of them.

> A villain his villainous bullet let fly
> He killed my sister beautiful.
> I climbed way up the hill so high
> My native village for to see.
> My vi-illage is in flames, in flames.
> My whole native la-and is on fi-ire! . . .

Stepan banged his fist on the table top.

"You don't love me, you don't pity me!" he said loudly.[1] "I respect you all, you ragged devils! I missed you badly."

In the doorway, through the haze of tobacco smoke, an accordion suddenly sobbed—somebody had had the foresight to fetch an accordion player. Everybody roared with approval . . . The song was drowned out. They climbed out from behind their spots at the table and did their best to fall into step to the "lowlands" folk dance. Everybody tried to stamp as hard as possible on the floorboards.

The womenfolk formed a circle and went round and round, dancing and singing. And the deaf girl went around waving her kerchief over her head. People pointed at her and laughed . . . And she laughed, too—she was happy.

"Verka! Ve-erk!" a fairly tipsy man shouted at her. "So give us a song, huh? You can't just walk around!" Nobody heard him, but he laughed anyway—he simply rolled with laughter—at his own joke.

Stepan's mother was telling some old woman about her dream.

"How she fell on me, heavens! I couldn't get my breath. I barely, barely lift my head up like this and I ask: 'Is it a bad omen or a good one?' And right in my ear she whispered: 'A good one!'"

The old lady shook her head.

"A good one?"

"A good omen, a good omen. She said so clearly: a good omen, she says."

"She warned you, all right."

"She did, she did. And here I'm still thinkin' come evenin': 'What kind of good omen,' I'm thinkin', 'did my neighbor foretell?' I'd only barely just thought that when the door opens—and there he is, on the threshold."

"Lord almighty," the elderly woman whispered and she dried her damp eyes with the corner of her scarf. "Of all things!"

The women dragged Yermolai into the circle. After a moment's thought, Yermolai began stamping one foot and tapping the floor with the heel of his other . . . And he kept repeating: "Op-pa, at-ta, op-pa, at-ta." And he stamped and stamped his foot so hard that the dishes in the cupboard shook.

"Come on, Yermil!" they shouted at Yermolai. "Today you got somethin' to dance about—kick up your heels!"

"At-ta, op-pa," Yermolai kept repeating, but his laborer's back, stooped from forty years of slaving over his workbench, couldn't straighten up all the way. So he danced the way he worked: slightly hunched over, with his big, gnarled hands hanging heavily at his side. But Yermolai was happy and he forgot all his sorrows—he had waited a long time for this day, well nigh five years.

Stepan, tapping out a heavy, uneven beat, elbowed his way through the circle toward his father.

"Come on, Pop . . ."

"Let's go, father and son! Kick up your heels!"

"Prison sure hasn't worn Styopka out—look at him go!"

"That's what he's been sayin': they had it good there. They gave 'em lots of grub. . ."

"Who you tryin' to fool? Next you'll say they gave 'em all seconds."

"At-ta, op-pa!" Yermolai kept repeating, trying to fall into rhythm with his son.

Neither of them knew how to dance, but they made out all right together—they gave it their best. Folks liked it, they enjoyed watching them.

And so everybody had a good time.

Later, nobody remembered seeing the district police officer make his appearance in the izba. They just saw that he went up to Stepan and said something to him. Stepan went outside with him. The partying continued in the izba: folks figured that that was how it was supposed to be. Stepan probably had to report to the village council and fill out all sorts of paperwork there. Only his deaf sister got worried all of a sudden. She began mumbling anxiously and started pestering her father. He brushed her aside drunkenly.

"Leave me alone! Get away with you! Go and dance over there."

They went out the gate. And stopped.

"Look, fella, have you lost your mind?" the police officer asked, peering into Stepan's face.

Stepan leaned up against the gate post and grinned.

"Think it's nuts? Okay . . ."

"You only had three months to go!"

"Nobody knows that better than me . . . Gimme a smoke."

The police officer gave him a cigarette and lit up himself.

"Let's go."

"Yeah."

"Maybe you'd like to tell the folks at home? . . . Or else they'll notice you're gone . . ."

"Not today—let 'em celebrate. You can tell 'em tomorrow."

"Couldn't wait it out three months so you ran away!" Again, the police officer was amazed. "Pardon me for sayin' it—I've seen a lot of fools in my day, but this takes the cake. Why'd you do it?"

Stepan walked along, his hands in his pockets, making out all the familiar peasant huts, gates, and wattle fences in the twilight . . . He breathed in the bracing spring chill in the air, familiar since childhood, and smiled pensively.

"Well?"

"What?"

"Why'd you do it?"

"You mean, escape? Wanna know why? Just to take a walk like this, even if I can only do it once. I got homesick."

"But you only had three months to go!" the police officer was almost yelling. "And now they'll tack on a couple of years."

"It doesn't matter . . . I've charged up my batteries. Now I can do my time. Or else those dreams would've done me in—every night I dream of the village . . . It's nice here in the spring, isn't it?"

"Mmm—yeah . . .," the police officer murmured thoughtfully.

They walked for a long time without saying anything, almost all the way to the village council itself.

"So you managed to escape! Were you alone?"

"There were three of us."

"And where are they?"

"I don't know. We split up right away."

"And how long did it take you to get here?"

"Two weeks."

"Jeez! . . . Well, to hell with you then, do your time if you want to."

At the village council building the police officer sat down to write his report. Stepan looked pensively out the darkened windows. His tipsiness had passed.

"Don't have a gun, do you?" the police inspector asked, breaking off from his report.

"In all my life I've never carried shit like that on me."

"What did you eat on your journey?"

"They'd gotten a bunch of provisions together, those two guys did . . ."

"And how much time were they servin'?"

"Lots . . ."

"They at least had a reason to escape, but what possessed you to do it?"

"All right, already! I've had it!" Stepan got mad. "Do what you've gotta do, I'm not stoppin' you."

The police officer shook his head and bent over his paper again. He added:

"To be quite honest, I didn't believe it when they called. I thought, it's some kind of mistake. Nobody's that stupid. Guess I was wrong."

Stepan looked out the window; he was calmly thinking about something.

"I imagine those other two guys laughed at you, huh?" the talkative officer asked again, unable to hold back.

Stepan didn't hear him.

For a long time the officer looked at him with curiosity. He said:

"Lookin' at you, I wouldn't say you were a fool." And he went on composing his report.

At that moment, Styopka's sister entered the council building. She stopped at the threshold, looked at the officer, and then at her brother with big, frightened eyes . . .

"Meh-mm?" she asked her brother.

Stepan was unnerved.

"Why'd you come here?"

"Meh-mm?!" his sister mumbled, pointing at the officer.

"So, is that your sister?" he asked.

"Yeah . . ."

The deaf girl went over to the table, touched the police officer on the shoulder and, pointing at her brother, she began to explain her question with her hands: "Why did you take him away?!"

The police officer understood.

"He . . . he," he pointed at Stepan, "escaped from prison! Escaped! Like this!" The police officer pointed at the window and showed how people escape. "Normal people use the door, but he went out the window and made off. And now he'll get . . ." The officer held up his fingers in the form of prison bars and pointed the deaf girl at Stepan. "Now he'll get this thing here again! Two!" He spread two of his fingers wide apart and shook them solemnly. "Two more years!"

She began to understand . . . And when she'd understood it all completely, her deep blue, frightened eyes blazed with such superhuman suffering, they reflected such pain, that the officer cut himself short. The deaf girl looked at her brother. He turned pale and froze up—he looked back at his sister.

"Now you tell him he's a fool, that normal people don't do things like that . . ."

She gave a guttural scream, flung herself at Stepan, and hung around his neck . . .

"Get her outta here!" Stepan begged hoarsely. "Get her out!"

"How'm I gonna do that?"

"Get her outta here, you creep!" Stepan began shouting in a frenzied voice. "Take her away, or else I'll split your head open with a stool!"

The officer leaped up and dragged the girl away from her brother . . . But she broke away and tore back to him and moaned. And she shook her head.

"Tell her that you fooled her, that you were jokin' . . . Get her outta here!"

"Damn you two! . . . What the hell am I botherin' with you for?" the officer swore, dragging Styopka's sister toward the door. "He'll come home in a moment, I'll let him say goodbye to you all!" He tried to make her understand. "He'll come home in a moment!" Finally he managed to drag her over to the door and push her out. "Damn, she's strong!" He closed the door and fastened the hook. "For cryin' out loud . . . Now look at the mess you've made. Satisfied?"

Stepan sat there, clutching his head in his hands, and stared into space.

The police officer put the unfinished report in his carrying case and went over to the telephone.

"I'm callin' for a car—we'll go to the district center, damn you all . . . Not a normal one in the bunch of you."

And through the village, down the middle of the street, the deaf girl walked back home, stumbling along and weeping bitterly.

1964

Ignakha's
Come Home

One lovely day at the end of August the Baikalov's son Ignaty came home. He was big, handsome, and wore a black suit made of Polish crepe. He kicked open the gate—he had a suitcase in each hand—stopped, looked around his parents' yard, and bellowed happily:

"Howdy, folks!"

The young, brightly dressed, dolled-up woman standing behind him said reproachfully:

"Can't you be a little quieter? . . . Where are your manners!"

"It's oka-ay!" Ignaty hooted. "You just wait and see, they'll be jumpin' for joy!"

A thickset old man with enormous hands came out of the house. He let out a quiet laugh and wiped his eyes with his sleeve.

"Ignashka! . . ." he said and went toward Ignaty.

Ignaty threw down the suitcases. They hugged and kissed each other three times—crisscross fashion—on the cheek. The old man dried his eyes again.

"So you made up your mind to come, huh?"

"Sure did."

"How long's it been? Must be well nigh five years. Mother's ailin', you know . . . Somethin's wrong with her back."

Father and son looked at each other, unable to get their fill of looking. They'd completely forgotten about the woman. She smiled and looked the old man over with interest.

"So this must be the wife?" the old man finally asked.

"Yep," Ignaty suddenly remembered. "Lemme introduce you."

The woman held out her hand to the old man. He shook it cautiously.

"Lyusya."

"Uh-huh," the old man said, taking Lyusya in with an appraising glance.

"Not bad, huh?!" Ignaty exclaimed with foolish pride.

"C'mon into the house, how come we're standin' out here?" The old man was the first to move toward the house.

"What should I call him?" Lyusya quietly asked her husband.

Ignaty roared with laughter.

"Listen here, Pop! . . . She doesn't know what to call you!"

The old man laughed.

"I guess this makes me her father . . ." He mounted the steps like a young man and bellowed out in the entrance way: "Mother, guess who's come to see us!"

In the izba a hook-nosed old woman, tanned and wiry, lay on a bed. She saw Ignaty and started crying.

"Ignashka, Sonny . . . you've come home . . ."

The son gave his mother a quick kiss and dug into his suitcases. His booming, powerful voice immediately filled the whole izba.

"I brought you a shawl . . . an Angora one. And for you, Pop, some boots. And this here's for Maruska . . . And this is for Vaska . . . Everybody around here alive and kickin'?"

His father and mother, for propriety's sake, smiled indulgently and watched their son's movements with interest. He kept on getting more and more stuff out of the suitcases.

"Everybody's well. Just your mother over there . . ." His father stretched his long hand out toward the boots, carefully picked one up, and began feeling, kneading, and stroking the high-quality calfskin. "Not a bad piece of work . . . Vaska'll wear 'em out. Nowadays I don't have any use for ones like these."

"You'll wear 'em yourself. Here's somethin' else for Maruska, some fabric for a dress." Ignaty spread everything out and sat down on a stool. The stool creaked plaintively under him. "Well, tell us how you're gettin' on. I've missed you folks."

"If you'd missed us, you'd have come sooner."

"Business, Pop."

"Business . . ." His father for some reason looked with displeasure at his son's young wife. "What kind of business could you have there . . ."

"All right, Father," his mother said. "He's come—thank God for that."

Ignaty couldn't wait to talk about himself, and he took the opportunity to raise objections to his father, who, by all appearances, didn't rate his town business very highly. Ignaty was a circus wrestler. In town he had a nice apartment, friends, money, a pretty wife . . .

"You say: 'What kind of business could you have there!'" Ignaty began, crossing one leg over the other and looking tenderly at his father. "How can I explain it to you? We Russians are a sturdy lot, you see. Just take a look at any other person and the devil only knows what you've got . . ." Ignaty stood up and paced up and down the room. "A Russian's shoulders are as broad as a barn, his chest—like a thoroughbred's: a real powerhouse! But as for learnin' how to control that strength, masterin' some kind of technique, appearin' in competitions somewhere? Not on your life! He'd rather go after a bear one-on-one! There's still a lot that's uncivilized in our people. They've no idea what the culture of the body's all about. They fear physical trainin' like the devil fears incense. I sure remember how we profaned it in school." With these final words, Ignaty turned toward his wife.

Somehow or other, Ignaty had once hit upon this idea—of the criminal disinclination of the Russian people to engage in physical training; he had stated it to somebody and been supported in it. From then on he had brought it up so often that, when he now began speaking about it again, his wife got bored and started looking out the window.

". . . So, Pop, think whatever you want, but my business is important. Maybe more important than Vaska's."

"All right," his father agreed. He'd been listening inattentively. "Mother, where we keepin' the money? . . . I'm goin' out for a bottle."

"Hold tight," Ignaty stopped him. "Why go out for a bottle?"

Having tasted the sweet fruit of his preaching, he would have liked to talk as well about how Russians need to break that habit, too: at the drop of a hat, they go straight to the store for a bottle. The question was: why is this so? But his father gave him such a look that he instantly backed off, gave it up, pulled a thick wallet out of his pocket, and plopped it down on the table.

"Here, take some money!"

His father raised his shaggy eyebrows in offense.

"Put that away, Ignakha! . . . You've come home, so sit still and hold your tongue. What're you tryin' to say—that we don't have our own money?"

Ignaty started laughing.

"All right, I get it. You haven't changed a bit, Father."

. . . They sat at the table and drank.

Old Baikalov softened up. He pawed his head with his gnarled palms and started singing:

> Why do you sit till midnight
> By a window opened wide?
> Oh, why do you sit . . .

But he broke off and fell silent. For a while he just sat there, with his head sunk in his hands. Then he said with unaffected sorrow:

"My life is endin', Ignakha. It's endin'!" He swore.

Ignaty's wife blushed and turned away to the window. Ignaty said reproachfully:

"Pop!"

"And you, Ignat—you aren't the same anymore," his father continued, not paying the slightest attention to his son's reproach. "'Course you don't notice it, but I could tell right away."

Ignaty looked at his father with sober eyes, listening attentively to his strange speeches.

"A little while ago you dragged out some boots for me. . . Thanks, Sonny! They're good boots . . ."

"That's not it, Father," Ignaty said. "What do boots have to do with it?"

"Don't take it wrong if I didn't put it right—I'm an old man. All right, it doesn't matter. Your brother'll be home soon—Vaska . . . He's gotten so strong! He'd crush you in a second, even with all your talk about that physical culture stuff. You're a real weaklin' next to Vaska. Clear as night and day."

Ignaty laughed: his good-natured, cheerful indulgence had returned.

"We'll see, Pops, we'll see."

"How 'bout another round?" his father proposed.

"No," Ignaty said firmly.

"Ah! Quite a husband you got there!" the old man said, not without some pride, addressing Ignaty's wife. "That's the Baikalov breed for you. Once they say no, that's it. Kaput! I was just the same. So's Vaska—he'll be here soon. And our Maruska's the same. She's prettier than you, even though she ain't all gussied up."

"Father, you're talkin' too much!" The old man's wife tried to make him be reasonable. "You're gettin' downright senile! The devil only knows what you'll say next. Don't listen to him, the old fool!"

"You be still, Mother," the old man snapped good-naturedly. "Be still, you're s'posed to be sick. I'm tryin' to have a conversation here and you're interruptin' us."

Lyusya got up from the table, walked up to the chest of drawers and started examining the record albums. She, obviously, was uncomfortable.

Ignaty also stood up. They cranked up the phonograph. They put on "Grushitsa."

They didn't say anything. They listened.

The elder Baikalov looked out the window. He was thinking gloomy thoughts about something.

Night was falling. The windows of the homes were lit up by a rosy, evening light. A herd of cattle passed along the street, bellowing and kicking up dust. The Baikalov's cow went up to the gate and tried to hook it with her horn, but couldn't get it open. She stood and mooed. The old man looked at her and didn't move. His celebration for some reason hadn't turned out. He'd waited for this day for a real long time—he thought it would be a big holiday. And now he sat there and didn't understand: why on earth hadn't the holiday come off? His son had come home a different person. In what way wasn't he the same? He'd brought presents, just like any other son would. But just the same, something was wrong.

Marya arrived—she was a robust young woman and looked a lot like Ignaty. Upon seeing her brother, a joyous, restrained smile lit up her face.

"Well, hello there, beautiful!" Ignaty boomed out, rather unceremoniously looking his now grown sister up one side and down the other. "Don't you look like a bride!"

"That's enough out of you," Marya said evenly and went over to make Lyusya's acquaintance.

Old man Baikalov watched all of this with sorrowfully screwed-up eyes.

"Vaska'll be comin' any minute now," he said. He kept waiting for Vaska. Why he needed his younger son to come home soon, he didn't know.

The young people went off to the other room and took the phonograph with them. Ignaty snatched up a bottle of red wine and some snacks to take, too.

"I'm gonna have a drink with my little sister, what the heck!"

"Go ahead, Sonny, it's all right. It's good for you," his father said peaceably.

Old friends and acquaintances of Ignaty started dropping by. Now this is when the big holiday should have started, but the holiday just wouldn't come. People arrived, exchanged greetings with the old man, and went into the other room, already smiling before they got there. Soon it got noisy in there. Ignaty's powerful bass boomed out, women laughed, the phonograph jingled away. Two of Ignaty's buddies ran to the store and returned with bottles and bags of stuff.

"Vaska'll be here any minute now," the old man thought as he waited. There was just plain no holiday in his soul—and that was all there was to it.

Finally Vaska arrived. He was an enormous fellow, with an open, strong face, suntanned and dirty. Vaska took after his father—he would look at you the very same way, sort of gloomily, but with kind eyes.

"Ignashka's come home," his father greeted him with the news.

"I already heard," Vaska said and smiled and shook his light, mussed-up hair. He set some iron implements down in the corner and straightened back up.

His father got up from the table and wanted to head toward the other room, but his son stopped him.

"Hang on, Pop, let me at least rinse myself off a bit. Or else it'll be real awkward."

"Well, go ahead," his father agreed. "Or else, you're right—he's all decked out like . . . like an actor."

But at this point, Ignaty came out of the other room with his wife.

"Little brother!" Ignaty roared, spreading his arms open wide. "Vaska!" And he went over to him.

Vaska blushed like a girl, laughed, and shifted from one foot to the other.

Ignaty hugged him.

"Look out, I'm gettin' you all dirty." Vaska tried to free himself from his brother's embrace, but his brother wouldn't let him go.

"It's oka-ay! It's honest workin' folk's dirt, bro. Lemme give you a kiss, dammit! I've missed you guys."

The brothers kissed.

Their father watched his sons and the tears rolled down his cheeks. He dried them and blew his nose loudly.

"He brought you some presents, Vaska," their father said loudly, heading toward the suitcases.

"Forget it, Pop. Who cares about presents! Well, go ahead—what's it you wanted to do? Wash up? Go ahead, but be snappy. We've got some drinkin' to do. There you go! Now take a look and see what the Baikalovs are like!" Ignaty said to his wife and lightly nudged her over to his brother. "Get acquainted."

Vaska blushed even harder than before—he didn't know if he should hold out his dirty hand to this dolled-up woman. Lyusya took his hand herself and shook it firmly.

"He's our shy one," their father explained.

Vaska coughed cautiously into his fist and gave a quiet short laugh. His father's explanations made him wish the earth would swallow him up.

"Pop . . . whatever."

"Go wash up," his father said.

"Yeah, I'll go real quick . . . uh . . ."

Vaska started for the entrance hall. Ignaty moved after him.

"Let's go, I'll wet you down for old time's sake."

Their father also went outside.

They decided to go to the Katun river to wash up—it flowed but a stone's throw away, just beyond the gardens.

"Let's have a swim," Ignaty suggested and slapped himself on his powerful chest with his palms.

They walked by way of the gardens along a winding, barely visible path through the luxuriant, leafy potato tops.

"Well, how're you gettin' on?" boomed Ignaty, waddling along between his father and brother.

Vaska again gave a quick laugh. He laughed kind of strangely: it was sort of a laugh, sort of an embarrassed cough. He was glad to see his brother.

"Not bad."

"We're gettin' along just fine!" their father exclaimed. "No worse than city folk."

"Well, thank God!" Ignaty said with feeling. "Vasily, they say you've gotten as strong as an ox around here."

Vasily again let out a laugh.

"Strong as an ox! . . . Whatever. How're *you* gettin' on?"

"I'm fine, boys! I'm absolutely fine. How do you two like my wife? Pop?"

"She's all right. I'm not an awful good judge, Sonny. I guess she's all right."

"She's a good woman," Ignaty said on her behalf. "She's a decent person."

"It's just, she's awful dressed up. What for?"

Ignaty gave a deafening roar of laughter.

"She's dressed normally! City style, of course. You folks are a bit behind in that regard."

"Somehow you sure do howl a lot, Ignat," the old man noted. "Like some blame fool."

"I'm happy, so I laugh."

"You're happy . . . We're happy, too, but you don't hear us brayin' like you. Does that mean Vaska over there's not happy or somethin'?"

"When are you gonna get married, Vaska?" Ignaty asked.

"First he's gotta do his army service," their father said.

"Vaska, you—here's the thing . . . When you go into the army, sign up for a sports club right away," the elder brother advised. "That's just how I started. If you're lucky enough to get a good trainer, it may give you a good start in life."

Vaska listened, smiling vaguely.

They arrived at the river.

Ignaty was the first to toss off his clothes, baring his beautiful, well-trained body. He tried the water with his foot and quietly gasped.

"Honest to God! Now that's what I call water."

"How's that?" Vaska also got undressed. "Is it cold?"

"Well, well, well—let's have a look at you," Ignaty said, intrigued. He went up to Vaska and started slapping him here and there and looking him over from all sides, like you would a stallion.

Vaska stood there patiently, looking off to the side, continuously adjusting his undershorts and chuckling.

"You'll do," Ignaty concluded. "How 'bout givin' it a try?"

"Lay off!" Vaska shook his hair discontentedly.

"What's wrong, Vaska? Wrestle with him!" Their father looked reproachfully at his younger son.

"Lay off, you guys, I mean it," Vaska said stubbornly and seriously. "What're we gonna go grabbin' at each other for? So people can laugh at us?"

"Phooey!" their father got mad. "Talk some sense into him, Ignat, for Christ's sake! He's just like a calf—shy about everythin'."

"What's there to be shy about here?" Ignaty said. "Sure, if we were some sort of weaklings we really would look like a couple of fools."

"That's it—explain it to him!"

Vaska scowled and walked toward the water. He threw himself right in and started swimming, his huge arms churning powerfully. The water seethed underneath him.

"He's strong, all right!" Ignaty said admiringly.

"That's what I've been tellin' you!"

They were silent for a while, watching Vaska.

"He'd lay you out flat."

"I don't know." Ignaty didn't answer right away. "He's got more strength—that's for sure."

His father angrily blew his nose, snorting forcefully into the sand.

Ignaty stood there a little longer and then also slipped into the water.

Their father set off lower down the river where Vaska was climbing back out of the water.

When Vaska came up on to the shore, they began to speak heatedly and in low voices about something. His father was trying to prove his point, even pressing his hands against his chest. Vaska muttered in reply. When Ignaty swam up to them, they stopped talking.

Ignaty crawled out of the water and started looking pensively at the far-away blue mountains, the numerous islands.

"Mother Katun," he said quietly.

Vaska and their father also looked at the river.

On the other side, a peasant woman was squatting on the bank, her skirt pulled way up. She was pounding her wash with a flat wooden paddle, her round, plump knees gleamed blindingly white.

"Hey, lower that skirt a bit!" the old man shouted.

The woman lifted her head, looked at the Baikalovs, and kept on pounding her wash with the paddle.

"Brazen hussy," the old man said with admiration. "Don't faze her a bit."

The brothers started getting dressed.

The alcohol had left Ignaty's head. He suddenly felt depressed.

"What's with you?" Vaska asked, feeling himself—in contrast to his brother—to be in a great mood.

"I don't know. It's nothin'."

"He didn't have enough to drink, that's his problem," the old man explained. "He's not drunk or sober."

"Hell if I know! Ignore it. Let's sit here and have a smoke . . ."

They sat down on the warm stones. For a long time they were silent, looking at the swift, flowing waves. The waves were murmuring by the bank in their own language and seemed to be hurrying somewhere.

The sun set on the other side of the river, beyond the islands. It was quiet. All that could be heard were the waves splashing, the river seething, and the strikes of the wooden paddle against the wet laundry—a dull, damp, smacking sound—carrying over the river.

The three men contemplated their native river, each thinking his own thoughts.

Ignaty had quieted down. He stopped guffawing, his voice no longer boomed out.

"What is it, Vasya?" he asked quietly.

"Nothin'." Vaska threw a little stone into the water.

"Still plowin'?"

"Yeah."

Ignaty also threw a stone into the water. They were silent for a while.

"You've got a nice wife," Vaska said. "She's pretty."

"Think so?" Ignaty perked up and looked at his brother cheerfully, with curiosity. Then he added vaguely: "It doesn't matter. Pop, see, doesn't like her."

"I didn't say that I didn't like her, what's your problem?" The old man looked disapprovingly at Ignaty. "She's a nice woman. I just thinks she's awful fancy."

Ignaty roared with laughter.

"And what do you know about fancy women?"

His father turned away toward the river and was silent for a long time—he was offended. Then he turned to Vaska and said angrily:

"You should've wrestled with him."

"Why do you keep pesterin' me about that!" Vaska was amazed. "What's with you?"

"Somethin's eatin' Pop," Ignaty said. "Somethin's not to his likin'."

"What don't I like?" His father turned toward him.

"I don't know. Somethin's not sittin' right with you, I can see it."

"Well, lookee here! You've become awful smart, there's no way 'round it. You see and understand everythin', don't you?"

"That's enough, you two," Vaska said. "What's gotten into you? This is a helluva time to fight."

"Oh, to hell with him." Their father snorted and started feeling around for his tobacco pouch. "He comes home, starts blowin' his own horn, brings a heap of presents . . . Like we're s'posed to be impressed!"

"Pop, what is your problem, really?"

Ignaty even half rose for a moment in astonishment. Vaska imperceptibly nudged him in the side—don't get into it. Ignaty sat back down and looked at Vaska questioningly. Vaska got up, shook the sand off his pants and looked at their father.

"Wanna go? Pop . . ."

"Do you have the money?" he asked.

"Yeah. Let's go . . ."

The old man got up and, without glancing around, set out, the first one to go along the path leading to the gardens.

"What's with him?" Ignaty was genuinely disturbed by their father's mood.

"He waited a long time for you to come home. It'll pass real soon. Sing some song with him." Vaska smiled.

"What song? I've plumb forgotten 'em all. Do you still sing songs with him?"

"I was just jokin'. I don't know what's eatin' him . . . It'll pass."

Again they walked single file through the gardens. No one said anything. Ignaty walked behind his father and looked at his stooped back, and for some reason thought about how his father's right shoulder was lower than his left. He hadn't noticed that before.

1962 (1963)

My Son-in-Law Stole a Truckload of Wood!

Venya Zyablitsky, a small man, high-strung and rash, had a knock-down-drag-out fight at home with his wife and mother-in-law.

Venya had arrived home from a haul only to find out that his wife, Sonya, had blown all the money he'd saved up for a leather jacket on a fake astrakhan fur coat for herself. This is how Sonya explained it:

"You see, they'd put 'em out—everybody started snatchin' 'em up . . . Well, I thought it over and thought it over and I picked one up, too. You don't mind, do you, Venya?"

"You picked one up?" Venya screwed up his face venomously. "It must be all right if you *thought it over* first and then picked one up." Venya's dream of someday putting on a leather jacket and going for a stroll through the village on his day off with the jacket open in front had now been put off for a long time. "Thank you. You were really thinkin' about your husband . . . Well you can just go and . . ."

"What's your problem?"

"Nothin', everything's just fine. Thank you, I said."

"How come you're cussin'?"

"Who's cussin'? I'm sayin', everything's just fine. You got nothin' but rags to wear, so of course you need a fur coat . . . Your kind can't do without a fur coat. How could you get by without a fur coat? Damn spongers!"

Sonya, round-faced and beefy, ran to her mother to complain.

"Mom, just look here and see what he's up to—all 'cause of that fur coat, he's callin' me every name in the book!" Sonya was already thirty but, like a little girl, would still go running to her mama. "He's callin' us spongers!"

Venya's mother-in-law came out of the other room. She also had a round face, was sixty years old and was tough in body, temperament, and in her way of looking at life—basically, she was just plain tough through and through.

"What's this all about, Venyamin?" she said reproachfully. "Any other husband would be happy . . ."

"I *am* happy! I'm so happy I could strip off all my clothes and flash the whole block outta joy!"

"If you don't quite get it, then listen to what you're bein' told!" The mother-in-law raised her voice. "A beautiful, well-dressed wife is an adornment to her husband. And really, you of all people should think about that, seein's you're not so handsome yourself."

It is true, Venya wasn't a handsome man (he was undersized, skinny, towheaded . . . and lame, to boot. As a boy he'd been a tractor hand; he dozed off one night on the trailer and fell into a furrow and the plough whacked him hard on the leg), and when he was reminded about this—that he wasn't a handsome man—Venya would tremble with indignation.

"Well, yes, of course you of all people know how to adorn others! You've already adorned two . . ." Both Venya's father-in-law and Sonya's former husband were doing time—the father-in-law for embezzlement, Sonya's husband for getting into a drunken brawl. Word had it in the village that Lizaveta Vasilyevna, the mother-in-law, had helped put away both her husband and her son-in-law.

"Shut up!" Lizaveta Vasilyevna said sternly. "Or else you'll have me to deal with! Babe-in-arms! Snivelin' wimp!"

Venya soared up over the earth in his fury. And from way up there, from on high, he circled down like a hawk onto his mother-in-law.

"What're you raisin' your voice for? What're you raisin' your voice for around here? Old whore . . ."

Sonya didn't yet understand that that was the kind of talk you could put somebody away for. She just got very offended for her mother.

"Young pup!" she exclaimed. "Twenty-eight years old and you're already actin' like an old fart!"

The mother-in-law, on the other hand, understood right away that that was *exactly* the kind of talk you could have somebody put away for.

"So . . . What was it you said? Whore? Good! Whore? . . Good. In front of witnesses." She ran to the other room to write a statement for the police. "I'll make you pay for that, for callin' me a whore!" she said loudly with a tremor in her voice. "I'll make you pay!"

"Go ahead, go ahead and write—you're an old hand at that." All the same, Venya got a little bit scared. Devil knows she's in with all the regional authorities. "You'd just as soon put somebody away as look at 'em."

"I helped organize the first kolkhoz farms and you say 'whore' to me!" his mother-in-law shouted loudly, appearing in the doorway.

"And I've been written about in the paper, that I drive heavy trucks, lame and all!" Venya shouted back. And he pounded his fist against his chest. "I have a fifteen-year work record!"

"Don't worry. It'll come in handy for you there."

Venya exploded again. He forgot his fear.

"Where's this 'there'? What 'there' are you talkin' about, whore? You just try and put me away first! That's when I'll think about where it'll come in handy for me and where it won't. You're a regular automated rattin' machine!"

"We'll put you awa-ay all right," his mother-in-law promised, again with a tremor in her voice. And she went off to write her report. But she came right back again and shouted: "Didn't you haul in a truckload of wood a little while back?! Where'd you get it from?! Where'd you get it?!"

"It was so *you* could warm yourself that I hauled it here . . ."

"Where'd you get it?!" Lizaveta Vasilyevna cried with all her might.

"I bought it."

"With what money? You turned all your pay over to us at home! You chopped down that wood in a government-owned forest, without payin' for it! You *stole* a truckload of wood!"

"Fine, we'll say that I did. Then how come *you* didn't go and report it right away? How come *you* burned those pieces of wood and held your tongue?"

"Because I've only just now realized with whom we are living under one roof."

"Uh-huh . . . Dodgin' the issue. If anybody's gonna do time, then we'll do it together. I stole, and you used the stolen goods. I'll get three years, you'll get one and a half minimum. There you have it. We also know the laws."

"Not quite, you don't know 'em yet. But when you've done your time, you'll know 'em all right."

His mother-in-law really did go with her report to the district police. But she said nothing, apparently, about the truckload of firewood. At the station she was advised to turn to the directorate of the sovkhoz with her complaint, since what they had at present was a family squabble and nothing more. You really just can't, with only one complaint, immediately institute criminal proceedings against a person. Now if this happens again and if he's under the influence . . . Lizaveta Vasilyevna flew off to the sovkhoz directorate.

Venya was called in.

Lying in front of the deputy director—a young man whom Venya respected for his youth and brains—was his mother-in-law's report.

"Well, what went on over there at your place? They've been complaining here . . ."

"Complainin'! They themselves are all dressed up like a buncha . . . They've got everything!" Venya began to recount honestly. "As for me—

what's on me right now, well that's all I've got. I wanted, just once in my life, to buy a leather jacket for a hundred and sixty rubles, even saved up for it, and she goes and buys herself a fur coat. And she's already got a good winter coat."

"Well, why all the name calling? Why all the cussing?"

"Anybody'd be furious at that! I'd saved and saved, for pete's sake . . . I even scrimped on my pint after the banya and she goes and buys a fur coat! And the thing is, she's already got a coat! If she didn't have one, that'd be one thing, but she's got a coat, you know! So what does she say there?"

"She says . . . She says a lot."

It was then and there that Venya realized his mother-in-law had kept quiet about the load of firewood.

"Does she say that she helped with collectivization?"

"Well, she does . . . Still, you . . . you shouldn't have. She's an elderly woman . . . So she bought a coat! She does work, too, your wife does, that is."

"She brings home sixty rubles and sits around where it's nice and warm. I bring home at least a hundred and twenty. I'm slavin' way above the norm. And I couldn't care less about the money! But just once in my life I should be able to get a little somethin', too! If only they'd wear the stuff. But they just buy it and stow it away in a trunk. And here I'm ashamed to show myself in what I've got."

The deputy director didn't know what to do. He believed that Venya was in the right—it was as clear as day.

"Still, you shouldn't, Venyamin. You see, you won't prove a thing doing that. Talk with your wife . . . See what she'll say. She'll understand—she's a young woman . . ."

"She won't say anythin'! . . . She's got no opinion of her own. It's that one you got there," Venya nodded at the report, "who's in charge of everything."

By and large, they talked on in this vein, and Venya left the office with a light heart. But his grudge and ill will toward his mother-in-law hadn't diminished one bit.

"A real snake in the grass," he thought. "She'd put you away without battin' an eye. How much spite there is in people! She's lived her whole life, and her whole life she's been spiteful. The whore . . . Why the hell are people even born like that?"

It was here that Kolka Volobuyev—not really a friend of his, but a good guy to pal around with—came across him.

"What's with you?"

Kolka somehow always spoke oddly, barely opening his mouth. And he'd look at everybody condescendingly, slightly squinting his eyes. A real type.

"What do you mean?"

"You look like . . . like a clipped sparrow. Where're you hoppin' from like that?"

"From the sovkhoz office." And Venya told him everything—about how he'd had to say goodbye to the leather coat, how he'd gotten in a fight at home and how his mother-in-law wanted to put him away.

"Gobblin' up two people's not enough for her," Kolka said through his teeth. "Let's go get a drink."

Venya went along gladly.

When they'd had a few drinks, Kolka screwed up his chilly gray eyes and started instructing Venya.

"You need to knock some sense into her. Just cover your tracks. Or else they'll sink their claws into you. When the old woman starts gettin' under your skin, give her a scare a time or two . . . Or else they'll saddle you like a horse. You're workin' like an ass for 'em . . ."

Venya's heart began to seethe vindictively. All the insults and injuries Sonya had inflicted on him came rushing back at once: how for a long time she hadn't wanted to marry him, how she'd kept him waiting by her gate and tormented him with neither a "yes" nor a "no," how she . . . No, everything's gotta be put right. Who the hell was master of the house anyway! He'd been playin' the ass, Kolka'd gotten *that* right.

"I'll go and see if I can't knock a few heads together," he said. And he soon limped off home. And he carried in his breast a heavy, malicious heart.

"They think they're dealin' with a fool! . . . The stupid bitches. And to top it off, she has to go runnin' to the police! Whore."

Sonya wasn't at home.

"Where is she?" Venya asked.

"How should I know?" his mother-in-law barked out. A cleaning woman from the office was quick to inform her that Venya had been let off easy. (There was something strange about this whole thing: by now, Lizaveta Vasilyevna had been retired for five years, but there were those who still regarded her as somebody to reckon with. They'd run to her and inform on folks. They were even kind of afraid of her.) "She doesn't give me a report on her whereabouts."

"Button it!" Venya shouted from the threshold. "We run our mouths way too much!"

Lizaveta Vasilyevna looked with amazement at her son-in-law.

"What's that? You been drinkin' or somethin'?"

Then an entertaining idea occurred to Venya. He went out into the yard, found a hammer in the shed and some large nails. He put them all in his pocket and went back into the house.

"What's that fabric doin' in there?" he asked amicably.

"What fabric? Where?" his mother-in-law answered, suddenly interested.

"In the outhouse . . . Tucked in up on the top. It's red."

His mother-in-law sped off to the outhouse. Venya followed.

His mother-in-law had barely stepped into the outhouse when Venya locked it, fastening the hook on the outside. Then he started boarding up the door with nails.

His mother-in-law started screaming.

"You just sit there a spell and think things over," Venya kept saying. "You like to put people away? Now you can try it for a while and see what it feels like." He drove in all the nails and sat on the step to wait for Sonya.

"He-elp!!" wailed Lizaveta Vasilyevna. "Good people, save me! Save me! Good people! . . . My son-in-law stole a truckload of wood! My son-in-law stole a truckload of wood! My son-in-law stole a truckload of wood!" his mother-in-law set in to howling.

Venya threatened:

"If you're gonna bawl, I'll put a match to you."

His mother-in-law fell silent. She only said:

"Come on, Venka! . . ."

"You threatenin' me?"

"I'm not threatenin' you, I'm not threatenin' you with anythin'. What do you want me to do—say thank you?"

Venya's eyes fell on a chunk of quicklime. He picked it up and wrote on the door of the outhouse:

"Sealed 25 July 1969. Handle with care."

"Come on Venka! . . ."

"Now I'm gonna wait for your Sonya, too . . . And she's gonna step lively for me. In her astrakhan fur coat. Did you think I was your dumb ass? All the money I dragged home, but did *you* ever even buy me one single decent suit?"

"But you came into a house that already had everything."

"And if I'd come stark naked, would I have gone around like that— naked? What—haven't I earned a single shirt for myself? You did away with the kulaks, but you're the biggest kulak yourself! Your trunks are burstin' at the seams with stuff . . ."

"No thanks to you!"

"And no thanks to you either! Who'd your man go stealin' for? And when he stopped bein' useful, you put him away. Now you can do some time yourself. You're gonna do three days. I'm gonna get my gun and I'm not lettin' nobody near. You can figure I've put you in solitary confinement. For bad behavior."

"Come on now, Venka!"

"That's that. And don't bawl, or else it'll be worse for you."

"You shouldn't torment an old woman."

"You've tormented people all your life—you did it when you were young and now that you're old, you're still at it."

Venya waited some more for Sonya, but then he couldn't wait any longer. He couldn't hold himself back. So he set off around the village to look for her.

"You sit there quietly!" he ordered his mother-in-law.

Fortunately, Venya didn't find his wife that day. His mother-in-law was released from "solitary confinement" by the neighbors.

The trial was stormy. It was held in the clubhouse—a show trial.

His mother-in-law wept at the trial, said once again that she had helped found the first kolkhozes, and talked about the emotional stress she'd suffered sitting in "solitary confinement"—she really wanted to put Venya away. But the villagers protested. Young and old alike said that they'd known Venya since he was a boy, that he'd grown up as an orphan, had always been obedient, had never laid a finger on a soul . . . Some punishment was necessary, of course, but not a prison term after all! Mikhailo Kuznetsov, an old soldier, a dignified, respectable man, who'd long been retired, put it well, with feeling.

"Citizen judges!" he said. "I knew Venya's father. He laid down his life on the field of battle. Venya's mother ruined her health workin' at the kolkhoz—it did her in. Venka himself went to work at the age of ten . . . Citizen Kiselyova, on the other hand . . . She may be cryin' now, and, sure thing, sittin' in the toilet in your old age don't strike anybody's fancy, but all the same, she's never known any hard times in her life. Yes and even to this day you don't know 'em—you got a pension bigger'n mine, and I'm all covered with wounds, I've been through three wars—"

"I'm from a poor peasant family!" Lizaveta Vasilyevna shouted, breaking into a squeal. "The first kolkhozes were my—"

"I'm from a poor peasant family, too," retorted Mikhailo. "You were the first to organize the kolkhoz, but I was the first to go work in it. What's so special 'bout your service to soci'ty? During the war you were in charge of the village co-op—so you sure didn't go hungry, we know *that's* a fact. Whereas this here fellow supported himself with his own labor. You gotta 'ppreciate that. You just can't do this. It's easy to put somebody away, but doin' time's a different matter!"

"He's gotten nothin' but commendations—ten or so of 'em! Every holiday he's held up as an outstanding worker!" people shouted from the hall.

But just then an official got up from the table. He was portly, wearing a light-colored suit. He scanned the hall with a knowing eye. Oh how he set to it, how he set into dressing them down! He said that with crime it's always better (and in the present case, simply more beneficial) to punish the petty crime than to wait for the serious one. He gave examples of guys who seemed perfectly harmless suddenly pulling a knife during a brawl.

"Where's the certainty, I ask you, that he, now that he's embittered, won't get drunk again tomorrow and take up an ax? Or a gun? There are two women in the house. You can just imagine . . ."

"He doesn't drink."

"What are you saying, that he took up a hammer and boarded up his mother-in-law in the outhouse after a couple of glasses of soda pop? An elderly, respectable woman with an excellent record! And for what? Because his wife bought herself a fur coat and, you see, they didn't buy *him* a leather jacket!"

The ground under Venya was getting shaky. And many in the hall made up their minds: Venka would have to do time in the slammer.

"No, comrades, our humanity lies precisely in the fact that we will not allow this misdemeanor to go by without taking action against the accused. It's better to do it now. We will protect him from a greater danger. For it is clearly lying in wait for him."

The official suggested giving Venka three years.

At that, Mikhailo Kuznetsov got up again.

"You, comrade, were absolutely right in everythin' you said. But, lemme give you one small example from the Great Patriotic War. We had this soldier with us, like Venka here, also a real runt, young, prob'ly about twenty. Well, we went on the attack and that soldier got all scared-like. He threw down his rifle, dropped to the ground and, you know, grasped his head with his hands . . . The unit Party officer wanted to shoot him right there on the spot, but we soldiers who were a little older didn't let him. We helped him to his feet and he ran on with us . . . And watcha think happened? All by his lonesome, right in front of everybody, he bayonetted two Nazis. And these Nazis coulda touched the ceilin', they were so tall. And that soldier—I've forgotten his name by now—was no bigger'n Venka. Where'd he get the strength? I'm sayin' this 'cause it often happens that some weakness or instinct'll come over a fella—you'd think, well, he's done for, completely done for . . . And it's just the opposite—don't be hasty, he'll get back on his feet. Did you happen to fight in the war yourself, comrade?" Mikhailo asked as he wound up.

Such a remarkable example didn't make the official lose his composure in the least. He gave a knowing smile.

"I did, comrade. That's in answer to your question. Now, as regards your example. It is . . . of course, striking, inspiring, but absolutely inappropriate. Here you are, as they say, trying to make a silk purse out of a sow's ear." The official gave a sharp laugh, making his ample, taut stomach shake slightly. "With an example like that you can prove the exact opposite of what you meant to say. By the way, did he stand trial, that soldier?"

Mikhailo didn't answer right away. Everybody even turned in his direction.

"He did," Mikhailo answered unwillingly. "But . . ."

"Quite right. But—"

"But they didn't take action!" Mikhailo raised his voice. "They just transferred him to a different unit."

"That's another matter altogether. The fact that he got up and ran along with you and then bayonetted two Nazis is a circumstance that speaks for itself and it must be taken into account, and, as we see, it was. But there are facts which . . . materially, so to speak, are impossible to take into account. The soldier got scared, threw down his arms and fell . . . He got scared—that's clear. But say you get scared all alone in the forest when you see a bear—well, then you'll have to put it in God's hands, as they say, or, to be more precise—in the bear's: will he tear you to pieces or won't he? But what we have here is a soldier, he wasn't going into the attack alone. He got scared, he struck fear into the hearts of the whole company."

"Nothin' doin'!" said Mikhailo. "We kept runnin' the same way we'd been runnin' before!"

"You ran in a different frame of mind. You yourselves weren't aware of it, but already fear was dwelling within you. The soldier who'd gotten frightened let you see, as it were, what kind of danger waited up ahead—possibly death . . ."

"As if we didn't know it without him."

"As regards the given concrete situation . . ."

Venka looked at the official, understanding poorly what it was he was saying. He only understood that this man also really wanted to put him away, although he wasn't at all spiteful like his mother-in-law and was seeing Venka for the first time. Venka had never been in court before. He didn't know that there were such things as public prosecutors . . . For him, a trial meant standing in front of a judge. And he simply could not fathom *exactly why* this man needed—no matter what—to put him, Venka, in prison for three years. The judge was silent, while that other man—for the umpteenth time already—was getting up and saying that they'd have to put him away, and there was no way around it. Venka was mute with amazement. When asked if he would like to give some sort of explanation to the court, he shrugged his shoulders and somewhat hastily and fearfully retorted:

"What for?"

The court withdrew for deliberation.

Venka sat there. He waited. He was paralyzed by terror. Not terror of prison. On his way here he'd done some calculating in his mind: twenty-eight plus three, well, four makes thirty-one or thirty-two . . .

But it was no good. Venka had been seized by terror of this man. He'd looked at him so hard that even now that he was no longer at the table, Venka could still see him as if he were there in the flesh: calm, intelligent, cheerful . . . And arguing, arguing, arguing that they needed to put him away. It was incomprehensible. How on earth could this man . . . eat supper later on, hug his kids, sleep with his wife? . . . Venya often used to get angry with people, but he'd never been afraid of them. Now he suddenly understood with horror that they can be—terrifying. Once in his life a couple of drunks had beaten Venya up. They beat him up and kind of grunted from time to time—from the exertion, he guessed. For a long time afterward, Venya remembered with loathing not the pain but precisely that quiet grunt after each punch. But those guys were drunk, out of their minds . . . This one—was an official, an educated man, and he was not at all angry, but rather was calmly convincing everybody that they had to put him away. Oh, Lord Almighty! His mother-in-law! . . . His mother-in-law was a snake and a fool. She was prepared to see to it that her son-in-law got not three years but five, and all the same you could understand that she was just that way— a real whore. But this one! How could he do this?

Venya was sentenced: he got two years probation.

Folks were happy for Venya.

But Venya was unusually pensive as he walked away . . . He kept seeing that official standing right before his very eyes, and Venka couldn't stop being amazed: did he really do that for a living?

For the time being Venya went to stay at Kolka Volobuyev's.

Again Kolka suggested they go drinking, but Venya refused. He went into the other room early, lay down on the sleeping bench and thought and thought.

The tricks life will play on you! In an instant everything had come crashing down just like that. To hell with that leather jacket anyway! And how come I suddenly wanted to buy a leather jacket so bad? I've done without one, and it was no big deal, I'd have kept on doin' without one. I should've lured Sonka away from my mother-in-law, we could've lived by ourselves . . . True, she was also a fool, she wouldn't have gone against her mother.

But whatever Venya thought about, however much his soul smarted that night, he kept remembering the official—how he had looked down at Venya from on high, from the stage, without malice, without yelling. His metal tie tack gleamed. He had black eyebrows, thick ones that grew slightly together across the bridge of his nose. His hair was slicked back and shone, except for several strands of hair that stuck together in a ringlet over his forehead and moved back and forth slightly and quivered when the man spoke. His face, although broad and round, was strong and when he smiled, dimples appeared on his cheeks.

In the morning Venya set out on a haul to the district center.

He left early, the sun had only just come up. But it was already warm, the ground hadn't cooled off during the night.

On the road Venya would always calm down. He'd start thinking about people as if they, the ones he knew, had stayed behind somewhere far away and no longer concerned him. He'd remember them all lumped together . . . He'd think: back there they've all gotten themselves in a terrible mess, they're all edgy, everything's all muddled and confused. He remembered yesterday's poor excuse for a trial like a bad, oppressive dream.

Twenty-seven kilometers into the trip, Venya saw a Volga up ahead with its hood up. The driver was poking around in the engine and next to him—Venya's heart skipped a beat in distress—was the official from yesterday's proceedings. For some reason Venya got flustered, he even took his foot off the gas . . . And when the official put up his hand to hitch a ride with him, Venya obediently stopped.

"Look here, how about a lift?" And he recognized Venya. "O-oh!" he said, also a bit flustered, or so it seemed to Venya. "An old acquaintance."

"Get in!" Venya said. In a flash, that certain confusion he'd glimpsed in the official's eyes infused him with a kind of impudent joviality. "Is this a bust?"

The official got nimbly into the cab and looked straight and also cheerfully at Venya. And already within a minute after they'd set off, Venya started doubting—had it really seemed to him that the official had been flustered at first?

"Well?" the man asked.

"What?"

"How's your mood? . . . I thought you'd have hit the bottle . . . for a good week. I'll give it to you straight, young fella: you drew a lucky card yesterday."

Venya was silent. He didn't know what to say. He didn't know how to behave.

"Of course you and your wife'll be getting a divorce, won't you?" the man asked knowingly. And again looked straight at Venya.

"Of course." Venya was again struck, as he'd been yesterday in court, how this man was so . . . tough perhaps, and smart, and pushy, and on top of all that—cheerful.

"Oh, kids, kids . . . Now you've done it. And you can't say the devil made you do it. You lived by your hard work and in one fell swoop you up and wiped it all out: you've destroyed your family, and your reputation's already not what it was. And you really loved your wife, didn't you?"

At that, Venya suddenly got angry.

"It's none of your business."

"Of course it isn't!" exclaimed the man. "It's yours. It's yours, pal, it's yours. If it were mine, my soul would be suffering. I'm just sorry for fools like you, that's the thing. You can get drunk on five little kopeks, but you'll need two rubles eighty-seven to pay for the consequences."[1] The man's stomach swayed slightly. "Was it really impossible to have a chat when you were sober? And your wife there sure is pretty, I saw that yesterday. A guy oughta be happy to live and let live . . ."

For a second it was as if Venya had gone blind—he suddenly realized, painfully and deep down inside, that he had actually lost his Sonka! For good! And he was terrified, as if he were falling headlong into the abyss . . .

"So what was this leather jacket like and where'd you want to get it?"

"In a district in Gorno Altai,[2] where else? There's a guy who makes 'em . . ." Venya was looking straight ahead. Up ahead was the bridge that crossed the Usha River. It was wide and long—every spring the Usha overflows its banks, like the Volga. "He makes 'em to order."

"How much does he charge for a coat? Do you have to bring your own material?"

"Uh-huh."

"How much does he charge?"

"It depends. I wanted one for about a hundred and sixty rubles. If it's good, it's more expensive."

"What do you mean, if it's good?"

"Well, the kind of leather varies, the quality varies . . . The quality can be high or low."

"Well, let's say, the very best? That is the very best kind of leather, and the very best quality. How much would that come to?"

"Maybe about three hundred rubles . . . He says he's done one for four hundred for some guy."

"Where is this district? Is it far?"

"No." It was strange. It was as if Venya were alone in the cab, having a conversation with himself—that's how it felt.

"Do you know the address then?"

"I know the address. I know it. . . Ekh!" Venya suddenly shouted, loudly, as if in a vacuum. "Are we gonna go slidin' off the bridge?!"

He stomped his foot on the gas and let go of the steering wheel . . . The truck lunged. Venya glanced at the public prosecutor . . . And glimpsed his eyes—large, white with terror. And this struck Venya as funny, he started laughing. But then the public prosecutor leaned into him with his side and seized hold of the steering wheel. And that's how they drove across the bridge, with Venya laughing and stepping on the gas and the public prosecutor steering. But once they'd driven across the bridge, Venya took his foot off the gas and took hold of the steering wheel. And he stopped.

The public prosecutor climbed out of the cab . . . He glanced once more at Venka. He was still pale. Evidently, he wanted to say something, but didn't. He slammed the door.

Venya put the truck back in gear and drove off. For some reason he was suddenly very tired. And—it was good, that he was all by himself in the cab, somehow it was more peaceful. It was better.

1971

Oddball

His wife called him "Oddball." Sometimes affectionately.

Oddball possessed one peculiarity: things were always happening to him. He didn't desire this, he'd suffer because of it, but time and time again he'd get into scrapes—minor ones, it's true, but vexing ones all the same.

Take these episodes from one of his trips, for example.

He'd gotten some time off and decided to go see his brother in the Urals. It'd been some twelve years since they had last seen each other.

"Where's that spoon bait? The one that looks like a fish." Oddball yelled to his wife from the storeroom.

"How should I know?"

"They were all lyin' right here!" Oddball tried to make his round bluish-white eyes look stern. "Don't you see, they're all here except that particular one."

"It looks like a fish?"

"Suppose so. It's for pike."

"I must've fried it up by accident."

Oddball was silent for awhile.

"Well, how was it?"

"What?"

"Taste good? Ha-ha-ha!" He was no good at cracking jokes, though he terribly wanted to be. "Still got your teeth? It's made of duralumin, you know!"

They spent a long time packing—all the way till midnight.

Early in the morning Oddball strode through the village, suitcase in hand.

"The Urals! The Urals!" he'd answer when asked where he was headed. "Need a change of scenery." And at that his round, meaty face and his round eyes would supremely express his couldn't-give-a-damn attitude about the great distance that stretched out before him. It didn't scare him. "To the Urals!"

But the Urals were still a long way off.

In the meantime he'd made it safely to the district capital, where he had to get his ticket and board the train.

He had lots of time on his hands. Oddball decided to buy a bunch of presents for his nephews—some candy and spice cakes. He dropped into a grocery store and got in line. A man in a hat was standing ahead of him, and ahead of the "hat" there was a plump woman wearing lots of lipstick. The woman spoke quietly, quickly, and heatedly to the hat.

"It's hard to imagine how vulgar and tactless a person can be. He's got sclerosis, fine, has had it these seven years, but nobody's ever suggested that he should retire. But this new guy—he's barely taken the reins at the collective and already he's saying 'Maybe, Alexander Semyonych, you'd be better off retiring.' What nerve!"

The hat agreed with everything she said.

"Yes, yes . . . They're like that these days. So what if he's got sclerosis? What about Sumbatych? Lately he can't seem to get his lines right. And how about what's her name?"

Oddball respected city folk. Granted, not all of them—he didn't respect hooligans and shop clerks. He was a little afraid of them.

His turn came up. He bought some candies, spice cakes, and three bars of chocolate. He stepped to the side so he could stow it all in his suitcase. He opened up the suitcase on the floor and started to arrange his things.

He happened to glance at the floor where people were lined up at the counter and there, lying at their feet, was a fifty-ruble bill. Just a silly piece of green paper, lying there by itself, and nobody had noticed it. Oddball even started trembling with joy, his eyes lit up. Quickly, so nobody could forestall him, he tried to come up with the most amusing and witty way to tell the folks in line about the bill.

"You live well, citizens!" he said loudly and cheerfully.

Everybody turned to look at him.

"Where I'm from, for instance, we don't just toss around bills like that."

At that, everybody got a little nervous. After all, this was no three-ruble bill, it wasn't a fiver. This was a cool fifty rubles, a good half-month's salary. And there was nobody to claim the bill.

"It's probably the guy in the hat's," guessed Oddball.

They decided to put the bill in a visible spot on the counter. "Somebody'll come runnin' in for it pretty soon," the shop lady said.

Oddball left the store in the highest of spirits. He kept thinking about how slickly and amusingly he'd pulled it off. "Where I'm from, for instance, we don't just toss around bills like that." Suddenly, he felt a rush of heat. He remembered that he'd been given a bill exactly like that one along with a twenty-five-ruble note at the savings bank back home. He'd just gotten change back from the twenty-five note, so the fifty should be in his pocket . . . He thrust his hand into his pocket—it wasn't there. He felt around—it wasn't there.

"That bill was mine!" Oddball said loudly. "Hang it all! That was my bill!"

A twinge of despair shot through his heart. His first impulse was to go back and say: "Citizens, it's my bill. I got two at the savings bank: one was a twenty-five-ruble bill, the other was a fifty. I just now broke the twenty-five, and the other one's not here." But he could only imagine how taken aback everybody'd be by his announcement and how many of them would think: "No doubt, since nobody's shown up to claim it, he's decided to pocket it himself." No, he just couldn't make himself, he couldn't stretch out his hand to take the damn thing now. Besides, they might not give it to him . . .

"Why, oh, why am I like this?" Oddball reasoned out loud bitterly. "What should I do now?"

He had to go back home.

He approached the store. He wanted to look at the bill, if only from a distance. He stood for a little while by the entrance . . . and didn't go in. It would be too painful. His heart might not be able to take it.

He rode along in the bus, swearing quietly as he braced himself for what lay ahead: he had some explaining to do when he got home.

They took out another fifty rubles from their savings account.

Oddball boarded another train, feeling crushed by his own worthlessness, of which his wife had, once again, made him abundantly aware. (She'd even whacked him a couple of times across the head with a slotted spoon.) But gradually the bitterness passed. Forests, copses, and little villages flashed by the window. Various people came and went, various tales were told. Oddball also told one to an intellectual-looking comrade while they were standing in the vestibule, smoking.

"We've also got a fool like that in one of our neighborin' villages. He grabbed a smolderin' log and goes after his mother. Drunk, of course. She's runnin' away from him, cryin': 'Your hands, Sonny!' she cries, 'Don't burn your hands, Sonny!' Here she is worryin' about him! But he keeps after her, the stinkin' drunk. After his own mother. It's hard to imagine how vulgar and tactless a person can be."

"Did you make that up yourself?" the intellectual comrade asked sternly, looking over his glasses at Oddball.

"What makes you say that?" He didn't understand. "It was in Ramenskoye village, just across the river from us . . ."

The intellectual comrade turned toward the window and didn't say anything more.

After the train, Oddball still had an hour-and-a-half flight by commuter plane ahead of him. He had flown once before, a long time ago. So it was not without a little trepidation that he climbed on board. "How can it be that not a single screw will go out of whack for a whole hour and a half," he thought. After they were under way, it was no big deal, he grew bolder. He even tried to strike up a conversation with his neighbor, who was reading a newspaper. But his neighbor was apparently so interested in what was in the paper that he didn't feel like listening to a live human being. Oddball, however, wanted to clear up the following. He'd heard that they give you food in airplanes. But for some reason nobody was bringing anything. He really wanted to have a meal in a plane—just to see what it would be like.

"They must've swiped ours," he decided.

He started looking down. There were mountains under the clouds. For some reason, Oddball couldn't say for sure if it was beautiful or not. But all around him people were saying: "Oh, how beautiful!" All he felt was the sudden, ridiculous desire to fall into them, into the clouds, as into cotton wadding. What's more, he thought: "Why aren't I amazed? After all, there's almost five kilometers below me." In his mind, he measured off those five kilometers on the ground and then stood them up on end in order to amaze himself. But even so, he wasn't amazed.

"That's man for you! The things he thinks up," he said to his neighbor.

His neighbor looked at him, said nothing, and started rustling his paper again.

"Fasten your seat belts," a nice-looking young woman said. "We've started our descent."

Oddball obediently fastened his seat belt. But his neighbor didn't pay any attention. Oddball cautiously touched his arm.

"They're tellin' us to fasten our seat belts."

"So what," the neighbor said. He put aside his newspaper, settled back in his seat, and said, as if recalling something: "Children are life's flowers—they should be planted head down."

"How's that?" Oddball didn't get it.

The newspaper reader burst into loud laughter and didn't say anything more.

They started to descend quickly. Soon the ground was just a stone's throw away and streaking past them. But the expected bump of the landing gear never seemed to come. As knowledgeable people later explained, the pilot had overshot the runway. When at last they touched down, everybody was tossed about so violently that you could hear the chattering and grinding of their teeth. The newspaper reader was thrown from his seat, butted Oddball with his bald head, smacked against the window, then ended up on the floor. The whole time he didn't make a single peep. And everybody around them kept quiet, too. That amazed Oddball. He had also kept quiet. They came to a stop. The first ones to come to their senses glanced out the window and discovered that the airplane was sitting in a potato field. The disgruntled pilot came out of the cabin and headed toward the exit. Somebody cautiously asked him:

"Seems we've landed in a potato field?"

"What's the matter with you, can't you see for yourself?" the pilot answered.

Their fear had subsided and the livelier ones were already timidly trying to crack jokes.

The bald reader was looking for his false teeth. Oddball unfastened his seat belt and started to look, too.

"This it?" he joyfully cried out and handed them over. The reader's bald patch actually turned purple.

"Was it absolutely necessary to touch them with your hands?!" he shouted lispingly.

Oddball fell apart.

"What else could I use?"

"Where am I going to boil them? Where?!"

Oddball didn't know that, either.

"Wanna come with me?" he offered. "I've got a brother who lives here. Are you afraid I got 'em all germy? Don't worry—no germs on me!"

The newspaper reader looked at Oddball in amazement and stopped yelling.

At the airport Oddball wrote his wife a telegram.

"We've touched down. A lilac branch fell on my breast, forget me not, Grusha, my sweetest. Vasyatka."

The telegraph worker was a severe, dried-up woman who, after reading the telegram, suggested:

"Write it differently. You're a grown man, not a kindergartner."

"Why?" Oddball asked. "I always write to her like that in letters. She's my wife, after all! You probably thought . . ."

"In letters you may write what you please, but a telegram will be sent over the wires. It's an open text."

Oddball rewrote it.

"Touched down. Everything's okay. Vasyatka."

The telegraph lady herself corrected two parts: "touched down" and "Vasyatka." It became: "Arrived. Vasily."

"'Touched down . . .' What are you—a cosmonaut or something?"

"Well, all right," Oddball said. "Might as well send it like that."

. . . Oddball knew that he had a brother, Dmitry, and three nephews. The fact that there also must be a sister-in-law somehow didn't cross his mind. He'd never seen her. And it was namely she, the sister-in-law, who ruined everything, the whole vacation. For some reason she took an instant dislike to Oddball.

While drinking with his brother in the evening, Oddball broke into song, his voice quavering:

> The poplar tre-e-es,
> The poplar tre-e-es.

Sofya Ivanovna, the sister-in-law, stuck her head out of the other room and asked nastily:

"Do you hafta yell? You're not at the train station, are you?" And she slammed the door.

Brother Dmitry was embarrassed.

"It's . . . The kids are sleepin' in there. Actually, she's a good woman."

They drank some more. They began to reminisce about their youth, their mother and father . . .

"Do you remember?" brother Dmitry asked joyfully. "Though who would you remember! You were just a baby. They'd leave me with you, and I'd smother you with kisses. You even turned blue once. They laid into me for that. After that, they didn't leave me with you. But that didn't matter. They just had to turn away, and there I'd be next to you, kissin' you again. Hell if I know what kind of a habit that was. I was just a little snot-nosed kid myself and already . . . it's . . . kisses."

"Remember," also reminisced Oddball, "how you . . ."

"Will you stop yellin'?" Sofya Ivanovna asked again, all nastiness and with an edge to her voice. "Who needs to listen to all your 'snot and kisses'? As if *you* were somebody special!"

"Let's go outside," Oddball said.

They went out and sat down on the porch.

"Do you remember? . . ." continued Oddball.

But now something happened to brother Dmitry. He burst into tears and started banging his fist against his knee.

"There you have it, that's my life! Did you see? How much nastiness there is in people! How much nastiness!"

Oddball began to calm his brother down.

"Stop it, don't get upset. You shouldn't. They aren't nasty at all, they're nuts. I have one just like her."

"But how come she took such a dislike to you? What for? You know, she took a real dislike to you . . . But what for?"

Only then did Oddball understand that, yes, his sister-in-law had taken a dislike to him. But what for, indeed?

"Here's why. It's 'cause you're no executive, no manager. I know her, the fool. She's crazy about those executives of hers. And who the hell is she? A snack bar girl in a government administration buildin'. A bump on a log. But she takes a good look 'round over there and then starts in . . . She hates me, too—'cause I'm not an executive, I'm from the country."

"What administration buildin' does she work in?"

"The mining . . . I can't even get my tongue 'round it now. But why did she marry me? Didn't she know who I was, or what?"

Now, Oddball was cut to the quick.

"And what's the point, when you get right down to it?" he loudly asked not his brother, but somebody else. "Yes, if you're really interested, almost all famous people come from the country. Just take a look at the obituaries and you'll read 'he was country bred.' You've gotta read the newspapers . . . No matter what kind of important person he may be, you understand, it's like this: 'he was country bred and started workin' early.'"

"And how many times have I tried to prove to her that in the country people are better, not so stuck-up?"

"Remember that Stepan Vorobyov? You used to know him."

"'Course I did."

"Well, there's country breedin' for you! Just like that—a Hero of the Soviet Union. He destroyed nine tanks. He rammed 'em. They're gonna pay his mother a sixty-ruble pension for the rest of her life. They learned, just recently, that he's listed among the missin' . . ."

"And Ilya Maksimov! You know, we left for the city together. There you go—he was awarded the Order of Glory, all three classes. But don't tell her about Stepan . . . It'll get her started."

"Okay. But how about that . . . ?"

The excited brothers continued on noisily for a long time. Oddball even paced next to the porch waving his hands.

"It's all thanks to country breedin', don't you see? What the air alone is worth there! You open up your window come mornin' and it's just like bein' bathed from head to toe in it, isn't it? If only you could drink it—it's so fresh and fragrant, all herbs and flowers."

Then they got tired.

"Did you put up a new roof?" The elder brother asked quietly.

"Yes." Oddball also sighed softly. "I added on a veranda. It's quite a sight. You go out on the veranda in the evenin' and your fancy takes off. If Mother and Father were alive, you could come with your kids and we'd all sit on the veranda and sip tea with raspberry jam. This year we've got tons of ripe raspberries. Now, Dmitry, don't you quarrel with her, or else she'll dislike me even more. And somehow I'll be a little sweeter, you'll see, she'll come around."

"She's from the country herself," Dmitry marvelled somewhat quietly and sadly. "And here she's gone and tormented the children, the fool. She tormented one on the piano, the other she signed up for figure skating. My heart bleeds for 'em, but I can't say a word or she cusses me up and down."

"Humph!" Once again Oddball got stirred up. "I can't for the life of me understand those newspapers. You see, there's one just like that who works in the store, rude as hell. Oh, she's a prize, all right! And she's no different when she comes home. That's where the real trouble is! I don't understand!" Oddball also pounded his knee with his fist. "I don't understand why they've all gotten so mean."

When Oddball woke up in the morning, there was nobody in the apartment. Brother Dmitry had left for work, so had his sister-in-law. The older children were playing in the courtyard while the little one had been dropped off at the nursery school.

Oddball made his bed, washed up, and started to think of something nice he could do for his sister-in-law. His eyes fell upon the baby carriage. "Aha," thought Oddball, "I'll paint pictures all over it." Back home he'd painted up the stove so well that everybody marvelled. He found the children's paint and a brush and got right down to work. In an hour everything was done, you'd never have recognized the baby carriage. Across the top of the carriage, Oddball put cranes—a flock in "V" formation—and along the bottom he put various little flowers, new grass, a pair of roosters, and some chicks . . . He looked the baby carriage over from top to bottom: it was a thing to behold. A real dandy among baby carriages. He imagined how pleasantly surprised his sister-in-law would be and grinned.

"And you say we're all hicks! Crazy woman!" He wanted there to be peace between him and his sister-in-law. "It'll be as if the baby were in a flower basket."

All day long Oddball roamed the city, window-shopping. He bought his nephew a boat, a real darling little boat, white, with a little light on it. "I'll paint it up, too," he thought.

About six o'clock Oddball arrived at his brother's. He soared up the steps of the porch and heard his brother Dmitry arguing with his wife. Actually, the wife was doing the arguing while brother Dmitry kept repeating:

"Really now, what of it! . . . All right, all right, Sophie . . . Don't go on about it . . ."

"Just make sure that by tomorrow that fool is outta here!" Sofya Ivanovna was shouting. "I want him out by tomorrow."

"All right, that's enough! Sophie . . ."

"No, it's not all right! It's not! He'd better clear out before I throw his suitcase the hell outta here right now and that'd be the end of that."

Oddball hurried down the porch stairs. But he didn't know what to do next. Once again he began to hurt. When people hated him, he felt very hurt. And scared. It seemed like this: well, it's all over now, so why go on living? And he'd want to go somewhere far, far away from the people who hated him or were laughing at him.

"Why, oh why am I like this?" he whispered bitterly, sitting in the shed. "I should've guessed that she wouldn't appreciate it at all, that she wouldn't appreciate folk art."

He sat there in the shed till it got dark outside. And his heart just ached and ached. Then his brother Dmitry came. He wasn't surprised, as if he had known that his brother Vasily had been sitting in the shed for a real long time.

"Here you are . . ." he said. "It's like this . . . She's blown up again. It's the baby carriage . . . You shouldn't have, you know."

"I thought it'd strike her fancy. I'll go back home, brother."

Brother Dmitry sighed . . . and said nothing.

When Oddball arrived home, a heavy, warm rain was falling. Oddball climbed out of the bus, took off his new shoes, and set off running along the warm, damp earth with his suitcase in one hand and his shoes in the other. He bobbed up and down and sang loudly.

> The poplar tre-e-es.
> The poplar tre-e-es.

One corner of the sky had already cleared up, become blue, and the sun was somewhere close by. And the rain began to taper off, only a few big drops splashed into the puddles; there they formed bubbles and burst.

In one spot Oddball slipped and almost fell.

. . . His name was Vasily Yegorych Knyazev. He was thirty-nine years old. He worked as a movie projectionist in the village. He adored detectives and dogs. When he was little, he'd dreamed of being a spy.

1967

Mille Pardons, Madame!

When city folk come to these parts to hunt, and they ask in the village who'd be able to go along and show them around, they're told:

"Ah, that'd be Bronka Pupkov . . . He's our expert as far as that goes. He'll make it lively for you." And the villagers smile kind of strangely.

Bronka (Bronislav) Pupkov, still a tough, well-built muzhik, is blue-eyed, always smiling, quick on his feet, and quick with his tongue. He's past fifty and was at the front. But that mutilated right hand of his—with two fingers shot off—was not from the war. Once, when he was just a kid out hunting, he'd gotten thirsty (it was in the wintertime), so he began picking at the ice by the riverbank with his rifle butt. He held the gun by the barrel, covering the muzzle with two of his fingers. The lock of the Berdan rifle was on safety, but it broke loose, and one finger blew clean off, while the other dangled by its skin. So Bronka tore it off himself. The two fingers—the index and the middle one—he brought home, burying them in the garden, even saying something like:

"My dear little fingers, rest in peace, till kingdom come."

He wanted to put up a cross, but his father wouldn't let him.

Bronka had raised plenty of hell in his day. He'd get in fights and often have the living daylights knocked out of him, but he'd just lick his wounds and be off again, tearing around on his deafening moped, not holding a grudge against a soul. He lived easy.

Bronka awaited the arrival of city hunters like a holiday. And when they came, he was ready—whether for a week or for a month. He knew the local country like the back of his eight-fingered hands. And he was a clever, lucky hunter.

The city folk weren't stingy with their vodka, and once in a while they'd even give him some cash, but if they didn't, that was okay, too.

"For how long?" Bronka'd ask, all businesslike.

"About three days."

"Everything'll suit you to a T. You'll rest a spell and calm those nerves of yours."

They'd go for three, four, seven days at a time. It was nice. City people were respectful, around them he wasn't tempted to pick a fight, even when they drank. He loved to tell them all sorts of hunting stories.

But it would be on the very last day, during their farewell supper, that Bronka would get down to his main tale. This day, too, he would await with great impatience, reining himself in with all his might. And when that long-awaited day would finally come, from morning on Bronka would feel a sweet aching in his heart, and he would be solemnly silent.

"What's the matter?" he'd be asked.

"So," he'd answer. "Where're we gonna have our farewell supper? Over on the bank?"

"We can do it on the bank."

Closer to evening time they'd choose a comfortable spot on the bank of the beautiful, swift river and set up a little campfire. While the bream fish soup simmered, they'd toss back the first round and chat.

After knocking back two aluminum cupfuls, Bronka'd light up.

"Ever been at the front?" he'd ask, as if he were just shooting the breeze. Almost everybody over forty had been at the front, but he'd ask the young ones, too: he needed to begin his tale.

"So that's from the front, then?" they, in turn, would ask, meaning his injured hand.

"No, I was a stretcher-bearer at the front. Yeah . . . The things I saw . . ." Bronka would remain silent for a long time. "Ever hear of the attempt on Hitler's life?"

"Uh-huh."

"Not that one. You're thinkin' about when his very own generals wanted to bump him off?"

"Yeah."

"No. A different one."

"What other one? Was there really another?"

"There was." Bronka would stick his aluminum cup under the bottle. "Hit me again." Then he'd down it. "There was, dear comrades, there was. A-hem! Here's how far the bullet missed his head." Bronka would hold up the tip of his little finger.

"When'd it happen?"

"July twenty-fifth, nineteen hund'erd'n forty-three." Once again Bronka would be lost in thought for a long time, as if remembering something that was his very own, distant and precious.

"Who shot at him?"

Bronka wouldn't hear the question. He'd just smoke and look at the fire.

"Where was this attempt, then?"

Bronka would remain silent.

Everybody would exchange glances in surprise.

"I did," he'd say suddenly. He would speak quietly, keeping his eyes on the fire for awhile, then he'd raise them. He'd look as if he wanted to say "Surprised? It even surprises me." And he'd smile kind of sadly.

Usually they'd keep quiet for a long time, glancing at Bronka. He'd smoke and tap pieces of coal back into the campfire with a stick. This was the most intense moment of all. It was as if a glass of the purest alcohol had been set coursing through his blood.

"Are you serious?"

"What do you think? That I don't know what they give you for distortin' history? I know, dear comrades, I know."

"Well, yes, but that's nonsense."

"Where'd you shoot? How'd you do it?"

"I had a Browning. It was like this: I squeezed the trigger and poof!" Bronka would gaze seriously and sadly—people were so distrustful. At this point he would no longer be joking or clowning around.

The doubting townsfolk would be at a loss.

"And how come nobody knows about this?"

"Even in another hund'erd years there'll still be a lotta things that ain't seen the light of day. Get it? 'Cause what you don't know . . . That's the whole tragedy, that many heroes are still under wraps."

"That kinda smacks of—"

"Just a minute. How'd it happen?"

Bronka knew that they would want to listen all the same. They always did.

"You'll blab, won't you?"

Once again they'd be thrown into confusion.

"We won't blab."

"Party's honor?"

"Of course we won't blab. Get on with the story."

"No," he insisted. "Party's honor? 'Cause in the village we have, well, you know what kinda people . . . They'll go and wag their tongues."

"Everything'll be okay!" By now, the people would be anxious to hear all about it. "Get on with your story."

"Hit me again, please." Once again, Bronka would hold out his cup. He'd look cold sober. "It happened, like I already said, on the twenty-fifth of July in 'forty-three. A-hem! We were on the attack. When you're on the attack, there's more work for stretcher-bearers. That day I lugged a dozen men into the field hospital. I carried in one badly wounded lieutenant and laid him down in the tent. There was some general already there. A major general. He was slightly wounded—in the leg, right smack above the knee. They were bandagin' him up. The general saw me and said: 'Hold on a minute, orderly. Don't go.'

"So I'm thinkin', he's gotta go somewhere and wants me to give him a hand. I wait. With generals, life's a heckuva lot more interestin'. Just like that, the situation's as plain as day."

By now the townsfolk are all ears. The cheery little fire sputters and smokes. Dusk steals out from the forest and creeps across the water, but in the middle, where the current flows most quickly, the river itself still sparkles and gleams, as if an enormous, long fish were being carried along by the current, her silvery body playing in the twilight.

"Well, they finished bandagin' up the general, and the doctor says to him, 'You need to stay in bed for awhile.' 'Like hell I will!' answers the general. Back then we were all scared of the doctors, but those generals sure weren't. Me and the general got into a jeep and took off somewhere. The general starts questionin' me. Where'm I from? Where'd I work? How many grades did I finish? So I explain it all in detail. I'm from such and such a place (I was born here), I worked, I say, at a kolkhoz, but I hunted more. 'That's good,' says the general. 'Are you a good shot?' Yes, I say, and, so's not to just blow hot air, I add: At fifty paces I can snuff out a candle with a rifle. And as far as schoolin' goes, well, there wasn't a heckuva lot. Ever since I was a little kid, my father took me with him around the taiga. 'Well, it doesn't matter,' he says, 'you won't need a college education where you're goin'. And you see,' he says, 'if you snuff out one particularly evil candle for us, one that has ignited a fire all around the world, your Motherland will not forget you.' This, you understand, was a light hint at weighty circumstances. Get it? But at the time, I don't have a clue."

"We arrive at a big dugout. After the general kicks everybody out, he keeps on questionin' me. 'Don't have any relatives abroad, do you?' he asks. 'Course not, I say. We've lived in Siberia since God knows when. We're descended from the Cossacks who built the Bii-Katunsk fortress not far from our village. That was back when Peter was tsar. We all go back to 'em, that is, almost the whole village does."

"Where'd you get a name like Bronislav?" one of the hunters suddenly asks.

"The priest thought it up while he was hungover. I let him have it though, the mangy gelding, while I was takin' him to the GPU in 'thirty-three . . .'[1]

"Where was this? Where'd you take him?"

"To town. We'd arrested him, but there wasn't anybody to take him there. 'Go ahead, Bronka,' they said, 'you've got a score to settle with him. You take him.'"

"But why? It's a nice name, after all."

"With a name like that, you gotta have a last name that fits it. And I'm Bronislav Pupkov.[2] Every time they'd call roll in the army, there'd be laughter. Now at home we've got a Vanka Pupkov and that's no big deal."

"Anyway, what happened next?"

"Next, let's see. Where'd I stop?"

"The general's questioning you."

"Yes. Well, he asked me about everythin', then says: 'The Party and the government commission you, Comrade Pupkov, with an assignment of the utmost importance. Hitler has come here, to the front lines, incognito. We have a chance to bump him off. We snagged this creep,' he says, 'who was sent to us on special assignment. He carried out his mission, but then he slipped up and got caught. He was supposed to cross the front line right here and hand over some very important documents to Hitler himself. Personally. And Hitler and all of his scum know this man by sight.'"

"And what do you have to do with it?"

"If you start to interrupt, I'll twist your you-know-what. Hit me again, please. A-hem! I'll spell it out. Me and that creep are as alike as two peas in a pod. Well, boys, here's where the good life begins." Bronka always abandons himself to his reminiscences with such ecstasy, with such smoldering passion, that an unconscious feeling of exquisite pleasure inevitably possesses his listeners. They smile. A kind of quiet rapture falls over them. "Right away they put me in a separate room next to the hospital and appoint two orderlies to look after me. One is a sergeant major by rank, even though I'm just a private. Well now, I say, comrade sergeant major, hand me over my boots. And he does. An order's an order, so he's gotta obey. Meanwhile, they're preparin' me. I'm undergoin' trainin' . . ."

"What kind?"

"Special trainin'. For the time bein' I can't give out any more than that. I've signed a statement. When fifty years is up, I'll be allowed to. But it's only been . . ." Bronka's lips move—he's counting. "It's been twenty-five. But that goes without sayin'. The good life goes on! In the mornin' I get up and there's breakfast: first, second, and third courses. If the orderly brings me some kind of lousy portvino, I send him packin'. So he comes back with pure alcohol—they had lots of it in the hospital, you see. I take it myself and dilute it just the way I like it, and he gets the lousy port. That's how a week passes. I wonder, how long is this gonna go on? Well, at last the general summons me and asks: 'Well, Comrade Pupkov?' I'm ready, I say, to carry out your assignment. 'Let's do it then,' he says. 'Godspeed,' he says. 'We'll expect you to return a Hero of the Soviet Union. Just don't miss.' So I say, if I miss, I'll be the lowest traitor and an enemy of the people! Either, I say, they'll have to lay me out dead next to Hitler, or you'll have to send out a team to rescue Hero of the Soviet Union Pupkov, Bronislav Ivanovich. The thing is that our mighty offensive was takin' shape. It was like this: the infantry went out from the flanks and the tanks made a powerful frontal attack."

By now Bronka's eyes always smolder and flare up like little coals. He doesn't even stick out his aluminum cup any more—he forgets to. Patches of firelight play across his weathered, well-proportioned face. He is handsome and nervous.

"I won't tell you, dear comrades, how I got across the front line and how I made it to Hitler's bunker. I just made it." Bronka stands up. "I just made it! . . . I take my final step as I go down the stairs and find myself in a large room made of reinforced concrete. A bright electric light bulb is burnin', there's a whole slew of generals . . . I quickly find my bearin's: Where is Hitler?" Bronka is all tensed up, his voice breaks, at times falling to a whistling whisper, at times becoming unpleasantly and tortuously shrill. He speaks unevenly, often stopping, breaking off in the middle of a sentence, swallowing his saliva . . .

"My heart's up here—in my throat. Where is Hitler? I had microscopically studied his foxlike mug and had marked out, in advance, where to shoot—right into that little moustache of his. I salute. 'Heil Hitler!' In my hand I've got a large package, in the package there's a Browning, loaded with explosive poison bullets. A general comes over and reaches for the package: 'Let's have it.' I politely wave him off. Mille pardons, madame, it's for the Fuehrer alone! In perfect German I say: 'For the Fyoorrar!'" Bronka swallows. "And then . . . *he* came out. I felt like I'd been jolted by an electric charge . . . I remembered my faraway Homeland . . . my mother and father . . . I didn't have a wife back then . . ." Bronka is silent for awhile, on the verge of breaking into tears, ready to let out a wail or rend the shirt on his breast. "You know, it happens that your whole life'll flash before your eyes . . . When you find yourself nose to nose with a bear it's like that, too. A-hem! . . . I can't go on!" Bronka weeps.

"Well?" somebody asks quietly.

"He's comin' toward me. The generals have all come to attention. He was smilin'. And right there on the spot I tore open the package. You laugh, scumbag! So take this for our sufferings! For our wounds! For the blood of the Soviet people! For the destruction of towns and villages! For the tears of our wives and mothers! . . ." Bronka is screaming, holding his hand as if he were shooting. Everybody feels ill at ease. "You were laughin'?! Now wash yourself with your own blood, you creepin' vermin!!" This is by now a heart-rending cry. Afterward, it's as silent as the grave . . . And then there's a whisper, hurried, nearly inarticulate. "I shot . . ." Bronka's head drops to his chest. For a long time he weeps quietly, grimacing and grinding his big teeth, shaking his head inconsolably. He raises his head. His face is all covered with tears. And once again quietly, ever so quietly, he says in horror:

"I missed."

Nobody says a word. Bronka's condition affects them so strongly, it surprises them so much, that it seems wrong to say anything.

"Hit me again, please," Bronka says quietly and insistently. He drinks it up and walks off toward the water. For a long time he sits alone on the bank, worn out by the agitation he's just experienced. He sighs and coughs. He refuses the fish soup.

In the village they can usually tell that Bronka has once again told about his "attempt."

Bronka arrives home rather gloomy, ready and willing to hear out the insults and do some insulting himself. His wife, a homely, fat-lipped peasant woman, pounces on him at once.

"How come you're draggin' yourself along like a whipped cur? At it again, huh?"

"Go to hell!" Bronka snarls listlessly. "Gimme some grub."

"You don't need no grub. No, what you need is a steel rod upside the head," his wife bawls. "I can't step foot outside the door without somebody pesterin' me about you."

"So stay home, then! Don't go gaddin' about!"

"No, I'll go all right! I'll go right over to the village council. Let 'em summon you again, you stupid idiot! They're gonna prosercute you sometime, you fingerless fool! For distortin' history!"

"They don't have the right. It's not a printed work. Is that clear? Now gimme some grub."

"They laugh! They laugh right in his face! They spit at him, but it don't faze him in the least. You filthy pig, you dumb ass! Don't you got a conscience? Or did they knock it outta you? Tfu!" She spits. "Right between your shameless little eyes! Boob-kov!"

Bronka levels a stern, malevolent look at his wife. He speaks quietly but forcefully.

"Mille pardons, madame! Now I'm gonna clobber you!"

His wife would slam the door and go off to complain about her "boob" of a husband.

She missed the mark, though, when she'd say that it didn't matter to Bronka. No. He'd feel it keenly, suffer, be in a vile mood. And he'd stay at home and drink for two days straight. He'd send his teenage son to the store for vodka.

"Don't listen to anybody over there," Bronka would tell his son guiltily and peevishly. "Get the bottle and come straight home."

He actually had been summoned to the village council several times where they shamed him and threatened to take measures. Cold sober by then and not looking the chairman in the eye, Bronka would say testily and incoherently:

"Okay, okay! Lay off! Well . . . what's the big deal, anyway?"

Afterward he'd drink a bottle at the shop, sit a little while on the porch till the alcohol went to his head, then get to his feet, roll up his sleeves, and announce loudly:

"All right, step right up! Any takers? If I rough you up a bit, don't take it personally! Mille pardons!"

And, by the way, it's true—he was a rare shot indeed.

1967 (1968)

Meditations

And it's like that every night!

As soon as the village quiets down a bit and people fall asleep—he begins . . . He starts up, the parasite, at one end of the village and walks toward the other. He walks along and plays.

And the accordion he has is some kind of special one—it bawls. It doesn't weep—it bawls.

People advised Nina Krechetova:

"Now you marry him and be quick about it! That devil is makin' life here impossible for us."

Ninka would grin enigmatically.

"So don't listen. Go to sleep."

"How can we sleep when he's pumpin' on that thing right under our windows. If he'd just play down by the river, the crazy devil, but no—he's gotta do it right here. It's like he's doin' it on purpose."

As for that thick-lipped beanpole, Kolka Malashkin, he'd just give you an impudent look with his small eyes and announce:

"I'm within my rights. There's no law against it."

The house of Matvei Ryazantsev, the local chairman of the kolkhoz, stood right on the very spot where Kolka would come out of the alley and turn down the street. It so happened that the accordion would begin its bawling in the alley, continue bawling as it passed the house, and could still be heard for a long time afterward.

As soon as it would start ringing out in the alley, Matvei would sit up in bed, swing his feet onto the floor, and say:

"That's it. Tomorrow I'll expel him from the kolkhoz. I'll find some pretext and expel him."

Every night he'd say that. And yet he wouldn't expel him. But, when he'd meet Kolka during the day, he'd ask:

"Are you gonna keep gaddin' about at night much longer? People are tryin' to get some sleep after workin' all day and you're wakin' 'em up, you damn bell ringer!"

"I'm within my rights," Kolka would say again.

"I'll show you rights! I'll find some rights for you!"

And that was all. On that note, the conversation would end.

But every night Matvei, sitting in bed, would vow:

"Tomorrow I'll expel him."

And then he'd sit there for a long time afterward and think . . . The accordion would disappear down the street and no longer be heard, but he'd keep on sitting there. He'd feel around in his pants on the chair, fish his cigarettes out of his pocket, and light up.

"Haven't you had enough fumes for one day!" his wife, Alyona, would grumble.

"Go to sleep," Matvei would reply tersely.

What did he think about? Why, actually . . . about nothing in particular. He'd reminisce about his life. But nothing specific, just dim snatches. However, on one such night, when the moon was bright and the accordion rang out and the bitter smell of wormwood, mixed together with the cool night air, poured in from the garden through the open window, he distinctly remembered another night. That night had been black as coal. He and his father and younger brother Kuzma were out haying about fifteen kilometers from the village in the Kuchugury foothills. That night Kuzma began wheezing. During the blistering heat of the day, when he was all covered in sweat, he'd drunk a dangerous amount of ice-cold spring water and during the night his throat swelled and clogged up. His father woke Matvei and ordered him to catch Igrenka (the most quick-footed gelding) and ride him for all he was worth to the village for milk.

"I'll light a fire while you're gone . . . When you bring it back, we'll boil it up—it'll help his throat, poor fella, or else I'm afraid we'll lose him," his father said.

Matvei made his way in the dark to where he heard the horses grazing, bridled Igrenka and, whipping him on his sides with the hobble rope, raced to the village. And now . . . Now Matvei was nearly sixty already—then he'd been just twelve or thirteen, and yet he remembered that night as if it had been yesterday. Horse and boy merged into one and flew into the black night. And the night flew back at them, striking their faces in dense waves heavy with the scent of grasses dampened by dew. A wild ecstasy gripped the boy; the blood pounded in his temples and hummed. It was like flying—as if he'd taken off from the earth and started to fly. He couldn't see anything around him: neither the earth nor the heavens, not even the horse's head—there was just the roaring in his ears and the sensation that the entire world that night had been torn from its place and was rushing to meet him. At the time he didn't think at all about his sick little brother. He didn't think about anything. His soul exalted, every fiber in his body pulsed . . . It was some sort of longed-for, rare moment of excruciating joy.

. . . Grief came later. He'd brought the milk, but his father kept circling the campfire, clasping his dear younger son to his breast, as if he were rocking him to sleep.

"Now, now Sonny . . . What's all this? Just hold on a little bit. Just hold on a little bit longer. We'll boil you up some milk now, you'll take a nice deep breath, my dear little boy . . . Here, Motka's brought you some milk! . . ."

But little Kuzma was already gasping for breath. He had turned blue.

By the time his mother arrived right on Matvei's heels, Kuzma was dead. His father sat there with his head in his hands, rocking back and forth slightly and uttering muffled, long-drawn-out moans. Matvei looked at his brother in astonishment and with a strange sort of curiosity. Just yesterday they'd horsed around in the hay and now an unfamiliar, bluish-white boy, who was somebody else's, lay there.

. . . Only, it was strange: why on earth did that damn accordion resurrect in his memory those events, and not others? That night, and not some other? After all, a whole lifetime of incidents had followed: marriage, collectivization, the war. And who knows how many other nights there had been! But everything had blurred together, had faded. All his life Matvei had done what needed to be done. When he was told that he needed to go work at the kolkhoz, he went; when the time came for him to marry, he got married; he had children with Alyona, they grew up . . . The war came, he went and fought. Because of a wound, he returned home earlier than the other men. He was told: "Matvei, you've gotta be chairman. There's nobody else." And so he did it. And somehow he'd gotten to like the job, and people got used to him and so to this day he'd slogged away at it. And all his life there was only one thing on his mind: work, work, work. And the war had also been work. And all his concerns, and joys, and sorrows were tied to work. When, for instance, he heard folks around him say "love," he didn't quite understand what they meant. He understood that love existed in this world. He himself had probably once been in love with Alyona (she'd been pretty in their courting days), but you couldn't say that he knew anything more about it, not really. And he suspected others of pretending: singing songs about love, suffering, he'd even heard of lovers shooting themselves . . . It wasn't so much that they were pretending, as it was some kind of a habit that people had: they had to talk about love—well, go ahead, then, talk about love. But it wasn't really love so much as the need to get married that was at the bottom of it. What about Kolka—was he really in love? 'Course he had a thing for that Ninka—she was a robust and shapely girl. But more likely the time had simply come for him to marry and so, fool that he was, he wandered around at night playing that damn wheeze box. And why not wander around? He was young, full of vim and vigor . . . It was the same old story . . . At least these days they didn't fight over girls anymore like they used to in the old days. Matvei himself had fought more than once. He'd been the same way—full of vim and vigor, his fists itching for a fight. You had to do something with all that energy.

One time, when Matvei had started thinking along those lines while sitting up in bed, he couldn't stand it any longer and nudged his wife:

"Listen here! . . . Wake up, I wanna ask you somethin' . . ."

"What's wrong?" Alyona was surprised.

"Have you ever really been in love? With me or anybody—it doesn't matter who with."

Alyona lay there for a long time, dumbfounded.

"You haven't been drinkin', have you?"

"'Course not! . . . Were you in love with me or did you just . . . marry me 'cause it was the thing to do? I'm serious about this."

Alyona saw that her husband wasn't tipsy, but she couldn't say anything for a long time—she didn't know either. She'd forgotten.

"What put that thought in your head?"

"There's somethin' I wanna understand, dammit. Somethin's botherin' me . . . I'm all stirred up inside. Like I'm sick or somethin'."

"'Course I was in love with you!" Alyona said with conviction. "If I wasn't, I wouldn't have married you, 'specially with that Minka Korolyov wooin' me like he was. But I didn't marry him. What're you doin' thinkin' about love in the middle of the night? You goin' off your rocker?"

"Go to hell!" Matvei was offended. "Go back to sleep."

"I forgot to tell you to drive the cow out to pasture tomorrow. I'm goin' berry pickin' with the other women early."

"Where?" Matvei pricked up his ears.

"Oh, not in any of your old hayin' fields, in case you're all worried we'll trample the grass down."

"If I catch you there, it'll be a ten-ruble fine."

"We know of a nice little spot where they're not hayin' that's all red with berries. So remember to let the cow out."

"Fine."

So what was it about that night, when he rode to get milk for his brother, that made it suddenly pop into his mind now?

"Must be gettin' senile," Matvei thought sadly. "Happens to everybody in their old age."

But the ache in his soul didn't let up. He noticed that he'd even begun to wait for Kolka and that singing wheeze box of his. When he didn't show up right away, Matvei would start to worry. And he'd get angry at Ninka: "Buxom heifer! She must be keepin' him!"

And he'd sit and wait. He'd smoke.

And then, way down the alley, the accordion would start to play. And the ache in his soul would rise up. But it was a strange kind of ache—one he longed for. Something was missing without it.

He also would remember different mornings . . . You'd be walking through the grass barefoot. It'd be all bluish gray from the dew. And only your trail would remain—a vivid green track. And the dew would burn your feet. Even now, when you recalled it, your feet would get chilly.

And then you'd suddenly start thinking about death—that soon it'll all be over. And you'd think about it without fear, without pain, but somehow with amazement. Everything would stay just the same, of course, but they'd carry you off to your grave and bury you. And that's what was hard to understand. How could everything here really just stay the same? Sure, it was plain that the sun would still rise and set—it always rises and sets. But the people there in the village would be different, people you'd never get to know . . . That was incomprehensible. Of course, for ten or fifteen years people'd still remember that there was this Matvei Ryazantsev, but then that would be it. And you'd really want to know how they'd be getting along here. You weren't sorry for yourself, nothing of the sort. You'd seen your fill of sunny days, you'd made merry on the holidays—it was all right, you'd had some good times, and . . . No, you weren't sorry for yourself. You'd seen a lot in your day. But just the thought that you're gone, that other people have taken your place, but you won't be there any longer . . . Surely it would be kind of empty for them without you. Or wouldn't it matter?

"Phooey! . . . No, I'm gettin' old."

These kinds of meditations even tired Matvei out.

"Listen here! . . . Wake up," Matvei tried to wake up his wife. "Are you ascared of death?"

"He's gone nuts!" Alyona grumbled. "Who isn't scared of the grim reaper?"

"Well, I'm not scared."

"Well then, go back to sleep. Why bother thinkin' about it?"

"Go to sleep yourself!"

But as soon as he would remember that black, deafening night when he flew on his horse, his heart would ache anxiously and sweetly. No, there was something to life, after all, something terribly poignant. It made you want to cry.

One night he waited for Kolka's accordion in vain. He sat and smoked . . . But it never ever came. He waited and waited, to no avail. It wore him out.

Toward daybreak, Matvei woke his wife up.

"Where'd that bell ringer of ours get to?"

"Why, he's finally gettin' married! The wedding's on Sunday."

Matvei became depressed. He lay down, wanted to fall asleep, but couldn't. So he lay there till sunrise, staring blankly at the ceiling. He wanted to remember something else from his life, but for some reason absolutely nothing came to mind. Once again worries about the kolkhoz came crowding in . . . Soon it'd be time to hay, but half of the mowers were at the blacksmith's with their shafts straight up. And that squinty-eyed devil, Filya the blacksmith, was on a binge. Now he'll tie one on at Kolka's wedding, too—might as well kiss the whole week goodbye.

"Tomorrow I'll hafta have a chat with Filya."

. . . Upon meeting thick-lipped Kolka the following day, Matvei grinned and said:

"So, brother, looks like you've played yourself into a tight spot, haven't you?"

Kolka broke into a smile that reached from ear to ear.

"That's it, Matvei Ivanych. I won't be wakin' you up at night anymore. I'm done for. I've dropped anchor!"

"Yes, indeed," Matvei said and set off on his own business, thinking to himself, "What're you so happy about, you bull calf? She's gonna take you by the horns now, that Ninka is. They're all like that, those Krechetovs are."

A week passed.

The light of the moon still poured into the windows each night, just as before, the garden smelled strongly of wormwood and young potato tops . . . And it was quiet.

Matvei slept poorly. He kept waking up and smoking . . . Sometimes he'd go to the front room for a drink of kvass. Or he'd go out onto the porch, sit down on a step, and smoke.

The village was bathed in moonlight. And it was terrifyingly quiet.

1967

Stenka Razin

His name was Vasyoka. Vasyoka could claim the following: twenty-four years from the day of his birth; exactly 185 centimeters to his height; a nose like a duck's bill . . . and an impossible character. He was a very strange guy, Vasyoka was.

There was no job he hadn't tried his hand at after the army! He'd been a shepherd, a carpenter, a boxcar coupler, and a stoker at a brick factory. At one time he had guided tourists around the neighboring mountains. He wasn't happy anywhere. After having worked a month or two at a new job, Vasyoka would go to the office and give notice.

"Can't make you out, Vasyoka. Why do you live like this?" they would want to know in the office.

Vasyoka, looking somewhere over the heads of the office staff, would give a brief explanation.

"'Cause I'm talented."

The office workers, being polite people, would just turn away, hiding their smiles. And Vasyoka, carelessly stuffing the money in his pocket (he held money in contempt), would leave. And he'd stride down the narrow street with an air of independence.

"Again?" he'd be asked.

"'Again' what?"

"Quit your job?"

"Yes, sir!" Vasyoka would give a salute, as if in the army. "Any more questions, sir?"

"Off to make more dolls, then? Heh . . ."

On that topic—dolls—Vasyoka wouldn't speak with anyone.

At home Vasyoka would hand over the money to his mother and say:

"That's it."

"Good heavens! . . . Well, now what am I gonna do with you, you bean-pole? You ganglin' crane! Huh?"

Vasyoka would shrug his shoulders: for the time being, he himself wouldn't know what to do, where else he could go work.

A week or two would pass and something would turn up.

"So are you gonna learn how to be a bookkeeper?"

"Maybe."

"Only . . . This is real serious!"

"What's with all the proclamations?"

Debit . . . Credit . . . Income . . . Expenditure . . . Overruns . . . Runarounds . . . And money! Money! Money! . . .

Vasyoka lasted four days. Then he got up and walked right out of class.

"What a lot of foolishness!" he said. He hadn't understood a single thing about the brilliant science of accounting.

Of late Vasyoka had been working for a blacksmith.

And now that he'd waved a heavy sledgehammer around for about two weeks, Vasyoka set it carefully down on the workbench and informed the blacksmith:

"That's it."

"What?"

"I'm off."

"Why?"

"There's no soul in this work."

"Windbag," said the blacksmith. "Get outta here."

Vasyoka looked with amazement at the old blacksmith.

"How come you have to get personal right away?"

"You're a babbler then, if not a windbag. What do you know about iron? 'No soul in it . . .' That really burns me up."

"But what's there to know? I can knock out as many of those horseshoes as you want without any of your 'knowledge.'"

"Then why don't you give it a try?"

Vasyoka heated a piece of iron, forged a horseshoe quite dexterously, cooled it in the water, and handed it to the old man.

"Have at it."

The blacksmith crushed it in his hands with ease, just as if it had been a piece of lead, and chucked it out of the smithy.

"Go shoe a cow with a shoe like that."

Vasyoka picked up a horseshoe that the old man had made and tried to bend it as well—nothing doing!

"What do you think?"

"Not bad."

Vasyoka stayed at the smithy.

"Vasyoka, you're not a bad guy, really, but you've got a big mouth," the blacksmith told him. "How come, for instance, you tell everybody you're talented?"

"It's true. I'm very talented."

"Where's your work to prove it?"

"I don't show it to anybody, of course."

"Why not?"

"They wouldn't appreciate it. Only Zakharych appreciates it."

"Bring it to me. I'll take a look at it."

The next day, Vasyoka brought to the smithy a thingamajig the size of a fist, all wrapped up in a rag.

"Here."

The blacksmith undid the rag . . . and placed upon his enormous palm a little man, carved out of wood. The little man was seated on a log with his arms propped on his knees. His head was in his hands, his face not visible. Sharp shoulder blades jutted out on the little man's back, under his cotton print shirt (blue with white polka dots). He was lean, his hands were all black, his disheveled hair was scorched in places. The shirt was also burned in several spots. His neck was slender and sinewy.

The blacksmith looked him over for a long time.

"A tarmaker," he said.

"Uh-huh," gulped Vasyoka, his throat parched.

"Aren't any like that around these days."

"I know."

"But I remember men like that. What's he doin'? Thinkin' or somethin'?"

"He's singin' a song."

"I remember men like that," the blacksmith said once more. "But how would a guy like you know 'em?"

"Heard stories about 'em."

The blacksmith returned the tarmaker to Vasyoka.

"He looks like one."

"That's nothin'!" exclaimed Vasyoka, wrapping up the tarmaker in the rag. "I've got other ones better than that."

"All tarmakers?"

"What do you mean? There's a soldier, there's an actress, a troika . . . another soldier—a wounded one. But right now I'm carvin' Stenka Razin."

"Who'd you learn how to do this from?"

"Nobody . . . I taught myself."

"What do you know about people? About an actress, for instance . . ."

"I know all about people." Vasyoka looked down proudly at the old man. "They're all terribly simple."

"You don't say!" the blacksmith exclaimed and started laughing.

"I'll soon be done with Stenka . . . Then you can have a look."

"People laugh at you."

"It doesn't matter." Vasyoka blew his nose in his handkerchief. "Actually, they love me. And I love 'em, too."

The blacksmith burst out laughing again.

"You're a fool, Vasyoka. Goin' around and sayin' people love you! Who does stuff like that?"

"What of it?"

"I'd think a fellow'd be ashamed to talk like that."

"Why ashamed? I really do love 'em, too. I even love 'em more."

"What song is he singin'?" the blacksmith asked, abruptly changing the subject.

"The tarmaker? One about Yermak Timofeyevich."

"And where'd you see the actress?"

"In a movie." Vasyoka snatched a piece of coal out of the forge with a pair of tongs and lit a cigarette. "I love women. Pretty ones, of course."

"And do they love you?"

Vasyoka flushed slightly.

"I'd have a little difficulty answerin' you there."

"Heh!" The blacksmith took up his position at the anvil. "You're an odd bird, Vasyoka! But it's sure interestin' havin' a chat with you. Tell me somethin': what do you get out of carvin' a tarmaker? No matter how you look at it, it's still just a doll."

At that, Vasyoka didn't say anything. He picked up his hammer and also took his position at the anvil.

"Can't answer?"

"Don't wanna. It gets on my nerves when people talk like that," Vasyoka answered.

. . . Leaving work, Vasyoka always strode along quickly. He'd swing his arms—he was lanky and ungainly. He wouldn't get the least bit tired at the smithy. He'd stride along in step—in the manner of a march—and would strike up a song:

> Let them say that I fix buckets,
> Oh, let them say I charge a lot!
> Two kopeks—for the bottom,
> Three kopeks—for the top . . .

"Hello, Vasyoka!" he'd be greeted.

"Howdy," Vasyoka'd answer. And he'd walk on further.

At home he'd hastily eat his supper, go off to the other room and wouldn't set foot out of it till morning: he was carving Stenka Razin.

He'd been told a lot about Stenka by Vadim Zakharovich, a retired teacher who lived in the neighborhood. Zakharych, as Vasyoka called him, was the kindest of souls. It was he who first said that Vasyoka was talented. He'd come over to Vasyoka's every evening and tell him stories from Russian history. Zakharych was lonely, he missed his work. Of late he'd taken to drink. Vasyoka deeply respected the old man. He'd sit cross-legged on a bench till the wee hours of the morning, not moving a muscle, and hear all about Stenka.

"He was a tough muzhik, broad shouldered, light on his feet, . . . a bit pockmarked. He dressed just like all the other Cossacks. He didn't care, you know, for those different kinds of brocade . . . and that sort of thing. What a man he was! When he'd suddenly turn around and glance at you from under those brows of his, it was enough to make the grass wilt. But he was a just man! Once it so happened that there wasn't any grub for his men. They boiled up some horseflesh. Well, there wasn't even enough horseflesh to go around. And Stenka saw one poor Cossack who was completely emaciated, sitting by the campfire, his head drooping: he was already at death's doorstep. Stenka nudges him and gives him his own piece of meat. 'Here,' he says, 'eat it.' The Cossack sees that the ataman himself is haggard from hunger. 'Eat it yourself, batka.[1] You need it more.' 'Take it!' 'No.' Then Stenka drew his saber so quickly that it whistled through the air. 'Damn you lousy sonuva . . . ! What did I just say: take it!' So the Cossack ate the meat. Isn't that something? . . . Oh you dear, dear man . . . You had a soul."

Vasyoka listened with moist eyes.

"And how about the business with that princess!" he exclaimed quietly, whispering. "He picked her up and flung her into the Volga . . ."

"The princess!" Zakharych, a frail little old man with a small, withered head, shouted. "Yes, that's exactly how he'd toss those potbellied boyars overboard! He always got the better of them. Do you understand? Get the rabble to the prow! And that's that."

. . . Work on Stenka Razin was progressing slowly. Vasyoka got all pinched in the face because of it. He didn't sleep at night. When things "came together" he wouldn't let up at the workbench for hours on end—he'd just whittle and whittle away. From time to time he'd give a snort and say to himself in a low voice:

"Get the rabble to the prow."

His back would ache. He'd begin to see double. Vasyoka would throw down his knife and hop around the room on one leg and laugh loudly.

And when things didn't come together, Vasyoka would sit motionless by the wide open window, his arms folded behind his head. He'd sit there for an hour, two hours, and look out at the stars and think about Stenka.

Zakharych would come by and ask:

"Is Vasily Yegorych home?"

"In here, Zakharych!" Vasyoka would yell. He'd cover his work with a rag and go meet the old man.

"Zdorovenki buly," Zakharych would greet him "in Cossack."

"Howdy, Zakharych."

Zakharych would cast a sidelong glance at the workbench.

"Not done yet?"

"No. Will be real soon."

"Can you show me?"

"No."

"No? Right you are. Vasily, you . . ." Zakharych would sit down on a chair, "you are a master. A great master. Just don't drink. It's the grave! Do you understand me? A Russian can let his talent go to waste. Where's the tarmaker? Give him here . . ."

Vasyoka would hand over the tarmaker and would himself fasten his jealous eyes on his creation.

Zakharych, wincing bitterly, would look at the little wooden man.

"He's not singing about Yermak," he would say. "He's singing about his own lot in life. You don't even know such songs." And he began singing in a surprisingly strong, beautiful voice.

> O-oh, freedom, oh my freedom!
> Oh, freedom, mine and free!
> Freedom is a falcon in the heavens.
> Freedom is my homeland, dear to me.

Vasyoka would get all choked up out of love and grief.

He understood Zakharych. He loved his native region, his mountains, Zakharych, his mother, . . . all people. And that love burned and tormented him, it cried out for release. And Vasyoka couldn't understand what it was he needed to do for people. To be at peace.

"Zakharych . . . dear," Vasyoka would whisper with colorless lips, turn his head, and wince in pain. "Don't, Zakharych . . . I can't take it anymore . . ."

Most often Zakharych would fall asleep right there in the room. And Vasyoka would turn back to Stenka.

. . . The day finally came.

One day just before sunrise Vasyoka woke Zakharych up.

"Zakharych! I'm done . . . Come. I've finished him."

Zakharych leapt to his feet and went over to the workbench.

Here's what was on the work bench.

. . . They'd taken Stenka unawares. They'd burst in during the night with shameless eyes and flung themselves at the ataman. Stenka, in his undergarments, rushed to the wall where his weapon was hanging. He loved people, but he also knew them. He knew the ones who had burst in on him. He had shared with them both joy and sorrow. But the ataman had no wish to share his final hour with them. These were rich Cossacks. Once things had become too hot for them, they'd decided to betray him. They wanted to live. This wasn't a band of sworn brethren who, drunk out of their minds, had broken in after midnight to carry away the ataman on their shoulders. These were Judases who had descended upon him. Stepan didn't waste his breath on the likes of them. He flung himself toward his weapon . . . but tripped on the Persian rug and fell. He wanted to leap to his feet but they'd already fallen on him from behind and were pinning his arms behind his back . . . A struggle ensued. They gasped. They swore quietly and dreadfully. With great effort, Stepan managed to raise himself slightly and butt one or two of them with his head . . . But then something heavy hit him on the head . . . The terrible ataman crashed to his knees and a sorrowful shadow fell over his eyes.

"Put out mine eyes, that I might not see your disgrace," he said.

They mocked him. They trampled on his mighty body. They crucified their consciences. They struck him in the eyes . . .

Zakharych stood for a long time over Vasyoka's work . . . and didn't utter a single word. Then he turned and left the room. And instantly returned.

"I wanted to go have a drink, but . . . I shouldn't."

"Well, what do you think, Zakharych?"

"I don't think anything." Zakharych sat down on a bench and started weeping bitterly and quietly. "How could they . . . huh? Why'd they do it to him? Why? What wretches they were, wretches!" Zakharych's weak frame shuddered from his sobs. He covered his face with his small palms.

Vasyoka winced in agony and began blinking back tears.

"Don't Zakharych . . ."

"What do you mean 'don't'?" Zakharych exclaimed angrily, and he turned his face away and began to mumble. "They're beating the life out of him, you know! . . ."

Vasyoka sat down on a stool and also started weeping—spitefully and heavily.

They sat there and wept.

"They got them . . . both him and his brother," Zakharych muttered. "I forgot to tell you . . . But, it doesn't matter . . . It doesn't matter, son. Oh, the wretches!"

"His brother, too?"

"His brother, too . . . His name was Frol. They got them both together
. . . But the brother—he . . . Ah, to hell with it. I won't tell you about the
brother."[2]

A radiant morning was beginning to break. A gentle breeze stirred the
curtains in the window.

In the village a cock crowed thrice.

1960 (1962)

All by Themselves

Harness maker Antip Kalachikov respected heartfelt sensitivity and kindness in people. In those moments when he was in a good mood and when a relative peace had fallen over the house, Antip would say to his wife tenderly:

"Marfa, though you're a fine, strappin' woman, you're a bit slow on the uptake."

"What makes you say a thing like that?"

"'Cause . . . you expect me to do is nothin' but sit and sew, day and night, don't you? But I've got a soul, too. My soul also wants to kick up its heels and have a little fun, it does."

"I don't give a darn about your soul."

"Ekh . . ."

"'Ekh!' 'Ekh!' What's *that* s'posed to mean?"

"Nothin' . . . I was just thinkin' of your kulak papa, may he rest in peace."

Marfa, domineering, big Marfa, put her hands on her hips and looked sternly down at Antip. Withered little Antip withstood her gaze without blinking.

"You leave my papa outta it . . . Understand?"

"Uh-huh, I understand," Antip answered meekly.

"That's more like it."

"You're an awful hardheaded woman, Marfynka. That's bad for you, dear. You'll put too much strain on that little heart of yours and up and die one of these days."

In all her forty years of conjugal life with Antip, Marfa had never been able to figure out when he was serious and when he was joking.

"Just sew."

"I am sewin', Mother, I am."

The ineradicable, strong odor of dressed leather, pitch, and tar permeated the Kalachikov's house. The house was large and light inside. Once it had resounded with the laughter of children, and then, later on, with weddings that had been held there. But the house had also witnessed doleful night hours of oppressive quiet when the mirror was shrouded and the weak

light of a wax candle cast a pale and feeble illumination over the profound
secret of death. All sorts of things had happened under that roof. Antip
Kalachikov and his mighty "other half" had brought twelve living children
into the world. Altogether they'd had eighteen.

The house's appearance had changed over the years, but Antip's work
corner always stayed exactly the same—it was to the right of the stove, behind a partition. There Antip sewed harnesses, bridles, saddles, and made
horse collars. And there, on the wall above him, hung his beloved balalaika.
The balalaika was Antip's passion, the silent, deep love of his life. Antip
could play it for hours on end, his head tilted to the side. And when he did,
it was hard to tell which it was: the balalaika telling him a story about something precious that he'd forgotten long ago, or him imparting to his instrument the unhurried thoughts of an old man. He could sit and play like that
all day long and would have, too, had it not been for the vigilant Marfa. But
Marfa absolutely needed him to do nothing but sew and sew for days on
end—money was her passion and she watched every kopek like a hawk. All
her life she'd waged war with Antip's balalaika. One time things got so bad
that in a fit of rage she flung it into the fire in the stove. Antip turned white
as a ghost and stood and watched it burn. The balalaika burst right into
flame, just like a piece of birch bark. It began to buckle . . . Three times it
let out a moan that was almost human—that was its strings snapping—and
then died. Antip went outside to fetch an ax and then chopped all the half-
finished horse collars, all the harnesses, saddles, and bridles into bits. He
chopped them up without saying a word, neatly. At his work bench. The
terrified Marfa didn't make a peep. After that, Antip drank for a week, not
once putting in an appearance at home. Then he came home, hung a new
balalaika on the wall, and sat down to work. Never again did Marfa touch
the balalaika. But she kept a close eye on Antip. She wouldn't stay long at
the neighbors, and on the whole tried not to be away from home. She knew
that the moment she crossed the threshold, Antip would take down his balalaika and play—he'd stop working.

One autumn evening they were sitting there—Antip in his corner, Marfa
at the table with her knitting.

Neither said a word.

Outside it was slushy, a light rain was falling. Inside it was warm and
cozy. Antip was hammering bronze nails into a horse collar: tap-tap, tap-
tap, tap-tap-tap.

Marfa set aside her knitting. She'd gotten lost in her thoughts, gazing
out the window. Tap-tap, tap-tap, Antip tapped away. The clock on the wall
was ticking, too, but in such a way that it seemed like it would stop any moment. But it didn't.

The rain streaked down the windows softly, with a muffled sound.

"What're you so sad about, Marfynka?" Antip asked. "Still thinkin' 'bout how to save more money?"

Marfa didn't say anything. She kept looking pensively out the window. Antip glanced at her.

"We're not long for this earth, no matter what you think. No matter what you think, a hundred rubles don't amount to much." Antip liked to talk when he worked. "I've been thinkin' all my life and all I ended up with is hemorrhoids. The work I've done! Ask me, what good have you seen? I'd say, nothin', really. People may've fought, they may've stirred up all sortsa rebellions, they may've been in the Civil War, the Great Patriotic War . . . They may've even died heroically at that. But I took my seat here when I was thirteen and I'm sittin' here to this day—soon I'll be sev'nty. What a patient soul I've been! Question now is: what did I do it for? I never been greedy 'bout money, don't give a darn about it. Didn't make a splash in the world, neither. And soon even my trade'll die its own death. Nobody'll need harnessmakers anymore. So question is: what was my life a-given me for?"

"For your children," Marfa said earnestly.

Antip hadn't expected that she'd take up the conversation. Usually she'd cut short his rambling with some offensive remark or other.

"For my children?" Antip perked up. "On the one hand, that's right, of course, but on the other, it's not, it's not right at all."

"In what way isn't it right?"

"In that you can't just live for your children. You've gotta live for yourself just a little, too."

"What would you have done for yourself?"

At first, Antip didn't know how to answer.

"What do you mean, what would I have done? I'd have found somethin' . . . Maybe I'd have become a musician. You know that fella from town did come here that one time and said I was a natural born talent. And a natural born talent's like a gold nugget—it's a rarity, that's how I see it. And what'm I now? Just an ordinary harnessmaker. When I might've been . . ."

"That's enough already!" Marfa waved him off. "You've gotten yourself goin' again. It's downright disgustin' to listen to you."

"So, you don't understand after all," Antip sighed.

They were silent for some time.

Marfa suddenly wept a few tears . . . She dried her tears with her hanky and said:

"Our dear children have all scattered to the ends of the earth . . ."

"Why should they stay by you all their lives?" Antip remarked.

"That's enough tappin' for one day," Marfa suddenly said. "Let's sit here and talk about the children."

Antip grinned and set aside his mallet.

"You're gettin' soft on me," he said cheerfully. "How 'bout if I play somethin' to cheer you up?"

"Go ahead," Marfa gave her permission.

Antip washed his hands and face and combed his hair.

"Gimme my new shirt."

Marfa got his new shirt out of a drawer. Antip put it on and wrapped a sash around his waist. He took the balalaika off the wall, sat down in the corner of the house where the icons were hung, and looked at Marfa.

"And now—for our concert."

"Just don't run off at the mouth," Marfa advised.

"Now we'll take a trip down memory lane," Antip said boastfully, tuning his balalaika. "Remember when they used to hold round dances out in the meadows?"

"'Course I remember, why shouldn't I? I happen to be younger than you."

"How much? 'Bout three weeks, give or take a day?"

"Not three weeks, two years. I was just a child back then, and you were already a real show-off."

Antip laughed amicably.

"I was a real catch in them days! Remember how you went after me?"

"Who me? Me? Lordy! And who was it my dear departed papa set his hounds on? Who was it left his pant leg behind him in the yard?"

"The pant leg, I'll admit, was mine."

Antip turned the last peg on his balalaika, tilted his small head toward his shoulder, and gave a strum . . . He struck up a song. And into the warm and empty gathering gloom of the izba poured the quiet, light music of the distant days of their youth. And other evenings came to mind, and it was both nice and sad at the same time, and thoughts about something essential in life were awakened, but in such a way that you couldn't really say what that essential thing was.

> Oh, Mommy, sew me no-ot
> A sarafan of red—

Antip sang softly and nodded at Marfa. She sang along:

> Dearest, for my dowry
> Don't harm the old homestead.

It wasn't that they sang all that harmoniously together, but the singing made them both feel surprisingly good all the same. Forgotten scenes arose in their mind's eye: the steppe opening out beyond their native village, the riverbank, the rustling poplar grove—dark and a little eerie . . . And there was something sweetly moving in all this. Gone were autumn and loneliness, gone also were cares about money and horse collars . . .

Then Antip struck up a lively little ditty. He hopped around the izba as if fawning before Marfa, playfully wiggling his bony hips.

> Oh, tum, rum-tuh-tum,
> My little rum-tuh-tums,
> Take a walk, kick up your heels,
> Have—some—fun!

Antip was touchingly funny in his gaiety.

He started bobbing up and down . . . Marfa laughed, then wept a few tears, but she dried them right away and laughed again.

"Just don't go showin' off, sakes alive! . . . After all, you're nothin' special to look at!"

Antip beamed. His intelligent, little eyes shone with a mischievous luster.

> Oh, Marfa mine, oh Marfynka,
> Don't give me heck for nothing-ka!

"Do you remember, Antip, takin' me to the town fair?"
Antip nodded.

> Oh, I remember it, Marfynka mine,
> I'd remember, come rain or come shine!
> Oh, laugh it up, tee-hee
> A lentil and a pea!

"You're a fool, Antip!" Marfa said tenderly. "Devil only knows what nonsense you'll say next."

> Marfushechka, you sure are grand,
> You're the joy of all the land!

Marfa simply rolled with laughter.
"Well, aren't you just the fool, Antip!"

> Oh, tum, rum-tuh-tum,
> My little rum-tuh-tums!

"Sit down and let's sing somethin'," Marfa said, drying her tears.
Antip was slightly out of breath . . . Smiling, he looked at Marfa.

"Not bad, huh? And you say your Antip is a bad one!"

"Not bad—just a bit on the foolish side," Marfa corrected him.

"So, you don't understand," said Antip, not the least offended by such a clarification of the point in question. He sat down. "What a life we could've had together, the two of us. Like two bugs in a rug. But you let yourself get all worried to death over that damned money. Now don't get mad . . ."

"It's not money that worried me, but that we don't have any—that's what worries me."

"There would've been enough . . . and you know it. But let's not get into it. What is your pleasure, mademoiselle frau?"

"The one about Volodya the Brave."

"That one? That one's too sad."

"It's all right. I'll cry me a few tears."

Antip began,

> Oh gulls, don't wing your way out o'er the sea,
> You'd have nowhere to rest, poor birds.
> To Siberia fly, to a faraway land,
> And carry these sorrowful words.

Antip sang from the heart, pensively. Just as if he were telling a story.

> Oh, 'twas twelve o'clock in the dark of the night
> When they killed him, Volodya the Brave.
> Next morning, his father with his younger son . . .

Marfa started sniffling.

"Antip, oh Antip! . . . Forgive me if I've ever done you wrong," she choked out through her tears.

"Don't be silly," Antip said. "Forgive me, too, if I'm to blame."

"I don't let you play . . ."

"Don't be silly," Antip said again. "If I was free to do as I pleased, I'd play day and night. That's not the way to go 'bout things, either. I understand."

"Want us to get you a pint?"

"That'd be nice," Antip agreed.

Marfa dried her tears and got to her feet.

"You go to the store and I'll get supper together."

Antip put on his rainslicker and stood in the middle of the izba waiting for Marfa to dig deep down into the enormous trunk, through all manner of stuff, and fish out their money. He stood looking at her broad back.

"There's this one other thing," he began offhandedly. "She's gotten so old . . . I should get a new one. Just yesterday they got some in at the store. Good ones! Lemme buy one—I'm goin' there anyway."

"Who?" Marfa's back stopped moving.

"A balalaika."

Marfa started moving again. She fished out the money, sat down on the trunk, and began counting it, slowly and laboriously, moving her lips and scowling.

"The one you've got still plays just fine."

"It's got a crack in it . . . It buzzes when I play."

"Then glue it together. You can take a little pitch and mend it nice and neat . . ."

"As if you can fix instruments with pitch! For God's sake!"

Marfa fell silent. She began counting the money all over again. She looked stern and preoccupied.

"Here." She held out the money to Antip. She didn't look him in the eye.

"Just for the pint?" Antip's lower lip drooped. "Yep . . ."

"That's right, yours'll still play. See how beautiful it played today!"

"Ekh, Marfa!" Antip sighed heavily.

"Ekh!' 'Ekh!' What's *that* s'posed to mean?"

"So . . . I guess it's passed . . ." Antip turned and headed for the door.

"So how much does it cost?" Marfa suddenly asked severely.

"Hardly anythin'—a few kopeks!" Antip stopped at the threshold. "'Bout six rubles."

"Here," Marfa said crossly, holding out six rubles to him.

Antip quickly stepped over to his wife, took the money, and left without saying another word: it was dangerous to talk or take his time. Marfa could easily change her mind.

1962 (1963)

A Roof
Over Your Head

In the evening, on Sunday, in the clubhouse in Novoye village, folks had gathered to discuss a play they'd just received. About twelve people had gathered there—all members of the amateur theatrical society.

Vanya Tatus, a short, brawny guy, ambitious, thin-skinned, and peevish, is making a speech. He has just this year completed a program of courses at the district school of culture and education and is a terrible show-off. He is the director of the amateur theatrical society.

"I've gathered you together in order to communicate an important piece of news to you . . ."

"Is an inspector general coming our way?"[1] That's Volodka Marov. Volodka is on friendly terms with nurse Vera, whom Vanya Tatus likes, but Vanya hides it, hoping that Vera herself will notice proud Vanya and leave that numbskull Volodka. If she does stay with Volodka, the driver, then she'll have only herself to blame. There will be reason enough later for her to suffer and repent. And Volodka knows—has sensed, perhaps—Vanya's secret intentions, and makes his life a misery. That's why he joined the theatrical society in the first place. Nurse Vera is sitting right here, too—she's wild about the society—and what irritates Vanya all the more is that, despite such love for the dramatic arts, she can't, the little fool, figure out that it's the director she should be in love with. It'd be interesting to know what she and Volodka talk about. Pistons?

"Marov, you can joke around later." Vanya knows that he shouldn't even notice Volodka, shouldn't engage him in conversation, but he can't hold back—he also tries to take a swipe at his rival. "We have received a play from the district committee. The play was written by our district author. We must rehearse it and perform it at the district art festival. Remember Marov, he laughs best who laughs last."

"Who is an ass," corrects Volodka.

"Exactly. First we must rehearse the play and then we can joke around and laugh . . ."

"Like children, amid labor and strife unrelenting . . ."[2]

"Stop it!" Vera says angrily. "What's the play about, Vanya? Are there any women's roles?"

"The play is taken from kolkhoz life. It hits upon . . ." Vanya glanced at the play's annotations. "It hits upon private ownership interests. The author himself hails from the dregs of the common folk and has a good knowledge of the modern kolkhoz village, its ways and customs. His word is as sound as . . . a shaft bow."

"What was that—'from the dregs'?" asked Vaska Yermilov, who is, by popular opinion, a bit on the dimwitted side and fond of drinking. Vaska is also a driver and a pal of Volodka's. Volodka had recruited him for the theatrical society to keep things from getting boring. Taking his cue from his buddy, Vaska figured that this was a place where you were supposed to joke around and make fun of everything. "Is he a lush or somethin'?"

"Vasya, be quiet, for God's sake!" Vera looks irately at Vaska.

"But I don't get it: what was it—'he hails from the dregs'? Dregs are what's left at the bottom of your glass of beer."

"We all talk about something, but the guy with lice can't quit talking about the banya," noted a married muzhik, who would leave his family—his children!—to run off and rehearse silly plays.

"So do *you* get it?"

"From the dregs means from the lowest classes, from the simple folk."

"There's no such thing as simple folk any longer. From the rank-and-file kolkhoz workers," Vanya corrected.

"Then they should've written it that way," grumbles Vaska. He isn't the least bit good at joking.

"This is how I'd have said it," the married muzhik persists. "From the working peasantry."

Old Yelistratych, a perpetual jester, also came to the society meetings. Among the young people he was considered a specialist on matters pertaining to the olden days and anything that came up in their plays concerning the peasantry—collectivization, for instance—directly concerned him. To this day he's sorry, for instance, that many, many kulaks in the village hadn't been dispossessed back in 1930. When the words "the peasantry" were uttered, Yelistratych jumped into the conversation.

"There aren't any peasants any more either—they're all kolkhoz workers." (He always said "kullkhoz.")

"Vanya, are there any women's roles?" asked an impatient Vera.

"Be quiet, comrades!" Vanya said, a tad sternly. "I'll give you a quick rundown of the play's contents and everything will be clear. Ivan Petrov, a good guy, comes back to the kolkhoz from the army. At first he . . ." Vanya reads the forward, "actively enters into the working life of the kolkhoz peasantry . . ."

"That's what it is: the kolkhoz peasantry!" exclaimed the married one.

"You could also say 'the working peasantry.' The kolkhoz peasantry is a working one. Moving right along: he actively enters into the working life, but then gets married . . . There are, as you can see, women. Otherwise, who do you think he would marry?"

"But maybe he's one of those . . . what're they called?" Vaska chimes in.

"Come on, let a person listen, will you?" Vera implored. "Honestly, they're all idiots! We still haven't found out what the play's about."

"Here's what I suggest," the married one got to his feet. "Whoever babbles on beside the point should be kicked out."

"Knock off the posturing," advises Volodka. "We're not at the police station, you know."

For some reason the married one suddenly burst out laughing.

"But I'm not saying—*haul in*. I'm saying *kick out*."

"Vanya, go on."

"He gets married and falls under the influence of his father-in-law and mother-in-law and, later, of his wife, too: he becomes a moneygrubber. He starts building himself a house and puts a high fence around it . . . The play is called 'A "Roof" Over Your Head.' 'Roof' is in quotation marks because the house is so large you can't really talk about its being just a roof over your head. Ivan gets reprimanded in the hopes that he'll become more modest in his aspirations. Ivan makes excuses, claiming that he's been subject to material stimulation, thus concealing his purely kulak views . . ."

"Are his father and mother alive?" Yelistratych jumped in again.

"Everybody's amazed: how did he get like this? The local paper rips him to shreds. The youth from the theatrical society compose denunciatory ditties about him . . . which is, by the way, just what I suggested we do with Ivanov, but I wasn't supported in it."

"Ivanov's a damn good worker."

"But what about this guy? The question is: who is this 'damn good worker' trying to benefit? Anyway, some mischievous gals perform these ditties on the clubhouse stage and the audience eats it up. But Ivan persists. So they look into the matter at a kolkhoz meeting. One by one, kolkhoz activists—Ivan's former comrades, elderly kolkhoz workers—step up to the tribunal. Their judgment is severe, but fair. Everybody explains to Ivan that, in erecting this so-called roof, he is in essence cutting himself off from the collective . . . What we must understand is that 'roof' here means fence. Roof-dash-fence. Is that clear?"

"And what position does his wife take?" That's Vera again.

"It was already stated that they acted jointly," said the married one. "As a group."

Yelistratych remembered a bit of folk wisdom. "A husband and a wife go hand in glove."

"Is she also present at the meeting?"

"And only here at the meeting," Vanya continues, "does Ivan realize what kind of a mire his in-laws have dragged him into. He leaps up and runs off to his unfinished house . . . He'd already put a roof on the house. He goes running up to the house and with trembling hands pulls out a match . . ." Vanya lowered his voice, paused for a moment, and announced: " . . . And sets fire to the house!"

Nobody had expected that.

"What?"

"He did it himself?"

"Is he nuts?"

"So *he* does it . . . Is there a fire wagon in the village?"

Vera is stunned by the play.

"It's a tragedy, right? Vanya?"

"If it's not a tragedy, then . . . it's at least a social drama."

"So are we gonna burn anything up?" a pyrotechnics buff wants to know.

"Yes, comrades," a gratified Vanya continues, "he himself sets fire to the house, which he himself with his very own hands had erected in his spare time."

"So did the house burn down?" asks Volodka, who is cut to the quick by Vanya's gloating. He can't believe that in a modern play a house would burn down.

"When does this thing happen?" The married one doesn't understand, either, how it could be that he'd set his own house on fire. "Is it summertime?"

"Calm down, calm down," says Vanya the actor. "He sets fire to the house, but the kolkhoz workers . . . Now here's the most intense moment of the play—the denouement. Pay close attention to the way the author approaches the finale—with bold strokes! Ivan leaps up, crying: 'The scum! What have they led me to?!' and runs out of the meeting. His wife . . ."

"But he'd already run out."

"His wife rushes after him."

"But he'd already run out!"

"After a while, his wife comes running back into the meeting, all pale . . . By this time, a different question had already been taken up at the meeting. She bursts in on the meeting and cries out, her voice breaking, 'Hurry! He's set fire to the house!' The kolkhoz workers leap up and run to the new house. One old man . . . At this point in the play it appears that we will take old Shchukar as our point of departure.[3] The old man runs off in the exact opposite direction—to Ivan's father-in-law's house. From behind the scenes he shouts: 'Are you on fire or not?!' Here we have an element of tragicomedy. We will be interpreting the whole play in a tragicomic key."

"But did the house burn down?" Volodka asks again.

"The kolkhoz workers save the house. They explain to Ivan that the house could be used as a kolkhoz nursery school. Ivan himself takes part in extinguishing the fire and keeps on repeating: 'The scum! What have they led me to?'"

"Now *who* is it he's talkin' about?" Vaska didn't understand it.

"Oh, for heaven's sake! His father-in-law and mother-in-law! How clear can it be!?"

"A powerful play!"

"And that's it? That's the end?" Volodka asks.

"In the end, Ivan, embarrassed but happy, signs, along with the other young people, a pledge to turn over the nursery school by New Year's."

"But where's he gonna live?" That's Volodka.

"He'll live for a while at his father-in-law's . . .," Vanya was on the verge of saying, but he suddenly remembered: the hero had just been cussing out his father-in-law and mother-in-law and calling them 'scum.' "He'll find somewhere to live."

"Where?"

"What's your problem? Doesn't the idea behind the play suit you?"

"The idea suits me fine. I'm asking about where he's gonna live."

"No, I think the idea itself doesn't suit you."

"Now don't you go hemming me in with politics. I'm asking where he's gonna live."

The married one was sick and tired of the two suitors' bickering.

"Let's suppose he'll build another house, one a bit smaller. Satisfied?"

"With what money? He builds one house, and now he's gonna build another?"

"The other house—is off camera," Vanya said sharply. "The other house doesn't even interest us. We have a play before us and we must approach it professionally. But I still think that what happens with the first house doesn't suit you . . ."

"At first he'll go to his father-in-law's," the married one said.

"There's no way he'd go to his father-in-law's!" Vaska exploded. "Are you nuts? After what's gone on between 'em, they'll cuss each other out to hell and back. After all, didn't he help him build the house . . . the father-in-law, that is? How could a soldier have any money? The father-in-law was helpin' him . . . But the son-in-law, one moment he's wantin' to burn it down, the next he's turned it over to the nursery school. And do you think that the father-in-law'll say to him after all that, 'Thank you, dear son-in-law'?"

"Don't measure others by your own yardstick."

"It's the father-in-law who worries me least of all," Vanya said stiffly.

The married one rose to his feet.

"Some folks around here just wanna slip another precious little idea in on us." And he sat down. He disliked Volodka because Volodka couldn't hold his tongue.

"Please continue," Volodka requested. "Why'd you stop? What precious little idea? Speak up."

The married one rose to his feet.

"Some folks around here just wanna show their sympathy for the father-in-law."

"The kulak father-in-law," Vanya corrected, for precision's sake.

An ugly silence ensued.

"I suggest we kick Marov out of the theatrical society," said the married one. "And Vaska, too. They're not rehearsing. They're just scoffing."

"What've *I* done?" Vaska was offended.

"No, leave Vaska out of it." The pyrotechnician felt sorry for him. "He'll come to his senses."

More voices rang out.

"Vaska's a real reliable worker. He's just under Marov's thumb."

The married one suggested another option.

"Issue Vaska a reprimand. And a warning: avoid the abuse of alcoholic beverages."

"Now you're talkin'!" Yelistratych took it up. "He deserves that. Holidays are one thing. But you, Vaska, hit the bottle on workdays. And you drive a truck—'fore you know it, you'll be in an accident."

"He should stop for good," the librarian put in her two bits. She was getting along in years, but was very nice looking.

"Wait a minute, for good? . . . Come on, you can't really mean for good?" doubted Yelistratych himself. "He's a muzhik after all . . ."

But at that the married one exploded.

"Well, so what if he's a muzhik? Go ahead and ask him why he drinks. He won't be able to tell you."

The storm clouds were thickening.

"Everybody drinks on holidays," Vaska mumbled. "I'm no worse than the next guy."

"Here's what we've got," Vanya summed things up. "Two of you are being stubborn, two of you are insisting on having your own way. I'm putting it up for a vote. Who's for—"

At that very moment, the widow Matryona Ivanovna crossed the room and sat down in the front row. She is a pensioner, the former director of the Department of Culture attached to the District Administration, and the behind-the-scenes chief and patron of the amateur theatrical society.

"Hello, comrades! Well, how are things coming along?"

"We're discussing the play, Matryona Ivanovna."

"Good, good."

"It's become apparent that the idea behind the play does not suit everybody."

"How can that be?" Matryona Ivanovna was surprised. "I read it—it's a good play. Who doesn't like the idea?"

"I like the *idea*," began Volodka, with a contemptuous glance at Vanya. "I just don't know where he's gonna live."

"Who?"

"The soldier."

"What soldier?"

"The hero of the play, Matryona Ivanovna," Vanya explained. "You need to express yourself more clearly, Marov. It's been a long time since his soldiering days."

"I was frightened for a moment there: how could you be asking 'where is the soldier going to live?' Do express yourself more clearly, indeed. Or else a person could think that our soldiers have no place to live. So why don't you like the idea?"

"Here's how it is. An ambiguous question is being posed: where is Ivan going to live?"

"Now don't you make it out to be ambiguous!" Volodka was enraged. "Ambiguous! The question's plain as day!"

"Go on."

"He's turned over his house to the nursery school. He can't go to his father-in-law's place after all that. So where's he gonna live?"

"Well, that's a fine thing to argue about! Just like a couple of roosters. The kolkhoz will provide him with housing. It's their duty to provide it. This man's turned over his house to the nursery school."

"But that's not in the play."

The widow thought it over for a moment.

"Well, what we may have here is an oversight on the part of the author. Here's what I'll do, children: I'll get in contact with the author by phone and ask him to add something about the housing arrangements. Or else it really would be possible to misunderstand things . . . You might come away thinking that they'd abandoned him to the whim of fate. I'll ask him to elaborate about the housing arrangements. As far as our undertaking his play, well I've already called him about that. He sends his congratulations and greetings to everybody. It's a serious matter, children. As the hunters say, we've got a chance here to bag the big one. If we win first place at the art festival . . ."

At that, there was an uproar.

"What then, Matryona Ivanovna?"

"Oh my, won't you tell us?"

"Matryona Ivanovna, do tell us!"

"The Title of the People's Theater?"

"Fancy that, for just one performance . . ."

"How can we do it!"

"Would they book a tour around the district for us?"

The widow, smiling, began clapping her hands.

"Quiet, children, quiet!"

"Come on and tell us, Matryona Ivanovna!"

"No, no, don't even ask." The widow smiled. "If you don't know, you'll work harder for it. That's how it is. That's more pedagogically sound. Get to work, my friends!"

A girl from the post office entered the club.

"Matryona Ivanovna, there's a telegram for you. I went by your house, but nobody was there."

Matryona Ivanovna put on her glasses and read the telegram.

"What a coincidence," she said. "We were just talking about him . . ."

"It's from the author?"

"Yes. He writes: 'Leave out the song "My Vasya." Stop. The heroine sings: "Look, someone's come down from the hill." Stop. Good luck. Krasnitsky.' His heart bleeds for his work."

"Does she really sing in the play?" Vanya asked.

"Who?"

"The heroine. In ours she doesn't sing."

"Yes, that's right . . . I don't remember her singing in ours. He probably got his plays mixed up. They're putting on another one of his plays somewhere else . . . Of course, he got them mixed up. I'll call and clear things up. But for now—get to work, my friends. Get to work!"

1969 (1970)

Wolves

Early Sunday morning, Ivan Degtyaryov had a visit from his father-in-law, Naum Krechetov, a still youthful muzhik, nimble, crafty, and charming. Ivan didn't like his father-in-law; Naum, sparing his daughter's feelings, put up with Ivan.

"Still asleep?" Naum began with animation. "Never seen the like! . . . Keep that up, Vanechka, and you'll sleep through the afterlife. Now that'd be a fine how-de-do."

"I didn't particularly wanna get there anyway. Never had my sights set on it."

"It's no use. Get up . . . Let's go and get some wood. I wrangled a couple of sledges out of the foreman. Of course, he didn't give 'em up for nothin', but to hell with him—we need the wood."

Ivan lay there for a bit, thought it over . . . and began to get dressed.

"Wanna know why young people are moving to the city?" he began. "Because once you've finished your day's work there you can go have a good time. They let a body take a break. Here you're at it like the damned. Can't rest day or night. Even on Sunday."

"Can't very well sit around without firewood can you?" Nyura, Ivan's wife asked. "They let him have a horse and he's still not satisfied."

"Far as I've heard, a fella's gotta work in town, too," his father-in-law remarked.

"Sure. If I had my way, I'd gladly go there and dig trenches, lay a water main. There you knock yourself out one time, but then your troubles are gone: you got water and heat at your fingertips."

"On the one hand, of course, it'd be good to have a water main. On the other—it'd be trouble: imagine how you'd sleep your life away then. Enough yakkin', let's go."

"Are you gonna have breakfast?" his wife asked.

Ivan turned it down—he didn't feel like any.

"Hangover?" Naum was curious.

"Yes sir, your Honor!"

"Ah-hah . . . That's how it is. And all this time you're talkin' about a water main to pipe in the heat . . . Well, let's go."

The day was sunny, bright. The snow was blindingly white. In the forest there was a stillness and otherworldly peacefulness.

They had to go a long ways—about twenty kilometers. Felling trees closer to the village was not allowed.

Naum's sledge was in front and his indignant voice could be heard all the time.

"Damndest thing I ever saw! . . . Gotta leave one forest and go into another just to get wood."

Ivan dozed in his sledge. The rhythmical sway of the ride was lulling him back to sleep.

They drove out onto an area that had been clear cut and went down into an open ravine and began going uphill. There, on the hill, the forest rose up again in a blue line.

They had almost driven out onto the hill when all of a sudden, not far from the road, they caught sight of them—five of them. They had come out of the forest and were standing there—waiting. Wolves.

Naum stopped his horse and began cussing quietly, in a singsong voice.

"Well I'll be a sonuva . . . Look at the gray little bastards. Struttin' your stuff, are you?"

Ivan's horse was young, skittish, it balked, stepped over the shaft. Ivan yanked on the reins, turning him. The horse snorted, stamped—but couldn't step back over the shaft.

The wolves moved down the hill.

Naum had already gotten turned around. He shouted:

"Well, c'mon!"

Ivan jumped out of the sledge and with difficulty managed to force the horse back in between the shafts . . . He fell back into the sledge. The horse turned by itself and took off.

Naum was already a long ways away.

"Rob-bers! Thie-eves!" he yelled, whipping his horse like a lunatic.

The wolves came bounding agilely down the hill like gray balls, trying to cut off the sledge.

"Rob-bers! Thie-eves!" Naum yelled.

"What's with him, is he losing his mind?" Ivan thought involuntarily. "Who's robbing whom?" He was frightened, but it was all somehow strange: there was both fear and a burning curiosity and a great urge to laugh at his father-in-law. His curiosity soon passed, however. And it was not funny any longer. The wolves reached the road about a hundred meters behind the sledge, spread out in a line, and quickly began to overtake them. Ivan clung tightly to the front of the sledge and looked back at the wolves.

A large, broad-chested one with a singed snout was running out in front of the pack. By now only fifteen or twenty meters separated it from the sledge. Ivan was struck by the dissimilarity between wolves and German shepherds. He'd never seen a wolf up close before, and he'd always thought that they were something like a German shepherd, only larger. But now Ivan understood that a wolf is a wolf, a wild beast. The fiercest dog can somehow still be stopped at the last moment: by fear, kindness, or even the unexpected sound of a human voice. This wolf, with the singed snout, could be stopped by only one thing: death. It wasn't snarling or trying to scare its victim . . . It was just chasing him down. And the look in its round yellow eyes was direct and simple.

Ivan glanced around in the sledge—there was nothing there, not even a measly twig. Both axes were in his father-in-law's sledge. There was just a small bundle of hay close by and the whip in his hand.

"Rob-bers! Thie-eves!" Naum shouted.

Real fear seized Ivan.

The wolf in front, obviously the leader, started to go around the sledge, making for the horse. It was some two meters away . . . Ivan stood up and, while holding on to the side of the sledge with his left hand, lashed the leader with his whip. It didn't expect that, snapped at the whip with its teeth, and leaped to the side. It stumbled and fell back . . . The others ran into it from behind. The whole pack reassembled around their leader. It squatted on its haunches and lashed out with its fangs at first one, then an-other member of the pack. Then, springing forward once again, it easily caught up with the sledge. Ivan got ready and waited for his chance . . . He wanted to get the leader once more. But the leader began to go around the sledge at a greater distance. And another one pulled away from the pack and also started to go around the sledge—from the other side. Ivan clenched his teeth, grimaced . . . "This is the end. Death." He looked ahead.

"Sto-op!" he yelled. "Father! . . . Throw me an ax!"

Naum was whipping his horse. He glanced back, saw how the wolves were surrounding his son-in-law, and quickly turned away.

"Slow down a little, Father! . . . Throw me an ax! We can beat 'em back!"

"Rob-bers! Thie-eves!"

"Slow down, we can beat 'em back! . . . Slow down a little, you bastard!"

"Throw somethin' at 'em!" Naum shouted.

The leader came up alongside the horse, waiting for the right moment to pounce. The wolves who were bringing up the rear were very close now. The slightest pause and they would fly straight into the sledge—and that would be the end. Ivan threw the small bundle of hay at them: the wolves didn't pay any attention to it.

"Father, you sonuvabitch, slow down, throw me an ax!"

Naum turned around.

"Vanka! . . . Look out, I'll throw it!"

"Slow down!"

"Look out, I'm throwin' it!" Naum tossed an ax to the side of the road.

Ivan judged the distance . . . He leaped out of the sledge and snatched up the ax . . . His jump startled the three wolves at the back of the pack, they leaped away and broke off their pursuit, intending now to rush at the man. But at that very instant, the leader, sensing a patch of packed snow beneath him, made his lunge. The horse shied to the side into a snowdrift. The sledge turned over: the shafts twisted the horse collar around, and put a stranglehold on the horse's throat. The horse began gasping for breath, it struggled against the shafts. The wolf that had overtaken the victim from the other side sprang up under the horse and, with one swipe of its sharp-clawed paw, opened up the horse's belly lengthwise.

The three remaining wolves rushed at the victim as well.

A moment later all five were tearing apart the flesh of the still quivering horse, dragging on to the blindingly white snow steaming tangles of bluish-purple intestines and growling. Twice the leader looked straight at the man with its yellow, round eyes.

Everything happened with such monstrous speed and ease that it all seemed more like a dream than reality. Ivan stood, ax in hand, looking in confusion at the wolves. The leader glanced at him once more . . . And that look—exulting, insolent—infuriated Ivan. He raised his ax, started yelling for all he was worth, and flung himself at the wolves. They reluctantly ran back a few paces and stopped, licking their bloodied chops. They did this so meticulously and with such absorption that it seemed the man with the ax didn't interest them in the least. The leader, however, looked directly at Ivan, watchfully. Ivan cussed it out, using the most terrible words he knew. He waved the ax and took a step toward it . . . The leader didn't budge. Ivan stopped as well.

"You win," he said. "Stuff your faces, you bastards." And he set off for the village. He tried not to look at the horse, now torn to pieces. But he couldn't resist, he looked anyway . . . And his heart contracted out of pity, and he was seized by absolute fury at his father-in-law. He strode off quickly down the road.

"Just you wait! . . . Wait till I get my hands on you, you goddam snake in the grass! We could've beaten 'em back—and the horse would still be alive. Selfish bastard!"

Naum was waiting for his son-in-law around the bend in the road. He was sincerely happy to see him alive and unharmed.

"You're alive? Thanks be to God!" His conscience must have been bothering him.

"I'm alive!" Ivan responded. "Question is: are you?"

Naum sensed ill will in his son-in-law's voice. He stepped over to his sledge to be on the safe side.

"Well, what're they up to there . . ?"

"Sending you their kind regards. Selfish bastard!"

"What's the matter? Why're you cussin' me out?"

"I'm not cussing you out, I'm gonna beat you up!"

Ivan walked toward the sledge. Naum lashed his horse.

"Stop!" Ivan shouted and started running after the sledge. "Stop, you parasite!"

Naum kept whipping his horse. Another chase began: this time it was man chasing man.

"Stop, you hear me!" Ivan shouted.

"Lunatic!" Naum shouted in reply. "Whatcha pitchin' into me for? What do *I* have to do with it?"

"So you had nothin' to do with it? We could've beaten 'em back, but you turned your back on me!"

"Now how would we have beaten 'em back?! What're you sayin'?"

"You turned your back on me, you snake! Now I'm gonna teach you a lesson! You won't get away from me, so you might as well stop. I can thrash you out here where nobody'll see and it won't be so shameful for you. Or I can thrash you in front of everybody. And tell them everything. You might as well stop!"

"Oh, sure! I'll stop all right!" Naum whipped his horse. "Damn freeloader . . . How we ever got saddled with you I'll never know!"

"Take my advice and stop!" Ivan's energy was beginning to peter out. "It'll go easier for you. I'll thrash you and won't tell anybody."

"We took you into our family when you didn't have a shirt on your back, you devil, and you go after me with an ax! Don't you have any shame?"

"First I'll beat the hell outta you, then we'll talk about shame. Stop!" Ivan was running slowly, he'd already fallen way behind. And finally he gave up the chase. He started walking.

"I'll find you, you won't get away!" he shouted to his father-in-law in parting.

When he got home Ivan didn't find anybody. The door was padlocked. He unlocked it and went into the house. He looked around in the cupboard . . . He found the bottle of vodka they hadn't finished off yesterday, poured himself a glass, drank it up and set off for his father-in-law's.

The unharnessed horse stood in his father-in-law's yard.

"So he's home," Ivan said with satisfaction.

He pushed on the door—it wasn't locked. He had expected it to be locked. Ivan went into the izba . . . They were expecting him: sitting in the izba were his father-in-law, Ivan's wife, and a policeman. The policeman was smiling.

"Well, what's goin' on, Ivan?"

"Ah-hah . . . Already gone runnin' to the authorities, have you?" Ivan asked, looking at his father-in-law.

"I did, I did. Seems you've already managed to booze up."

"I took a slug . . . for eloquence's sake." Ivan sat down on a stool.

"What's all this about, Ivan? Are you outta your mind, or what?" Nyura started in. "What's the matter with you?"

"I wanted to give your daddy a lesson . . . on how to be human."

"Drop it, Ivan," the policeman began. "Well, so something unfortunate happened, you both got scared . . . Who on earth expected that it'd turn out like that? It's the law of the jungle."

"We could've easily beaten them back. I was all by myself with them afterward . . ."

"Didn't I throw you an ax? You asked me to—and I did. What more was I s'posed to do?"

"Not much. Just act like a human being, that's all. But you're just a self-ish bastard. All the same, I'm gonna teach you a lesson."

"So now we got a teacher in our midst! Snot-nosed kid . . . He came with nothin' to his name into our home where everythin' was ready and waitin' and now he's makin' threats. And what's more, he's findin' fault. We ain't got no runnin' water here, you see!"

"That's not what this is all about, Naum," the policeman said. "What's running water got to do with it?"

"Life's bad in the village! It's better in the city," Naum went on. "So how come you up and forced yourself on us in the first place? To show off your dissatisfaction? To ageetate the population?"

"The son of a bitch!" Ivan was amazed. And he stood up.

The policeman also stood up.

"Drop it, you two! Let's go, Ivan . . ."

"You know where they put ageetators like that?" Naum wouldn't let it go.

"I do!" Ivan answered. "Head first into an ice hole . . ." And he took a step toward his father-in-law.

The policeman took Ivan by the arm and led him out of the izba.

Outside they stopped and lit up.

"How's that for a real parasite!" Ivan was still amazed. "He had the nerve to lay into *me!*"

"Forget it, for cryin' out loud!"

"I can't—I oughtta beat the hell outta him."

"And you'd be the one who'd get it in the end. And all because of that shit."

"Where are you taking me?"

"Let's go. You'll spend the night with us. It'll give you time to cool off. Or else you'll make matters worse. Steer clear of him."

"No way, that's . . . What kind of person acts like that?"

"You can't do anything about it, Ivan. You won't prove anything with your fists."

They set off down the street in the direction of the village lockup.

"You couldn't give it to him out there?" the policeman suddenly asked.

"Couldn't catch him!" Ivan said, annoyed. "I wasn't able to catch him."

"Well, that takes care of that . . . It's too late now. You can't do it now."

"I feel sorry for the horse."

"Yeah . . ."

They fell silent. For a long time they walked without speaking.

"Listen, let me go." Ivan stopped. "Why should I spend Sunday locked up? I won't touch him."

"No, let's go. Let's go. Or else you'll wind up in more trouble. I'm saying this for your own good. Let's go play a game of chess. Do you play chess?"

Ivan spat his cigarette butt on the snow and dug around in his pocket for another one.

"I do."

1966 (1967)

Alyosha at Large

His name wasn't Alyosha, he was Kostya Valikov, but everybody in the village called him "Alyosha at Large." And here's why they called him that: it's because it was rare in our day to see irresponsibility and unmanageability like his. However, that irresponsibility wasn't without its own limits: five days a week he was a reliable worker, and what's more, a diligent, skillful one at that. (During the summer he'd take the kolkhoz cattle to pasture, while in the winter he cared for them indoors, working in the stables and sometimes even delivering calves during the night.) But once Saturday rolled around, that was it. Alyosha would throw off the harness. For two days—Saturday and Sunday—he wouldn't work at the kolkhoz.

Folks had even forgotten when it was that he'd established such a regime for himself. They just knew that this righteous Alyosha had been like that all his born days—that is, on Saturday and Sunday he wouldn't work. They tried, of course, time and again, to pressure him, but they never got anywhere. Basically they felt sorry for him: he had five kids—only the oldest had made it to the tenth grade so far, while the rest of the bunch were still somewhere in the second, third, or fifth . . . So they just washed their hands of him. After all, what could you do? Try as you might to convince him, it was like beating your head against a brick wall. He'd just look blankly at you.

"Well, is it clear, Alyosha?"

"How's that?"

"You just can't let yourself do the things you do! You don't work in a factory after all, you work in agriculture! How can you carry on like this? Well?"

"How's that?"

"Quit playin' the fool. You're bein' asked in plain Russian: are you gonna work on Saturday?"

"No. By the way, as for me bein' a fool—you know, I can also . . . give you one upside the head, and you won't be able to find a single criminal statute against it. We know the laws, too. If you insult me verbally, I can give you one upside the head: that's what they call reciprocity."

Just try and talk with him! He wouldn't even go to meetings on Saturday.

So what on earth did he do on Saturday?

On Saturday he'd heat up the banya. That's all. Nothing else. He'd make the banya piping hot, wash up, and start steaming himself. He'd steam like a madman, like a steamship. He'd steam himself for five hours straight. He'd take a breather, of course, and a smoking break . . . But still, you'd have to be as strong as a horse to do that!

On Saturday he'd wake up and in a flash remember what day it was. And instantly a quiet joy would wash over his soul. His face would even brighten up. He wouldn't bother to wash. Instead, he'd go straight out to the court-yard to chop wood.

He had the heating of the banya down to a science. For example, the wood used in the banya had to be birch: it gives off a lasting heat. He would cut the wood carefully, enjoying every minute of it.

Here, let's suppose, is a story of one such Saturday.

The weather, as it turned out, was tedious—chilly, damp, and windy. The end of October. Alyosha loved weather like this. Long before morning he had heard it sprinkle—there had been a gentle, steady pattering on the windowpanes, then it stopped. In the upper right corner of the house—it always happened in the same place—a moaning could be heard, the wind had picked up. And the shutters began a-rattling. Then the wind died down somewhat. But, all the same, in the morning it still blew slightly. It was a cold one, bringing snow along with it.

With ax in hand, Alyosha went out to the yard and began choosing birch logs to split. The cold crept under his sweater. But Alyosha got right down to swinging his ax and warmed up. He chose slightly thicker chunks from the wood pile . . . He would choose one and pick it up like a suckling pig and carry it to the thick stump where he split logs.

"Well, just take a look at you," he'd tenderly address the chunk of wood. "What an ataman[1] you are . . ." He'd set the "ataman" on the stump and hack away at its head.

Soon he'd chopped up a big pile. For a long time he stood looking at that pile. The logs were all whiteness and sappiness, with an inner purity to them. And their aroma! Fresh, visceral, slightly dank, foresty.

It took several trips for Alyosha to lug them into the banya, where he stacked them neatly close to the stone stove. Next there would be the task of lighting the fire—this was also a pleasant task. Alyosha would even get all anxious while lighting the fire in the stove. On the whole, he really liked fire.

But the water still needed to be hauled. Although you couldn't really call this a pleasant task, there wasn't anything disagreeable about it either. Alyosha tried his best to haul the water quickly. So he'd mince along while carrying full buckets on a yoke, bending his tall figure over in such a way so as to keep from splashing water out of the buckets. It made people laugh to see him. The village women at the well always watched him. And they'd exchange remarks.

"Take a look, just you take a look at him, bendin' and straightenin' up like a spring.. A gen-u-ine acrobat!"

"And he doesn't spill a drop, you know."

"Where's he rushin' off to like that?"

"Well, he's firin' up his banya again."

"But it's still early, after all!"

"You'll see, he'll busy himself with the banya all day long. He really is 'at large,' that there Alyosha is."

Alyosha would fill to the brim the kettle on the stove, two large tubs, and a galvanized bath tub as well, which he'd bought some fifteen years ago, a tub in which all his kids had been bathed when they were babies. Now he'd put it to use in the banya. And it worked great. It rested on the end of the shelf for steaming, not taking up much space—it didn't get in the way of a person's steaming, and water was always at hand. When Alyosha felt like he was burning up on the shelf, when the hair on his head crackled from the heat, he'd dunk his head right into this tub.

Alyosha hauled in some water and sat down on the threshold for a smoke. That was a precious moment, too—sitting for a spell and smoking. Here, Alyosha liked to look over his setup in the banya's changing room and in the little shed built as an addition to the banya. He kept all sorts of things there. Old scythes without handles, old rakes, pitchforks . . . But there was also a joiner's bench and there were tools in good working order: a plane, a hacksaw, gouges, and chisels. But all that was for Sunday. Tomorrow was the day he'd putter around out here.

For now it was gloomy and not at all cozy in the banya, but the banya's pungent, cold scent was already mingling with the aroma of birch logs—so delicate, barely perceptible—and this was the herald of Alyosha's impending holiday. Now and again, joy would flood Alyosha's heart—he'd think, "Any minute no-ow." The banya still had to be washed. Alyosha didn't let his wife do even that. He had at the ready a bundle of leafless birch twigs and a little jar of sand. Alyosha took off his sweater, rolled up his sleeves, and got right to work, got right down to scrubbing. He washed everything down, scrubbed everything with his twigs, rinsed it with clean water, and wiped it dry with a rag. He rinsed out the rag and hung it on the branch of a maple tree which grew next to the banya. Well, now, the banya could be heated. Once more Alyosha lit up . . .

He looked at the gloomy sky, at the dismal, distant horizon, at the village. Nobody else's banya had been heated up yet. Later, toward evening, they'd all do it in a haphazard, slapdash way, puff! puff! They'd inhale the suffocating, bitter black smoke and steam themselves. A guy'll steam himself like that—and get poisoned by the charcoal fumes. Then he'll come in and flop down on his bed, barely alive—and he'll think that that's what a banya's like. Hah! Alyosha tossed down his cigarette butt, ground it into the damp earth with his boot, and set to heating the banya.

He put logs into his stove the same way everybody else did: two like this, one like that, crosswise, and then one on top. But in the embrasure thus created, where people usually put kindling and paper, and then doused it with kerosene, Alyosha, to the contrary, put nothing. And the log he'd placed across the top, well, he'd have notched the center with an ax, and that was all. Then he'd ignite the notches and it'd catch fire. That was a thrilling moment, too—the moment it would burst into flame. Oh, what a glorious moment! Alyosha squatted in front of the stove, his eyes glued to the fire, as it went from a small, timid flickering to a bigger, steadier flame.

Alyosha would always become thoughtful while staring into the fire. He'd think, for example: "Now you people want everybody to live in exactly the same way. But take two logs—they won't even burn up in exactly the same way, and yet you want people to live their lives like that!" Or else he'd make a discovery. A person who is dying will—at the very end—suddenly want to live, will feel a rush of hope, will rejoice at the chance to take some special kind of medicine! Everybody knows that. But it's exactly the same way that any stick, burning out, will suddenly burst into flame, and the whole thing will light up, and cast off such a crown of fire that you just marvel: where on earth did that final strength come from?

The wood was burning steadily and so now it was possible to go have some tea. Alyosha washed up at the basin, dried himself off, and with a light heart went to the house.

While he'd been busy with the banya, the kids, one after another, had shuffled off to school.[2] Alyosha time and again heard the door slam and the gate creak. Alyosha loved children, but nobody ever would have imagined that that was the case because he never showed it. Sometimes he'd stare at one or another of them for a good long time, and he'd get an aching in his chest from love and delight. Nature always amazed him: where did man come from? From almost nothing, from some kind of tiny particle. He especially loved children when they were still real little and helpless. Truth be told, a child's like a slender little stalk. Hang in there with all your might, little stalk, and climb on up! All sorts of things lie in store, but the future's not ours to see! And so they grow, they climb. If it'd been up to Alyosha, he'd have turned out five more, but his wife was plumb worn out.

While they drank tea, he and his wife chatted.

"It's sure gotten cold. Wait and see, it'll snow," said his wife.

"It'll snow all right. And it wouldn't be a bad thing, either, if the ground weren't wet."

"Did you fire it up?"

"Uh-huh."

"Kuzmovna dropped by . . . to borrow some money."

"Well? Did you give it to her?"

"I did. 'Till Wednesday,' she says, you know that's when she'll get paid for her potatoes."

"Well, that's fine." Alyosha was pleased that they had, for instance, money to lend out. Somehow it made it a lot more fun to look people in the eye. And yet they'd all taken to calling him "Alyosha at Large." Stupid people. "How much did she ask for?"

"Fifteen rubles. 'On Wednesday,' she says, 'we'll get paid for our potatoes.'"

"Well, fine. I'll go back and carry on."

His wife didn't say anything to that. She didn't say, "Well, go on, then," or something along those lines. But she didn't say anything different either. She used to say something about it and they'd end up quarreling. She'd start in, "You need to do this, you need to do that, you can't heat up the banya the whole livelong day!" Alyosha wouldn't budge. On Saturday it was the banya or nothing. Period. Come hell or high water! For better or for worse! "So what am I supposed to do, cut my soul up into little pieces?" Alyosha would shriek wildly in those days. And that frightened Taisya, his wife.

The thing is that, in a similar circumstance, Alyosha's older brother Ivan had shot himself. And Ivan's own wife had driven him to it. They'd also been quarreling on and on and it got so bad that Ivan started banging his head against the wall, saying over and over, "How long am I gonna suffer like this? How long?! How long?!" His fool of a wife, instead of calming him down, took to egging him on. "Come on, come on . . . Harder! Well now, which is harder, your head or the wall?" Ivan grabbed for his gun. His wife collapsed in a faint. And Ivan blasted himself in the chest. He'd left behind two children. That's when they warned Taisya: "Watch out! Who knows, maybe it runs in their family." So Taisya backed off.

After drinking up his tea, Alyosha had a smoke in the warmth near the stove and once again went out to the banya.

The banya was completely heated up.

Streaming smoothly upward, smoke poured out the door, evenly and strongly, looking like a bending river. This marked the first stage. Later, when more and more heat would build up in the stove, the smoke would dissipate. It's crucial that you toss more wood in at just the right time, so as not to be down to the coals already, but it was important not to pack it in too tight either—a fire needs room to breathe. It needs to burn freely, heartily, in all corners of the stove at once. Alyosha ducked under the stream of smoke as he made his way to the stove, sat down on the floor, and remained there for a spell, staring into the blazing hot fire. The floor had already warmed up a bit, it was steaming. The heat was even beginning to burn his face and knees, he'd have to cover them up. But that was okay—right now it wasn't the best of ideas to sit here. You could get carbon monoxide poisoning without even realizing it. Alyosha skillfully poked at the charred logs and crawled out of the banya. There was still a lot to be done. The birch switches had to be readied, kerosene had to be poured into the lantern, some pine branches had to be gathered. Quietly humming something indistinct, he clambered up to the ceiling of the banya, took down the thicker of the birch switches from the stake up there, then on the stump where he split logs, he chopped off some pine branches, the ones that were smoother and didn't have twigs, and laid the bunch in the changing room. So that's taken care of. What else? The lantern!

Once again, Alyosha dove under the smoke, carried out the lantern, and shook it slightly—it needed more kerosene. There was some in it, but . . . he didn't want to have to think about doing it later. Alyosha hummed away. What a welcome peace had settled down into his soul. Heavens! The kids weren't sick, he hadn't quarreled with anybody, people'd even borrowed money from him . . . Life! When is it most precious? Maybe during wartime. Alyosha had served, been wounded, recovered, fought out the war, and then for the rest of his life remembered it with loathing. He wouldn't go see a single movie about the war—it sickened him. He was amazed at people who could just sit there and watch it.

Nobody would have believed it, but Alyosha seriously pondered life. What sort of mystery did it hold? Should you regret its passing, for instance, or could you die in peace, knowing there was nothing much special left? He would even stretch his imagination like this: he would pretend to fly high, high up and from there look down at the earth. But things didn't get any clearer. He could make out his cows in their pasture, they were as small as little bugs. But as for those people and the lives that they lived, there was no illumination. Nothing dawned on him. So how was it then: should you regret your life or not? And do you suddenly, in your very last moment, cry out that you didn't live as you should have, that you didn't do everything that you should have done? Or doesn't it happen that way? After all, other people are turning up their toes and it's no big deal—they go quietly, peacefully. Well it's a shame, of course, it's sad. After all, it's not so bad here. And Alyosha would remember—right when the thought would come to him, that it's not so bad here after all—he'd remember an episode from his own life. This is what he'd remember:

He was coming back from the war. The journey was long, stretching nearly across the whole country. But they all traveled boisterously, just the way he liked to. At some small station, still beyond the Urals, a young woman on the platform approached Alyosha and said:

"Listen here, soldier, take me with you—like I'm your sister, like we met here by chance. It's urgent that I get on the train, but I just haven't been able to."

The woman was from a place far from the front line. She was pleasantly plump, had a birthmark on her neck, and was wearing lipstick. She was well dressed. Her mouth was small and her upper lip downy. She looked at Alyosha as if she were touching him, stroking him. She seemed a bit embarrassed, but kept on looking at him so very shamelessly, caressingly. During the entire war, Alyosha hadn't touched a single woman. Yes, and even before the war he hadn't been very lucky. At parties he'd only get to kiss the girls. That's all. And now this one was standing there, looking at him strangely. Alyosha's heart ached so bad, he got so keyed up, that he couldn't hear a thing, and his tongue wouldn't move.

All the same, they set off.

The soldiers in the car would have gotten all keyed up, too, but she, tender thing that she was, clung to Alyosha in such a way that it would have been awkward to approach her. And it turned out that she had just a very short distance to travel. In two stops she was already there. It happened to be nearly evening. In a sad voice, she said something like:

"I've just got a little ways to walk from the station, but I'm scared. I don't rightly know what to do . . ."

"And who's at home, then?" Alyosha's mouth began to function again.

"Why, nobody. I'm all by myself."

"Well, then I'll walk you there," said Alyosha.

"But how on earth can you?" The woman was surprised and happy.

"I'll go on a different troop train tomorrow. It's not like there aren't a lot of them, you know"

"Yes, a whole lot do go by each day . . ." she agreed.

And off they went to her place. Alyosha first snatched up the stuff he was taking home: two pairs of officer's boots, an officer's field shirt, and a German rug, and off they went. Alyosha would often recall that very path to her house, that sinful night. A terrible force—joy, or was it something else—that was a fever and muteness and horror, all paralyzed Alyosha while he walked along with that tender creature.

The weather was oppressive and heavy. It was as if the June sky, which had warmed up during the day, had sunk. Alyosha could barely move his leaden feet. He had a hard time breathing and his head was all in a jumble. But even now Alyosha remembered everything down to the last trivial detail. Alya—that was her name—slipped her arm through his. Alyosha remembered what her arm was like—so soft and warm under her rough dress of crepe de Chine. It's true that he couldn't remember what color her dress was, but he always did remember the sharp little bumps of that particular crepe de Chine, its warm roughness, and he remembered it now. It was somehow both prickly and slippery, that crepe de Chine was. And Alyosha remembered the watch on her arm. It was small (a war trophy), its band cut into the softness of her arm. What stunned him at that time was that this woman herself—simply, trustfully—had slipped her arm through his and walked off with him, her soft side touching his . . . And it was warm—where her arm touched his—he remembered that. Yes . . . Well, what a night it was! In the morning, Alyosha found neither Alya nor his stuff. It was only later, while Alyosha was riding along in the car of another troop train (she hadn't taken his documents), that he figured out she made a living this way, that she'd meet the troop trains and target the stupidest soldiers. But here's the deal—if in the morning she had just asked, "You know, Alyosha, why don't you give me the German rug, the field shirt, the boots," he'd have done it. Well, maybe he'd have kept one pair of boots.

It was that crepe-de-Chine Alya whom Alyosha would remember when he was all by himself. And he'd grin. Alyosha had never told anybody about this incident, but he loved her, that Alya. That's how it was.

The firewood had all burned up. Now a golden, hot mountain of coals simply breathed, simply radiated heat. From time to time a blue flame streaked across the stove's fiery mouth—that was the charcoal fumes. Well now, let's make everything here hot as hell: the walls, the sweating shelf, the benches . . . Soon it'll be so hot, you won't be able to touch anything!

Alyosha tossed some pine branches onto the floor. In a little while, it'd be just like Tashkent in a forest.[3] The branches would be so aromatic, the air so easy to breathe. Damn it all anyway, it'll be glorious! Alyosha always tried not to bustle around at the last minute, but he never managed to pull it off. He walked around the yard, put away his ax, then poked his head back into the banya—not yet, it was still smoky in there.

Alyosha went to the house.

"Gimme my underwear," he said to his wife, all the while trying hard to hide his delight—for some reason it irritated everybody, that Saturday joy of his. To hell with those people! They do one stupid thing after another, they're mired in their stupidity, but when it comes to his joy on Saturday, you see, they're all surprised, they snort, they don't understand.

Without saying a word, his wife Taisya opened a chest and stuck her head under the lid. This was Alyosha's second wife. The first, Sonya Polosukhina, had died. She hadn't had any children. Alyosha thought about them least of all, that is, Sonya and Taisya. He stripped down to his underwear, sat for a little while on a stool with his bare legs pulled up close to his body, experiencing a certain pleasantness in this position. It'd sure be nice to have another smoke. But he had long ago broken the habit of smoking at home—when the kids had come along.

"Why'd Kuzmovna need that money?" Alyosha asked.

"Don't know. Hers ran out—so she needed more. Prob'ly didn't have any to buy bread with."

"Did they have a lot of potatoes?"

"They hauled away two loads . . . 'Bout twenty bags."

"They'll rake in the dough."

"Sure will. They just keep savin' it . . . You don't think they got nothin' in their savin's account, do you?"

"Oh, c'mon! The Solovyovs always have lots!"

"Do you want warmer drawers or will cotton ones do for now?"

"Gimme the cotton ones, the cold doesn't bite yet."

"Here."

Alyosha took the fresh underwear, set it on his lap, and sat there a little while longer thinking about what it must be like in the banya at that very moment.

"So . . . Well, fine."

"Kolka's got strep throat again."

"Then why on earth did you let him go to school?"

"Well . . ." Taisya herself didn't know why she'd let him go. "Why should he miss class? He's a bad enough student as it is—just barely squeaks by."

"True enough."

It's strange, but Alyosha never worried too much about his children's sicknesses, even when they were seriously ill. He didn't think about bad things. Such thoughts would somehow just never occur to him. And not a single child, thank God, had died. But if he didn't worry about their health, Alyosha did want his children to do well in school, go to the big city, and rise in the world to positions of honor and respect. And then in the summertime, when they would come visit the village, Alyosha could fuss over them—over their wives, husbands, kids. You know, not a soul understood what a kind, considerate person Alyosha really was, but those city folk would notice it right away. The grandkids would run around here in the yard . . .

Yes, there is a purpose in living. The fact that we don't always know how to live is an entirely different matter. This last point in particular applied to the pigheaded numbskulls of the village—now there's a stubborn bunch for you. And take even your local educated folk—agronomists, teachers. There's no person more puffed up than one of your own, a villager who has gotten an education in town and has come back here again. She goes walking along, you know, not seeing anybody at all. However short she may be, she does her best to look right over other folks' heads. The city folk, on the other hand, now they somehow manage, the sonuvabitches, to parade their erudition without humiliating anybody. They're the first to say hello to you.

"So . . . Well, fine," said Alyosha. "I'm off."

And Alyosha left for the banya.

He really loved walking from his house to the banya in weather like this, when it was cold and damp. He always walked along just in his underwear, walking slowly, on purpose, so's to get good and cold. On the way, he'd also find some kind of odd job to do. He'd untangle the dog's chain or go and close the gate carefully. This was to make sure he'd really get good and cold.

In the changing room he stripped and quickly looked himself over. Not bad—he was still a robust muzhik. But his heart really ached—he was longing to enter the banya. Alyosha grinned at his own impatience. He stayed a little longer in the changing room. His skin got all goosebumpy, just like that crepe de Chine, hah-ah . . . Oh, hell's bells, the things that happen in life! This is why Alyosha loved Saturdays. On Saturday he would meditate, reminisce, and ponder, as he could on no other day. Do you really think he'd give up this Saturday for any set of values, admirable though they may be? Well?

> I'll catch you, I'll catch you, I'll catch you,
> Habiba, I'll catch you!

Alyosha sang quietly, opening the door and stepping into the banya.

Ah, life! . . There was a public banya in the village and Alyosha had gone there once—just to check it out. How funny, how pathetic it was! That day there were gypsies bathing there. They weren't really washing themselves so much as drinking beer. The muzhiks would growl at them, and they in turn would cuss right back. "You just don't understand what a banya is!" As if they understood! It was true, though—in a banya like that, a public one, all you could do was sit around and drink beer. That's no banya, God only knows what it is. It's a good thing he hadn't gone on one of his Saturdays. That very Saturday he heated up his own and washed away to the devil and the deep blue sea all recollection of the public banya.

And so life—as concrete and tangible as it was inexplicable—went on, brimming with what was familiar and dear.

Alyosha went to move his basins and buckets. He began to fix up his "little Tashkent." Alyosha was set completely free from all harmful stress. Petty thoughts vanished from his mind. A kind of wholeness, greatness, and clarity settled over his soul. Life became intelligible. That is to say, life was close by—just beyond the little window in the banya—but it could no longer touch him, its bustle and its fury could not reach him. He became expansive and indulgent.

And Alyosha loved—out of this sense of fullness and peace—to sing a little before he got down to steaming himself. He'd pour water into a small basin, listen to the heavenly clear sound of the stream of liquid, and without even realizing it, he'd be singing quietly. He didn't know any songs, he just remembered some village folk ditties and also snatches of songs that the children sang at home. In the banya he loved to purr out these ditties:

> I'm looking among the people
> My sweetheart, he's not there;

sang Alyosha, and he scooped up more water.

> With a forelock large and curly
> Like Voroshilov's hair.

And he scooped out more, and sang some more.

> Mama's heated up the banya
> And she sends me off to steam;
> I'm in no mood for the banya, Mommy—
> My sweetheart will soon be wed.

Alyosha poured some water into the small basin. And for the time being he put the birch switch into another basin of boiling water to let it soften up in the steam. He began to wash up. He washed for a long time, taking breaks. He sat on the warm floor, on the branches, splashing himself and purring:

> I myself am on my way,
> My thoughts, however, go astray;
> Sweetheart, you shouldn't have said with pride
> That I was soon to be your bride.

And while he was sitting there, it was as if he were floating down a stream—a smooth and warm stream—and he floated along kind of strangely, nicely, in a seated position. And it seemed as if warm currents flowed somewhere near his heart.

Then Alyosha lay for a while on the shelf, for no particular reason. And suddenly he thought: well, what do you know. I'll stretch right out exactly like this someday . . . Alyosha even folded his hands on his chest and lay in that position for a little while. And he was just about ready to make an effort to picture himself like that in his grave, and already something like that had begun to loom in his imagination: a pillow indented where his head lay, a new suitcoat . . . But his soul wouldn't let it go any further. Alyosha got up and, experiencing a slight feeling of disgust, doused himself with water. And to cheer himself up, he once again sang:

> Oh, I'll catch you, I'll catch you, I'll catch you!
> Habiba, I'll—catch—you!

Well, to hell with it! It'll come, it'll come all right, why should he practice it before its time? All the same, it was strange that when Alyosha was at war he hadn't thought about death at all. He hadn't been afraid of it. Of course, he avoided it as best he could, but he hadn't gone into it in such detail then. Well, let the devil take it! It'll come, it'll come, there's nowhere to hide. But that's not the point. The point is that this holiday on earth really isn't a holiday, and you shouldn't view it as a holiday, either, you shouldn't wait for it like you do a holiday. Instead you should calmly accept everything and not, as they say, "fuss too much under your client." A little while back, Alyosha had heard an anecdote about how an experienced madam in a brothel instructed her girls: "The most important thing is not to fuss too much under your client."[4] Alyosha laughed for a long time, thinking: "For sure, we do fuss too much under our client." It's nice here on earth, it's true, but that doesn't mean you should caper about like a goat. Besides it's far more delightful when you're not waiting for this joy to come, not preparing for it. Saturdays were another matter. He awaited the arrival of Saturday all week long. But it also often happens this way:

Some odd morning, when you're out of sorts and fed up with everything, you head out of the village with the cattle and the sun peeps through the clouds, some bush lights up with a faint fire from above . . . And you're suddenly warmed all over by such a feeling of unexpected joy, you suddenly feel so good, that you stop and stand there without realizing that you're just standing there and smiling.

Of late, Alyosha had started noticing that his love for things was something he could consciously feel. He loved the steppe beyond the village, the sunset, a summer day . . . That is, he became completely aware that he—

loved. A peacefulness began to settle in his soul, he began to love. People were harder to love, but as for children and the steppe, for instance, he loved them more and more.

This was the sort of thing Alyosha would think about and while he was thinking, his hands would keep busy. He took the steamed, fragrant birch switch out of the basin, which he rinsed out and into which he poured cooler water. Then he scooped a dipper of hot water from the kettle and tossed it on the stove—this was the initial, test dipper. The stove gasped and started hissing and the steam curled upward. The heat clutched at his ears, crawled down his throat. Alyosha sat down for a moment and waited for the first onslaught to subside, and then he just clambered up onto the sweating shelf. To keep the planks of the shelf from burning his sides and back, he doused them with water from the small basin. And he began lightly lashing himself all over with the birch switch.

The big mistake people make is that they start switching themselves real hard with the birch branches. First you have to brush yourself a bit—flick the switch down your back, along your sides, arms, legs . . . So it feels like the gentlest, the merest of whispers for the time being. Alyosha knew just how to do this. He shook the birch switch lightly next to his body, and its leaves, just like somebody's small hot palms, touched his skin, excited him, and put him into a frenzied state in which he wanted to switch himself all over. But Alyosha wouldn't allow himself that. No. Instead, he rinsed himself off and lay there for a while. He tossed another half dipper on the stove, held the switch over the stove in the steam, and then pressed it several times to his sides, under his knees, and to the small of his back.

He got down off the shelf, cracked open the door, and sat down for a moment on the bench to have a smoke. Now even the tiniest traces of carbon monoxide, if there were any left, would be sucked out with the first damp steam. The stove would dry out, the coals would once again get piping hot and then, without endangering yourself, you could steam to your heart's content. That how it's done, ladies and gentlemen.

. . . It was already getting dark by the time Alyosha came in from the banya. He was a new man, rejuvenated and light on his feet. He kicked off his galoshes at the threshold and, walking along the clean mat, he crossed into the side room. And he lay down for a bit on the bed. He wasn't aware of his own body, the world around him rocked gently in time with his heartbeats.

"Hope you had a nice bath," said Boris.

"Wasn't bad," answered Alyosha, looking straight ahead. "Go on out yourself and have a go at it."

"I will in a minute."

Boris, his son, had, for some time now, begun, well, not really to be ashamed, but to feel somewhat uncomfortable or something, was somehow bothered by the fact that his father tended and grazed cattle for a living. Alyosha had noticed this but held his tongue. At first it offended him deeply, but after thinking it over, he didn't even show any sign that he'd noticed the change in his son. He understood—his son was young, full of great aspirations. Let him be that way. After all, he'd turned out to be a strapping, handsome kid and maybe—God willing—he'd even get some brains. That'd be nice. So, he's ashamed his father's a herdsman . . . Ah, the dear boy! Well, go ahead, go ahead. If you've set your sights higher, then keep your eyes open and you may make it somewhere. He's a good student. His mother said he's even seeing some little gal. Everything's just as it should be. It's amazing to think of it, but everything's just as it should be.

"Go on out yourself and have a go at it," said Alyosha.

"Is it hot out there?"

"How could it be hot now!? . . It's nice. Well, if it seems hot, open the vent."

Alyosha hadn't managed to teach his sons how to steam themselves—they just didn't want to do it. They took after their mother's side of the family, that is, after the Korostylyovs.

His son went off to get ready for the banya, and Alyosha kept on lying there.

His wife came in and once again bent over the chest—to get some underwear for their son.

"Remember how," asked Alyosha, "when our Manya was real little, she made up a poem?"

> The little white birch
> Stands out in the rain.
> Green burdock will cover her up.
> The little birch will be warm and happy there.

His wife turned from the chest and looked at Alyosha . . . She thought over his words for a moment or two. She didn't understand anything, didn't say anything, and once again leaned into the chest, which smelled of mothballs. She got out the underwear and started for the entry room. On the threshold she stopped and turned toward her husband.

"Well, what of it?" she asked.

"What?"

"That she made up that poem . . . What're you tryin' to say?"

"It's funny, you know, that poem is."

His wife was going to leave because she didn't think it was necessary to waste time on empty words, but she remembered something and looked back again.

"The hog's gotta be driven in, and fed, too. I got the slops all ready over there. I'll go get the kids ready for the banya. Rest up and then take care of it."

"Okay."

The banya was over. Saturday wasn't over yet, but the banya already was.

1972 (1973)

Critics

Grandpa was seventy-three; Pyetka, his grandson, was thirteen. Grandpa was a wiry, nervous man and suffered from deafness. Pyetka was independent and tall for his age. He was bashful and stubborn. They were friends.

They loved movies more than anything else in the world. Half of Grandpa's pension went for tickets. Usually, having counted up his money toward the end of the month, Grandpa would inform Pyetka bitterly and merrily:

"Between the two of us, me and you've blown five rubles."

Pyetka would feign astonishment for propriety's sake.

"It's okay. They'll feed me," Grandpa would say. ("They" meant Pyetka's father and mother. He was Pyetka's grandpa on his father's side.) "We're doin' this for our own good."

They always sat in the front row: it was cheaper and also Grandpa could hear better there. But all the same he couldn't make out a good half of the words and would try to guess what they were saying by following the actor's lips. Sometimes Grandpa would suddenly roar with laughter for no rhyme or reason. Even though nobody else in the auditorium was laughing, Pyetka would elbow him in the side and shush him angrily:

"What's the matter with you? They'll think you're a fool . . ."

"So what'd he say there?" Grandpa would ask.

Pyetka would repeat the lines for his grandpa, whispering right into his ear.

"'Without dropping his pace . . .'"

"Hee-hee-hee," Grandpa now laughed quietly at himself. "Sure didn't sound like that to me."

Sometimes Grandpa would cry when some innocent person got killed.

"Confound you . . . people!" he'd whisper bitterly and blow his nose in his handkerchief. Overall he liked to speak his mind about what he saw on the screen. When there was passionate kissing, for instance, he'd grin and whisper:

"Oh you devils! . . . Just take a look at that . . . Hah!"

If there was fighting, Grandpa would grab hold of his armrests and, all tensed up, follow the fight closely. (As a young man, it's said, he was fond of fighting. And he was good at it.)

"No, that one there's not . . . it's just . . . he's a weaklin'. But this one's not bad, he's quick on his feet."

However, he could sniff out any kind of falseness.

"C'mon," he'd say resentfully. "They're just playin' around."

"But he's bleedin'," Pyetka would object.

"Sure, he's bleedin'. So what? The nose is real weak. All you gotta do is tap it and it'll bleed. That don't count."

"How can it not count?"

"'Course it don't count."

They'd be shushed from behind and would quiet down.

The real argument would begin once they'd left the club. Especially when it came to films set in the countryside, Grandpa was categorical—even brutal—in his judgments.

"That's a load of bull," he'd declare. "It don't happen like that in real life."

"Why not?"

"So, did you really like that fella?"

"Which one?"

"The one with that accordion. Who was tryin' to get in through the window."

"He wasn't tryin' to get in through the window," Pyetka corrected. He would remember everything that had happened in the film perfectly, but Grandpa would get things all mixed up, and that irritated Pyetka. "He was just tryin' to get over to the window to sing a song."

"Fine, so he was tryin' to get over to the window. Back in my day I remember one time I was gonna do that . . ."

"So, you don't like him?"

"Who?"

"What do you mean, who?! That guy, the one tryin' to get over to the window. You were the one who brought him up in the first place."

"Not a bit. Not even this much." Grandpa held up the tip of his little finger. "Some sort of Ivan the Fool. He goes around singin' his head off . . . We had an Ivan the Fool like that—he went around singin' all the time."

"It's 'cause he's in love!" Pyetka started to get upset.

"So what if he's in love?"

"That's why he's singin'."

"Huh?"

"I said, that's why he's singin'."

"Yeah, and folks should've made a laughin' stock outta a fella like that long ago! They shouldn't have given him a moment's peace about it. So he's in love . . . When folks're in love they're all bashful. But this one goes around shoutin' it from the rooftops . . . What kind of fool would go and marry him? He's not a serious feller. Back in our day, I remember if you liked a girl, you wouldn't come within two blocks of her—'cause you were all bashful 'bout it. So he's in love . . . Well, be in love as much as you like, what's the use . . ."

"What's the use of what?"

"What's the use of makin' people laugh at you? Back in our day, I remember—"

"There you go again: 'back in our day.' People are different now!"

"What do you mean, they're different? People are always just the same. Have you seen a lot of fools like that 'round here?"

"But it's just a movie—it's not real. You just can't compare 'em."

"I'm not comparin' 'em. I'm sayin' that that fella's not like anybody I ever seen. There you have it," Grandpa stood his ground.

"But everybody liked it! They were laughin'! I even laughed."

"You're still a young 'un, that's why you think everythin's funny. You won't catch me laughin' at just any old thing."

Grandpa rarely argued about art with adults—he didn't have the knack. Right away he'd start getting upset and call people names.

Only once did he really get into it with adults, and this one single time brought the roof down on his head.

Here's what happened.

He and Pyetka had seen a movie—a comedy. They came out of the club and in no time picked it to pieces.

"And you know what really bugs me: they're howlin' with laughter themselves, them actors are, the devils, and you sit there and it don't do a thing for you, you can't even crack a smile!" Grandpa was bitter and indignant. "Did you crack a smile?"

"No," Pyetka admitted. "Only once, when they turned over in that car."

"There you go! And here we paid good money for it—two rubles in old money! And they were the only ones laughin'."

"And to think they call it a comedy."

"Comedy! . . . They should get it in the teeth for a comedy like that."

They arrived home in a foul mood.

At home, everybody was watching some TV movie about village life. Pyetka's aunt, his mother's sister, had come for a visit. With her husband. From the city. And everybody was sitting around and watching television. (Grandpa and Pyetka couldn't stomach television programs. "It's like when I was still a bachelor, see, and my brother Mikita was married. I liked to sneak up to their room, you know, and peek through a crack at 'em. That's what that TV of theirs is like. It's just like peekin' in on somebody,"

Grandpa said after watching a couple of television programs.)

Anyway, everybody was there, sitting around, watching TV.

Pyetka immediately went off to the entrance room to do his homework, but Grandpa stopped and stood behind everybody, watched five minutes of the tedious flashing coming from the television tube and announced:

"That's a load of bull. It don't happen like that in real life."

Pyetka's father took offense.

"Be quiet, Pop, don't butt in."

"No, this is interesting," said the polite man from the city. "Why isn't real life like that, Grandfather? How is it not like that?"

"Huh?"

"He's hard of hearing," Pyetka's father explained.

"I asked: why isn't real life like that?! What *is* it like?!" the man from the city repeated loudly, for some reason smiling in anticipation.

Grandpa looked at him contemptuously.

"Here's how real life's not like that. You there are watchin' and you think he's a real carpenter. As for me, when I take a look, I can tell right away: there's no way on earth he could be a carpenter. He don't even know how to hold an ax right."

"He and Pyetka are our critics," Pyetka's father said, hoping to soften Grandpa's harsh tone a little.

"Interesting," the man from the city began again. "And how did you decide that he's holding the ax wrong?"

"'Cause I been a carpenter myself my whole life. That's 'how I decided.'"

"Grandfather," Pyetka's aunt jumped into the conversation, "does that really matter?"

"What *that* are you talkin' about?"

"For me, the man himself is much more interesting. Do you see? I know he's not a real carpenter—he's an actor. But I think it's interest . . . I think it's much more interesting . . ."

"That's the kind of person who writes letters to movie studios," Pyetka's aunt's husband said with a smile again. They—Pyetka's aunt and her husband—were very clever and knew everything. They smiled when they talked with Grandpa. That made Grandpa furious.

"It's not important to you, but it is to me," he snapped. "They can bamboozle you—that'd be child's play—but they can't bamboozle me."

"Ha-ha-ha," the man from the city burst out laughing. "He got you there!"

Pyetka's aunt also grinned.

Pyetka's father and mother felt very embarrassed for Grandpa.

"You're hard to please, you know, Pop," Pyetka's father said. "Why don't you go in to Pyetka and help him out." He bent over to the man from the city and explained quietly, "He helps my son with his lessons and he doesn't know beans about them himself. They duke it out. It's enough to kill you!"

"He's an interesting old man," the uncle from the city agreed.

Once again everybody started watching the movie. They'd forgotten all about Grandpa. He stood behind them as if in disgrace. He stood there for a little while longer and then went off to join Pyetka.

"They're laughin'," he told Pyetka.

"Who?"

"In there . . ." Grandpa nodded toward the living room. "'You don't understand anythin',' they say, 'you old coot.' As if *they* understand!"

"Don't pay any attention," Pyetka advised.

Grandpa sat down at the table, he was silent for a while. Then he started in again.

"'You're a fool,' they say, 'you're gettin' senile . . .'"

"What, did they really say that?"

"Huh?"

"Did they really say you're a fool to your face?"

"They're sittin' there grinnin'. As if they know an awful lot!" Little by little, Grandpa was getting "all worked up," as Pyetka liked to put it.

"Don't pay any attention," Pyetka advised him once again.

"They've come visitin' . . . know-it-alls!" Grandpa stood up, dug around in his trunk, took out some money, and left.

He came home an hour later, drunk.

"Uh-oh!" Pyetka was surprised. (Grandpa rarely drank.) "What'd you do that for?"

"They still watchin'?" Grandpa asked.

"Yup. Don't go in there. Lemme help you get undressed. How come you went and got drunk?"

Grandpa sank heavily onto the bench.

"They understand, you see, but you and me don't!" he started in loudly. "'Grandfather,' they say, 'you're a fool! You don't understand anythin' about life!' As if they do! Got lots of money?!" Grandfather was already yelling. "If you do, then don't go around with your nose up in the air! I been workin' my butt off all my life! . . . And now I'm s'posed to just sit around and be quiet. And you in all your livelong days haven't so much as held an ax in your hands!" Grandpa was talking to the door behind which the others were watching television.

Pyetka was at a loss what to do.

"Don't, Gramps, don't," he tried to calm down his Grandpa. "Lemme take your boots off. To heck with them! . . ."

"No, stop. I'll tell him . . ." Grandpa wanted to stand up, but Pyetka held on to him.

"Don't, Gramps!"

"City flibbertigibbets." Grandpa seemed to have gotten calmer, he'd quieted down.

Pyetka pulled off one of his grandpa's boots.

But then Grandpa tossed back his head once more.

"Pokin' fun at me?" Once again his eyes began glittering recklessly. "Well I got somethin' I can tell you!" He picked up his boot and went into the living room. Pyetka couldn't hold him back.

Grandpa entered the room, wound up his arm, and flung the boot at the television set.

"This is for you! . . . And your carpenters!"

The screen was smashed into smithereens.

Everybody jumped up out of their seats. Pyetka's aunt even screeched.

"Pokin' fun!" Grandpa started shouting. "Have you ever held an ax in your hands?!"

Pyetka's father tried to get his arms around Grandpa, but Grandpa put up a fight. Chairs went flying with a crash. Pyetka's aunt screeched again and flew out of the house.

Pyetka's father nonetheless managed to overpower Grandpa. He twisted his arms behind his back and started tying them together with a towel.

"Now you've gone and done it, dear parent!" he said spitefully, securely tightening Grandpa's hands. "Thank you."

Pyetka was scared to death. He was watching it all with wide-open eyes. The man from the city stood off to the side and shook his head now and again. Pyetka's mother was picking the glass up off the floor.

"Now you've gone and done it," Pyetka's father kept saying, clenching his teeth unpleasantly.

Grandpa lay on the floor face down, rubbing his beard against the painted floorboard and shouting:

"You poke fun at me, but I got somethin' to tell you! I'll tell you and then you'll shut up. If I'm a fool, like you say—"

"Did I ever say that?" the man from the city asked.

"Don't talk to him," Pyetka's mother said. "He won't hear you now. He's shameless."

"You don't wanna sit me at the table with you—fine! But tell me . . . Fine, be that way!" shouted Grandpa. "But tell me, then: have you ever in all your life built an izba? Hu-uh!? And you go and tell me I don't know nothin' about carpenters! I built half this village with my own two hands! . . ."

"Now you've gone and done it, dammit," Pyetka's father kept saying.

At that point, in walked Pyetka's aunt and a police officer, a local muzhik, Yermolai Kibyakov.

"Well, what do we have here!" Yermolai exclaimed, smiling broadly. "What'd you do that for, Uncle Timofei? Huh?"

"He went and did it all right," Pyetka's father said, getting to his feet.

The police officer hemmed, scratched his chin with the palm of his hand and looked at Pyetka's father. Pyetka's father nodded in agreement and said:

"Do it. Let him spend the night there."

Yermolai took off his cap, hung it carefully on a nail, got a piece of paper and a pencil out of his carrying case, and took a seat at the table.

Grandpa quieted down.

Pyetka's father began telling about everything that had happened. Yermolai smoothed back the thinning hair on his large head with his calloused, dark palm, coughed, and began to write, leaning his chest on the table and tilting his head to the left.

"'Citizen Novoskoltsev, Timofei Makarych, born . . .' What year was he born?"

"Ninety."

"'Born in one thousand ninety, formerly a carpenter, now retired by occupation. No distinguishing characteristics . . . On September twenty-fifth of this year, the aforementioned Timofei showed up at home influenced by strong alcohol. At that time his family was watching television. And there were guests there as well.' What was the film called?"

"I don't know. We turned it on after it'd already started," father explained. "It was about a kolkhoz."

"'. . . They don't remember the title of the film. They do know one fact: it was about a kolkhoz. Timofei also began watching television. Then he said: "There aren't any carpenters like that in real life." Everybody asked Timofei to get control of himself. But he continued in his state of excitement. Once again he said that there aren't any carpenters like that in real life, it's a pack of lies, he said, "Carpenters' hands," he says, "aren't at all like that." And he began shoving his own hands at them. Again he was asked to get control of himself. Then Timofei pulled his right boot (size 43–45, calfskin) off his foot and carried out a blow to the television. Consequentially, he knocked it in completely, that is, the place you usually look at.

'Chief Sergeant of Police KIBYAKOV.'"

Yermolai got up, folded the report in half, and put it away in his carrying case.

"Let's go, Uncle Timofei!"

Up until the very last moment, Pyetka hadn't understood what was happening. But when Kibyakov and his father began lifting his grandpa up, he realized that in a minute they were going to take his grandpa to the lockup. He burst into tears, crying loudly, and rushed to defend him.

"Where are you takin' him?! Grandpa, where are they takin' you! . . . Don't, Pop, don't let 'em!"

Father pushed Pyetka away, and Kibyakov laughed.

"Feel sorry for your grandpa, huh? Just you wait, we're gonna put him in jail. Just you wait . . ."

Pyetka cried even louder. His mother led him away to a corner and began trying to calm him down.

"Nothin'll happen to him—what're you cryin' for? He'll spend the night there and then he'll come home. Tomorrow he'll be ashamed of himself. Don't cry, Sonny."

They put Grandpa's boots on him and led him out of the izba. Pyetka sobbed. His aunt from the city went over to him and also began trying to persuade Pyetka.

"What's the matter, Pyetenka? It's just the drunktank they're taking him to, the drunktank! He'll come home soon. Do you know how many people they take to the drunktank where we live in Moscow?"

Pyetka remembered that it was she, his aunt, who had brought the police officer. He rudely pushed her away, climbed on to his berth on the stove and there he cried bitterly for a long time more, his face buried in his pillow.

1963 (1964)

Passing Through

The blacksmith Filipp Nasyedkin—a calm man, well respected in the village, a no-questions-asked worker—suddenly took to drinking. Actually, he hadn't taken to drinking at all, rather this is how it was—he'd started having the occasional nip or two. It was his wife, Nyura the Worry Wart, who decided that Filya had taken to drinking. And it was she who flew off to the kolkhoz governing board and kicked up such a fuss that everybody decided: Filya's taken to drinking. And everybody decided that Filya must be saved.

The main thing that put them all on guard was that Filya had hooked up with Sanya Nevyerov. Sanya was a very strange man. There wasn't a spot on his body that didn't ail him or that hadn't wound up under the surgeon's knife (he had pleurisy, a perforated stomach ulcer, liver problems, colitis—the devil only knows what he didn't have—including hemorrhoids). So he lived accordingly: I'm alive today but tomorrow's still up in the air. That's how he put it. He didn't work, of course, but he had money from somewhere. Folks would gather at his place for a drink. He took everybody under his wing.

Sanya's izba stood at the edge of the village overlooking the river, nestled down with its back facing the steep slope of the bank and its two little window-eyes looking far, far away—across the river, into the blue mountains. The yard was small with some old logs lying around and a couple of birch trees . . . But there, in that yard, your soul could really find peace.

You couldn't say that Sanya knew all that much or had seen a lot in his lifetime. (Anyway, he didn't talk about himself. He talked very little.) He just somehow spoke very wisely about life and about death . . . And he was a genuinely kind man. You were drawn to him, to this near and dear, solitary, fatally ill man. You could sit for a long time on a warm old log and look into the distance at the mountains. Whether or not you thought any thoughts, everything would become fine and clear in your soul, as if suddenly—and for just a moment—you had become immense and free and could touch with your hands the beginning and end of your life—as if you had measured something valuable and understood everything. Well, and what of it? Everything's all right! That's the sort of thing that would come to you there.

The married women hated Sanya from the very day he made his appearance in the village. He arrived this spring, took a liking to a ramshackle izba owned by some gypsies, bargained for it, bought it, and began living there. And right away, as was the custom, folks gave him a nickname—"passing through." Sanya, of course, was short for Alexander. Folks were even a little afraid of him. And all for nothing. When Filya spent time at Sanya's, he always felt like he was holding in his hands a weak but still warm sparrow, with drops of blood on its broken wings—a trembling, living, little bundle of life. And when folks said bad things about Sanya, everything would boil up within him—all his good and bad impulses.

This is what Filya said at a meeting of the kolkhoz governing board.

"Sanya—is a person, too. Leave him alone, let him be."

"He's a drunk," corrected the female bookkeeper, a middle-aged, but still nice-looking Party activist.

Filya glanced at her and it suddenly struck him that she wore lipstick. Somehow he'd never noticed that before.

"Fool," Filya said to her.

"Filipp!" the chairman of the kolkhoz raised his voice sternly. "Watch your tongue."

"I've been goin' to see Sanya and I'm gonna keep on goin'," Filya repeated stubbornly, aware of a wicked strength within him.

"Why?"

"What business is it of yours?"

"You'll go outta your mind there! He's got . . . at most a year and a half left, it doesn't matter to him how he lives it out. But what about you?!"

"He'll outlive you all," Filya said for no particular reason.

"Well, fine. That may be. But why should you take to drink?"

"Just try and make a drunk outta me," Filya grinned. "You'll be bankrupt before a week's through. Have you ever even once seen me plastered?"

"It always starts that way!" they all exclaimed—the chairman of the kolkhoz, the bookkeeper, the young female agronomist, and the foreman Naum Sarantsev, who himself was really fond of wetting his whistle. "It always starts with the little things!"

"The dangerous thing about that kind of poison, Filipp," the chairman began elaborating on his thought, "is that it doesn't scare you at first. Just the opposite—it leads you on. Never happened to play cards at the bazaar after the war, did you?"

"No."

"Well, I have. I was comin' home from the front, bringin' some odds and ends with me: a 'Pavel Buré' watch, an accordion . . . I had to change trains in Novosibirsk. For lack of somethin' better to do, I went to the flea market. I see they're playin' cards. The old three-card guessin' game. C'mon, they say, frontliner, try your luck! I'd already heard from the guys, how they cheat soldiers like us. No, I say, play without me. C'mon and give it a try, they say! We-ell, I think, I can drop thirty rubles . . ." The chairman became animated. Everybody was listening to him, smiling. Filya twirled his cap between his knees. "All right, I say! Only no cheatin', now, you devils! What you had to do, see, was guess one card . . . First off, he shows 'em to you, then shuffles 'em right in front of your eyes, see, and he spreads 'em out face down. All three of 'em. You have to guess one, the ace of diamonds, for example. And, you know, he does everythin' right before your very eyes, the parasite! He showed me all three cards face up. Got 'em in your head, he says? I do, I say. Keep your eyes on 'em! . . . Plop, plop, plop—he tosses 'em down. I'm keepin' track of the ace of diamonds. Which one is it, he asks? I put my finger on it . . . We turn it over—the ace of diamonds. I won. They let me win about three or four more times . . . But that was it: by evenin' it was as if my accordion, watch, and money had all vanished into thin air. I lost everythin'. I'd have tried to take my stuff back by force, but there were too many of 'em there. So I showed up home empty-handed. That's how, Filipp, any kind of sickness starts—you don't notice it. You see, they let me win at first, and only then did they start takin' me to the cleaners. You see, I kept wantin' to win back what I'd lost, I kept hopin' . . . And see where it got me. Vodka works the same way. First off, it'll humor you, lull you, and then it'll take a hold of you for good. So you watch out, Filipp—don't be taken in."

"I'm not an eighteen year old."

"Vodka doesn't ask for your vital statistics! It doesn't care . . . You're a good worker, and for now all's well at home . . . We're just warnin' you. Don't go and see that Sanya! He may be a decent person, but see how many womenfolk here are complainin' about him!"

"They're all fools!" Filya said once again.

"You sound like a woodpecker, hammerin' away at the same thing: 'they're all fools.' So is your Nyura a fool, then?"

"Yes, my wife's a fool, too. What's all the foamin' at the mouth for?"

"Because she doesn't want her family to be destroyed!"

"Nobody's destroyin' it. She's the one runnin' around and destroyin' it."

"Well, watch out. You've been warned. As for that Sanya, we can just clear him out of our village if it comes to that . . . That's how he'll end up."

"You don't have the right—he's a sick man."

"We'll find the right! So he's sick . . . If he's sick, then he shouldn't drink. Go back to work, Filipp."

"Did you get called in?" Sanya asked in the evening, his left eyelid twitching nervously.

"I did." Filya was ashamed for his wife, the chairman, and the entire governing board as a whole.

"Did they forbid you to come?"

"Yeah . . . What do they take me for—a kid or somethin'?"

"Uh-huh," Sanya agreed. "Of course." And his eyelid kept on twitching. He looked at the distant mountains. He had an expression on his face, as if he were expecting the sun to reverse its course and rise from that spot instead of setting there. "At night, after eleven, the nightingales sing. Ah, the little devils! . . . What a show they put on. Trying to impress each other, I suppose."

"It's their matin' call to the females," Filya explained.

"They've got a pretty mating call. It's beautiful. People don't have pretty mating calls. We rely on strength."

What strength can you rely on? Filya thought.

"I respect strong people," Sanya went on. "When I was a kid, a boy thrashed me—he was stronger than me. My father advised me: work out, lift something heavy—in a month, you'll be thrashing him. I began lifting a wagon axle. I lifted it for three days—and ruptured my innards. My belly-button came untied."

"You should've gotten a weight—seein's you were the weaker one—and tied it to a strap and knocked him in the noggin with it. I was also a quiet little boy, and, well, this fella also started pickin' on me, he just wouldn't lay off. So I treated him once to a knock on the head with a weight from a clock—he left me alone after that."

Sanya was getting drunk. His eyes were clouding over . . . They moved from the faraway blue mountains to take in the river, the road, and the wild raspberry bush at the foot of the wattle fence. They grew warm and became joyful.

"It's good, Fillip. I'm fifty-two. Let's not even count the first twelve years, when I was still unaware of things—that leaves forty . . . Forty times I've seen the spring, forty times! And only now do I understand how good it is. In the past I used to put everything off, I never had enough time—I was in a hurry to learn a lot, I wanted to make a big name for myself . . . Now it's—stop the car! Let me feast my eyes on everything. Let me have my fill of joy. And it's good that I've got a little time left. I understand a whole lot now. That's enough! You can't understand more than that. There's no need to."

From below, by the river, the air was getting colder. But the chill was barely perceptible, wafting up from the river . . . It was merely the weak breath of decay that was destroyed by the enormous, calm warmth from the earth and the sky.

Filya didn't understand Sanya and he didn't make an effort to. He also felt that it was good here on earth. That basically it was good to be alive. He would hold up his end of the conversation out of politeness.

"So are you all alone in the world?"

"What makes you say that? I've got relatives, but, as you see, I'm ill." Sanya wasn't complaining. He never complained in even the most subtle way. "And then there's this weakness of mine—for the bottle . . . I get in their way. That's natural . . ."

"You've probably had a rough time gettin' by . . ."

"Not always. Sometimes I used a weight on somebody . . . Sometimes they used one on me. And now the end has come. However, maybe not . . . Right now I can feel eternity. As soon as it starts getting dark and it's warm—I can feel eternity."

This went completely over Filya's head. Another muzhik was sitting there with them, Yegor Sinkin, who had a beard because he'd been wounded in the jaw during the war. All this went over his head, too.

"You must've done time in prison, then?" Yegor asked, fishing for information.

"Lord almighty! You'll make a convict outta me yet. It's just that I lived and didn't understand that it's wonderful to be alive. Well, I haven't done much with my life . . . I really loved art. I wasted a lot of time and energy. Now I'm at peace. I was an artist, in case you're interested. But not much of one." Sanya laughed sincerely, quietly, good humoredly. "Now I've really confused you . . . Don't let it bug you. There are lots of us eccentrics and strange people in this world! My brother sends me money. He's rich. That is, he's really not rich, but he's doing all right. And he gives me some."

The muzhiks understood this—his brother felt sorry for him.

"If only I could start all over again!" Sanya clenched his teeth, causing small ridges to appear on the sharp cheekbones of his thin, dark face. His eyes glittered feverishly. He was agitated. "I'd like to explain what I now know: man is . . . an accidental, beautiful, agonizing attempt on Nature's part to know itself. But a fruitless one, I assure you, because right alongside me there are also hemorrhoids in nature. Death! . . . And it's inescapable, and we will ne-ever understand that. Nature will never understand itself . . . So it's gone on a rampage and is avenging itself in the form of man. It's like an evil . . . mmm . . ." Sanya went on, talking only to himself, indistinctly. The muzhiks got tired of straining to hear him and started talking about their own things.

"Love? Yes," Sanya muttered, "but it only muddles and complicates everything. It makes the attempt a torment—that's all it does. Long live death! If we aren't in the position to comprehend it, then to make up for it, death at least allows us to understand that life is wonderful. And, no, it's not sad at all . . . Meaningless, maybe, yes . . . Yes, it's meaningless . . ."

The muzhiks realized that Sanya was already soused. And they went their separate ways.

Filya wandered through the alleys and back streets and little by little the fervent belief that life was wonderful diminished in his breast.

All that was left was an aching pity for the man who had remained sitting on the log all by himself . . . sitting and muttering under his breath something that he thought was very important.

A week later, Sanya died.

He died sober. During the night. Filya was with him.

Sanya knew all along that he was dying. Sometimes he'd just drift off— as if completely lost in thought. He'd stare at the wall and wouldn't hear Filya . . .

"Sanya!" Filya would call out. "Don't you go daydreamin'. It'll be worse for you. Maybe you should get up and walk around a bit. Let me walk you around the izba . . . Okay, Sanya?"

"Hmmm?"

"Snap out of it . . . Stretch your legs a bit . . ."

"Filipp, go . . . and get me a sprig from the raspberry bush . . . It grows at the foot of the wattle fence. Just don't shake the dust off it . . . Bring it here."

Filya stepped out into the darkness and it stunned him with its boundlessness. It was the dead of night. A spring night, warm and heavy . . . and vast. Filya had never feared anything in his life, but now he suddenly grew timid . . . He hastily broke a young branch off the raspberry bush, moist from the night dampness, and hurried back into the izba. He thought: How can there be dust on it? There isn't any yet . . . there isn't any dust. The roads are still muddy. Where would dust come from?

Sanya raised himself slightly up on his elbow and stared straight at Filya, fixedly. And waited. When Filya entered the izba, those eyes were all that he saw. They blazed in pain, they beseeched him, they called out to him.

"I don't want to, Filipp!" Sanya said clearly. "I know everything . . . I don't want to! I don't want to!"

Filya dropped the branch.

Sanya, weakened, fell back on his pillow and quietly and quickly added:

"Lord, Lord . . . What an eternity! Just one more year . . . half a year! I don't need any more."

Filya's heart contracted in pain. He realized that Sanya would die that night. That he would die soon. He kept silent.

"I'm not afraid," Sanya said quietly, hastily, marshalling his last reserves of strength. "It's not terrifying . . . But just one more year—and I'll accept it. You have to accept it, after all. But it can't just be so . . . so . . . It's not an execution, after all! What's the meaning of it?"

"How about some vodka, Sanya?"

"Just half a year more! Another summer . . . I wouldn't ask for anything, I'd just look at the sun . . . I wouldn't crush a single blade of grass. Who needs this to happen, if I don't want it to?" Sanya wept. "Filipp . . ."

"What Sanya?"

"Who needs this to happen? It's just stupid, stupid! Death's a fool! Some kind of senseless wheel."

Filya also wept—he felt the tears running down his cheeks. He wiped them angrily with his sleeve.

"Sanya . . . don't call it names, maybe it'll . . . um . . . back off for a while. Don't cuss at it."

"I'm not. But it's all so stupid. So vulgar . . . and there's no helping it! Oh, the fool."

Sanya shut his eyes and fell silent. And he was quiet for a long, long time. Filya even thought that it was already over.

"Turn me . . ." Sanya asked. "Turn me toward the wall." Filya turned his friend so he was facing the wall.

"Fool," Sanya said once more very softly. And again he fell silent.

Filya sat in his chair for roughly an hour without moving. He waited for Sanya to ask for something. Or to start speaking again. But Sanya didn't say anything else. He was dead.

Filya and some of the other muzhiks buried Sanya. They buried him quietly, without a lot of superfluous words. They drank a toast to his memory.

Filya planted a birch tree at the head of his grave. It took root. And when the warm south winds blew, the birch tree swayed and rustled, rustling its multitude of little green palms—as if it were struggling to say something. And couldn't.

1969 (1970)

Stubborn

It all began with Monya Kvasov's reading in some book that the perpetual-motion machine was an impossibility. For this, that, and the other reason, not the least of which was the existence of friction. Monya . . . By the way, at this point it's necessary to explain why they called him Monya. His name was Mitka, that is, Dmitry, but his granny called him Mitry and made it Motka and Motya when she was being particularly affectionate. And his pals turned it into Monya—it was simpler that way, and besides, the name Monya somehow fit the fidgety Mitka better, it set him apart from others, it emphasized his restless and obstinate character perfectly.

Monya read that the perpetual-motion machine was an impossibility . . . He read that many, many people had tried and tried to invent just such a machine . . . He carefully inspected the diagrams of those perpetual-motion machines that had, at various times, been proposed . . . And he became thoughtful. The part about friction and the laws of mechanics—well, he skipped all that stuff and threw himself headfirst into inventing a perpetual-motion machine such as the world had never seen. For some reason he couldn't believe that such a machine was an impossibility. It somehow so happened with him that, when confronted with all kinds of sober ideas, he'd just brush them aside and think his own thoughts: "Let them say what they want, what do I care?" And now he also thought: "Who the hell do they think they are? . . . What do they mean—impossible?"

Monya was going on twenty-six. He lived with his granny, even though he had parents somewhere, a mother and a father. When he was still little, however, his granny had taken him away from his parents and brought him home with her (his parents were forever breaking up and getting back together again), and it was she who raised him. Monya finished the usual seven years at the village school, studied for a year and a half at the agricultural-tech school, didn't like it, dropped out, and worked in the kolkhoz till his time for military service came up. He did his time in the army, was trained as a driver there, and now worked as a driver in the sovkhoz. Monya was a towhead with high cheekbones and deep-set, small eyes. His large lower jaw protruded noticeably forward, which was why Monya always had an arrogant and stubborn look about him. This stubborn look pretty well suited him to a T. Once an idea had gotten set in his mind (whether it was to learn to play the accordion or, like last year, to fight for their garden plot—not the amount of land prescribed by law, but the extra one-twentieth of an acre he and his granny already had, which caused the village council to propose they move their wattle fence closer to their house), then that idea would completely possess Monya. He could no longer think of anything but how to learn to play the accordion or how to keep from turning over that wretched one-twentieth of an acre. And he would always manage to pull it off. And this is exactly how it was with the perpetual-motion machine: Monya stopped seeing and understanding what went on around him and devoted himself completely to this great venture in invention. Whatever he happened to be doing—driving a truck, eating supper, watching television—all his thoughts were on one thing alone: the perpetual-motion machine. He'd already roughed out a dozen or so versions of the machine, but rejected them all, one after the other. His brain worked feverishly. At night, Monya would leap out of bed and draw yet another wheel . . . In all his conjectures he kept returning to the wheel—the wheel had been his point of departure—and he kept looking for new ways of making this wheel go on turning continuously.

And finally the way was found. Here it is: take a wheel, say, from a bicycle, and fasten it to a vertical axle. Fasten a chute securely to the rim of the wheel at an incline (about a forty-five degree angle to the hub of the wheel); this was so that some kind of weight—say, of one kilogram—could slide freely down the chute. Now, if you take the axle that the wheel's fastened to and securely attach an iron pivot to it in such a way that the free end of the pivot crosses over the chute where the weight slides . . . That is, if the weight, rushing down the chute, bumps up against this pivot, then it will jog it—well, not jog it—press on it, on the pivot! And the pivot is joined to the axle. The axle will start spinning, and the wheel will start spinning, too. In this way, the wheel will keep spinning all by itself.

Monya thought this up during the night . . . He leaped up, drew the wheel, the chute, the pivot, the weight . . . And he didn't even experience any special joy, he was just surprised. How come they'd spent so much time racking their brains over it? He paced the room in his undershorts, proud and calm deep down inside. He sat on the window ledge and lit up. A hot wind was blowing in through the window. The young birches by the garden fence swayed and rustled; it smelled of dust. In his mind, Monya suddenly pictured the enormous expanse of his homeland, Russia, as an unending plain, and he saw himself on that plain, walking calmly down a road, with his hands in his pockets, glancing around . . . There was nothing special about it, he was just walking, nothing else, but in this walk Monya fancied he could get a sense of his own greatness. That's how a body walks the earth—without a lot of shouting, without making proclamations; he takes a look at everything here, and takes his leave. And then folks realize: What a man he was! What a man! What a man! . . . Monya paced the room some more. If he'd been in his pants instead of only his undershorts, he'd already have stuck his hands in his pockets and walked a bit like that—that's what he felt like doing. But he was too lazy to put on his pants. Not lazy, really, but he felt too embarrassed to go to all the fuss. A calm, a powerful calm, had seized Monya's soul. He lay down on the bed, he lay there till morning without falling asleep. He didn't do anything more to his invention—everything was already all figured out. He just lay on top of his blanket and looked out the window at the stars. The hot wind tapered off toward morning. It was warm, but not stifling. The dense sky began to lighten, it turned light blue, like a faded piece of calico . . . Outside, that special quiet peculiar to daybreak—timorous and fleeting—leaned in through the window. But it was soon scared away—close by, a gate creaked, the chain on the well clanged and, with a squeal, the pail was lowered down into it . . . People were beginning to get up. Monya kept on lying in bed, looking out the window. Although nothing had really changed, how welcome and dear life had suddenly become. Why the heck doesn't anybody ever notice how wonderful, simple, and infinitely dear everything here on earth is? Monya lay there another half an hour and got himself out of bed. It was early, but there was no way he was going to fall asleep now anyway.

He took a seat by the table and looked over his sketch . . . It was strange that he was neither agitated nor happy. A sense of calm still filled his soul. Monya lit up, threw himself back in his chair, and began to pick his teeth with a match—just for the heck of it, on purpose, so as to emphasize by this insignificant action the enormity of what had occurred during the night and what was now lying on the table in the shape of those small drawings. And Monya experienced a sense of pleasure: on the table lay a sketch of the perpetual-motion machine, and here he was picking his teeth! That's how it goes, dear comrades! You were the ones, after all, who chose to labor away at daybreak in those hot feather beds with your wives, to sweat and pant and go into raptures of ecstasy. Small-minded people! And then in the daytime, they'll go around looking pleased with themselves, doing trivial little tasks, knitting their brows, and pretending to be deep in thought. Ooh-la-la! As if you even know how to think! Give it up! However, it's true, they did, after all, invent the washstand, for instance. And, really, you'd have to be quite a genius to do that . . . Oh people, people! Monya grinned, and went over to man's proud invention—the washstand—to wash up.

And after that, all morning long, Monya was in this ironic state of mind.

His granny noticed that he'd been off in another world ever since getting up . . . She was a cheerful, sturdy old woman, and loved her Motka, but didn't show it. She also thought about people in uncomplicated terms. They live, earn their daily bread, and when the time comes—they die. It was important not to take a false step during difficult times, and to figure out how to get by. During the war, for instance, this is how she'd coped: she noticed a crack in the floor of one of the kolkhoz granaries and saw that, little by little, grain was seeping through. The back wall of the granary faced the road, but it was shielded from the road by thickets of stinging nettles and tall weeds. During the night, that crafty old Kvasova would make her way through those thickets with a bag, getting stung all over in the process but making it to the grain. The granary was a tall one, the floor was high off the ground—a person could just crawl underneath it. Old Kvasova gathered up the grain and whittled away at the crack with a knife . . . For about a week she would crawl under the granary at night with her little bag, and carry away a fair amount of grain. And during the great famine she pounded that grain with a mortar at night, mixed some pine bark into the flour, and baked bread. That's how she sidestepped death. Motka was like a son to her, probably even dearer because by then she didn't have anybody else (her two sons had both been killed in the war). There was, of course, her daughter—Motka's mother—but she was so completely wrapped up in her complicated relationship with her husband and so caught up in the whirl of city life that basically nothing came of the woman. She never showed her face here in the village, and so it was as if Granny had a daughter and yet didn't, at the same time.

"What you goin' around like that for today?" Granny asked when they were sitting down eating breakfast.

"Like what?" Monya inquired calmly and condescendingly.

"All satisfied-like. You're narrowin' your eyes like a cat in the sunshine . . . Did you have a nice dream or somethin'?"

Monya thought for a little bit . . . And then said enigmatically:

"I dreamed that I found a briefcase with ten thousand rubles."

"Oh go on with you!" The old woman grinned, was silent for a moment, and then asked, "Well, what would you do with it?"

"What? . . . What would *you* do?"

"I'm askin' you."

"Hmmm . . . No, what would you do? What do you need, for instance?"

"I don't need nothin'. Maybe I'd have 'em take the house apart, get rid of the rotten logs, and put it back together again."

"You'd be better off buildin' a new one. What's there to take apart and put back together? It's rotten through and through."

Granny sighed. She was silent for a long time.

"That may well be, but I'll live out my days here. There ain't many of 'em left. I've already thought everythin' over, 'bout how they'll carry me outta here."

"Here you go again!" Monya said with displeasure. He also loved his granny—although he probably wasn't too aware of it—but one thing about her irritated Monya: all her talk about her impending death. If it had been prompted by feebleness, sickness, or feelings of doom there'd be some excuse for it—but no, his granny really wanted to live. She hated death, but pretended to be resigned to it. "How come you're at it again?"

The clever old woman assumed a mournful grin.

"Why not? What—am I gonna live two lifetimes? She'll come all right, death will . . ."

"'Course she'll come—let her come. How come you gotta talk about it beforehand?"

But the old woman felt like talking about it. It was just too bad that Motka couldn't bear such talk. She liked talking with him. She thought he was a smart fellow and was only surprised that other folks in the village didn't think so, too.

"So what'd you dream then?"

"I didn't dream anything . . . I'm just . . . The morning's so nice, I'm just happy."

"Well, well . . . Go ahead and be happy while you're young. Old age'll come, and you sure won't be happy then."

"Let it come!" Monya said carelessly and loudly, finishing his breakfast. "We'll have things figured out. We'll get our two bits in."

And Monya left for the garage. But along the way he decided to drop by to see the engineer from the repair and maintenance station, Andrei Niko-layevich Golubyev, a young specialist. He was a newcomer, intelligent, a little on the gloomy side, it's true, but to make up for it he didn't run off at the mouth. Monya had talked to him a couple of times and liked him.

The engineer was in his yard, busy with his motorcycle.

"Howdy!" Monya said.

"Hello." The engineer didn't respond right away. And he looked at Monya disapprovingly, he probably hadn't liked Monya's familiarity.

"You'll have to put up with it," Monya thought. "You're still young."

"I just dropped by to say my two bits," Monya continued, entering the yard.

The engineer looked at him again.

"What two bits?"

"What do scientists think about the perpetual-motion machine?" Monya got his question out right away. He sat down on a log, pulled out his cigarettes . . . And looked at the engineer. "Well?"

"What kind of perpetual-motion machine?"

"You know, that there 'perpetuum mobile.' The regular perpetual-motion machine, which nobody's ever been able to invent . . . "

"Well, what of it?"

"What do they think about it nowadays?"

"What 'they' do you have in mind?" The engineer began to get annoyed.

"The scientific world . . . In general. Have they given up on this problem?"

"They don't think about it at all. As if they don't have anything better to do with their time . . ."

"So, they've completely given up on the problem?"

The engineer once again bent over his motorcycle.

"Right."

"Isn't that a little premature?" Monya wouldn't let him duck out of the conversation.

"What do you mean, 'premature'?" The engineer turned to glance at Monya again.

"That they've given up. On the problem."

The engineer looked closely at Monya.

"What, did you invent a perpetual-motion machine or something?"

Monya looked back just as closely at the engineer. And just as if he were driving a stick into an anthill, Monya blurted out right into that little diploma-filled head of his:

"I did."

The engineer, still squatting, stared harder at Monya . . . Then he smiled right in Monya's face—and returned the "stick" to him. Every bit as distinctly and a little spitefully, he said:

"Congratulations."

Monya became anxious. It wasn't that he suddenly had doubts about his invention; rather, what worried him was how apparently deep the notion that the perpetual-motion machine was an impossibility had sunk into people's consciousness. It seemed that even if you'd already invented it, they'd still insist it was impossible. Arguing with people was upsetting and depressing. All of Monya's obstinacy, all of his stubbornness, was aimed at keeping people from hurting him when his own trustful and compliant nature left him open to insult and injury.

"So now what?" asked Monya.

"In what sense?"

"Well, you congratulated me . . . What next?"

"Next—send it through the usual channels, try to get it approved . . . Have you already made it? Or have you just thought it up?"

"I've just thought it up."

"Well, then . . ." The engineer grinned, and shook his head. "Then move things along now . . . Write the experts or something. I don't know."

Monya was silent for a bit, cut to the quick by the engineer's grin.

"Well, and how come you're not even interested in findin' out what kind of machine it is? You should at least learn the principle behind the work. You're an engineer, after all. Aren't you even curious?"

"No," the engineer said firmly. "I'm not."

"Why?"

The engineer abandoned the motorcycle, dried his hands with a rag, threw the rag on a log, and dug into his pocket for his cigarettes. He looked down at Monya.

"Look . . . Correct me if I'm wrong, but didn't you say you studied awhile at the tech school?"

"A year and a half."

"So how come you're sitting here talking such gibberish? You're a driver, you're familiar with machinery . . . You don't really believe in this invention of yours, do you?"

"You haven't even found out the principle behind the work and right away you say it's gibberish!" Monya was astounded. That was it. From this point on, he dug in his heels. He recognized the familiar trembling in his chest, the revolting chill and trembling.

"And I don't want to find out."

"Why?"

"Because it's stupid. And you yourself should understand that it's stupid."

"And suppose it isn't stupid?"

"Test it. Test it and *then* come here . . . with the principle behind the work. But if you want my advice, don't waste your time."

"Thanks for the advice." Monya stood up. "And all the kind words . . ."

"Just as I thought," the engineer said with a touch of sympathy, but adamantly. "A person can't say a word to your kind. Next you'll be telling me that what they taught me at college was wrong . . ."

"What's college got to do with it? I didn't come to you for a patent, af-ter all . . ."

"Well then, what's with all this . . . this homegrown science?" the engineer exclaimed. "Almost nine years of education and you still think you've made the perpetual-motion machine! What kind of B.S. is that? You should know better . . . Don't you think that if the perpetual-motion machine were a possibility somebody would have invented it by now?"

"But that's just how everybody looks at it: it's impossible, end of conversation. So everybody's just thrown in the towel . . ."

"No, they haven't thrown in the towel, they've proven long ago: it's an im-pos-si-bil-ity. It'd be one thing for a person with a fourth-grade education to go on like this . . . But you've had eight and a half years! You should know better." The engineer was fed up, really angry. And he didn't hide the fact that he was angry. He looked at Monya crossly and severely. And he lectured him: "What the heck did you do for eight and a half years?"

"Picked my nose and scrubbed my toes," Monya said, also crossly. And he looked the engineer straight in the eye. "Where do you come off makin' speeches? We're not at a meetin', you know. What're you showin' off for? I'm not lookin' to nominate you for anything."

"There you go . . ." The engineer was a little taken back by the obstinate spite he encountered, but he didn't let go of his own spite either. "You're well spoken—so you aren't such an ignorant guy. Can't you see it doesn't make a damn bit of sense to fuss around trying to make a perpetual-motion machine? You're making a laughingstock out of yourself." The engineer threw down his cigarette, stepped on it, ground it into the dirt, and went to start up his motorcycle.

Monya left the yard.

The engineer had stunned him. And he was ashamed to have been scolded that way. Genuine malice toward the engineer grew within him . . . Most awful of all was the fact that doubt in his perpetual-motion machine had arisen. He headed straight for home—back to his sketch. He stepped briskly and looked at the ground. He'd never been so ashamed. He was also ashamed of his cockiness that morning, his serenity and self-satisfaction. All the same, he should have tested everything through and through. And what a damn state of serenity he'd shown up in at the engineer's! He should have tested it, of course.

Granny wasn't at home. Good. She'd have been all anxious and pestered him with questions. Monya took a seat at the table and pulled the sketch over to himself. Well, now what? The weight—here it is—presses down on the pivot . . . Does it really press down on it? It does. How on earth could it not press down! What else could it do? Monya remembered the engineer's words: "What the heck did you do for eight and a half years?" He fidgeted nervously in his chair and turned his attention back to his machine. Well? The weight presses down on the pivot; the pressure will cause the pivot to move . . . It'll move. And it's welded at the other end to the axle . . . So what's so friggin' impossible? Monya was worried now. He was definitely worried. He was seized with impatience. That's right, he'd gone to school for eight and a half years, absolutely true. But—take a look at this! Monya leaped out of his chair and paced around the room . . . He didn't understand what they were talking about. Well, let them prove that the weight won't press on the pivot, and the pivot won't move because of it. Why wouldn't it move? Anybody would agree it would move! Then the axle . . . Phooey! Monya didn't know what to do. He had to do something, or else his heart would burst from all this, his skin would split open from the stress. Monya picked up his sketch and left the house, not knowing himself where he was headed. He'd have gone to the engineer's had the engineer not already left. But maybe he hadn't left yet? So Monya set off for the engineer's again. Once more he walked briskly. He was no longer ashamed, but was seized by such impatience that he practically ran. Monya actually did run a little bit—on a street where there weren't any people.

The motorcycle wasn't in the yard. Monya got annoyed. He stepped into the engineer's house anyway, more out of reflex than for any real reason. The only one at home was the engineer's young wife. She'd just recently gotten out of bed, was still in her bathrobe. She was all rumpled from sleep and hadn't combed her hair yet.

"Hello," said Monya. "Has your husband left?"

"Yes, he has."

Monya wanted to leave, but stopped.

"You're a schoolteacher, aren't you?" he asked.

The engineer's wife was surprised.

"Yes. What about it?"

"What subject?"

"Math."

Without paying any attention to the mess (which any housewife would have been ashamed of) and without paying any attention to the housewife herself (that she'd not tidied herself up yet), Monya walked over to the table.

"Take a look at this . . . I had an argument with your husband about it . . . Come here."

The young woman stood indecisively for a moment, looking at Monya. She was very cute and a little on the plump side.

"What's the matter?" Monya asked.

"What's this all about?" the teacher asked, walking up to the table.

"See," Monya began to explain things, pointing to his sketch, "this here little chute is made from steely . . . tin. Follow me? It—just like this—is fastened at a slant to the rim of this wheel. If we set the weight here, right here, at the top . . . And this here would be the pivot, it's fastened to the axle. The weight'll slide and move the pivot . . . It will move the pivot, won't it?"

"It'll press on it . . ."

"Right! It'll move away from the weight, right? The pivot, that is. And what's the axle gonna do? Start spinnin'? And what about the wheel? The wheel is fixed tight to the axle . . ."

"What is this, a perpetual-motion machine or something?" the teacher asked in surprise.

Monya sat down on a chair. He looked at the teacher. He was silent.

"What is it?" she asked.

"You said it yourself already!"

"A perpetual-motion machine?"

"Uh-huh."

The teacher curled her rosy lips in surprise and looked at the sketch for a long time . . . She also drew up a chair for herself and sat down.

"Well?" Monya asked, lighting a cigarette. Once again there was a trembling in his breast, but this time it was from joy and impatience.

"The wheel won't turn," the teacher said.

"Why?"

"I'm not quite sure yet . . . This needs to be calculated out. It's not supposed to turn, though."

Monya pounded his knee hard with his fist . . . He stood up and started pacing around the room.

"Well, you guys are too much!" he began. "I don't understand, but either you've had a bit too much learnin' or . . . Why won't it?" Monya stopped, looking steadily at the woman. "Why?"

The woman looked back at him, she was a little anxious. You could see that she was even a little bit frightened.

"So you need it to turn?" she asked.

Monya chose to ignore that she'd asked something really stupid and repeated his own question.

"Why won't it turn?"

"How did my husband explain it?"

"Your husband . . . didn't. Your husband chose to humiliate me." And again Monya turned eagerly to the sketch. "You tell me why the wheel . . . Does the weight press on it or not?"

"It does."

"It does. This pressure makes the pivot . . ."

"You know what," the teacher interrupted Monya, "what are we doing here just guessing when the physics teacher, Alexander Ivanovich, could easily explain it all to us. Do you know him?"

"Yes, I do."

"He doesn't live very far from here."

Monya picked up the sketch. He knew where the physics teacher lived.

"Just wait for me, okay?" the teacher asked. "I'll go with you. I'm getting interested myself."

Monya sat down on a chair.

The teacher hesitated.

"I need to get dressed . . ."

"Ahhh . . ." Monya guessed. "Well, of course. I'll wait on the porch." Monya went to the door but glanced back from the threshold and said with a smile: "Interesting stuff, huh?"

"I'll be ready in a minute," the woman said.

The physics teacher was a very nice man, one of the Germans from the Volga region, by the name of Gekman. He listened with a smile to Monya's excited explanations. He examined the sketch. He heard him out.

"Here! . . ." he said to the young teacher with unfeigned delight. "See how everything is well thought out! And you always say there aren't any—" He turned to Monya. And little by little he also got excited and started explaining things. "Watch this: I'll hardly change anything in your design. I'll just make a few little adjustments. I'll take away (he pronounced it 'take avay') your chute and your weight . . . Instead of attaching the chute to the rim of the wheel, I'll fasten the pivot, too—vertically. Like this . . ." Gekman drew his own wheel and fastened the pivot to its rim. "Now here's where we'll fix it . . . All right?" Gekman was very pleased. "Now I attach a spring to this vertical pivot . . . Like this . . ." The teacher sketched a spring, too. "And with the other end . . ."

"I've already seen a machine like that in a book," Monya stopped the teacher. "It's not gonna spin when it's like that."

"Ah-h!" exclaimed the happy teacher. "Why?"

"The spring presses each end just the same."

"So that makes sense to you, huh? Now, let's take your version: there's a weight. The weight lies on the chute and presses on the pivot. But, after all, the weight is the same thing as the spring, and you already know why the spring won't work. The weight presses just the same way on both the pivot and the chute. The force is equal at either end. The wheel will stop."

This seemed monstrous to Monya.

"How can that be?!" He turned to him. "What're you sayin'? It just slides along the chute—the chute can be made steeper—and it'll fall onto the pivot. How can you say it's the same?!" Monya looked ferociously at the teacher. But the teacher was still in the grip of his strange joy.

"Yes!" he also exclaimed, smiling. Probably the inexorability of the laws of mechanics delighted him. "It's the same. The difference in force is illusory. What we have here is perfect equilibrium . . ."

"Well then, why don't you and your perfect equilibrium just all go to hell!" Monya said bitterly. And he grabbed his sketch and went off.

He went out into the street and strode home quickly again. It was all like some sort of conspiracy. The devil only knows what it was! It was as if they'd made a pact among themselves. Why it was clear as day, a child could understand it: the wheel can't but revolve! "No, you see, it's NOT SUP-POSED to turn." What on earth does that mean?

Monya made it home again, wrote a note saying that he didn't feel well, found his granny in the garden, and told her to take the note to the sovkhoz office. He didn't say anything more to his granny. Instead he went into the shed and started to make his perpetual-motion machine.

. . . And, indeed, he did make it. He worked like a dog all day long, till it got dark. He put the final touches on it by lantern light. He'd demolished a bike (he needed the wheel), made a chute out of an old galvanized pail, bolted the pivot to the axle instead of welding it . . . Everything was done according to plan.

Monya hung the lamp a little higher, sat down on a stump next to the wheel, and lit up . . . And, without the least agitation, he gave the wheel a shove with his foot. For some reason he wanted to start the perpetual motion with his foot, no other way would do. And he leaned against the wall. And with a look of condescension, he began to watch the wheel spin. The wheel spun and spun for some time—and stopped. Then Monya set it into motion with his hands . . . For a good long time—with astonishment, hostility—he watched the bright circle of the wheel with its flashing spokes. It stopped again. Monya concluded that there wasn't enough counterweight. He needed to balance the chute and the weight! He made the necessary adjustments. Once again, putting everything he had into it, he set the wheel into motion. Once again he sat there looking down at it and waited. Once again the wheel stopped. Monya wanted to smash it into bits, but decided not to . . . He sat there for a little while longer, stood up, and slowly went off somewhere, utterly dispirited.

. . . He came to the river, sat down by the water, groped around for some small rocks, and flung them into the dark current. No calm descended on him from the river. It gushed, plashed against the rocks, and sighed in the dark by the opposite bank . . . All night long it moved restlessly, murmured to itself—and kept flowing and flowing. Out in the middle, in the mainstream, its undulating back gleamed, and here, by the bank, it kept jostling small rocks, rustling among the bushes, sometimes sputtering angrily and sometimes almost laughing quietly under its breath.

Monya wasn't suffering. He even liked being all by himself. Everybody laughed behind his back and would doubtless continue to do so in the future. After all, though folks pull stupid stunts in the village from time to time, nobody there had ever yet tried to invent the perpetual-motion machine! This would give them all something to talk about for a couple of months. Let them. People have to have their laugh. They work hard, there's not much to entertain them around here—let them have their laugh. It didn't matter. For some reason that night Monya even felt love for them, for all the people in the village. He thought of them calmly, with pity. He even thought he shouldn't argue with them so much. Why argue? We've all gotta live and bear our cross in silence . . . And he began to feel a little sorry for himself, too.

Monya waited till dawn began to break. He put his failure behind him, washed his face and hands in the river, went up the slope, and set off down the street that ran along the river bank. He wasn't headed anywhere in particular. He didn't feel like sleeping. I should get married, Monya thought, have children—say, three—and watch them grow up. And find peace, and walk around just like this—slowly and deliberately—and look at everything serenely, condescendingly, a little ironically. Monya really liked the men in the village who were calm like that.

It was already completely light outside. Monya hadn't noticed that he'd come upon the engineer's house. He hadn't come on purpose, of course. He'd just been walking by and saw the engineer in his yard. The engineer was once again busy with his motorcycle.

"Good mornin'!" Monya said, stopping by the fence. And he looked at the engineer amicably and happily.

"Howdy!" replied the engineer.

"And yet it does spin!"[1] Monya said. "The wheel, that is."

The engineer tore himself away from his motorcycle . . . He looked at Monya for some time. It wasn't that he didn't believe him—it was more like he neither believed nor understood him.

"You mean, your perpetual-motion machine?"

"Sure do. The wheel . . . is still spinnin'. It's spun all night long . . . And it's spinnin' now. Got tired of watchin' it so I went out to stretch my legs."

The engineer didn't know what to think. Monya had a tired and honest air about him. And he didn't look ashamed in the least, but even seemed radiant.

"Are you serious?"

"Let's go—you can see for yourself."

The engineer left his yard and set off for Monya's.

"Is this some kind of trick?" He still couldn't believe it. "What kind of contraption have you built?"

"What do you mean, trick? It's in our shed . . . It's on the floor, spinnin' away."

"Where'd you get the wheel?"

"From a bike."

The engineer stopped for a moment.

"Well, you're right there. A bike wheel would have a good bearing—it would spin for a good long while."

"Yes," said Monya, "but not all night!"

They set off again.

The engineer didn't ask any more questions. Monya also kept quiet. His blissful mood hadn't yet left him. He was in such a good mood that he himself wondered about it.

"And it's been spinning all night?" the engineer couldn't help asking once more, when they were right outside Monya's house. And he fixed his eyes on Monya. Monya, cool as a cucumber, met his gaze and said, apparently also amazed:

"All night! From about ten at night when I gave it a shove till . . . what time is it now?"

The engineer didn't look at his watch. He followed Monya. He was extremely perturbed, though he tried not to show it—so as to uphold the calling of an engineer. Monya was amused every time he looked at him, but also tried not to show it.

"Get ready!" he said, stopping in front of the door to the shed. He looked at the engineer and pushed the door open with his foot . . . He stepped to the side to let the engineer pass by him to see the wheel. And then he also entered the shed. He'd become extremely curious to see how the engineer would take it when he discovered that the wheel was not spinning.

"Well, now," the engineer said. "I thought you'd at least come up with some kind of trick. This isn't funny."

"Sorry 'bout that," said a contented Monya. "Let's go—I've got a little brandy left in the house. Wanna have a glass with me?"

The engineer looked at Monya with interest. He grinned.

"All right."

They went into the house. Cautiously, trying not to make any noise, they crossed the hallway . . . They'd almost made it when Granny heard them.

"Motka, where you been all night?" she asked.

"Go back to sleep," Monya said. "Everythin's fine."

They went into the other room.

"Have a seat," Monya invited. "It'll take me just a moment to rustle somethin' up—"

"Don't bother. You don't need to rustle anything up!" the engineer said in a whisper. "Forget it. Why go to all the fuss so early in the morning?"

"Oh, all right," Monya agreed. "I wanted to get us a meat pie or somethin' . . . but that's okay."

When they'd drunk their glass of brandy and lit up, the engineer once again gazed curiously at Monya and screwed up his intelligent eyes as he grinned.

"Just couldn't take my word for it, huh? You had to make one yourself . . . Probably worked all night on it, didn't you?"

Monya sat there, however, pensive and calm—as if he already had three children and were watching them grow up.

"I killed all day yesterday on it . . . But that's not what gets me," Monya began, and he spoke without any petty regret or sorrow, but rather with a deep and sincere curiosity. "What gets me is that I still don't understand why it won't keep spinnin'. It really should keep spinnin'."

"No it shouldn't," said the engineer. "That's the whole point."

They looked at each other . . . The engineer smiled and it became clear that he wasn't a spiteful person at all. His smile was kind, trusting. Probably it was just that they'd dumped tons of work on him at the sovkhoz because of his youth and conscientiousness, and therefore he'd forgotten how to smile and speak courteously—he didn't have time for it.

"You need to go back to school, educate yourself," the engineer advised. "Then things'll make more sense."

"School, education . . . What's that got to do with it?" Monya said with dissatisfaction. "You sound like a broken record: school, education . . . Are you tryin' to tell me that there's no such thing as a fool with a college degree?"

The engineer laughed . . . and got up.

"Sure there is. But there are a lot more fools without one. Present case excluded, of course. Take care!"

"Don't you want another glass?"

"No. And I don't advise you to, either."

The engineer left the room and once again tried to cross the hallway without making any noise. Granny, however, was no longer asleep. She was watching him from her berth on the stove.

"No need to tiptoe," she said, "I'm not sleepin' anyhow."

"Good morning, Granny!" the engineer greeted her.

"Mornin', dearie. How come you're not gettin' your sleep? You should be gettin' your sleep while you're young. You'll be old 'fore you know it."

"But then what'll we do when we're old?" the engineer asked cheerfully.

"Well, you sure won't be gettin' a good night's sleep."

"Well, I guess we're all fated to sleep sometime, somewhere."

"True enough, we'll all sleep someday . . ."

Monya sat in the room and looked out the window. The upper part of the window was already bathed in red—the sun was rising. The village was waking up: gates were slamming, cows were mooing and gathering in a herd. People were talking with each other, somewhere somebody was yelling at somebody else . . . Everything was just as it should be. Thank God at least here everything made sense, Monya thought. The sun rises and sets, rises and sets—unattainable, inexhaustible, eternal. And down here folks busied themselves with this and that: shouting, hurrying, working, watering their cabbages . . . Counting their blessings . . . Monya got all choked up . . . People, dear people . . . Good day to you!

1972 (1973)

Let's Conquer the Heart!

About three days before New Year's, in the dead of night, in the village of Nikolayevka, the sharp report of two shots cut through the frozen stillness. One after the other they rang out . . . from a high caliber rifle. And somebody shouted:

"Let's conquer the heart!"

The shots echoed throughout the village for a long time. Dogs started barking.

In the morning everything became clear—Veterinarian practitioner Alexander Ivanovich Kozulin had fired the shots.

Vet practitioner Kozulin had only lived in this village for half a year. But even when he'd first appeared on the scene, he'd failed to excite the slightest bit of interest on the part of the Nikolayevites. He was an uncommonly inconspicuous person. He was about fifty, portly, flabby . . . He walked, however, at a good clip. And he'd keep his eyes on the ground. He'd greet people hastily and immediately lower his eyes. He didn't say much, and when he did, he spoke quietly and unintelligibly, always as if he knew some sort of secret about people and was afraid he'd give himself away if he looked them in the eye. Not out of fear for himself, but out of shame and delicacy. Even the village women, though they generally respected sober, quiet muzhiks, didn't like him. Folks also didn't like the fact that he was single. Why he was single nobody knew—it was just bad, that's all. Fifty years old and no family, nobody at all.

And now this very man had popped out of his house after midnight and blasted twice into the air with his gun. And shouted something about the heart.

Everybody was at a loss.

At noon, a corpulent district police officer with a red, weather-beaten face drove up to the veterinarian's office to see Kozulin.

"Hello, comrade Kozulin!"

Kozulin looked with surprise at the police officer.

"Hello."

"We've gotta . . . um . . . go over to the village council. To file a report."
Kozulin's eyes guiltily searched the floor for something.

"What sort of report? What for?"

"What?"

"Why a report? I don't understand."

"Did you fire your gun yesterday? Or rather, in the middle of the night?"

"I did."

"That's why we've gotta file a report. The chairman of the village council wants to, um . . . have a chat with you. How come you opened fire? Somebody scare you or something?"

"No, not at all . . . There's been a great breakthrough in science, so I fired off a salute."

The officer looked at the practitioner with genuine interest and amusement.

"What sort of breakthrough?"

"In science."

"Go on."

"I fired a salute. What of it? I did it out of joy."

"They fire salutes in Moscow," the officer explained for Kozulin's edification. "But here—it's a violation of public law and order. We're fighting against that."

Kozulin removed his robe, put on his coat and hat and indicated that he was ready to go explain things.

A motorcycle with a sidecar was at the gate to the veterinarian's office.

The chairman of the village council was waiting for them.

"So what happened, as it turns out, is that during the night a salute was fired," began the officer, and once again looked with amusement at Kozulin. "Comrade Kozyulin here explained to me . . ."

"Kozulin," corrected the practitioner.

"What?"

"That's right—Kozulin."

"But what diff . . . A-ah!" the officer understood, and started laughing. And he sat down heavily in a large leather chair. And he pulled a form for filing a report out of a carrying case. "Sorry, it was unintentional."[1]

The chairman squeaked his calfskin boots and adjusted the strap of his field shirt with his right hand. (From the other sleeve protruded the perfect lacquered palm of a prosthesis.)

"Take a seat, comrade Kozulin," he invited the practitioner.

Kozulin also sat down in a deep chair.

"So now, what happened? Why was the gun fired?"

"Yesterday in Cape Town a man received a heart transplant," Kozulin pronounced triumphantly. And fell silent. The chairman and the officer waited for what was to follow. "A dead man's heart was given to a living human being," finished Kozulin.

The officer's face fell.

"What's that?"

"The heart they put in the live man came from a dead man. A corpse."

"What, they went and dug up a corpse and . . . ?"

"C'mon, why the heck would you go dig somebody up if a man's just died!" Kozulin exclaimed irritably. "They were both in the hospital, but one died . . ."

"Sure, it happens, it happens," the chairman agreed patronizingly. "They do transplant certain organs. Kidneys, among others."

"Others—yes, but it's the first time for the heart. We're talking about the heart here!"

"I fail to see a direct connection between this . . . pathological event and two shots fired during the nighttime," the chairman noted sternly.

"I was rejoicing . . . I was stunned. When I heard the news, I happened to see my gun, so I ran out into the yard and fired it . . ."

"During the nighttime."

"What of it?"

"What of it? Why, that's a violation of public law and order."

"What time did this take place?" the officer asked sternly.

"I don't know exactly. About three."

"What's the matter with you, do you really listen to the radio at three o'clock in the morning?"

"I couldn't sleep, so I was listening . . ."

The officer shot the chairman a significant glance.

"There's no *Moscow* radio station that airs programs at 3:00 A.M., is there?" he asked again.[2]

"'The Lighthouse' does."

"'The Lighthouse' is on all night," the chairman corroborated, but he kept his eyes fixed attentively on the practitioner. "Who gave you the right to disturb the village with gunshots at 3:00 A.M.?"

"Forgive me, I wasn't thinking at that moment . . . I'm a schizo."

"A what?" the police officer didn't understand.

"A schizo. You know, it just comes over me . . . I lose all self-control." As if lost in thought, the practitioner touched his forehead and then his eyes. "Shirvo kolo shirvo . . . Tooth powder et cetera."

The police officer and the chairman exchanged puzzled glances.

"Now, we here forgive you, comrade Kozulin," the chairman pronounced sympathetically, "but what about those workers? Some of them have to get up at 5:00 A.M. You're a man with an education, you really should understand these things."

"By the way," the officer added good-naturedly, growing more animated, "how come you had to go rushing out and fire a salute? After all, it's not in your field—the breakthrough, that is—you're a veterinarian, you know. They didn't give a mare a heart transplant."

"Don't you dare talk like that!" the practitioner suddenly started shouting. And he flushed. He was silent for a few moments and asked quietly and bitterly: "What makes you say a thing like that?"

For a while everybody was silent. The chairman was the first to speak.

"There's no need to get all hot under the collar. Of course it's a great achievement for scientists. It doesn't matter who got the heart transplant. All of us, when it comes right down to it, are part of the animal kingdom. What's important is the achievement itself. What's more important is that it was performed on a human being. But, comrade Kozulin, I'm telling you one more time: that unauthorized action of yours with the nighttime salute is a flagrant disturbance of the peace. Who knows what sort of achievements the future may bring us! You'll make psychopaths out of all us citizens. Remember that, once and for all. By the way, how's your firewood situation?"

The practitioner was thrown for a loop by the unexpected question.

"It'll do for now, thank you. I've got everything I need for now. I like it here." The practitioner kneaded his hat in his hands and frowned. He was ashamed of his outburst. He looked over at the officer. "Forgive me—I couldn't help it . . ."

The officer got all embarrassed.

"Well now, forget it . . . "

The chairman started laughing.

"It's all right. As they say, forgive and forget."

"But if *you* forget," the officer threatened jokingly, "we won't forgive. We won't file a report, but we will remember this. Good enough, comrade Kozulin?"

"What's a report got to do with it," the chairman said. "He's an educated comrade . . ."

"Educated is as educated does . . . but should it get back to our boys down at the station . . ."

"We won't keep you any longer, comrade Kozulin," said the chairman. "Go back to work. Drop by if you need anything."

"Thank you." The practitioner got to his feet, put on his hat and headed toward the exit.

At the threshold he stopped . . . and turned. And suddenly he made a wry face, closed his eyes and surprisingly loudly—just as if he were standing before a battalion—he drawled out the commands:

"R-r-right dress! 'Ten-tion!"

Then he touched his forehead and eyes and said quietly:

"It came over me again . . . Goodbye." And he went out.

For a short time afterward the police officer and the chairman sat there staring at the door. Then the officer turned heavily in his chair, so he was facing the window, and watched the practitioner walking off down the street.

"We used to say guys like that've had one too many knocks on the head," he said.

The chairman also looked out the window.

Vet practitioner Kozulin was walking along at his usual quick clip. He kept his eyes on the ground.

"Gotta take away his gun," said the chairman, "or the devil only knows what could happen . . ."

The officer coughed hesitantly.

"What do you think? Is it true that he's 'not all there'?"

"What else?"

"He's faking it. I can see it in his eyes . . ."

"What for?" The chairman didn't understand. "Why would he need to? Now, anyways?"

"What else? That way he's not responsible for anything. Now if you go ahead and ask him for proof of his mental illness he won't have any. I'd bet my life he doesn't have a certificate attesting that he's a schizo. What he *does* have . . . is a hunting license. Take away his gun, you say . . . But he's doubtless got a hunting license. Let's make a bet! I'll go right now and check if he's got a license. And his fees are all paid. How about it?"

"All the same, I don't get it. Why would he need to go slandering himself like that?"

The officer started laughing.

"For no particular reason—just to be on the safe side. In case something comes up, he'll say 'I'm a schizo.' We're on to all those little tricks."

1967 (1970)

Vanka Teplyashin

Vanka Teplyashin was laid up in bed at the rural hospital with a gastro-intestinal ulcer. He had been laid up for a long time. The doctor called Vanka in when some man from the district center came to the hospital. The doctor and this other man turned Vanka around, kneaded and pressed on his stomach, and pounded him on the back . . . The two of them talked about something between themselves and then said to Vanka:

"How would you like to go to the city hospital?"

"What for?" Vanka didn't understand.

"For treatment. You'd be laid up a bit there just like you are here. Sergei Nikolayevich here would treat you."

Vanka agreed.

He was comfortably set up at the city hospital. Everyone there started calling him the "research case."

"So where's that research case?" the nurse would ask.

"Probably smoking in the lavatory," Vanka's neighbors would answer. "Where else could he be?"

"Smoking again? What are we ever gonna do with that research case?"

Somehow Vanka didn't like being in the city hospital. He'd told his neighbors in the ward everything that had happened to him in his life, how last year they'd wanted to take away his driver's license, how he'd once lost a truck in the river . . .

"The ice up ahead was swollen just like this—like a small hill . . . I opened the door and gave it some gas. Suddenly, I started goin' down!" When Vanka tells a story, he hurries through it, waves his arms around, jumps from one thing to another. "So I'm goin' down. Natural as can be, like goin' down a little hill. The water was beatin' against my windshield! A big block of ice slammed into my door and jammed it shut. And I'm headin' straight to the bottom, natural as can be, and I can't get the door open. And I'm already swimmin' in the cab. Then I groped around and found the other door. I crawled outta the cab and I started lookin' around . . ."

"Right—you make it sound like it was a banya you fell into, not a river. 'I crawled out and started lookin' around.' Knock off the lies, huh?"

Vanka looked at him from where he was lying in bed, his honest eyes bulging out.

"Me, lie?!" For some time, words even failed him. "Of all the . . . How can you say that? Whatcha mean lie? Of all the . . ."

It was true—if you took a good look at Vanka, it was clear. He didn't know how to tell lies. After all, that's something you have to learn how to do, too—lying, that is.

"Well, what happened next? Go on, Vanka. Don't pay any attention to him."

"As I was sayin', I'm lookin' up. I see there's this light blue hole, that's where I fell through . . . So I swim in that direction."

"So how long was it that you were under water?"

"How'm I s'pposed to know? Not long, I'd say. I'm just takin' a long time tellin' about it. And I keep gettin' interrupted to boot . . ."

"Well, what happened next?"

"Well, I crawl out . . . Folks are already runnin' toward me. They took me to the nearest izba . . ."

"Did they give you some vodka right away?"

"First off, they rubbed me down with cologne . . . For a whole week after that I reeked of 'Red Carnation.' After that, they ran off to get vodka."

. . . Vanka couldn't say when it was that he started getting depressed. He'd stand at the window by the hour, and he'd watch the hustle and bustle of the street below, one so completely alien to his heart and mind. Life down below was strange. People bustled and shouted and nobody heard anybody else. Everybody was in a hurry, but since from up above everybody looked just the same, it seemed that nobody was getting anywhere. It was all some sort of mysterious running in place. And Vanka soon got used to casting his eye over the street, the people, the cars . . . Some floozy in a short skirt would pass by, swinging her hips, and Vanka would follow her with his eyes. But besides that, everything was the same. And so Vanka got depressed. He felt all alone.

You could just imagine, then, his surprise and joy when, down in this world below, he suddenly caught sight of his mother . . . She was trying to cross the street and was glancing all around, afraid. Oh dear, sweet mother! You knew you should come!

"My mama's comin'!" he shouted joyfully to everybody in the ward.

This was so unexpected, it had popped out so freely, this human joy, that everybody burst out laughing.

"Where, Vanya?"

"Over there! There, the one with the bag!" Vanya hung out the window and shouted: "Mom!"

"You go and meet her downstairs," they told Vanka. "Or else they won't let her in. Today's not a visiting day, see."

"Sure they'll let her in! She'll say she's come all the way from the village . . ."

They started guessing what would happen.

"Fat chance! If what's-his-name is on duty, that skinny guy with the red eyes, it'll be a cold day in hell before he lets her in."

Vanka ran downstairs.

His mother was already standing next to the skinny guy with red eyes, asking him to let her in. Red Eyes wasn't even listening to her.

"That's for me!" Vanka said while still at a distance. "That's my mother."

"Wednesday, Saturday, Sunday," Red Eyes droned woodenly.

Upon seeing Vanka, his mother was also overjoyed. She was even about to go over to him, but Red Eyes detained her.

"Back off."

"But she's here to see me!" Vanka shouted. "What's your problem?!"

"Wednesday, Saturday, Sunday," the . . . orderly—or whatever you call them—ticked off again in triplicate.

"But I didn't know," his mother pleaded, "I'm from the village . . . I didn't know, comrade. Can't I just set a spell with him somewheres . . ."

For the first time in his life, Vanka was stunned—his attention was caught—by how his mother's voice had suddenly acquired a pitiful tone, an artfully pitiful tone, one put on by habit, and how immediately she had jumped to this tone . . . And Vanka became ashamed that his mother was begging in such a humiliating way. He ordered her to keep quiet.

"Be quiet, Mom."

"But I'm explainin' things to the comrade here . . . What's the matter?"

"Be quiet!" Vanka ordered once again. "Comrade," he addressed the orderly politely and with dignity, but the orderly didn't even look in his direction. "Comrade!" Vanka raised his voice. "I'm speaking to you!"

"Vanya," his mother cautioned, knowing how her son could fly into a rage at the drop of a hat.

Red Eyes kept on looking apathetically askance, just as if there wasn't anybody there next to him and he wasn't being petitioned on all sides.

"Let's go on over there and sit for a bit," Vanka said calmly to his mother, though it took all his strength to do so, and he pointed to a bench behind the orderly. And he walked past him.

"Get ba-ack!" the orderly said, even with a touch of repulsion in his voice. And he tried to grab Vanka by the sleeve.

Vanka had been waiting for just that. As soon as Red Eyes touched him, Vanka knocked the orderly's arm away with a sharp upward jerk of his arms, and, though already turning pale, he still managed to tell his mother calmly:

"Right over here, on this bench here."

But that wasn't all Vanka had been waiting for—he also expected that

Red Eyes would grab him from behind. And Red Eyes did. By the collar of Vanka's striped pajamas. And he jerked it so hard that it hurt. Vanka caught his hand and squeezed it so painfully that Red Eyes curled his lip.

"I'm gonna tell you once more, if you don't keep your hands to yourself," Vanka began, speaking quietly into his face, unable to find weighty words right off the bat, "I'll . . . You and I are gonna have a very serious talk."

"Vanya," his mother pleaded, almost in tears. "Lord almighty . . ."

"Sit down," Vanka ordered, his voice a little husky. "Sit down right here. Tell me, how's everythin' at home?"

For some short moment Red Eyes was dumbfounded. Then he moved into action and sounded the loud voice of alarm.

"Stigneyev! Lizaveta Sergeyevna! . . ." he shouted. "Over here! We've got lawlessness here!" And he spread his arms wide open, as if he were trying to catch a dangerous lunatic, and made for Vanka. Vanka stayed put, he just braced himself and looked up at Red Eyes. And that gaze stopped Red Eyes in his tracks. The orderly glanced around again and shouted: "Stigneyev!"

Out of the door to a side room popped stocky Yevstigneyev in a white lab coat, with a roll in his hand . . .

"What?" he asked, not understanding where the lawlessness here was, or what that lawlessness was about.

"Over here!" Red Eyes yelled. And spreading his arms out wide, he started to go after Vanka.

Vanka met him head on . . . The orderly went flying backward. But by now Yevstigneyev had already seen what the lawlessness was about and rushed at Vanka.

. . . Vanka didn't give them the chance to get their hands on him. He didn't run away, but he didn't let them get ahold of him even though this Yevstigneyev was a hefty guy, and he and Red Eyes were trying with all their might. Vanka was careful to send as few chairs and tables as possible flying across the room. But despite his efforts, the orderly's table went flying anyway and a decanter sitting on top went flying with it and shattered into pieces. The shouting and noise increased. Some more white coats came running. Sergei Nikolayevich, Vanka's doctor, came running up as well. They had a hard time quieting down Red Eyes and Yevstigneyev. Vanka was taken upstairs. Sergei Nikolayevich took him. He was very upset.

"Well, how could you, Ivan?"

Vanka, on the contrary, had even become tranquil. He understood that now he was going to go home. He'd even instructed his mother to wait for him.

"What in the devil did you get into it with him for?" Young Sergei Nikolayevich could make neither head nor tail of it. Vanka greatly respected the doctor.

"He wouldn't let my mother in."

"But if you'd just told me I'd have taken care of it! Go to the ward and I'll bring her up."

"No need to. We're goin' home right now."

"What do you mean, home? What are you saying?"

But Vanka suddenly displayed a resoluteness that surprised even himself. It was because he was going home that he'd calmed down so much. Sergei Nikolayevich began trying to talk him out of it in his cramped little office. He even said this:

"Let your mama stay at my place for now. Three days or so. However long she wants! I've got enough room for her. We haven't seen your case to its conclusion. Understand? You're letting me down. Don't pay attention to those idiots! They're hopeless. Your mama can come visit you as much as she likes . . ."

"No," Vanka said. He remembered his mother asking Red Eyes for permission in that humiliating way. "No, not on your life."

"And what if I don't discharge you?"

"Then I'll jump out the window . . . I'll run away in my pajamas in the middle of the night."

"Come now," Sergei Nikolayevich said in disappointment. "You're making a mistake."

"It's okay." Vanka even felt cheerful. He was only a little sorry that the doctor . . . that he'd taken it so hard. "You'll find somebody else with an ulcer . . . There's that red-headed guy over there by the window, he's got an ulcer, too."

"That's not the point. You're making a mistake, Ivan."

"No." Vanka was feeling better and better. "Don't take it personal."

"Well, that's it, then . . ." Sergei was still very upset. "Keeping you like this won't help either. Maybe you'll think things over? When you've calmed down . . ."

"No. My mind's made up."

Vanka darted to the ward—to gather up his belongings, such as they were.

In the ward they started vying with each other to see who could let him have it the most.

"You fool! What do you mean you're leavin' . . ."

"They would've cured you here, you know. Sergei Nikolayevich would've seen you through."

They didn't understand, these people didn't, that soon he and his mother would get on the bus and in about an hour or so Vanka would be home. For some reason they couldn't understand that.

"All because of some idiot you're gonna ruin your health. You're a fool, Vanka."

"You gotta be human," Vanka said with a certain vindictive calm bordering even, perhaps, on solemnity. "Is that clear?"

"It's clear, it's clear all right . . . But you shouldn't be in such a hellfire hurry. You really shouldn't."

"You should've slipped him a fifty-kopek piece, that old Red Eyes, and everything would've been fine. What's wrong with you?"

Vanka cheerfully said his goodbyes to everybody, hoped everybody would get better, and skipped off down the stairs, light at heart.

He still had to get his clothes downstairs. And it just so happened that it was Yevstigneyev who was issuing clothes that day. Without a trace of ill temper he looked at Vanka and even said sympathetically:

"Kicked you out, huh? Well, that's too bad . . ."

And when he handed over the clothes, he leaned over to Vanya and said quietly, with belated reproach:

"You should've given him fifty kopeks and that'd be that—and there'd have been no fuss at all. You young people are all alike . . . Is it really that hard to figure it out?"

"You gotta be human and not try to squeeze fifty-kopek coins outta people," Vanka said again with an air of importance. But there, in the basement, in the midst of all the clothes hangers, in the close-smelling cloud of mothball fumes, these words didn't sound so solemn. Yevstigneyev didn't pay any attention to them.

"These shoes here—are they yours?"

"Uh-huh."

"You're not well yet and you're going."

"I'll get well at home."

"At home! How are you gonna get well at home?"

"Take care, Mr. Bear!" Vanka said.

"You take care. You should've asked that doctor . . . Maybe they'd keep you. You shouldn't have gotten into it with that fool."

Vanka didn't bother to explain anything to Yevstigneyev, but hurried off to his mother who was most likely sitting by Red Eyes and crying.

Vanka was right. His mother was sitting on the bench behind the orderly's desk and drying her tears with her shawl. Red Eyes stood by his stand and was watching the corridor—on the lookout. He was standing straight as an arrow. Vanka's heart began to pound in excitement when he saw him. He even slowed down—he wanted to say something to him in parting. Something with a sting to it. But he just couldn't come up with the right words.

"Take care!" Vanka said. "Twerp!"

Red Eyes blinked in surprise but didn't turn his head—he kept his eyes fixed on his post.

Vanka picked up his mother's bag and they went straight out of the city hospital, so praised and overrated, where, as rumor had it, they'd almost found a cure for cancer.

"Don't cry," Vanka told his mother. "What's the matter with you?"

"You can't seem to find any place where you can get your feet under you," his mother said, putting her bitter thoughts into words. "It was like that back at the tech school . . ."

"Lay off! To heck with them and all their tech schools. And another thing, don't go askin' anybody for stuff the way you did with that Goggle Eyes back there. Don't ever ask anybody for anythin'. Is that clear?"

"Well, you won't get very far if you don't know how to ask proper."

"But not the way you were askin'. I was ashamed to listen to it."

"He's the one that oughtta be ashamed! . . . I gotta go get my papers for my pension all signed—just try runnin' around to get that done without knowin' how to ask right . . . Think you'll get very far?"

"All right, all right . . ." It was impossible to outtalk his mother. "How're things there, at home?"

"Okay. Are you goin' back to our hospital?"

"Um-mm . . . I don't know," Vanka said. "I feel better already."

A little while later, they got on a bus at the station and set off for home.

1972 (1973)

In the Autumn

Ferry operator Filipp Tyurin finished listening to the latest news on the radio, hung around at the table some more, and was sternly silent . . .

"There's just no stoppin' 'em!" he said angrily.

"Who you railin' at this time?" asked Filipp's wife, a tall, old woman with manly hands and a man's deep booming voice.

"They're bombin' again!" Filipp nodded at the radio.

"Who're they bombin'?"

"The Vietnamese, who else?"

The old woman didn't approve of her husband's passion for politics, and, what's more, this foolish passion irritated her. From time to time they'd had some serious quarrels because of politics, but the old woman didn't feel like quarreling now—she didn't have time for it. She was getting ready to go to the bazaar.

Filipp, in a stern, intense frame of mind, put on some warmer clothes and set off for the ferry.

He'd been a ferry operator for a long time, ever since the war. He'd been wounded in the head and had to give up carpentry because it hurt to bend over his work. So he became a ferry operator.

It was the end of September, the wind had picked up after the rains, bringing with it cold, nasty weather. The ground squelched underfoot. From the loudspeaker in the village store you could hear an exercise program being broadcast. The wind mixed with snatches of music and the buoyant voice of the Moscow trainer. Even so, the village pigs and roosters managed to hold their own, their squealing and crowing piercing through the other sounds.

The villagers Filipp met on his way nodded their greetings to him and hurried on, either to the village store for bread or to the bus—they were in a hurry to get to the bazaar, too.

Filipp was used to making the trip from his house to the ferry each morning; he'd complete it without thinking. That is, he'd think about something, but not at all about the ferry or who, for instance, he might be ferrying across the river that day. Everything was clear as far as that was concerned. Right now he was thinking about how to keep those Americans in check. He was surprised, but he never asked anybody, why it was we didn't force them back with our missiles. Everything could be resolved in a couple of days.

In his youth Filipp had been very active politically. He'd taken an active part in the new life after the revolution, he'd been an activist in the organization of the kolkhozes . . . He hadn't dispossessed any rich peasants, it's true, but he'd done a lot of arguing and shouting, trying to convert the unbelievers and getting himself all worked up in the process. But he hadn't become a Party member either. Somehow that had never come up in conversations with the comrades in charge of everything, but still those in charge could never manage without Filipp. He helped them with all of his heart. And he was secretly proud that there was no way they could manage without him. He liked, for instance, on the eve of elections, to sit around in the village council and talk to the district comrades about how best to hold the elections: who should take the ballot box home, who would come on their own to vote, and of all things not to forget to run and remind them in the morning . . . Of course, there'd also be those who'd start getting all pigheaded about things as soon as you tried to get them to vote: "And did they lend me a horse when I asked for one so's I could go get firewood?" Such words would absolutely amaze Filipp. "What're you talkin' about, Yegor," he'd say to the muzhik. "There ain't no comparison! Any fool can see that! What we got here is a political matter, and you're goin' on about some horse! They're as alike as a pie and a pussy." And he'd rush all over the village, arguing his point. And folks would also argue back, they liked sparring with him. They wouldn't take offense. Rather, they'd say "Now, you tell 'em over there . . ." Filipp would feel the importance of the moment, he'd get all worked up, and take everything personally. "Well, that's the common folk for you!" he thought, completely wrapped up in his great cause. "They're all a bunch of backwoods blockheads." As the years passed, Filipp's political activism subsided, his head wound began to bother him again, so he no longer had the strength to be an activist and get all worked up. However, he continued to take all political and social issues to heart, as he'd done formerly, and he worried a lot.

By the river the wind blew in strong gusts. It whipped and blustered . . . The cables creaked. But at least the sun peeped out, and that was nice.

Filipp went back and forth across the river. He ferried the people across who were in the biggest hurry and then, later on, things went more easily, without a lot of jumpy nerves. And Filipp was just about to turn his thoughts back to the Americans when a wedding party drove up . . . the kind they have nowadays, with everybody in cars all decked out with ribbons and balloons. This city-style wedding party had also become the fashion in the village. Three cars drove up . . . The wedding party piled out on the bank. They were loud, slightly tipsy, and very, very showy and swaggering. Although it was the fashion—to go in cars with ribbons—it was still a rare sight. It was often the case that not everybody could get a hold of the cars.

Filipp watched the wedding party with interest. He didn't know these people—they weren't locals, they were going to visit somebody. One guy in a hat was pulling out all the stops, trying to attract attention to himself . . . It looked as though he was the one who'd managed to get the cars. He kept wanting everything to come off in a big way, with some dash to it. He made the accordion player perform on the ferry, and he was the first one to break into a dance—he shouted, tapped out a beat with his feet, and looked at everybody with the proud gaze of an eagle. Only, it was uncomfortable to look at him, it was embarrassing. And it was embarrassing for the bride and groom—they were more sober than the others, more self-conscious. No matter how much that fellow in the hat showed off, he didn't infect anybody with his put-on gaiety, and he soon got tired . . . The ferry made it to the other side, the cars drove off, and the wedding party rolled away down the road.

And Filipp began thinking about his own life. Here's how his marriage had come about when he was in his youth. There had been a girl in the village, Marya Yermilova, a beauty, round faced, rosy, friendly . . . She'd take your breath away. She was the kind of bride you could only dream about at home, while lying on your sleeping bench. Filipp loved her very much, and Marya also loved him—it looked like they'd end up marrying. But Filipp got involved with the Komsomol workers . . . And it was the same story then as later. He wasn't a member of the Komsomol himself, but he shouted and worked to overturn things just as much as they did. Filipp liked the fact that the Komsomol workers had risen up against the old villagers, against their hold on power. There was one conflict in particular: all the young, politically aware people declared their opposition to church weddings. The unheard-of had happened . . . The village elders couldn't do anything, they got angry, reached for their whips, meaning to set those upstarts back on the straight and narrow with whips alone if need be, but instead they only succeeded in making them all the more dogged in their persistence. It was an exhilarating time. Filipp, of course, was all on the side of the Komsomol. He was also against church weddings. But that wasn't the case with Marya—she wasn't against them at all. Marya's mother and father were tough as flint on that issue, and she herself had bowed out of the ranks of the progressive-minded once and for all. She wanted to have a church wedding. Filipp found himself in a very difficult position.

He tried to persuade Marya in every possible way (he was a masterful talker, which was probably why Marya loved him—it was a rare talent in the village). He tried to convince her, to thwart her peasant ignorance. He read her various articles, instructional and satirical. He made fun of her, but with a pain in his heart . . . Marya wouldn't budge. It was a church wedding or nothing. Now, looking back on his life, Filipp knew that back then he'd been hopelessly stupid. He and Marya ended up parting ways. Filipp didn't change later on. He'd never been sorry and wasn't sorry now that he'd been able to participate to the best of his abilities in the restructuring of life in the village. But he was sorry about Marya. All his life, his heart bled and ached. Not a day went by without his remembering Marya. At first it was so hard on him that he wanted to lay hands on himself. And as the years passed, the pain didn't go away. He already had a family—the wedding ceremony had been a civil one—and kids . . . But his heart longed and longed for Marya. When his wife, Fyokla Kuzovnikova, detected in Filipp this constant sorrow of his, she came to hate him. And that deep-seated, quiet hatred took up permanent residence in her. For his part, Filipp didn't hate Fyokla. No . . . But during the war, for instance, whenever they were told "You are defending your mothers and your wives . . . ," instead of Fyokla, Filipp would picture Marya. And if he had ended up getting killed in the war, he'd have died thinking about Marya.

The ache didn't go away as the years went by, but, of course, it didn't burn anymore the way it had burned those first years of his marriage. By the way, he started talking less back then, too. He was an activist, as he'd been before; he spoke out because people had to be convinced, but all along it seemed as if all of his talk originated in his profound, bitter thoughts about Marya. He'd be ever so pensive, then he'd suddenly snap out of it and once again he'd be trying to make people understand, once again trying to open their eyes to the new and the unprecedented. As for Marya . . . Marya was taken away from the village at that time. Some guy came to see her (not just some guy, later on Filipp met him many times), a rich fellow from Krayushkino. His family came, made the match, and took her away. Of course, they had a church wedding. After a year had gone by, Filipp asked Pavel, Marya's husband, "Weren't you ashamed? Draggin' yourself into a church . . ." At which Pavel acted surprised, then said: "And why should I be ashamed?" "You gave in to the old folks." "I didn't give in," Pavel said, "I wanted a church wedding myself." "That's what I'm askin'," Filipp was at a loss. "Weren't you ashamed? The old folks can be pardoned, you know, but what about you? We'll never crawl out of the dark that way." At that, Pavel started cussing. He said: "Get the hell outta here!" And he wouldn't talk with Filipp any more. But here's what Filipp noticed: when they'd meet, Pavel would look at him with some sort of suppressed rage, with pain even, as if he wanted to understand something and just couldn't. Rumor had it that Pavel and Marya weren't getting along well, that Marya was unhappy. This was the last straw for Filipp. He even went on a drinking binge to quell the new pain welling up within him, but afterward he quit drinking and learned to live with his pain. He looked at his pain as if it were a snake that he constantly carried inside himself, and no matter how much it bit him, he put up with it.

These were the melancholy thoughts that the wedding party on wheels had resurrected. These were the thoughts Filipp ferried from shore to shore, back and forth, and it occurred to him that he'd probably need to drink a glass of vodka with his lunch—the wind cut to the bone and his soul had begun to whimper for some reason. It started to ache outright; it became alarmed and anxious.

"I'll do two more turns and go have lunch," Filipp decided.

As he approached "their" bank (for Filipp, there was "our" bank, where his native village was, and "their" bank, opposite), he saw a covered truck and a small group of people by the truck. Filipp's experienced eye immediately guessed what kind of vehicle it was and who was being transported in it: a dead person. People transport their dead in exactly the same fashion. Waiting to board the ferry, they always climb out of the truck, away from the coffin, and somehow just stand there like that and stare at the river and keep quiet, so that it's clear from the start what kind of group it is.

"Who could it be?" Filipp wondered, peering at the people. "They're from some village up the river, seein' as we haven't heard about anybody 'round here dying. But why on earth are they bringin' the body here from somewhere else? Maybe the person didn't die at home, and so they're bringin' him home to bury?"

When the ferry got closer to shore, Filipp recognized one of the men beside the truck—it was Pavel, Marya's husband. And suddenly Filipp realized who they were bringing . . . They were bringing Marya. He remembered that in the beginning of the summer, Marya had gone to visit her daughter in town. She and Filipp had talked while they rode on the ferry. Marya said that her daughter in town had had a baby and that she needed to help her out for the time being. They'd had a nice chat back then. Marya told him that they were doing fine, quite well, that the children (there were three of them) were all settled, she herself was getting a pension, Pavel was also getting a pension, but he still worked, he did a little cabinetmaking at home. They didn't keep a lot of livestock, but somehow they had everything they needed . . . They'd gotten into breeding turkeys. Last year they'd taken their house apart and replaced the bad logs; their sons had come and helped. Filipp also said that they, too, were doing well for the time being, he was also getting a pension, had no complaints about his health, though his head would ache a bit when the weather was about to change. And Marya said there was something the matter with her heart . . . She was suffering from some sort of heart problem. Sometimes she'd be feeling just fine and then suddenly her heart would constrict and feel so heavy . . . It would happen at night. It would squeeze so bad, it was enough to make you cry. And now, Marya clearly had met her end. As soon as Filipp saw Pavel, he moaned under his breath. He felt a sudden rush of heat.

The ferry bumped up against the rickety dock. They threaded the chains for the ferry through the rings on the dock and secured them with metal bars . . . The front wheels of the covered truck were already touching the logs of the dock, the logs shook, creaked, and moaned . . .

Filipp stood by his rudder as if bewitched, he was looking at the truck. Oh God, it's Marya they're bringing, Marya . . . Filipp was supposed to show the driver how to park his truck because two more were rolling up from behind, but he'd become rooted to the spot, he kept looking at the truck, at the back of the truck.

"Where do you want me to put it?!" the driver shouted.

"Huh?"

"I said, where do you want me to put it?"

"Put it over there . . ." Filipp gestured vaguely. He just couldn't really believe that they were transporting Marya's body . . . His mind was all in a whirl, his thoughts were disjointed and couldn't focus on this one sorrowful turn of events. First he remembered how Marya told him—right here, on the ferry—that they were doing well . . . Then he saw her as a young woman, when . . . Oh, God . . . Marya . . . Is it really you?

At last Filipp tore himself away from the place where he'd been standing and went up to Pavel.

Life had bent Pavel over. His face was fresh, his eyes were intelligent and clear, but his bearing was very poor. And there was a great, peaceful sorrow in his intelligent eyes.

"So, Pavel?" Filipp asked.

Pavel glanced momentarily at him, as if he didn't understand what he'd been asked, and again he began looking down, at the planks of the ferry. Filipp felt awkward about asking again . . . He turned back to his rudder. And as he went, he walked around to the back of the covered truck, glanced in—and saw the coffin. And his heart started aching openly, and his thoughts came together. Yes, this was Marya.

They floated along. Filipp mechanically steered the rudder and kept thinking: "Maryushka, Marya . . ." The dearest person in the world to him was making her last crossing with him . . . All those thirty years that he'd been a ferry operator, he knew exactly how many times Marya had ridden on the ferry. Basically, she'd keep going to town to see her children, either when they were studying there or when they were setting up house or when they had kids . . . And now—Marya was no more.

He steamed up to the shore. Once again the chains rattled, the engines roared . . . Once again Filipp stood by the rudder and looked at the covered truck. It was incomprehensible . . . Never in all his life had he thought what it would be like if Marya died. Not once had he ever thought about that. This was the one thing he hadn't been ready for, her death. When the covered truck began to drive off the ferry, Filipp felt an unbearable anguish in his chest. He was seized by anxiety. Shouldn't he do something? After all, they were taking her away right now. For good. He couldn't just let it go at that; he couldn't just see her off with his eyes and that's all. What was he thinking? And anxiety took hold of him all the more, but he didn't budge, and because of that, he became altogether out of sorts.

"Why, I should've said goodbye!" he realized, when the covered truck was already climbing up the slope. "If I could just say goodbye! If I could just take one last look. The coffin hasn't been nailed shut yet, I could still take a look!" And it seemed to Filipp that these people, who had driven Marya past him, well, that they shouldn't have done that—just driven by and that's all. After all, if it was anybody's grief, then more than anybody else's, it was his grief. Marya was in the coffin. Where were they taking her? . . . Everything that life had not wiped out, that was unravaged by time, unforgotten, painfully dear, crashed down on Filipp . . . His whole long life passed before his eyes—the most important part, the most necessary part, what he'd lived for . . . He didn't notice that he was weeping. His eyes kept following that monstrous truck where the coffin was . . . The truck made it to the top of the slope and turned down the street and disappeared. And now life would go on differently somehow. He had been used to the fact that Marya was here on the earth with him. When things were difficult, when times were hard, he'd remember Marya and wouldn't feel so alone in the world. How on earth would he get along now? Oh God, what emptiness, what pain!

Filipp quickly got off the ferry, while the last truck off the boat was still lingering close to the dock for some reason. Filipp went up to the driver.

"Catch up with that covered truck . . . the one with the coffin," he asked, climbing into the cab.

"How come? What for?"

"You just have to."

The driver looked at Filipp, didn't ask anything else and took off.

While they were driving through the village, the driver leveled several sidelong glances at Filipp.

"Those are Krayushkinites, right?" he asked, nodding at the covered truck up ahead.

Filipp nodded in silence.

"A relative of yours?" the driver asked again.

Filipp said nothing at that. Once again his eyes were glued to the covered truck. From where he was, you could see the coffin in the middle of the truck bed. The people who were seated along the sides of the truck bed suddenly seemed alien to Filipp—both to him and to this coffin. What in the heck were they there for? After all, it was Marya who was in the coffin.

"Want me to go around, or what?" the driver asked.

"Pass it . . . and let me out."

They passed the vehicle. Filipp climbed out of the cab and raised his hand. And his heart began pounding, as if right here and now something was going to happen that would make it clear to everybody, Filipp included, who Marya had been to him. He didn't know what would happen, he didn't know what words he'd say when the truck with the coffin stopped . . . He just wanted to see Marya so badly, it had become something necessary and important. It was impossible for her to go off like that—after all, his life had also passed by, and now there wouldn't be anybody for him any more . . .

The truck stopped.

Filipp got in at the back . . . He grabbed onto the side and climbed up the little set of iron steps which was at the base of the truck bed.

"Pavel . . ." he said pleadingly, not recognizing his own voice. He hadn't planned on speaking so pleadingly. "Let me say goodbye to her . . . Open it, if only for a glimpse."

Pavel stood up abruptly and stepped toward him . . . Filipp managed to see his face up close . . . It was a changed face. The eyes, which had not long ago been filled with sorrow, had now suddenly turned malevolent . . .

"Get outta here!" Pavel said quietly and harshly. And he shoved Filipp in the chest. Filipp hadn't expected that. He almost fell. He grabbed onto the side of the truck and held on. "Go!" shouted Pavel. And he shoved him again and again—he shoved him hard. Filipp hung onto the truck with all his might. He looked at Pavel. He didn't recognize him. And he didn't understand a thing.

"Hey, hey, what's the matter?" The others in the back got all alarmed. A young man, the son, probably, took Pavel by the shoulders and dragged him away from the rear of the truck. "What are you doing! What's the matter with you?"

"He'd better clear outta here!" Pavel said, dripping with venom. "He'd better clear out now! I've got my eye on you! He comes slitherin' up . . . the snake! Get outta here! Outta here!" Pavel stomped his foot. It was as if he'd gone mad with grief.

Filipp climbed down from the truck bed. Now he understood what the matter was with Pavel. He also looked malevolently up at him. And he spoke, not aware himself what it was he was saying, and yet, as it turned out, saying the very words he'd been carrying inside him, words that had been waiting to come out.

"What, feelin' a little bitter? You snatched up what didn't belong to you, and now you're all bitter about it. Were you happy about it back then?"

"As if you were any happier!" Pavel said from the back of the truck. "Or maybe I don't know how happy you were!"

"That's what happens when you try to build your whole life on somebody else's misfortune," Filipp continued, not listening to what was being said to him from the back of the truck. It was important to get everything out, very important. "Did you think you were gonna live in clover? No-o, it doesn't happen that way. Now I see what it was you got for your pains . . ."

"So, did *you* live in clover? You? Yourself? Then how come you're so old and bent over yourself? If you did live well—how come you're so bent over? From livin' the good life?"

"Were you happy back then? Well, now you can see what that happiness has brought you. You're just a beggar! A lousy beggar!"

"What's the matter with you two?!" The young man became angry. "Have you lost your minds? A fine time you've picked!"

The truck started up. Pavel still managed to shout from the back:

"*I'm* a beggar? You spent your whole life whinin' like a dog at the gate! I'm not the one who's a beggar, you are!"

Filipp slowly started back.

"Marya," he thought, "oh, Marya, Marya . . . Here's how you bent all our lives out of shape. A coupla fools snarlin' at each other . . . Both of us are beggars, Pavel, so don't get so shook up. If you aren't a beggar, then why are you so angry? What should you be angry at? You carved out a piece of happiness in your youth—so live and be happy. But you didn't know joy either. She didn't love you, that's why the grief came rushin' out of you like that. There was nothin' for you to snatch up back then. You just showed up and took her away . . . and everybody was overjoyed about it."

Filipp was sick at heart. But now vexation at Marya got mixed in with his bitter gall.

"You were a fine one, too. Just couldn't wait, so you rushed off to Krayushkino! All impatient-like. And there was no sense in it, either . . . And now what?"

"I'll tell you what there is now . . ." Filipp said to himself in conclusion. "There's nothin' now. Except to find some way to live out my days . . . And get ready, too—to follow in her footsteps. You can't undo the past."

The wind had slackened noticeably, the sky had become clear, the sun shone, but it was cold. All around it was somehow barren and cold. Well, it was autumn, after all. Why would it be warm?

1972 (1973)

Strangers

I just happened to come across a book that told about Tsar Nicholas the Second and his relatives.

It was a pretty angry book, but a fair one I think. Here's what I'm going to do: I'm going to excerpt a rather large passage from it, then I'll explain what I'm up to. It's about the tsar's uncle, Grand Duke Alexei:

> From childhood, Alexei had been destined, by his father, Emperor Alexander the Second, for service in the royal navy and he was therefore enrolled in the Naval Academy. But he did not go to classes and instead made the rounds of various theaters and shady restaurants in the lively company of French actresses and dancers. One of them, by the name of Mocure, had him completely wrapped around her little finger.
>
> "Won't you advise me," Alexander the Second asked his minister of war, Milyutin, "how to force Alexei to attend his classes at the academy?"
>
> Milyutin answered:
>
> "There is only one way, your Majesty. Appoint Mme. Mocure as a teacher. Then you won't be able to drag the Grand Duke away from the academy."
>
> Such was the highly qualified naval officer whom Alexei's own brother, Emperor Alexander the Third, had not the least qualm about appointing as Admiral General—the head and overseer of the Russian navy.
>
> Now, being involved in the building of battleships and ports was a gold mine for any dishonest person wishing to line his own pockets with public property. For some twenty years, Admiral General Alexei, forever in need of money for gambling and women, had been involved in an overhaul of the Russian fleet. He personally stole shamelessly from its treasury. And his lovers and those who procured them for him stole every bit as much as he.
>
> Alexei did not understand a thing about maritime affairs and did not bother himself with his department at all. His style of command soon spread throughout the ranks, from top to bottom. Theft and ignorance among the officers grew with each passing year, and went completely unpunished. Life became unbearable for the sailors. The authorities robbed them at every turn: in their rations, their drink, their uniforms. And to keep the sailors from taking it into their heads to mutiny against the rampant robbery going on all around them, the officers intimidated them with harsh disciplinary actions and rough treatment. And this outrage went on unchecked some twenty-odd years, no more no less.

Not a single contract passed through the Navy Department without Alexei and his loose women skimming [here I would have said "ripping off"—V.Sh.] half of the revenue, sometimes more. When the war with Japan broke out, the Russian government contemplated buying several more battleships from the republic of Chili. The Chilean battleships arrived in Europe and were docked at the Italian city of Genoa. There they were inspected by Russian naval officers. These were battleships such as our navy had never even dreamed of. The Chileans were asking very little for them, almost cost value. But what came of it? Because of the low asking price, the deal fell through. The Russian plenipotentiary, Soldatenkov, gave a candid explanation:

"You should ask for at least three times that much. Otherwise why should we go to all the bother? As it now stands, the Grand Duke will receive six hundred thousand rubles off the selling price of each battleship. Four hundred thousand must be given to Mme. Baletta. So what will be left over for us—the members of the Naval Ministry?"

The Chileans, indignant at the impudence of these Russian bribe takers, declared that their government refused to negotiate with middlemen known to be unscrupulous. Now as soon as the Russian deal fell through, the Japanese quickly bought up the Chilean battleships. Later on, these very battleships sank ours at Tsushima.

Mme. Baletta, for whom Soldatenkov demanded four hundred thousand rubles from the Chileans, was Alexei's last mistress, a French actress. Without giving an enormous bribe to Mme. Baletta, not a single entrepreneur or contractor could hope that the Grand Duke would even receive him, let alone hear him out.

A Frenchman, for instance, had invented an unusual torpedo. It would create a waterspout that could sink ships. The Frenchman offered his invention to the Russian government. He was summoned to St. Petersburg. But here—just to have the opportunity to demonstrate in Alexei's presence what the torpedo could do—he was asked for twenty-five thousand rubles for Mme. Baletta. The Frenchman did not have that kind of money, so he headed back home, having gotten nothing for his pains. Back in Paris, a Japanese functionary presented himself to the Frenchman and bought his invention for a goodly sum.

"You understand," the Japanese man said, "a few months ago we would have paid you a lot more, but now we've already invented our own torpedo, which is more powerful than yours."

"Then why are you buying mine?"

"Just to keep it out of the hands of the Russians."

Who can know whether it was not just such a torpedo that capsized the *Petropavlovsk,* thus drowning the crew together with Makarov, the only Russian admiral worth his salt, a real sailor.

During the last ten years of his life, Alexei became a mere pawn in Baletta's hands. Before her, the Admiral Generalette had been Zinaida Dmitriyevna, the Duchess of Leichtenberg, née Skobeleva (the sister of the renowned White General).[1] Unbeknownst to Alexei, members of the Navy Department went straight to her with actual documents. And he carelessly signed everything his lovely lady wanted him to.

The war with Japan put an end to the good life for Admiral General Alexei. It turned out that the Japanese had high-speed cruisers and battleships on the Pacific Ocean while our ships were no better than old galoshes. How well the Admiral General had trained his navy can be judged on the following evidence: the *Tsarevich* fired its guns *for the first time* in the very battle in which the Japanese shot it so full of holes that it leaked like a sieve. The officers did not know how to give orders. The ships did not have maritime maps. The cannons misfired. Time and again the Russians either drowned their own men or ran up against their own mines. The Pacific squadron ran aground at Port Arthur like a crab caught in a tide pool. The Baltic squadron under Admiral Rozhdestvensky's command was sent to the rescue. But when Rozhdestvensky realized that it meant risking his own skin, he reported to the tsar that they had nothing to go into battle with. As it turned out, only the outer layer of the armor plating on the battleships was metal—underneath it was only wooden. At this, the tsar is alleged to have said to Alexei:

"It would have been better, Uncle, for you to have stolen twice as much if that's what it would have taken to put real armor plating on."

After the sinking of the *Petropavlovsk*, Alexei was foolish enough to show himself at one of the Petersburg theaters with his mistress Baletta, all draped in diamonds. The public nearly killed them both. They chucked orange peels, playbills, whatever they could get their hands on, at the pair. And shouted:

"Those diamonds were bought with our money! Hand them over! Those are our cruisers and battleships! Give them here! That's our fleet!"

Alexei stopped going outside his palace, because people on the streets would whistle at him and fling mud at his carriage. Baletta beat a hasty retreat abroad. She took with her several million rubles in cold hard cash, nearly a mountain of precious stones, and a rare collection of Russian antiques, mementos, doubtless, of the Russian people whom she and Alexei had stolen blind.

Tsushima was the end of Alexei. Since that time, never in all the world has a single fleet ever suffered a more stupid and pathetic defeat. Thousands of Russian men went to the bottom of the sea along with their old galoshes-ships and the cannons that couldn't shoot far enough to hit the enemy. It took the Japanese but a few hours of firing to reduce the product of twenty years of thieving done by Alexei and company to nothing but splinters of wood floating on the waves. Everything was revealed in an instant: the robbery practiced by the scoundrel shipbuilders, the ignorance of the talentless officers, and the hatred the tormented sailors felt toward them. The tsar's uncle fed the fish in the Yellow Sea with the bodies of Russian men in sailor suits and soldiers' greatcoats.

After his resignation, Alexei migrated abroad with all of his stolen riches, hastening to the warm side of his Baletta. He bought up palaces in Paris and in other fine cities, and he threw about the gold he stole from the Russian people on women, wine, and games of chance, till one day he croaked from a cold that he happened to contract.

I read this, and I remembered our cattle herder Uncle Yemelyan. In the morning, before the sun was up, you could hear from afar his kind, slightly mocking, powerful voice:

"Women, send out your cows! Your cows, women!"

As soon as you began to hear that voice in the spring, in May, your heart would simply pound with joy. Soon it would be summer!

Then, later on, when he'd gotten too old to graze the cattle, he loved to go fishing on the Katun River. I also loved to fish, and we would stand side by side in the backwater, silently, each of us looking after his own fishing line. In our parts, you fish without floats, and you have to keep an eye on your line. Once it starts twitching against the water and vibrating, give it a tug—you've got a bite. The fishing lines were wound out of horse hair. You had to contrive to pull some white hairs from a horse's tail. The horses wouldn't let you do it without a struggle; sometimes the odd gelding or two would try to get you with their hind legs—they'd kick you if you didn't get the knack of it. I got some hair for Uncle Yemelyan and he taught me to twist a line on my knee.

I loved to fish with Uncle Yemelyan. He didn't goof around, but rather went about his fishing in a serious, wise fashion. There's nothing worse than when adults begin to play around, hoot with laughter, kick up a fuss . . . They'll arrive, a whole mob of them, with a seine. They'll scream, make a lot of noise. In three or four hauls, they'll rake in enough fish to fill a bucket, and—pleased as punch—they'll return to the village, where they'll fry them up and get drunk.

We'd go off somewhere a bit farther away and stand barefoot in the water. We'd stand there till our feet were about ready to drop off. That's when Uncle Yemelyan would say:

"Let's break for a smoke, Vaska."

I would gather dry kindling, light a fire on the bank, and we would warm our feet. Uncle Yemelyan would smoke and tell some story. It was back then that I learned that he'd been a sailor and had fought against the Japanese. And that he'd even been a Japanese prisoner of war. That he'd fought didn't surprise me—almost all our old men from the village had fought somewhere sometime—but the fact that he was a sailor, that he'd been a Japanese prisoner of war—now that was interesting. But for some reason he didn't like to talk about it. I don't even know what ship he served on. Maybe he told me and I've forgotten it, or maybe he didn't. I was too shy to pester him with questions, I've been that way all my life. I'd listen to what he had to say and that was all. He wasn't one to talk a lot. It was like this: he'd remember something, tell about it, and then we'd be quiet again. I can see him now: tall, lean, with a large frame and broad cheekbones, his piebald beard all tangled up . . . He was old, but still seemed powerful. Once he looked real closely at his hand, the one holding his fishing pole. He grinned, motioning with his eyes for me to take a look.

"Look at it tremble. Shriveled old thing . . . Used to think it'd never wear out. Used to be a strong son of a gun! When I was a young feller I floated rafts for a livin' . . . I'd pick 'em up at Manzhursk and float 'em to Verkh-Kaitan, and there townsfolk would take the lumber home in carts. I knew this woman in Nuima, a real looker . . . She was a smart gal, a widow, but better'n any of them young girls. But the Nuimites—it stuck in their craw that I was goin' to see her . . . well, payin' her calls. Mostly it was the muzhiks that got their noses all outta joint. But I didn't give a rat's ass about 'em, them fools, I kept goin' and that's all there was to it. Whenever I'd be floatin' by Nuima, I'd moor my raft, tether it with cables, and be off to her place. She was real sweet to me. I'd have married her if I hadn't been drafted so soon. And what do you s'pose them muzhiks were all so hot under the collar about? 'Cause some stranger's taken to goin' there . . . Ever'body had a thing for her, but they were all married. That didn't matter—it was always 'you stay away.' But that's not all they did. One time when we'd just moored, my raftin' partner set off to visit this clever old gal he knew—she made some wicked moonshine—and I went to my sweetheart's. I'm goin' up to the house and there they are a-waitin' for me, 'bout eight of 'em. Well, I thinks to myself, I can send that many of 'em sprawlin'. So I walk straight toward 'em . . . Two come toward me: 'Where d'ya think you're goin'?' I grabbed 'em both by the front of their shirts, shoved 'em into the ones waitin' on the sidelines—and laid five of 'em out flat. They came flyin' at me in a heap and my heart started a-racin'. I got down to knockin' heads. Soon as I got ahold of one, I'd send him flyin' across the road, and lemme tell you that sure was a purdy sight. More folks came a-runnin' up to help 'em, but they couldn't do nothin' . . . So they started grabbin' up fence stakes. I also managed to yank one up and kept on a-fightin'. It was an out-and-out battle. The pole I had was a long one—they couldn't get at me. So they started a-throwin' rocks . . . Shameless people. Those Nuimites've been shameless since the day they were born. The old-timers, it's true, tried to calm 'em down—you can't have a fistfight with rocks, they hollered. Twelve against one is bad enough without throwin' rocks to boot. We fought a long time, I was workin' up a sweat. And then some woman shouted from the sidelines 'the raft!' They'd chopped through the cables, the dogs, and the raft was bein' carried off downstream. There were rapids downstream, the raft would be smashed to smithereens, and my day's work would be wasted. I threw down the fence pole and started chasin' after the raft. I chased it all the way from Nuima to Bystry Iskhod without stoppin' to catch my breath—'bout fifteen kilometers. Sometimes I ran along the road, sometimes I ran right on the rocks—I was afraid of lettin' the raft outta my sight. You might outrun it and you wouldn't even know, so I tried to keep to the bank. Did I ever run! In all my life I never ever ran like that again. Like a stallion. I caught up with it. I swam out and clambered on board—thanks be to God! But the rapids would be upon me any minute now. Two fellers could just barely manage 'em, and here I was all by myself. I'm runnin' back and forth like a tiger, from one oar to the other. I throw off my shirt. But I made it. Could I ever run in them days!" Uncle Yemelyan grinned and shook his head. "Nobody believed I caught up with it at Bystry Iskhod. Can't be done, they said. But if a feller wants somethin' bad enough, he can do it."

"How come you didn't marry her later on?"

"When?"

"Well, when you came home from the service . . ."

"How could I have? Do you know how long we had to serve back in them days? I came home early, bein' a prisoner and all, but even so . . . She was already thirty five—what's she gonna do, wait for me? Oh, she was a smart gal, she was! When you grow up, get yourself a smart one. A woman's beauty now, it can only turn a muzhik's head at first. But later on . . ." Uncle Yemelyan was silent for a little while, looking pensively at the fire. He puffed hoarsely from his home-rolled cigarette. "Later on you need somethin' different. I had a woman with a head on her shoulders, too, I can't complain."

I remembered Yemelyan's wife. She was a kind old woman. They were our neighbors, a wattle fence divided our yard and their garden. Once she called over to me from the other side of the fence:

"Com'ere, com'ere!"

I went over.

"Your chicken's laid her eggs—just look how many there are!" She pointed to ten or so eggs she was holding in the hem of her skirt. "See, she dug a little hole under the fence and lays her eggs over here. Here, take 'em. Give five to your mooter (mother) and five"—the old woman glanced around and quietly added, "take to them's on the track (the highway)."

Back then, convicts worked on the highway (the Chuisky Tract) and we kids were allowed to approach them. We took them eggs, bottles of milk. . . .

One of the convicts, in those prison jackets they all wore, would drink up the milk right there on the spot straight out of the bottle, wipe off the top with his sleeve and order:

"Give this to your mother and tell her: 'Uncle said to say thank you.'"

"I remember your wife," I said.

"Yup . . . she was a good woman. She knew how to cast charms."

And Uncle Yemelyan told me the following story.

"Our marriage had been arranged—me and my older brother Yegor went together to make the proposal. She was from over there in Talitsa (it's across the river). They brought her. Well we had the widdin' (wedding) . . . We're havin' a good old time. I'd just had a new jacket made, a good jacket, outta heavy felted wool . . . I had it sewed 'specially for the widdin', Yegorka gave me the money, 'cause I'd come to her as poor as poor can be. And right there at the widdin' somebody pinched that jacket. I almost sat down and cried. But my wife says, 'Just you wait, don't you go grievin'! They'll bring it back.' Oh sure, they'll bring it back, I'm thinkin'. There were so many folks there . . . One thing I did know—whoever it was wasn't from our village, but from Talitsa and that's for sure. Where could one of ours ever wear it? Back in them days they sewed 'em right there in your house. The tailor would come with his sewin' machine. He'd cut it out right there and sew it. I remember he sewed for two days. He ate and slept right there in the house, too. So what's my wife do? She takes a scrap of fabric—there was lots of scraps left over from my jacket—wraps it up in birch bark and seals it with clay in the mouth of the stove, right where the smoke bends into the stove pipe, right where the thickest smoke goes. I didn't understand at first. 'What're you up to?' 'Well,' she says, 'every mornin' now, see, he's gonna writhe, that thief is. Soon as we light the stove, he'll start writhin' like this here piece of birch bark.' And whatcha think happened? Three days later a feller comes over from Talitsa, some kin of hers, my wife's that is . . . with a sack. He came, put his sack in a corner and as for himself—boom, there he was down on his knees in front of me. 'Forgive me,' he says, 'the devil made me do it. I was the one who walked off with your jacket. It struck my fancy.' He pulls out my jacket and a big "gander" filled with wine—now it's just called a three-liter bottle, but back then it used to be called a "gander." That's how it was, see . . . 'I can't live like this,' he says. 'I feel like I'm done in.'"

"Did you give him a beating?" I asked.

"What for? He came himself . . . Why should I have? We drank up that gander of his, and I even got us another one, and we drank that one up, too. Not all by ourselves, mind you, I invited Yegor and his wife, and then some other muzhiks came by—it was almost like a whole new widdin'! . . . I was outta my mind with joy—it was a good jacket after all! I wore it well nigh ten years. That's the kinda person my old woman was. Back in them days she wasn't an old woman, but still . . . She knew about that jacket. God rest her soul."

They had five sons and one daughter. Three were killed in the last war, and the others moved to the city. Uncle Yemelyan lived out his days all by himself. His neighbors would take turns firing up his stove, giving him something to eat . . . He'd lie on the stove, he wouldn't moan, he'd just say:

"God bless you . . . It'll be taken into account up there."

One morning they came and he was dead.

What was my reason for writing down such a large excerpt about Grand Duke Alexei? I'm not sure myself. I want to spread open my mind, like a pair of arms—and embrace these two figures, bring them together, perhaps, in order to mull them over in my mind—that's what I wanted to do from the start, to mull them over in my mind—but I just can't. One is stubbornly hanging out somewhere in Paris, the other is on the Katun River with his fishing pole. I tell myself over and over again that, after all, they are children of one people, even if it might make me furious, and yet it doesn't. Both of them have long been lying in the earth now—the talentless Admiral General and Uncle Yemelyan, the former sailor . . . But what would it be like if they met somewhere over *there*? After all, I imagine there are neither epaulets nor jewels over *there*. Nor palaces either, nor mistresses, nothing like that at all. Two Russian souls would meet. And yet even *there* they'd have nothing to talk about, that's the thing. You see, once strangers, always strangers— forever and ever. Vast and great is our Mother Russia!

1974

From the Childhood Years of Ivan Popov

Siberian Pies

My very first memories begin with the following incident.

A sultry midday. Haymaking. There's not a soul in the streets in the village. Just once in a while somebody on horseback will gallop by, or a cart will rattle by, and once again a dry, hot quiet will settle in for a long time.

I'm sitting by the side of the road in the soft, silky dust. I'm making pies. It's easy to do. You've got to bring a dipper of water from home and splash the water on the dust a little at a time, and what you get are sticky blobs of mud. You can mold pies out of them. But pies are pies . . . You make them in order to put them in a line stretching across the road, so you can wait for some muzhik to come riding up. You have to wait for ages. Finally, a muzhik in a wagon appears at the end of the street. I crawl into the nettles by the fence. (Our nettles grow really high, as tall as a man and only the top part stings. You can hide comfortably down below.) And from there I watch the wagon draw near. It's coming closer and closer—my heart stops beating—in a moment it'll run over my pies. The muzhik has caught sight of the pies, glanced around, and has lazily urged his horse on . . . It is with some kind of incomprehensible, anxious agitation that I see first the horse's hooves sending my pies flying and then the four wheels running over them. I spring out of the nettles and stand over my pies. Almost all of them have perished. The ones off to the side have remained intact, but the middle ones have all perished. I get down to making pies all over again and arranging them in a line stretching across the road. There is some meaning in this work. This is probably it: the muzhik doesn't see my pies till the last moment, but I know that they're there, and I also know that upon seeing them, the muzhik will look around. I know this and wait in advance for him to look around. And I am seized by a sweet ecstasy and agitation when he does look around. What's more—sitting in the dust is very pleasant. Of course, my legs are all chapped, but that's something for Mama to worry about. In the evening she'll wash me off by the well.

I was at just such an occupation, sitting peacefully and making pies, when the neighbor's young bull cornered me. He liked to butt a lot, he butted like the devil, and I was scared to death of him. We kids were all scared of him. We teased him from a distance and when he charged with his head lowered, we scattered in all directions. And here I'd been so busy with my pies that I'd failed to notice him. I saw him when he was about five paces away. He stood there and looked at me. I was about to leap up and run away when I sat down instead—my legs refused to move. The calf kicked up his hind legs, bellowed ominously and rushed at me. It seems that I'd fallen on my back in advance. So he began rolling me toward the road. I didn't make a peep. Then my voice returned and I started yelling. I yelled so loud that the calf jumped back, stood with his front legs spread apart, and looked stupidly at me for a long time. Somebody came running out of an izba and rescued me.

In the evening, a dirty, withered gypsy woman with large thieving eyes appeared in our izba. I was lying on a berth on the stove, and the gypsy rustled her skirts in a corner by the stove and whispered rapidly. Mama looked at her full of hope and suspicion. The gypsy melted some wax in a spoon and poured the wax into a glass of water—there it turned into a yellow, formless blob. The gypsy began nodding her little jackdaw head rapidly. I don't remember what she said, but she was saying something. I do remember Mama saying: "It was a calf that scared him, not a dog." Then they talked about our rooster. For some reason the gypsy shouted. Mama also got angry and said: "So that's the kind of person you are!" Then I drank the warm water from the glass, which the gypsy had cast a spell over, and I fell asleep.

Later I can remember myself at the following occupation.

It was obvious that we were having a tough time getting by. We weren't getting enough to eat. Mama would go off to work and would leave me and my sister at Grandpa and Grandma's. We ate there. And so . . . Grandpa is planing wood in the shed, Grandma is weeding the rows in the garden.

I'm sitting by the workbench linking the golden, sunny rings of the wood shavings together. And suddenly I remember that Grandma has some tasty rolls in the cupboard. I go out of the shed and head for the house. The padlock is hooked on the door—for no particular reason, without being locked with a key. (My sister is in the garden with Grandma.) If I pull the padlock out of the loop and open the door, Grandma will hear and ask: "Whatcha doing there, Vanka?" And Mama had ordered us—I remember this well—not to pester Grandpa and Grandma, especially Grandpa, and not to ask for food. However much they gave us would have to do.

A window in the izba was open. From inside came the smell of freshly baked bread and of the whitewashed hearth. In the corner stood the potbellied cupboard with dully gleaming glass panes—that's where the rolls were.

I crawl in through the window and carefully tiptoe across the painted floor . . . I open the cupboard, take the smallest roll and clear out of the izba the same way I'd come. I can't remember if I'd ever stolen anything before that or not. But I do remember sneaking through the izba on tiptoes. Somehow I knew that that's what you were supposed to do.

In the evening, Grandma, chuckling, told Mama about my climbing through the window (she'd seen it all from the garden). Mama didn't laugh. She looked displeased.

"In all your livelong days, you'd never think of givin' him any yourselves . . . You two are awful stingy, Mom, so darn stingy!"

Grandma took offense.

"We feed 'em, you know . . . What do you mean stingy? He wasn't really hungry. He was just bein' a nasty brat."

I also remember this.

A frightening little man with a red beard is standing in the middle of our izba—Yasha Goryachy—he's shaking his finger and saying: "Don't you threaten me, you hear, don't you threaten me—we've had it with your threatenin'." But Mama is standing right in front of him and says quietly: "Well, you watch it . . . I'm not threatenin' you . . . You shouldn't carry your activism so far."

Then Yasha climbed up to the sleeping benches and began throwing down birch logs. Chopping trees from the birch grove near the village was forbidden, but everybody did it anyway and hid the wood wherever they could. But Yasha Goryachy, the village Party activist, went from home to home searching for it.

And here's another thing I remember.

Our calf had disappeared. I don't remember the calf itself, but I do remember looking for it. We set off with Mama, beyond the village toward the lakes. It was already getting dark. We called and called for it: "Prusya! Prusya!" The calf was nowhere to be found, it had just vanished. Suddenly, Mama sat down on the ground and said: "Oh, Sonny, I don't feel very good . . . Lord almighty. Can you find your way home? Run as fast as you can to Grandma's . . ."

I said I could. I remember running. I imagined that I was riding a horse. I shouted to myself "Giddy-up," kicking up my legs. I neighed . . .

Granny got all scared. I suggested that she also get on the horse, and we'd go as fast as the wind. But she just brushed me off and went trotting along on her own two feet.

Mama met us not far from the village. She was walking real gingerly down the road and was clutching at her chest.

She and Grandma began talking about something, and I went along behind them, this time "on foot."

Another incident took place at the nursery school.

The nursery school had two stories. The windows were open. So I climbed up on a windowsill on the second floor, sat down and dangled my legs . . . And then I saw Mama. She says to me quietly from down below: "Vanya, climb down from the window, Sonny. Climb down, I'll watch you. Just climb there into the house . . . Go on . . ." I climbed down from the windowsill.

Then Mama ran in, picked me up in her arms and carried me off. But our nursery school worker ran into us on the stairs. She was a plump young woman. Mama put me down and the woman ran away from us. Down the stairs we go. I thought it was all funny.

"Big fat cow!" Mama wasn't afraid of anything. Later, when I'd already grown older, I heard the story of how they'd wanted to evict us from our izba. They arrested my father and sent him to the district center, to the "lockup." They said: "The bastard wanted to go stir up an uprising." Many others were also "taken" from the village. We never saw them again. They were all rehabilitated in 1957 "for lack of corpus delicti."

We were left behind with Mama. I was a little over three, Natashka, my sister, was seven months. Mama was twenty-two. And the next day two men came to our place: "Clear outta here."

We were little and didn't understand the seriousness of the moment. Besides, we had nowhere to go. Mama refused point-blank to clear out. Natashka and I kept quiet. One of them pulled a revolver out of his pocket and told us once again to clear out. Then Mama picked up a steel rod and stood in the doorway. And she said, "Go on with you! What good's that revolver of yours if I smack you in the noggin with this steel rod?" And she didn't let them in—they went away. Later on Mama said, "I knew he wouldn't shoot. He's not that stupid, is he?" But when they took father, she wept like a child. She kept waiting for them to release him. They didn't. They took him to Barnaul. Then my mother and another young woman set off for Barnaul. They rode in some freight cars, they rode for two days and nights. (Now people get there in six hours.) They got there. They went to the prison. They dropped off their care packages.

"I should've given 'em everythin' right away, but I'd divided it up to make for two trips, thinkin' that way he'll know I'm still here, maybe it'll make it easier on him," my mother told me. "But I arrive the next day— and they're not takin' things. We don't have such a person, they say."

Then they went to see some chief warden. He's sitting there, she says, a gray-haired, tired, kind-looking man. He glanced in a book and asks: "Any children?"

"Yes, two."

"Don't wait for him, make yourself a new life somehow. He's got a death sentence."

For some reason he was lying. Father was posthumously rehabilitated in 1956, but documents indicate that he died in 1942. What they accused my father of, I really don't know. Some say acts of sabotage in the kolkhoz, others say he allegedly incited the muzhiks to start an uprising against Soviet rule.

However it may have been, our father was no more.

. . . So we began a new life. We endured much hunger and cold. Throughout my entire life, I have always preserved a particular love for my mother. I was always terribly afraid that she would die—she was often ill.

Then another father appeared in our izba. Life became easier.

But then the war broke out and our other father was no more, he was killed in the Kursk encirclement.

Once again, hard times came upon us . . .

First Acquaintance with the City

Right before the war, my stepfather moved us to the city of B——. It was the closest one to us—almost entirely wooden, a merchants' town in former days, flat and dirty.

How sorry I was to leave our village! I disliked my stepfather for it and although I didn't remember my own father, I thought: If he were with us, our own Pop, we wouldn't have been getting ready to go anywhere. To spite my stepfather (I now know that he was a man with an unusually big heart—kind, loving . . . A young bachelor, he married my mother with her two children, moreover "children of an enemy of the people," since our Pop left us "along the lines of the GPU" and was liquidated, or so they say), anyway, to spite my stepfather, that is, to spite Papka—so he'd fly into a rage and fall into despair—I rolled an enormous cigarette, went into the outhouse, and began puffing away—smoking. Smoke poured out of all of the cracks in the outhouse. Papka saw it . . . He never beat me, but he always threatened to lay into me. He flung open the outhouse door and, with his hands on his hips, started looking at me without saying a word. He was a very handsome man, swarthy, strong, with intelligent brown eyes . . . I threw down the cigarette and started looking back at him.

"Well?" he said.

"I was smokin' . . ." If only he had hit me, if only he had popped me once across the face, I could have put up such a howling then and there, I could have grabbed my head and frightened Mama . . . Maybe then they'd have had a fight and maybe Mama would have informed him that she wasn't going anywhere, if that's the way he was—a child beater.

"I can see that you were smokin'. You're bein' stupid, Vanka, stupid . . . Who are you hurtin' most? Think it's me? I'm gonna go right now and tell your mother . . ."

That hadn't figured into my plans and could make everything turn out all wrong—Mama, after all, would give me a licking, no doubt about it. I ran after Papka . . .

"Papka, don't, don't go!"

"So how come you're smokin' at such an early age, dummy? Just think how much nicotine you'll build up startin' that early! You think it over, cabbage head. Say that you won't do it again and I won't go to your mother."

"I won't. I swear to God, I won't."

"Well, then watch it."

. . . And so we're going to town—we're moving. Our stuff is on the wagon, Talya and I are sitting on top of it all, Mama and Papka are walking. Our cow, Raika, is walking behind, tethered to the wagon.

Talya, my little sister, is happy that we're going, that we've still got a long, long ways to go. It's never crossed her mind that we're leaving our home. All in all, I'm also really enjoying the ride. All around, the steppe is so free and spacious . . . In the grasses there is a ceaseless chirping. Thousands of tireless little grasshoppers are beating and beating their ringing anvils with their tiny hammers, and from above, from the hot blueness, stream spiraling silver strands . . . Probably the little grasshoppers are forging these delicate strands on their anvils and then spreading these sparkling webs out on the grass. Early in the morning, when the sun comes up, somebody threads emerald beads on these strands, stretching them from blade to blade—and then the green garments of the steppe shine with precious adornments.

We stop to eat.

Papka unharnesses our horse and lets it wander about on the bank. Raika also has gone off happily to graze on the lush array of grasses. We make a small fire—to cook some millet cereal. Everything's fine! I even forget that we're leaving our home. Papka reminds us!

"This is the last time our river comes up to the road. Farther on it bends to the west."

For some time we all look at our native river without speaking. I grew up on it, was used to hearing its steady, muffled, powerful roar day and night . . . Now I was not to sit on its banks with a fishing pole any more, or frequent the islands where it is peaceful and cool, where the bushes are groaning with all sorts of berries: currants, raspberries, blackberries, bird cherries, sallow thornberries, hawthorn berries, and guelder-rose berries . . . I was not to make my way with enormous difficulty—so that my legs would get all bloodied and I'd have to leave my pants behind in the bushes—along the towpath dragging the boat far upstream and now, perhaps, I was never to experience the greatest bliss of all—the return trip home, downstream. How I liked it, what a grown-up muzhik—slightly weighed down by concerns about my family's welfare—I felt myself to be when we were getting ready to go upstream for an overnighter. It was important not to forget matches, salt, a pocket knife, an ax . . . Nets, seines, and heavy sweaters are piled in the prow of the boat. There's bread, potatoes, and a kettle. There's a gun and a stiff, heavy ammunition belt.

"Is that everything?"

"Looks like it . . ."

"Let's go, it's already late. We've still gotta set up camp for the night. Let's get a move on."

The slyest one among us—the owner of the gun or boat—heads for the stern, the rest—two or three of us—take hold of the tow rope. Actually, it's true, I even preferred being with the tow rope. Then you can snatch up a handful of currants as you're walking along, or crawl up to the river on all fours and put your burning lips into the water, or wade across the river bed—waist deep—or even slip off a slimy boulder and find yourself in over your head. The best part is precisely that it all happens on the way, it's not intended, it's not for the fun of it. And the main thing is that you, and not that guy in the stern of the boat, are doing the real, the important work . . .

Oh, Papka, Papka! And what if everything doesn't go so well for him in town? After all, we're going there to give it a try. It's still not clear where he'll find work there and what kind it'll be. He wasn't very educated, nor did he have a trade. And so what does he do? He's hellbent on going to town and has gone and dragged three people off with him, to boot! And he himself doesn't know what it'll be like. He just went there, made arrangements for an apartment, and that was it. And Mama, too . . . Where was she agreeing to go? Of late, I'd heard them whispering back and forth all the time at night. It seems she wasn't agreeing to it. But she wanted to learn how to be a seamstress, and in town they had classes . . . He wore her down with those classes. She agreed. Let's give it a try, he says. It'll be okay, he says, we won't sell anything. The extra stuff that we don't need we'll push off on our relatives for storage and we'll go and give it a try.

And Papka was terribly anxious to get hired on in some factory or work-shop—he wanted to become a worker there and that was that. So here we are, riding to town.

. . . We arrived in town after dark. I couldn't even see it. By some mira-cle, Papka found his way. We turned down dark side streets, our wheels rumbled along the cobblestone streets . . . A couple of times he just asked people we met for directions, and when these people explained something to him, it sounded like gibberish. We had to keep going till the end of Osoaviakhimovskaya Street, then turn toward Kazarmy, then you'll come to Degtyarny . . . Papka came back over to us and said that everything was all right—we were going the right way. Talya, Mama, and I quieted down. Papka was the only one who tried to act brave, he spoke loudly . . . Proba-bly it was to cheer us up.

Large buildings behind fences flanked the dark streets and alleys. The windows were brightly lit.

"Good Lord, when will we finally get there?" Mama couldn't hold back. This very thing amazed me, too. We seemed to have passed through five villages the size of ours just while we were making our way through all these streets. That's the city for you!

"Soon, soon!" Papka tried to be cheerful. "We'll turn down one more street, then down an alley and we'll be home."

Home! . . . Papka sure is a brave man. I respect him. But all the same, I can't accept this undertaking of his with the city. It's frightening here, ev-erything is alien, you could easily get lost.

We didn't get lost. We drove up to a large building, Papka stopped the horse.

"We're here. I'll tell 'em that we're here . . ."

"Don't be long in there," Mama orders.

"I won't be! I'll just tell 'em . . ."

It's dark in the alleyway. I can sense that Mama's scared, and I also start getting scared. Only Talya isn't the slightest bit fazed.

"Mom, are we gonna live here?"

"Yes, daughter . . . We're stuck now!"

"Talk him into goin' back home," I advise.

"It's too late now . . . What a fool I am, a fool!"

As ill luck would have it, Papka's gone for a long time. There's a light on in the house, but the fence is high and it's impossible to make out anything in the windows.

Finally, Papka appeared . . . There was some muzhik with him.

"Hello," the muzhik says, not very cordially. "Drive on in, I'll show you where you can put the wagon. Do you have a lot of stuff?"

"How could we! Some clothes and beddin'."

"Well, drive on in."

While they are lugging in our stuff, Talya and I sit on a trunk in the corner of a large, brightly lit room. A lanky boy came into the room . . . with a toy airplane. I became rooted to the trunk.

"Wanna hold it?" the boy asked.

The plane was light, like a bit of fluff, with delicate, sweeping wings and a propeller in front . . . Talya also reached for the airplane, but the lanky boy wouldn't give it to her.

"You'll break it."

Talya began whining and kept reaching for the airplane—she also wanted to hold it. The lanky boy was implacable. And suddenly there awoke in me a monstrous urge to brownnose, so I said sternly:

"Well, whatcha want! You'll break it and then what?!" I wanted to hold the airplane one more time, and for the lanky boy to give it to me, it was necessary that Talya didn't reach for it and snatch it away unexpectedly.

That's when the grownups came in. The father of the lanky body said:

"Go to bed, Slavka. Don't get underfoot."

When we were left by ourselves, I suddenly discovered that the light came from the ceiling! Dangling from the ceiling on a cord was a glass light bulb, resembling a cucumber, and inside the light bulb was a bright spider web. I even cried out:

"Look at that!"

"What about it? It's electricity. Vanka, you're gonna have to stop yellin' so much now—you're not at home."

At that, Mama intervened.

"So, the boy can't even say a word, now?"

"Sure, he can say however much he wants—just quietly. What's with all the shoutin'?"

They talked a bit more in that vein—they conversed that way fairly often.

"Look where you've gotten us—aren't you satisfied yet?"

"Sure, let's say at every step: 'Lookee! Look at that!' People'll start laughin' at us."

"Well, don't hush the boy every time!"

"Just you wait and see, he's gonna hang on you like a millstone if you're gonna be that way . . ."

How's that, I'd like to know? His own father had beat him half to death during haymaking once because, as a little boy, he had been too scared to take the hobbles off of a mischievous mare—it liked to kick with its hind legs . . . All Papka had to do was remember it, and he'd get all indignant. Back then his mother—our step-grandmother—had had a hard time reviving him.

So, don't worry, I'm not going to be a millstone around anybody's neck, you can rest easy there.

We went to bed.

I couldn't get to sleep for a long time. I was all anxious inside. On the other side of the wall, our landlord snored loudly and made a whistling sound; wires hummed strangely outside; groups of young guys and girls walked down the street and talked and laughed loudly. For some reason I remembered how our grandfather, when he drinks a lot of sweet, home-brewed beer, always asks me:

"Vanka, what's the longest word in the world?"

I know which one he means, but in order to hear him say it once more, I pretend not to:

"I don't know, Grandpa."

"A-ah! . . ." And he begins: "Intre . . . internatzal . . ." And only then does he manage to get his tongue around it: "In-ter-na-ti-o-nal!"

We roll with laughter—that is, Mama, Talya, and I.

"There you go! Think it's funny?" Grandfather gets offended. "Well, go right ahead and laugh."

I guess I could write that on that first night I dreamed about large buildings, the airplane, and the light bulb . . . I guess I could write that, but I don't remember whether I dreamed at all. Maybe I did.

In the morning I woke up because right under our window the owner of the apartment was loudly blowing his nose and muttering:

"Damnation! . . . Blew my nose so hard I'm seein' stars."

Mama and Papka weren't there. Talya was sleeping. I began wondering what life was going to be like now. I won't have any pals—the boys here are hooligans, or so they say, and what's more, they really give a hard time to a kid on his own. There's no river, either. There *is* a river, Papka said, but it'll be a long ways away from us. The woods, he says, are nearby, that's where we're going to graze our cow, he says. But the woods aren't ours, and there aren't any islands—there's just a pine forest, and I was kind of scared of it. And you know what? There's only one kind of mushroom in that pine forest.

Then suddenly people began running around and shouting in the landlord's side of the apartment. From their shouting I figured out that Slavka had got a pea stuck in his ear. The whole family went rushing off to the hospital. I got up and went into their room—to see what city stoves are like. Folks said that they were marvelous contraptions. I opened the door . . . yet it wasn't the stove that my eyes fell upon, but a nice white roll on the table. Later on, I found out that they're called "saikas." Nobody was in the room. I went up to the table, took the saika, and went back to Talya. She had just woken up.

"Oh!" she said. "Give it to me."

"The whole thing?"

"No. Measure it with a thread and cut it in half. Did Mama buy it?"

"They gave it to me. Slavka did."

We broke the saika into pieces and started eating, sitting on the bed. I'd never eaten such delicious bread before. It was slightly salty and so incredibly fragrant and soft that it was even too bad we had to eat it. I kept an eye on how much was left. We didn't hear the door open . . . What we did hear was:

"Up to no good already, huh?" Slavka's mother was looking at us from the doorway. Something snapped inside me. "Why'd you take the saika?"

And—I swear to God, I'm not lying—I said:

"I thought it was somebody else's."

"Somebody else's . . . It's not nice to do that. That's called stealing. I'm going to tell your father and mother."

I was at my wit's end. Suddenly, I asked:

"Did they get the pea out?"

"What a child!" The woman was amazed. "Already learned how to stall for time."

And she left.

It all became too much for me.

"Wanna go home?" I suggested to Talya.

"In a minute, only let's finish eatin' first," she quickly agreed. She firmly remembered Mama's order: don't eat and walk at the same time. Instead, sit down, eat up what you've got, then you can walk or run around.

I saw from the window that Slavka's mother had gone into a shed, so I hurried Talya up. She was about to turn stubborn on me, but she went anyway.

I remembered that we had approached the gate from the left, so if you face it, it meant we had to go to the right now. So we set off to the right. We came to an intersection . . . I didn't know where to go from there. We asked some man:

"How can we get to the Ch—— Tract?"

"Why?" the man asked.

"Our mama told us to go there. She's waitin' for us there." Before learning anything else that would make this life considerably easier, I had long since learned how to lie. And when I lied and people didn't believe me, I almost wept out of wounded pride. The man looked closely at me, then at Talya . . . And he pointed out the way:

"Go straight till the intersection, then the street turns to the left. Go along it and at the spot where you come to a great big water tower, ask somebody else."

A nice woman pointed out the way from the water tower. She even went a little ways with us.

Whether it was a long or a short walk, we finally came out on the

Ch——Tract. We sat down on a little hill there and waited for somebody to come along who could take us back to the village. It was there on the little hill that Mama and Papka found us—by then, it was nearly evening. Talya was crying—she was hungry—and despair had gradually taken hold of me, too . . .

"Talenka! . . . My little girl!"

I thought I would really get it. But they didn't do anything.

Soon the war began. We returned to the village. Papka was called up for service.

In 1942 he was killed.

Gogol and Raika

During the war, from the very beginning, two hardships plagued us kids more than anything else: hunger and cold. They would both bear down on us just as soon as our endless Siberian winter with its blizzards and vicious cold set in. During the summer it was a different story. In the summer I'd go and put out three or four seines for the night and, you know what, come morning there'd be a couple of burbots in them. (To this day your heart shudders when you remember the live, quivering tug of the tow rope in your hands and the way it slaps against the water when it begins to "pull.") Or I'd go and find magpie eggs, cook them up in the embers of the fire, and I'd be full. There was so much for the taking! If you're clever with your hands and have a noggin on your shoulders you can feed yourself and have something left over to bring home. But the winter! . . . May he be thrice accursed, Old Man Winter! How he howls and howls over the rooftops and bangs around in the woodpiles! No matter how many rags you stuff in the crack under the door, no matter how hard you try to keep the heat from escaping out the windows, by evening all the warmth that had been in the izba in the morning—every bit of it—is blown out through the cracks. Or it gets so bitter cold that the entry room frosts over and it seems that any minute now, if it gets just a little bit colder, the glass window panes will crack. If you run out into the yard for a minute, out to the cattle pen, it feels just like you've been tossed buck naked into a snowdrift and your mouth's been sealed by some icy palm. But the cow's out in the pen . . . and the really sad thing is that there's no hay to spare and in such bitter cold she needs to have something to chew on constantly, but where can you get more hay when it looks like winter will never end? So you do your little deed and you speed inside like a shot—to get away from the burning cold and because you feel this unbearable pain for the cow. If only you could keep from seeing her, with her head drooping, all covered with hoarfrost and looking at you with her sad eyes. And you feel no peace inside: here—

poor and badly off though you may be—you can at least warm up, but she has to stand out there . . . And we can only give her one armload of hay to last her through the night, that's all. And so you keep picturing those endlessly sad cow's eyes—they look straight into your soul. You see, she provides for us. In the spring she'll produce milk and a calf. And when our cow Raika is on the verge of calving, what a time of joyous fussing it is! Spring is here, it's already getting warm out and soon right here, God willing, a little baby calf will be skidding along the floor on its tender little hooves. (Last year, we turned a baby calf over to the kolkhoz. In return, we got flour, lots of crushed sunflower-seed cakes left over from making oil, and a pot of honey. Of course, we had to wait a long time for such a holiday—summer, winter, and then summer again—but that made it all the more precious, the holiday, that is. And there was something to look forward to.) On such days in spring, such a hullabaloo goes on in our izba that your soul gets all wound up from the exultant feeling of having important work to do. Time and again I run out to look at Raika and feel her warm belly, although this doesn't tell me a darn thing. Talya also runs along with me, she also touches Raika's belly . . . Raika, turning her head, looks at us with her smoke-colored, damp eyes, her tender eyes—she's also waiting for the calf to come along. She probably understands our fussing and anxiety.

"Soon, Vanya?"

"She'll probably have it tonight."

All night long our light is on. Mama goes over to Raika and also touches her belly . . . She comes back and says:

"It's real close . . . You can feel its legs movin' and movin' around, but nothin' else seems to be happenin'. Could she be in trouble? Mother, Queen of Heaven, don't let us starve. What would we do then?"

It is an anxious, terrible night.

But early in the morning our grandfather looks at Raika and tells us all:

"Whatcha goin' crazy for? It won't happen till nightfall . . . You're a-scarin' the children, silly fool!" That is meant for Mama because by morning Talya and I have tear-stained faces. How much happiness our grandfather brought us!

But for now—it's still winter. I had marked a row of lines on the wall to show how many days are left till March. Each evening I cross out one, but there are still so many left!

Still, I did have one joy—a unique, great joy—even in the winter. During the long evenings I read books to Mama and Talya from my berth on the stove.

There's a whole story behind me and books. I somehow learned to read before going to school. My Uncle Pavel taught me. (He himself was wild about reading and even tried to compose some poems, and he says that when he was in the war, some of his verses were published in a frontline newspaper. He probably isn't telling the truth, he likes to brag a little. When I recently came across a notebook of his verses recently, they struck me as being absolute nonsense.) In short, as soon as I'd already kind of gotten the hang of it at school and begun to read pretty well, I got carried away with books. I read whatever the librarian gave me, indiscriminately, one book right after another. She was surprised and didn't believe me.

"You've already finished it?"

"Yes, I have."

"That's not true. If you're going to check out books, little boy, you need to read them all the way to the end. Take it back and finish it."

What could I do? I took the book, waited around for a couple of days, and went back. Then I got good at stealing books from the school bookcase. It stood in the hall, the bookcase did, and during the summer, when the school was being repaired, it was easy to slip into the hall later on in the evening. Once inside, it was even easier. The bookcase was a folding one with a ringlet on the edge of each of the two folding halves, and a padlock . . . If you opened up the folding halves slightly, the crack was wide enough for you to stick a hand in and you could pick any book you wanted. I'm ashamed to admit it, but I had a ball doing this. Later on, I also pinched some other little things, snuck into other folks' gardens, but never did I experience such burning passion as I did with those books.

Mama liked the fact that I read a lot. But then she found out that I was doing really poorly in school. The teacher herself came to our house and told Mama. Right then and there the teacher and Mama fixed upon the reason for my lagging behind so terribly in my studies—it was all because of those books. (After all, I was a bright enough boy.) And also some fool of a woman told Mama that boys shouldn't read so much, that it sometimes happens that they read themselves silly. Mama started to fight mercilessly against my books. They took away my library privileges, and my pals were forbidden to give me books checked out in their names. Of course, they gave them to me anyway. But Mama kept an eye on me at home. She took away all my books and gave me a thrashing . . . Little by little, I began taking books down from the attic, the ones I'd stolen from the school bookcase earlier on. (By that time they'd put an end to that stunt of mine. The loss was discovered, and the lock was redone. The carpenters were accused of stealing the books. Why, they were asked, were they taking and tearing up books that the school needed so badly, just to make their home-rolled cigarettes? There are old newspapers for that. The carpenters swore they hadn't the slightest idea where the books had gone—they hadn't taken them.) I would take books down from the attic and reread what I'd read before. Here's how I did it: I'd put a book inside the cover of my math book and read it as calmly as you pleased. Mama would see me with my math book in my hands and would leave me alone and, what's more, was probably happy that I'd sat down at last to do my homework. Had she happened to think about it a minute or two, she'd have realized that nobody reads a math book for that long or with such ecstacy, in which case I'd have gotten another whipping.

Fortunately for me, a young teacher from among the Leningrad evacuees[1] (I'm ashamed to say I've forgotten her name by now) learned about my trouble with books. She came to our house to see us and began discussing it with Mama and me. (Our women—all the inhabitants of the village—really respected those Leningrad evacuees.) The Leningrad teacher had found out how I went about my reading and explained that this really was doing me harm. The main thing was that all my reading wasn't bringing me any benefit. Out of all the heaps of books I'd read, I hardly remembered a thing. All I was doing was killing time at it and falling behind in school. However, she convinced Mama that I should be reading, but reading sensibly. She said she'd help us. She'd compose a list and I would start borrowing books at the library from this list. (Really, the devil only knows what I had been reading: even the works of the academician Lysenko—from the stolen books. I also adored brochures. I liked the fact that they were so slender and neat. I'd zip through one in a single sitting and put it aside.)

From that time on I began reading good books. Less often, it's true, but it was always a real holiday. And what's more, Mama—and after her, Talya—also showed an interest in books. In the evening we three would climb up onto the spacious stove and take a lamp with us. And I'd start . . . Good Lord, what a burning delight I experienced! As if I'd lived a long, long life, like an old man, and I'd sat down to tell various stories to my relatives, who were extremely interested, grateful people. It was as if I wasn't holding a book close to the lamp, but rather that I knew all of it myself. When Mama would say in surprise, "Oh, good heavens! You don't say! The things that happen in the world!" I'd almost groan with happiness and I'd say hastily and with a touch of exasperation: "Just you wait and see, just listen what happens next!"

"What happens next, Vanya?" would come flying out of snub-nosed Talya's mouth. I'd shush her, call her stupid, and then Mama'd say that I shouldn't do that.

"Well, how come she keeps askin'?"

"Well, when we don't understand, we ask. Now don't you get cross, just tell us—you're the one who knows. Your teacher doesn't call *you* stupid, does she?"

"Can't she figure out that I don't know what's gonna happen next myself?"

"She's still little. Keep readin'."

Oh what holidays they were! (I keep exclaiming here "Happiness, Joy! Holidays!" But it's true—it was like that. Maybe that's because it was childhood. But also, I guess now, that in the difficult, bitter times of our lives we experience joy—be it a small joy or a rare joy—more keenly, more purely.) These were the holidays that I have cherished all my life afterward, the holidays that themselves grow in endearment with the years. There have been no better holidays since.

Here's the only thing that clouded our holidays: Mama—and right after her, Talya—would fall asleep too soon. Here you've just gotten into it, you've just settled down to read all night, and lo and behold, Mama's already sneaking a yawn. And right after her, her carbon copy also covers her mouth with a tiny palm—she's imitating Mama. I look at them almost in tears.

"Go ahead, keep readin'! What, is yawnin' not allowed?"

"But you're just gonna fall right to sleep!"

"No, we won't. Just keep readin'."

But I know they'll fall asleep. I read further . . . Mama fights to stay awake, her eyes keep closing, she's weakening. Darn! . . . In just a couple of minutes my listeners will be sleeping soundly. I sit there bitterly wounded . . . It never crossed my mind, fool that I was, that Mama had worn herself out from working all day, that she'd gotten chilled to the bone. And this little one doesn't care a hill of beans about my books. She just wants to be like Mama, that's all. I try to read by myself—it's not the same. And I'm also beginning to nod off . . . And there was one other thing that disturbed our holidays: thinking about Raika. That she'd soon eat up that armful of hay and stand there, freezing till morning. Just the thought of it made me feel cold and sad and ashamed to be perched up on the warm bricks of that stove. And these thoughts were painful and troubling for Mama, too, and she'd sigh from time to time while I read.

I know what she's sighing about. But what can we do, what can we do? Where can you get more hay?

On one such evening we were reading "Viy." I read, dying of fright myself.

"'He looked at her wild with fright and rubbed his eyes. But, indeed, she was no longer lying, but sitting up in her coffin. He looked away and once again in horror directed his gaze back at the coffin. She stood up . . . and started walking around the church with her eyes closed, continually stretching out her arms, as if wishing to catch hold of someone.

"'She was coming straight toward him . . .'"

Mama was the first to give in.

"That's enough, Sonny, don't read any more. We'll finish it tomorrow."

"Come on, Mom . . ."

"No, don't, darn them . . . Now tomorrow we'll invite Grandfather over to spend the night and you can read the whole thing to us. What's it called?"

"Gogol. But there's all sorts of different ones here. This one's 'Viy.'"

"Good heavens . . . Don't read any more."

We lay there for a long time with the light on. Talya was already sleeping, but Mama and I couldn't fall asleep. To be quite honest, I couldn't have read any further. Now that's a book for you! My teacher had marked on the table of contents which ones to read in the volume, but she hadn't marked this one. But for some reason (maybe because it was forbidden fruit?) I started with none other than "Viy." And there you have it: right off the bat you've got incomprehensible, soul-clutching, thrilling horror. You can't tear yourself away from it, but it's terrifying. If only grandfather wouldn't be sick tomorrow, if only he'd come, smoke, lie on a bench covered with his sheepskin coat (he couldn't sleep in a bed under a blanket), if only he . . . We'd . . . I'd begin reading that "Viy" again and read all the way to the end.

"Don't you be afraid, Sonny, go to sleep. A book is just a book. It's all made up. Who is this Viy?"

"He's the chief devil. The other day in school I snuck a peek at the end."

"Now there aren't such things as Viys! They make 'em up, those darned people do—and scare kids. I've never heard of any Viy. Or why wouldn't our old folks have known about 'em?"

"Well, 'cause it was a long time ago! Maybe he croaked a long time ago."

"All the same, the old folks know about everythin'. They heard about things from their fathers, their grandfathers . . . Does your grandfather tell you all sorts of stories? He does. And so will you to your kids, and later on, maybe to your grandkids . . ."

Such an extraordinary thought makes me laugh. Mama also laughs.

"Here's what we're gonna do," she says, "you two'll be by yourselves for a little bit and I'll go and gather up some hay. A little while back, when we were haulin' hay, I dropped about a bale in the street by old Sosnina's house. She gets up early—she'll see it and pick it up. And that'd be a shame—it was a good-sized bale. Will you be all right if you stay with her a bit by yourself?"

"'Course I will."

"You stay with her. I'll be back real soon. Don't put out the light. And don't get down off the stove."

Mama quickly got ready to go, told me not to be afraid, and left. I began thinking about how I once again hadn't made good on my debt (seventeen babki[2]) to Kolka Bystrov—so as not to think about Viy. This was not a cheery thought either (for a week now I hadn't been able to give them to him); still, it was better thinking about that than . . . But my thoughts return stubbornly to Viy. I get this invincible desire to look down into a dark corner. In despair, I start fighting this desire, I turn away toward Talya, I encourage myself with bits of conventional wisdom: that while you're on the stove, you have nothing to fear from any evil spirit, they can't climb up on the stove, it's not within their powers—they can call out as much as they want, rage at you, scare you from their hiding places down below, but they can't climb up on the stove, that's been verified. They hover around nearby until the first cock's crow and then disappear. I lie there and try to think cheerfully about this. But it's as if somebody's pulling your hair—the back of your head twists from the desire to look down into the corner. I don't have the strength to fight it. I'm already thinking: well, I'll take a quick look! Let them try climbing up on the stove! Just let them try . . . And at that moment, I hear hurried steps in the entry room. I freeze in horror . . . Who's there? Mama can't have made it to old Sosnina's . . . Something was already taking hold of the hook at the door . . . I yanked the blanket over my head—just don't let me see it . . . Good Lord! . . . I'll study hard, obey Mama . . . The door opened and I hear Mama's voice, a little tense from walking quickly.

"Are you asleep, Sonny?"

The hazy, persistent chill of terror drained from my heart.

"Is it you, Mom? How come you're back so soon?"

"Well, I thought how come I went all by myself? I won't be able to carry it home all by myself—it's a good-sized bale of hay . . . Let's go and we'll take some rope. We'll tie up two bundles and carry 'em home. It'd be a pity to leave 'em. Is Talya asleep?"

I'm off the stove in a flash.

"Yep. I'll be ready in a sec. She's sleepin' like a log."

And so we walk along the dark street, keeping close together . . . We don't talk. We hurry. I'm counting how many houses remain before we get to old Sosnina's. Five. There's the little street. Here are four izbas and the long garden of the old woman herself.

"The hay's good! It's real fluffy . . . It'd be a shame to leave it. When we drove by there a while ago there wasn't anybody in the street, and so I tossed some off my load. What's it to them, the kolkhoz workers? They've got more than enough to last 'em till spring . . ."

"If it's a good bunch of hay it'll be enough for three or so feedin's."

"There's enough for four there. Back when they were puttin' the hay on the wagon, I thought maybe we'd be late gettin' to the village—it'd be gettin' dark, we'd drive around a corner and I'd toss it off. And so I put a bi-ig old bale on top."

"And what if somebody'd come along?"

"Well, then . . . I'd have carted it off to the work brigade. There'd be nothin' else to do."

"Gosh, now she'll really have somethin' to eat! Real fresh stuff . . . It'll warm her right up. Can we give her some right away?"

"'Course! Didn't cost us a thing . . ."

Well, there it was, the old woman's izba. Between the izba and the banya there's this secluded spot. During the summer, the nettles there grow as tall as a man, and in the winter the dead stalks stick out of the snow and turn black. In the evening there's no way you could notice any hay around there, and not just because it was nighttime.

We quickly bind up two large bundles . . . The hay is fragrant, it rustles in our arms and pricks us. I can just picture our Raika burying her muzzle into this stuff.

We walk back. And suddenly—as if it were the devil's doing—the Chuyev's dog appears out of nowhere. She'd run up, unseen and unheard, and how she started barking! I jumped, yet didn't drop my bundle. But Mama dropped hers and sat right down on it. As soon as she'd recovered from her fright, we set off. Mama scolds:

"Darned thing! Nearly gave me a heart attack! You okay, Sonny?"

"I'm all right. Made my legs feel weak at first, but I'm fine now."

We keep walking for a while longer.

"Maybe we should run a bit, Sonny? That way this'll get done sooner. Or else Talya'll wake up there . . ."

"Okay."

And so we trot down the street. I think it's funny how the bundle—just like a big, dark hump—bounces around on Mama's back.

Raika mooed upon hearing us . . . I put down my bundle and dropped a big armful of hay with a thud at her feet. Raika shook her head and started munching away at the scrumptious hay.

"Eat up, darlin', eat up," Mama says. "Eat, my dear." And for some reason she burst into tears and right then and there dried them and said: "Well, let's go, Vanya, or else Talyukha in there'll miss us . . . We did it!"

Talya's still asleep! She didn't even move a muscle when we noisily and happily got undressed and climbed up on the stove.

"Howdy, Viy!" I said under my breath and looked down into the far dark corner.

Somehow we made it to spring, but then our Raika was no more . . . Even now I don't have it in me to tell what happened in detail. In our izba a little bowlegged calf tottered about—a little girl calf!—spraying an endless stream onto the straw bedding. We ate potatoes and washed them down with milk.

Of course we didn't have enough hay. But there were now only two weeks left before we could drive the cattle out to graze. If only we could somehow get through these two weeks . . . Mama tried to get somebody to give her a small bundle of hay, but nothing doing! Raika now needed a lot because she was giving milk. And we'd let her out the gate so she could go gleaning along the street. Maybe somewhere a wisp of old hay would poke out of the snow, or she'd come across a spot where loads of hay were transported to the kolkhoz farm and bits would catch in the wattle fences . . . Sometimes a good-sized handful would get caught in the pickets. So we let her go wandering about. But somewhere, apparently, she wandered into somebody else's yard and settled down by their haystack . . . Lots of people still had haystacks: those who had a man in the house, or those who had gotten ahold of a load of hay through the right connections, or those who had bought some, or . . . God only knows how they did it. Late one evening, Raika arrived at our gate with her intestines hanging out of her belly, dragging along after her. She'd been run through with a pitchfork.

So . . . It meant we had to wait for our little calf to grow up. We also called her Raya.

Harvesting

The year is probably 1942. (That would make me thirteen years old.) It's summer, the time of backbreaking work at harvest time. The heat is hellish. And there's absolutely no chance to hide anywhere to get away from the heat. The shirt on your back is scorching hot and when you turn around, it burns you.

Sashka Krechetov and I are reaping. Sashka's older, he's fifteen or sixteen years old, he sits on "the machine"—on the harvester (in these parts we call it the reaper). I ride goose-fashion. Riding goose-fashion is when a troika is harnessed to the harvester, with a pair of horses side by side—one on either side of the shaft (the *vodilo* or *vodilina*)—and the third at the end of a long strap out in front. Usually a boy about my age would ride in its saddle, guiding the pair of draft horses—and, in turn, the machine—precisely along the swath cut through the stubble.

The machine rattles deafeningly, making clanking noises, ringing out, and waving its white-hot, polished blades. (When you look at the harvester from a distance, it seems as if somebody's gotten lost in the tall rye and is motioning you over to him with his hands.) Behind it, golden-gray dust hangs suspended like a curtain in the air over the strip you're harvesting. You ride along and are continually assailed by the dry, hot scent of ripe grain, hay, heated grass, and the last vestiges of dust—for even though the golden curtain from a moment ago has settled, a new one from behind rises up and remains suspended, unmoving in the air.

The heat is bad enough, but we're also just dying for a nap. We'd gotten up when it was barely light, and it's now nearly lunchtime. Again and again I drift off in the saddle, and then the gelding—which isn't trained for this kind of work—turns off into the grain to brush the gadflies off its legs against the stalks of rye. Sashka yells:

"Vanka, I'm gonna clobber you!"

His whip is a long one—he could reach me with it. I cuss quietly and bring my horse back into line . . . But sleep, monstrous, longed-for sleep, again bends my head down to rest against the horse's mane and I don't have the strength to fight it.

"Vanka!" Sashka also cusses. "I'm about to fall off my seat myself! I'm gonna burst a blood vessel in my brain any second now! Hang in there!"

"How 'bout just a five-minute nap?!" I suggest.

"Three more turns—and we're unharnessin' 'em."

Three enormous turns! . . . But the machine rattles and rattles along, and my horse steps evenly and pulls at the reins and snorts, and it feels just as if a buttery pancake has been placed on your head and the hot butter is flowing in streams down your shirt and into your pants . . . The saddle is wet with sweat and everything else has gotten scorching hot and smolders.

"How 'bout it, Sanya?! Or else I'll fall under the reapin' machine, just you wait and see!"

Sashka is also worn out. He's still swaggering a little, singing some songs, then he pulls on the reins.

"Who-oa! Five minutes, Vanka! Or else they'll catch us at it."

Good heavens, I don't need more than that! That's an eternity in itself. I fall off my horse and crawl on all fours as far as I can into the rye so that I won't get run over by the machine in case the horses start up on their own—I still manage to think about that . . . Then the warm, fragrant earth presses itself to my face and nestles up to me. The sound of the harvester still rings in my ears, but it fades away. Overhead, the cast-bronze ears of grain rustle—and that's it. The world of sounds has closed, I depart into a soft, swaying quietness. For some time longer it's as if my whole body is gently rocking, like I'm in the saddle. My blood hums pleasantly, then I'm out of my body swimming somewhere, and I experience a sensation of perfect bliss. It's strange, but I am aware that I'm sleeping—I am consciously, sweetly asleep. The earth carries me swiftly along on her bosom, but I am sleeping, I know that. Never again in all my life have I slept like that—with my whole body, to my heart's content, without measure.

I do not know how long we slept, I just woke up suddenly with a sense of impending danger. In a flash somehow, as if I'd been pushed, I swam up from the depths of nonexistence to the surface . . . Somebody was shouting . . . I jumped up. All the same, we'd been caught in the act. The chairman of the kolkhoz himself, Ivan Alekseich, was running through the stubble after Sashka, but since one of the chairman's legs was wooden, there was no way he could catch up with Sashka and only threatened him with his lash from a distance and swore. Having caught sight of me, the chairman was about to make a dash after me, but I shot out of my spot so fast that he stopped right away.

"Counter-revolutionaries! You'll answer to me! . . . You get back to reapin' this minute!"

"Move away from the reaper and then we will." Clearly, Sashka had come under the chairman's lash before—he was scratching an old scar on his back.

"You get back on that reaper now! Whatcha tryin' to do, get me in trouble with the law?!"

"Move away from the reaper . . ."

The chairman, swearing, headed toward his light carriage, which was standing off to the side.

Once again the harvester began creaking and grinding, once again the sun started baking us, but now our spirits felt so much lighter, we were even merry. We'd snatched a moment or two for a nap.

The chairman stood there a little bit longer, looked at us, and then drove off.

He was a strange man, our chairman Ivan Alekseich was. That leg of his had been like that for a long time on account of a threshing machine. He'd wanted to pack the sheaves more tightly under the drum and his leg got pulled in along with the sheaves. By the time they managed to get the driving belt off the pulley, his leg was all torn to pieces by the teeth of the drum; later on they removed it above the knee. We weren't a bit scared of him, that chairman of ours, though he swore something awful and sometimes managed to get us with his lash. Back then we didn't realize that we young folk were still wet behind the ears—we swore like muzhiks among ourselves and with the chairman, too. He didn't have an easy time with us. As I now understand, he was a good-natured man with great patience and a big conscience. He'd camp out there on the plowing fields with us, he'd fix the rope harnesses himself, cussing a blue streak the whole time. Sometimes he'd forcefully throw down a breast-band that had been mended over and over again, stamp on it with his good leg and weep angrily.

That day the chairman really gave us a good laugh.

We all gathered late in the evening in the house that served as quarters for the work brigade, sat wherever we could find a spot and gulped down some *zatirukha* (tiny pieces of dough—little blobs—boiled in water). Then there was supposed to be a meeting. The chairman had amassed lots of instances of our disgraceful behavior: how somebody else, besides Sashka and me, had slept on the job; how, the night before, somebody had run home for a steam in the banya without permission; how somebody, after having reaped a field, went chasing quail with a whip, thereby losing precious time . . .

While we ate supper, the chairman covered a long table under an over-hang with a red cloth, sat at the table all by himself, and kept glancing sternly in our direction—he was waiting. A tongue-lashing was coming up.

We rinsed out our cups, lit up, and got ready to listen.

"Today, four lazy bums," the chairman began, "were caught sleepin' on the job. They are Sanka Krechetov, Ilyukha Chumazy, Vanka Popov, and Fatherless-Vaska. Do you realize what you're doin'?! And then that bean-pole—Kolka, I'm talkin' about you!—he felt like goin' and havin' a steam in the banya, see!"

(Kolka, Moisei's grandson, caught a louse on my shirt yesterday and tried to get me to run off to the village in the evening with him for a steam in the banya, returning by daybreak. I refused.)

"Felt like steamin' himself, see, the stallion! What a numbskull! You'd spend the whole night runnin' there and back, and durin' the day, you'd be sleepin' on the job!"

"I wasn't sleepin'."

"Oh, I'll give you a nap, all right! I'll give you a nap, you devils! I'll have you stackin' ricks for me at night, too!"

Far away, beyond the forest, the large red sun slowly sinks into the deep blue haze. It's good here on earth, pensive, peaceful. Under the chairman's table, Borzya, our infinitely good-tempered scamp of a dog, lies curled up, sleeping peacefully.

The chairman is simply incapable of flying into a rage on demand, it all comes out sounding wishy-washy—nobody gives a hang. We all sit there nodding off.

"Next, just what kind of a fad have you taken up—whippin' quail?! You buncha brutes . . . First of all, they destroy all sorts of larvae . . . And you're wastin' time, you know, you devils! When you finally catch it and smack it with your whip, just think how much time has slipped away! Next, Lyonka-the-Jap, that sonuvabitch, ran over a stump and broke a blade. What were you gawkin' at?! I'm gonna dock you fifteen days' pay and then maybe you'll start lookin' where you're goin'! Go straight to the blacksmith's, so's tomorrow, just as soon as old Makar wakes up, they rivet that blade back on."

Lyonka-the-Jap is mighty pleased. He'll have a short stay at home. What a lucky runt! Maybe he ran over that stump on purpose? But he's wily—he doesn't let us see how pleased he is. Instead, he just scowls guiltily.

"Next, if I sees somebody else—"

At that point, along came an unexpected guest. On the road, from behind the hillock, the district committee representative's buggy came into sight. We knew his stallion well. He was coming to pay us a visit.

Boy did our chairman leap to his feet then (he was terribly afraid of the representative), and he started banging his fist on the table and shouting.

"For some time now, I've been noticin' among you counter . . . counter . . ."

But then the chairman stepped on Borzya's tail with his peg leg. Borzya let out an otherworldly howl. The chairman had to shout over the dog:

"For some time now I've been noticin' counter-revolutionary elements among you!"

The dog is howling, still underfoot beneath the table. For some reason the chairman can't move his leg off of him, either because he's agitated or . . . God only knows. Good-tempered Borzya starts biting the peg leg. We're writhing with laughter. The scene is enough to kill you. (Later on, when we all recalled the incident, Lyonka-the-Jap admitted that he'd suddenly had an accident—he'd pissed in his pants, he was laughing so hard.)

The representative drove up. He looks at us and can't understand anything. The chairman quickly walks over to meet him. A berserk Borzya flies out from under the table with a yelp and rushes off . . . And he goes straight at the legs of the district committee's stallion. The beautiful stallion snorts wildly and rears, almost slipping out of its collar. The representative jumps out of his buggy; the chairman was about to hop after Borzya on his peg leg, but he returned and began calming down the stallion.

We were all rolling on the ground with laughter. We were also kind of afraid of the representative, but there was nothing we could do with ourselves now—we were dying of laughter.

"What's this all about?!" the representative asked sternly.

"Um . . . it's our meetin'—about results," Ivan Alekseich explained. "We had a little comedy with the dog . . ." And he shouted at us: "Tomorrow you'd better clear that flea-bitten mutt outta here!"

"I can see it's a comedy and not a meeting. Maybe it's a little early to be enjoying yourselves?!" the representative asked us. "Maybe you should be crying, instead?!"

We gradually quieted down. Now, it seems, we're going to get a real tongue-lashing. But for some reason the representative cancelled the meeting. In an unexpectedly kind voice he said:

"Fine—you've worked and laughed. Now go get some sleep."

We slept on bunk beds in the building. That evening we were unable to calm down for a long time. We kept remembering Borzya and Ivan Alekseich and laughed loudly into our pillows. Ivan Alekseich had a chat by the campfire with the representative. A couple of times he came over to us and whispered angrily:

"Are you gonna sleep or not? There'll be no wakin' you up again tomorrow! Lazy bums. You'd think you'd be a little ashamed . . ."

Then the representative left.

One after another we drift off to sleep . . .

When I—later than the others, probably last of all—step out to take a leak, the moon is already shining and somewhere nearby a night bird cries out.

The chairman is sitting by the campfire, quietly clinking his spoon against his aluminum cup—he's gulping down some *zatirukha*. His prosthesis has been unfastened, it's lying next to him . . . His thin stump of a leg shows up white against the grass somewhat unnaturally. Ivan Alekseich often bends over and blows on it—apparently he'd worked so hard that day that it had started hurting, but now his hot stump could finally rest.

All around it's warm and clear. Way, way up high somebody has nailed a light blue canvas to the sky with golden nails, and a pure, bluish white, gentle light shines—pours—through it in a never-ending stream.

And some night bird keeps crying out in the marsh. Could it be calling someone?

The Ox

I worked for a while on a tobacco plantation, or *tabachok,* as we called it around here. I watered the tobacco plants.

Water had to be hauled from the marsh.

As soon as the sun was just beginning to rise, we would hitch water carriers onto the oxen and all day long we'd haul water.

My ox was unusually stubborn and lazy. Since my harness was made of rope, it would break from time to time. So there you are going up a slope, the ox will give it all he's got—and the collar snaps in half. But the ox walks on. And I'm left standing there in the middle of the road with the water barrel. I catch up with the ox, turn him around somehow or other, tie the collar back together, harness him, and we just barely make it up the slope. On several occasions he'd dump me and the barrel over. He'd be walking and walking along the road and then for some reason he'd feel like veering off to one side. He'd turn and the barrel would go awry. I'd beat him with whatever I could get my hands on. I'd beat him and weep angrily. The other boys were able to put in enough work in one day to get paid for a day and a half while I could barely squeak out a day's pay with an ox like that. I'd beat him and he'd stand there calm as can be, gazing at me with his big, stupid eyes. We hated each other.

One time—after lunch—when it was time to hitch up the oxen, my ox turned up missing. The foreman Petrunka Yarikov—a cross-eyed, slightly built muzhik, yelled at me:

"Where the heck could yours have gotten to, the lousy friggin' piece of cowhide?! Vanished into thin air, or what?"

I scoured every out-of-the-way corner and secluded spot—the ox was nowhere to be found. Well, I thought, just let me find you, you snake in the grass, I'll show you a thing or two.

I found him in the millet—he was lying there panting away in the shade. I took a running start and gave it to him right smack in the snout with my boot. How he bellowed, how he jumped, and how he gave it to me right in the rear! I flew nearly three meters and thought I'd met my end. But he just spread his legs wide, lowered his head, and looked at me. I looked back at him . . . It seemed to me that we looked at each other like that for a long time. I was afraid to move a muscle. I was thinking it was like a standoff with a dog. If you get up, he'll rush you again. Then I began slowly getting up anyway . . . The ox just stood there. He was watching me. I got all the way up and backed away from him. I somehow managed to hobble back to the work brigade. My rear end felt like it was on fire . . . It's a good thing he didn't get me with a horn as well (he had real wide ones, but he'd butted me with his head instead)—I'd have been stuck on his head like a sheath of grain on a pitchfork.

The foreman was furious with the ox. He snatched an iron kingpin out of a cart and ran off to the millet field. Five minutes later, we see our foreman running like hell with the ox on his heels. The foreman is running and yelling:

"Shoot him! Shoot, whatcha standin' there for?! He's gonna rip me to bits!"

In his fright, he'd forgotten that nobody had a gun—they were all taken away from us once the war began.

At the sight of the enraged ox, the boys and women scattered in all directions. I was lying on my stomach next to an izba. The ox thundered on by me, not paying me any attention. It was obvious that Petrunka had nailed him real hard with the iron kingpin. The ox was so close to me as he ran by that the ground shook. My heart sank to my boots.

Petrunka ran first one way, then another, but the ox kept on his heels, chasing him around the yard. He chased him into a corner. Petrunka flew up the wattle fence like a bird—and made it to the other side. The ox, without stopping, without even pausing, jabbed his horns into the fence as hard as he could, tore it up pickets and all, carried it a few paces and tossed it aside. Only then did he stop. Somebody threw a noose around his neck, pulled it tight, wore him down, then threaded the rope through a ring, and tied him to a post.

In keeping with a long-standing tradition (strange as it may be, it was kept even during the war), after the tobacco is harvested, dried, and transported to the tobacco factory in town, the work brigade has a party. They'd knock off some cow and cook it—roast it . . . They'd bring in home-distilled vodka from the village—and the party would be under way.

This time they butchered my ox. Three muzhiks took him and led him onto an open patch of grass—not far from the izba. The ox followed them submissively. But they were carrying a sledge hammer, knives, and a strip of clean, unbleached linen . . . I ran away from the work brigade so as not to hear him bellow. I heard anyway—quietly, indistinctly, briefly, just as if he'd said: "Oh!" A bitter lump rose in my throat. I dug my hands into the grass, clenched my teeth, and screwed up my face. I kept seeing his eyes . . . At the moment when he'd stood there, legs spread wide, and looked at me, at where I'd been thrown to the ground—he'd spared me then, spared me.

I didn't eat any of the meat—I couldn't. And I was mad at myself for not being able to eat my fill, as I should have—you don't get eats like that too often.

The Airplane

We four boys—Shuya, Zharyonok, Lyonka, and I—are walking uphill carrying our little trunks. We are enrolling in the Automotive Tech School. In three and a half years we'll be service technicians—mechanics who specialize in the maintenance and operation of motor vehicles. The school is in town, or to be more precise, it's about seven kilometers outside town in a former monastery. To get there you have to walk along the steep right bank of our wide river. This is my second trip to town. My soul is aching a little bit—I'm a little anxious and want to go home. Still, you do have to make your way in the world. Back then I didn't know that I was leaving my native village for good. That is, I would still come back later on, but just to catch my breath . . . I couldn't know all that yet!

The town boys didn't like us country boys; they laughed at us and held us in contempt. They called us "stags" and "devils" (if anybody's a devil, then I'd have to say they fit the bill better). To this very day, I don't know what they meant by "stag"[3] and I'm just too lazy to find out. It probably has something to do with the "devil" who has horns. At fourteen it hurts to have to deal with contempt, especially when you know—when you can already feel—that you've got a little strength inside. An irresistible desire for revenge boils up within you. Later on, once we'd begun to feel at home, we didn't let anybody treat us bad. I remember Shuya—a real bruiser of a guy, easily ruffled, full of vim and vigor—landing one on some gangly city punk's face and the guy flying back just like a bird, only not chirping. And then there was Zharyonok and the frightening moment when he had to decide whether to take the plunge—and did. He went for his knife . . . The guy who confronted him and who also had a knife was really surprised. And that very thing—the fact that he was only surprised—was enough for me to rush him with my bare fists. You had to defend yourself—so we did. Sometimes we did it any old which way—foolhardily, but other times we did it with striking inventiveness.

But that was all later on. For the time being, we were walking along carrying our trunks uphill. And walking along with us—traveling light—were the boys from town. They were also going there to enroll. It was our trunks that really got under their skin.

"Whatcha got there, Vanya? A hunk of 'good ol' fatback' and a jar of 'that there honey'?"

"If you're stingy about it, you devils, we'll shake it outta you!"

"So where'd you hide your money? Lousy kulaks! In your eye with a stinkin' cow pie!"

Where did this malice come from? This was so premeditated and hurtful for fourteen year olds. Didn't they know that there was hunger in the countryside? In the city, at least, they had some kind of ration cards, they were looked after, but out there in the country there's nothing—you're on your own. We kept quiet, amazed and depressed by such open hostility. I'd have liked to pitch it down the hill, that damn trunk, in which there was neither "that there honey" nor "good ol' fatback," and which now burned shamefully in my hand.

But then, there on the hill, just as we reached the top, we saw . . . nothing less than an airplane, resting on a level, open spot. And so close! There was an airfield there. And it had appeared so unexpectedly, this neat airplane had, and it was so close and nobody was around, that you could walk right up and touch it, if you wanted to. In the past—on rare occasions— we'd seen an airplane or two up in the sky. When one flew over the village, people would pour out of all the homes and make a fuss. "Where?! Where is it?" Good God, what a sight! I let out a gasp. Hell, we all flipped. Even the city boys. After all, it's not like they saw airplanes every day, now, is it? But soon they covered up their excitement, the fakers.

"It's a crop-duster, the bitch."

"Just sittin' there . . . Must be outta fuel."

And they walked on, without looking at the airplane any longer.

We followed them and also tried not to look at the airplane. We couldn't show them that we really were just a bunch of absolute backwoods hicks. And yet, nothing would have happened at all if we'd just stood there for a little bit and looked at it. But we walked along without looking back. When I couldn't hold out any longer and looked back anyway, one of the guys tugged hard on my sleeve.

Later I dreamed about it, about that airplane. Many times afterward I had to walk that hill right past the airfield, but the airplane was never there—it was flying. And now I can see it in my mind's eye—big, light, and beautiful . . . A beautiful two-winged creature from a distant, distant fairy tale.

The Letter

At the age of fifteen, I wrote my first letter to a sweetheart. It wasn't the kind of letter you'd normally write to your sweetheart. While I was writing it, my head was spinning, and I felt like I was burning up, but I wrote it anyway.

Here's how I fell in love.

She was a newcomer to the village—that struck my fancy. For some reason that always struck me. Before and after her, newly arrived girls made me all nervous, and I'd do all kinds of stunts in order to attract their attention. For me, each time it was as if they'd stepped right off the pages of a book and I would momentarily stop being myself: I affected indifference, I went overboard in making a show of my bravery. I couldn't care less what people thought of me. But I was afraid to approach them. When I was all by myself I was tormented by shame; it seemed that all the same they'd noticed that I was just showing off. I always noticed it myself when people were faking and even as an onlooker I'd be embarrassed for them. But just as soon as a new girl would appear, I couldn't help myself—I showed off.

This time I really got worked up. Right away I fell in love with everything about this girl: her eyes, her braids, the way she walked . . . I liked the fact that she was quiet, that she was a student at the village school (I was no longer a student there), that she was a Komsomol member . . . And when a guy at their school tried to poison himself because of her (later on, folks said that he was just trying to scare her a little), I completely lost my head.

I don't remember now how it came about that I started walking her home from the club.

I remember it was spring . . . I didn't even show off, I didn't say any-thing. My heart was bouncing around in my chest, like a potato in boiling water. I couldn't believe that I was walking with Maria (that was her name—Maria, and I also liked that terribly). I was amazed at my courage and afraid that she'd change her mind and say, "You don't need to walk me home," and walk off by herself . . . And I was miserable—good heavens, was I ever miserable—that I wasn't able to say anything. I was as quiet as the grave. I wasn't able to squeeze a single word out of myself. But, you know, I could tell a fib when the need arose, and . . .

At parting, I just clasped her tightly to my chest and beat a hasty retreat home—I flew home as if I had wings. Dammit, I thought. Try and get me now! I felt so strong that night, so kind—I loved everybody . . . And my-self, too. When you love somebody, you love yourself at the same time.

Then, for about three days I didn't see Maria, she didn't go to the club. That's all right, I thought. I'll build up my courage in the meantime. I managed to get in a fight with this dimwit.

"You been walkin' Maria home?" he asked.

"Yup."

"Pup! Not any more! I'm gonna now."

He was a dense, belligerent guy with a real nasty smirk . . . But he was pretty tough. Still I knew how to "crack beans"—that is, butt somebody in the head. While he was waving his mitts around, I cracked beans with him a couple of times, and he left me alone.

But there was still no Maria. (Later on we found out that her father started not allowing her to go out at night.) I thought that she hadn't taken the least liking to me and that she didn't want to see me again because I was such a clam. Or, it was also possible that she was avoiding me, thinking that if she went out, I'd tear into her for not wanting to be my girl. That was how they did it around here. If a girl didn't want to be with some guy, she went out of her way to avoid him until a protector turned up.

And so back then I sat down to write a letter.

"Listen here, Maria," I wrote, "what are you doing going with that Ivan P.? You must be out of your mind! You really don't know that guy—he'll take advantage of you and dump you. You should avoid him like the plague, because he's already rotten through and through. And you're a ten-der girl. And his father is an enemy of the people and he goes around mak-ing enemies of everybody himself. So you watch out. Here's my advice: find yourself a nice boy, a modest one. You can walk to school with him and go out with him while you're at it. But make sure you get that fool out of your head—he's dangerous. Why did he drop out of school? Do you think it's true that it was because his family is poor? He spent some time in town, hung out with crooks, and now he's headed on a one-way road to prison. So you watch out. How are you going to look people in the eye when you go to school after the traveling circuit court meets at the clubhouse and sticks him with five years? You'll just burn with shame. What will your own mother and father say when he's taken off to prison? Stay away from him. Don't ever go out with him, steer clear of him. He runs around with the kind of people who are capable of cleaning out your apartment, especially since you're all on the wealthy side. He'll case your home for his friends. And if it should happen to be a night job, they could slit your throats. And he'd just watch and smile. You'll never find out who wrote you this, but it's a person in the know. And he only wishes you well."

There you have it.

Many years later, Maria, my ex-wife, looking at me with her sad, kind eyes, said that I had ruined her life. She said she wished me all the best, advised me not to drink too much—and then everything would work out fine for me.

This was unbearably painful for me—I felt sorry for Maria and for myself, too. I felt sad. I didn't answer her.

And that letter back then—I never sent it.

1968–1974

Uncle Yermolai

I remember an incident from my childhood.

It was harvest time. The threshing was finished early that day because it looked like rain. The sky was a dark, dark blue, and the wind was already blowing in gusts. We kids were glad about the rain, glad to get a break, but Uncle Yermolai the foreman kept glancing at the clouds with displeasure and dragged his feet.

"There won't be any rain. It'll blow over with the storm." He wanted to finish threshing the grain rick. But . . . everybody was already getting ready to go, and he, grudgingly, also started to get ready.

It was about a kilometer to the house which served as quarters for the work brigade. Once we made it there, the horses were let loose and we ate supper. By that time, the thick blueness of the sky had spread far and wide, but there was no rain. A strong wind blew in, kicking up dust . . . In the gloom, lightning trembled and flashed and thunder roared. The wind tore at you, carrying things in its path, but there was still no rain.

"Just the kinda night for thievin'," Uncle Yermolai said. "Well now Grishka . . ." Uncle Yermolai looked around and his eyes fell on me. "Grishka and Vaska, you go to the threshin' floor—you'll be spendin' the night there. To make sure somebody don't drive up on a night like this and make off with the grain. This'd be the night if ever there was one."

Grishka and I set off for the threshing floor.

The kilometer or so that we'd covered in just a flash a short while back now seemed long and dangerous to us. The storm had broken out in full force. Lightning blazed and thunder crashed all around us. An occasional raindrop stung our faces. It smelled like dust and something sort of scorched—sharp, bitter, like when you strike steel against flint trying to make a fire.

When the lightning flashed overhead, everything on the ground—the grain ricks, trees, mounds of sheaves bound together, motionless horses—seemed to hang in the air for an instant, then the darkness would swallow it all up again. Peals of thunder boomed out, as if huge boulders were tumbling off a mountain into an abyss, colliding and bouncing.

We finally wound up getting lost. We lost our way and couldn't find the rick we'd been threshing next to. There were lots of them. We'd stop and wait until the sky would light up. Once again it was as if everything would jump and hang for a quick moment in the dark blue glaring light, and once again everything would disappear, and in the pitch dark the thunder would roar.

"Let's climb into the very next rick we come across and spend the night there," Grishka suggested.

"Yeah, sure."

"And in the mornin' we'll say that we spent the night at the threshin' floor, nobody'll know the difference!"

We climbed into the warm, pungent straw of a rick that had already been threshed. We talked for a little bit, and instructed ourselves to wake up real early . . . And without noticing it, we fell right to sleep, and didn't hear it rain during the night.

The morning turned out to be clear, quiet, and refreshed after the rain. We had overslept. But since everything had gotten good and wet during the night, we knew our brigade wouldn't be out early to thresh. We set off for the house.

"Well, night watchmen," Uncle Yermolai asked when he saw us, and it seemed to me that he gave us a searching glance. "How'd your night go?"

"Fine."

"Everythin' out there okay? At the threshin' floor, that is?"

"Everythin's okay. What's the matter?

"Nothin'. Just askin' . . . I was the one who sent you, so I'm askin'. That's 'what's the matter.'" And he kept on looking at us. I started feeling uncomfortable. "Is the grain intact?"

"Yep." Grisha had round, bright eyes; he could look right at you without blinking. "What's the matter?"

"C'mon, where were you?! At the threshin' floor?"

The tip of my spinal chord, the tail bone, began to ache. Grishka also lost his composure . . . His eyes started blinking away.

"What do you mean, where were we?"

"Well, were you there?"

"We were. Where else would we be?"

And at that, Uncle Yermolai hit the roof.

"Oh no, you weren't there, you sons of bitches! You spent the night somewhere under a buncha bundled-up sheaves and are only sayin' you were at the threshin' floor! I'm gonna grab you two by the scruff of the neck like a coupla mangy cats and send you flyin' face first to the threshin' floor, face first! Where'd you spend the night?"

"How . . . What's the matter with you?"

"Where'd you spend the night?"

"At the threshin' floor." It was obvious that Grishka had decided to stick to his guns. I felt better.

"Vaska, where'd you spend the night?"

"At the threshin' floor."

"Of all the no good, friggin', low-down double-dealin'!" Uncle Yermolai even seized his head with his hands and winced in pain. "Just look at what they're tryin' to cook up! You weren't at the threshin' floor—you were missin'! I was there myself! Well?! A coupla good-for-nothin's, that's what you are! I went right after you did. I was wonderin' if you'd made it. And you weren't there!"

But this didn't rattle us in the least—the fact that he, as it turns out, had been at the threshing floor.

"Well, what about it?"

"What?"

"Well, um . . . we were there, too. We just got there a little later, that's all. We kept gettin' lost . . ."

"A little later where?!" Uncle Yermolai cried out. "A little later *where?!* I waited there till the rain ended! I didn't leave till it started gettin' light out. You weren't there."

"We were . . ."

Uncle Yermolai went berserk. Maybe in his eyes we had also popped up all of a sudden and were hanging in midair like yesterday's ricks and horses, and that's why his eyes had gotten so round and full of amazement.

"You were?"

"We were."

He seized a bridle and we tore off in different directions. Uncle Yermolai stood there for a moment, bridle in hand, then tossed it down, winced in pain, and went off, wiping his eyes with the palm of his hand. He wasn't in very good health.

"Good-for-nothin's," he said on his way out. "They weren't really there at all. And still they stand there and lie right to your face. I hope you croak 'fore your time. I hope you . . . end up marryin' a coupla real witches! . . . Good-for-nothin's. They stand there and lie right to your face—and it don't bother 'em at all! Oh! . . ." Uncle Yermolai turned to us. "Now you coulda told me honest-like: you got a-scared, mebbe you couldn't find it. No, they look you right in the eye and lie. Good-for-nothin's . . . If that's the way you're gonna be, I'm dockin' you five days' pay."

During the afternoon, while we were threshing, Uncle Yermolai approached us once more.

"Grishka, Vask . . . 'fess up: you weren't at the threshin' floor, were you? I won't dock you five days' pay. You weren't really there, were you?"

"We were."

Uncle Yermolai looked at us for some time . . . Then he asked us to come with him.

"Com'ere. Come on, come on. Now right here's where I hid to get outta the rain." He pointed. And looked at us entreatingly. "And where did *you* hide?"

"We were over on that side."

"What side?"

"Well, *that* one . . ."

"So where the heck is this other one?! Where is this other one?" Again he began to lose patience. "I shouted for you! I called your names! I walked all around it, the rick, that is. The lightnin' was flashin' so bright you could find a needle, to say nothin' of people. So where were you?"

"Here."

Uncle Yermolai needed every last bit of his strength to keep from hitting the roof again. He winced once more.

"Well, all right, all right . . . Mebbe you're afraid I'll scold you, huh? I won't. Just tell me honest: where'd you spend the night? I won't dock you the five days' pay . . . Where'd you spend the night?"

"At the threshin' floor."

"Where at the threshin' floor!!" Uncle Yermolai exploded. "Where at the threshin' floor?! Where, when I . . . Aaah, you good-for-nothin's!" He looked around for something to whack us with.

We ran off.

Uncle Yermolai went behind the rick . . . most likely to shed a few tears. He would cry when there was nothing else he could do.

Later on we did the threshing. He never did dock us five days' pay.

Now, many, many years later when I'm home visiting and I come to the graveyard to pay my respects to my deceased relatives, I see on one cross:

"Yemelyanov, Yermolai . . . vich."

Yermolai Grigoryevich, Uncle Yermolai. And I pay my respects to him, too. I stand over his grave and think. And my thought about him is a simple one: he'd always been a hard worker and a kind, honest man. As were, by the way, all the folks here, like my granddad and grandma. A simple thought. Yet with all my schooling and books I can't think it through to the end. For instance, was there some sort of greater meaning in this, in their lives? In the very way they lived their lives? Or was there no meaning at all, just work and more work . . . They worked and bore children. Since then I've seen all kinds of people . . . You couldn't call them sluggards, no, but . . . they look at their lives differently. And I also look at mine differently now! But it's just that when I look at those little mounds, I'm not sure any more. Which of us is right, who is smarter? No, that's not it—not who is smarter, but—who is closer to the Truth. And it's absolutely agonizing—it drives me to despair and fury—that I can't understand. Wherein lies the Truth? You see, it's just for the sake of looking educated, and slightly out of cowardice, that I wrote it like that—honored it with a capital letter, even though I don't know what *it* is. I'd like to take my hat off to somebody, but to whom? I love these people, under these mounds of earth. I respect them. And I feel sorry for them.

1970 (1971)

Text Notes

I Believe!

1. From Terence (Publius Terentius Afer), Roman comic dramatist (190?–159 B.C.): "Homo sum; humani nihil a me alienum puto" ("I am a man; I count nothing that is human indifferent to me").

2. This was a popular belief in old Russia.

Cutting Them Down to Size

1. The colonel should have said that it was Count Fyodor Rostopchin, the Russian governor and military commander of Moscow, who was alleged to have ordered the burning of the capital in the first days of its occupation by the French during the War of 1812.

2. Fili (now a suburb of Moscow) was an outlying village where a military council was held on 1 September 1812, at which the Russian commander in chief, General Mikhail Kutuzov, decided to abandon Moscow to the French, rather than risk the Russian army in defending it. Gleb is implying that the question they are debating is not of the same momentous importance as the one discussed in Fili.

3. The Russian titles are "Klub veselykh i nakhodchivykh," a quiz show, and "Kabachok trinadtsat' stul'ev," a sitcom. These two shows enjoyed great popularity throughout the sixties even as they were constantly criticized for their light, diversionary content.

Styopka

1. Styopka is quoting the first line from a poem by Sergei Esenin (see Glossary): "You don't love me, you don't pity me" ("Ty menia ne liubish', ne zhaleesh'").

My Son-in-Law Stole a Truckload of Wood!

1. Two rubles eighty-seven kopeks was the price of a half-liter bottle of cheap vodka in the 1960s.

2. *Aimak*—translated as "a district in Gorno Altai"—is a Turkic word for "district." Its use here suggests that the maker of "illegal" leather coats is a member of the native Altai minority.

Mille Pardons, Madame!

1. The year 1933 is a pointed reference to the time of Stalin's rural purges.

2. Pupkov comes from *pupok*, which means navel, or belly button. Bronislav, on the other hand, is an uncommon, old-fashioned name, slightly reminiscent of imperial Russia.

Stenka Razin

1. *Batka* (literally, "little father") is the Cossacks' endearing form of address for their leader.

2. Frol Razin claimed at the last minute to know the location of hidden booty, thus putting off his execution. In Shukshin's novel on Razin, *I Have Come to Give You Freedom*, Frol's act is depicted as a betrayal that tarnishes Stepan's own proud acceptance of his death sentence. Frol was decapitated five years later in 1676, shortly after Tsar Alexei's death.

A Roof Over Your Head

1. Vanya Tatus's statement is very evocative of a line from a play by Nikolai Gogol (see Glossary) called *The Inspector General* (1836) about a small provincial town whose corrupt leaders are roused to action by the news that a government inspector is coming to check up on them. Hence, Volodka's rejoinder.

2. ". . . like children, amid labor and strife unrelenting" ("kak deti, sredi upornoi bor'by i truda"). This quote is taken from a movie song by Isaak Dunaevsky and V. Lebedev-Kumach called "Marsh" ("A March") from the 1934 film *Veselye rebiata (Happy-Go-Lucky Guys)* by director G. V. Aleksandrov, whose films enjoyed great success in Stalinist Russia. Aleksandrov's movies and Dunaevsky's songs, while very entertaining for their Soviet audiences, were also highly propagandistic, orthodox productions that adhered closely to the precepts of socialist realist art. The whole stanza from which the line is taken goes as follows:

> We can sing and laugh like children,
> Amid labor and strife unrelenting,
> Nowhere and never surrendering,
> Since that is the way we were born.

3. Old Shchukar is a garrulous, clownish character from a novel by Soviet writer Mikhail Sholokhov, *Virgin Soil Upturned* (1931–1960). Sholokhov (1905–1984) was awarded the 1965 Nobel Prize for Literature for his novel *And Quiet Flows the Don* (1928–1940).

Alyosha at Large

1. *Ataman* is a Cossack term for leader.

2. Children attended school six days a week.

3. Alyosha means that soon it would be as fragrant as a forest and as hot as Tashkent, the capital of the former Soviet republic of Uzbekistan in Central Asia.

4. Shukshin is citing a well-known joke here. Due to censorship, however, he had to change "under the client" to "in front of the client," in the Russian text of his story. His readers, of course, understood what lay behind the euphemism.

Stubborn

1. Here, Monya is invoking a comment supposedly made by Galileo. In April 1633, the aged astronomer was brought before the Inquisition in Rome and, under threat of torture, was forced to recant his claim that the earth revolved on its axis. Legend has it that he muttered *"Eppur si muove!"* ("And yet it does move!") under his breath as he left the hall after making his recantation.

Let's Conquer the Heart!

1. This mispronunciation has several possible connotations. Kozyulin calls to mind *kozyulya*, an endearing form of the word *kozyol*, meaning "ass" or "goat," but also slang for "homosexual." *Kozyulya* is likewise a regional dialectal word meaning *gadyuka*, or "a vile, dastardly person." In addition, Kozyulin evokes the word *kozyavka*, which means "snot" or an "insignificant person."

2. The officer suspects that Kozulin is listening to a foreign radio broadcast, such as the Voice of America or the BBC.

Strangers

1. The White General was Mikhail Skovelev (1843–1882), a hero of the Balkan War (1877–1878). The nickname "White General" was given to him in the ancient Russian sense of supreme purity, as in "White Russia," "White Tsar," and "White [Orthodox] Faith."

From the Childhood Years of Ivan Popov

1. During World War II, many inhabitants of cities under siege or attack, like Leningrad, were evacuated to remote safe havens, where their skills were put to use locally.

2. "Babki" are cattle knucklebones used in a rural Russian children's game that resembles marbles. Kids compete to win the most babki by using them to knock as many other babki as possible out of a designated area.

3. The Russian term is *rogal*, which, like *rogach*, refers to the male of various species of animals with horns or antlers, such as deer or rams.

Glossary

Banya. The banya or (steam) bathhouse is a small log building that stands some distance away from the izba or peasant house, to protect the latter from fire. A stone stove *(pech-kamenka)* in which the fire is built occupies one wall. Stones, placed on top of the stove and heated, are in turn used to heat water for washing. The water is then poured over these same stones to generate steam. You wash yourself on a built-in bench (called a *lavka*) and steam yourself on a steaming shelf *(polok)*. While steaming, you switch yourself with a bundle of birch twigs (called a *venik*), which is supposed to improve circulation. The typical banya has no chimney (the smoke is supposed to escape through the door), so it is important to wait until the fire has burned down—and in the process, has completely heated the banya—before taking your bath. In Russia, the banya was not only a traditional means of cleaning yourself, but was also an important ritual associated with physical and spiritual health and served as a mark of the banya owner's hospitality toward his guests. This information has been summarized from Genevra Gerhart's *The Russian's World: Life and Language,* 2d ed. (New York: Harcourt Brace Jovanovich, 1995), 43–45, to which the reader is referred for more details.

Esenin, Sergei. 1895–1925. Most famous of Russia's peasant poets. Of peasant descent himself, Esenin wrote poems resonant of the rural Russian countryside, including ballads about animals and nature such as the poem about the maple tree sung by the priest in "I Believe!" Believing the Russian Revolution might offer a new order that would further the peasants' cause, Esenin threw his support behind the Bolsheviks, only to be bitterly disillusioned by their emphasis on the urban proletariat. In his own encounter with the city, Esenin often led a profligate life, keeping company with drunkards, prostitutes, and drug addicts. His disastrous marriage to the American dancer Isadora Duncan supplied scandal sheets with much material. Esenin eventually returned to the countryside, where his despair over his own unhappy life and the unhappy lot of his countrymen only deepened. He eventually committed suicide in a Leningrad hotel room, writing a farewell poem "Goodbye, my friend, goodbye" in his own blood. The Soviets suppressed publication of his works (deemed insufficiently informed by the spirit of the Party) until 1955. At the beginning of the "thaw" in Soviet culture, new editions of his work began to appear. Many of his poems were put to music and became popular as songs.

Gogol, Nikolai. 1809–1852. One of Russia's greatest prose writers. Best known for his play *The Inspector General* (1836), his novel *Dead Souls* (1842), and his short stories. Set in St. Petersburg, the most famous of these stories tell about downtrodden clerks, a renegade nose, and a stolen overcoat. "Viy," one of Gogol's fantastic tales, was first published in his collection *Mirgorod* (1835). Although early Russian and later Soviet critics hailed Gogol as the father of Russian realism, Gogol's own use of fantastic elements and his singular ability to spin whole narratives out of seemingly insignificant trivia lend his characters and stories a grotesqueness that often verges on the absurd. Gogol's dark sense of humor has been described as one of "laughter through tears."

GPU. An abbreviation for an earlier incarnation of the KGB.

Great Patriotic War. The Soviet name for World War II.

Izba. The traditional Russian peasant house. Made of logs, the izba consists of the following rooms: the entrance room *(seni);* the main room where the stove, sleeping benches, dining table, and icon corner are located; often an extra room *(gornitsa)* that can serve as a bedroom or a place to receive guests; and a cellar. The izba typically has no running water and no plumbing; izba dwellers clean themselves in the banya and use an outhouse. The izba usually has a small fenced yard *(dvor)* that, if large enough, can include shelter for chickens or livestock. Next to the izba is located a garden plot.

Kolkhoz (sovkhoz). The kolkhoz (*kollektivnoe khozyaistvo* or "collective farm") transformed private agriculture into a publicly owned, collectively run industry in the 1920s and 1930s, but was to a large extent replaced by the sovkhoz (*sovetskoe khozyaistvo* or "state farm") in the 1950s and 1960s. The sovkhoz was meant to transform the kolkhoz into a more disciplined operation, treating the collective farmers like hired workers and paying them a strict wage. The practice on the kolkhoz farm had been to allow farmers to participate in management responsibilities and to provide them a share of the farm's crops as part of their wage.

Komsomol. Communist Youth League for persons aged from fifteen to twenty-six. It was "designed to produce adults who accepted the fundamental ideological commitments and values of the Party proper and were habituated to its standards of unquestioning discipline." From Donald W. Treadgold, *Twentieth Century Russia,* 5th ed. (Boston: Houghton Mifflin, 1981), 268.

Kulak. A rich peasant. Kulaks were dispossessed of all their property during the implementation of collectivization (1929–1938). It was often hard to determine who should be considered a kulak, since peasant prosperity varied widely from region to region. The label was often applied for arbitrary, political reasons having little to do with a peasant's actual wealth. Villagers themselves were sometimes guilty of settling scores with each other by denouncing their enemies as kulaks. After collectivization, the term was used pejoratively to designate any peasant with material aspirations.

Lysenko, Trofim. 1898–1976. Soviet botanist who claimed that biological traits acquired environmentally could be passed on hereditarily. This view fit Marxist theory giving prominence to environment over other considerations and was largely responsible for Lysenko's rise, under Stalin, to a position of authority in the Academy of Sciences. Lysenko set back Soviet biology (and, consequently, agricultural practices) for decades and ruined the careers of many scientists who disagreed with him. After Stalin's death, Lysenko was removed from his post, only to be restored to a position of authority in 1957 under Khrushchev. Although removed from all high-level policy-making positions after Khrushchev's fall in 1964, Lysenko remained in charge of a major experimental station through the early 1970s.

Muzhik. A Russian peasant man. The word can simply denote a country-bred villager who generally works in agriculture, it can be used pejoratively to describe an ignorant, crude man, or it can serve as a colloquial term for man or husband.

Razin, Stenka. 1630?–1671. Don Cossack leader of the 1670 peasant rebellion during the reign of Tsar Alexei Mikhailovich Romanov. Although this widespread rebellion, which occurred some twenty years after the consolidation of serfdom in Russia (1649), enjoyed early success, it was put down in 1671. The handing over of Razin by the Cossack leadership, anxious to avoid reprisals from Moscow, marked the beginning of the subjugation of the Cossack host to Moscow rule. Razin was tortured, then publicly quartered and beheaded. The Russian Orthodox Church, under orders from the tsar, officially anathematized Razin, but the rebel leader remained an extremely popular figure in Russian folklore and epics. The well-known folk song "Iz-za ostrova na strezhen'" (From beyond the island to the deep stream) was popularized in the late nineteenth century. It relates Razin's drowning of a Persian princess, whom he had kidnapped to be his concubine during a raid of plunder. Razin throws her overboard—from one of the *strugi* used by Don Cossacks to execute their raids—when his men grumble that she has supplanted them in his affections.

Shock Labor. "The idea of 'socialist competition' . . . was first put forward by Lenin. In April 1929, a Communist Party conference passed a resolution on the organization of socialist competition, and in May the Central Committee approved a special resolution laying down the rules for displays of 'mass enthusiasm.' Thus was born a superior way for the laboring masses to 'demonstrate their enthusiasm and readiness to work,' known as 'shock work.'

"A shock worker was an outstanding employee who produced more than the economic plan demanded. . . . The word *udarnik* (shock worker) originally referred to the part of the breech of a rifle or gun that detonates the cartridge's percussion cap when the weapon is fired. During the First World War, the idea of 'shock' military units to carry out special operations and inflict concentrated 'shocks' on the enemy was developed. This use of a term from the military lexicon was no accident, since labor was being depicted as a war for socialism." From Mikhail Heller, *Cogs in the Wheel: The Formation of Soviet Man* (New York: Alfred A. Knopf, 1988), 119–20.

Sleeping Bench. High, raised platforms called *polati* located in the main room between the stove and the wall in the typical peasant house (izba). In an essay about his native region, Shukshin singles out these polati as an important part of his childhood memories: "Nowadays, you don't see *polati* any more (even in the most out-of-the-way villages), and when I conjure up my country (which I think I know quite well) in my mind's eye, I see the Altai—as if it were these dear *polati* from my childhood, a special world, tremendously dear to me. It may be that I always have this feeling of being perched high because the village I come from is on a rise, in the foothills, and perhaps it is just that these high beds, these *polati*, are associated with the dearest part of my life . . ." ("The Place Where I Was Born," in Eduard Yefimov, *Vasily Shukshin*, trans. Avril Pyman [Moscow: Raduga, 1986], 217–18. The Russian is "Slovo o maloi rodine" in Shukshin's *Voprosy samomu sebe* [Moscow: Molodaia gvardiia, 1981], 66.)

Sovkhoz. See Kolkhoz.

Stove. The traditional Russian *pech* or *pechka* is the center of the izba. Made of clay or brick, it serves not only as the place where food is cooked and bread is baked, but it also heats the entire izba and is large enough to provide sleeping berths for children and older members of the household. The stove is made to use fuel very efficiently. Most of its surfaces are only warm to the touch, hence the otherwise unimaginable ability of Russian peasants to "sleep on their stoves." The sleeping berths on the stove are considered the privileged spots to pass the night, especially during the long Russian winter. The stove is an important symbol of home and hospitality in the Russian folk imagination, and is often referred to as *matushka-pechka* or "mother stove."

Timofeyev, Yermak. ?–1584. Leader of a band of Cossacks. In 1581–1582, during the reign of Ivan the Terrible, he conquered vast territories in western Siberia that were promptly incorporated into the Russian Empire. Yermak's daring exploits in battle against various Siberian tribes became the subject of Russian folk songs and epic tales.

Vlasov, Lt. General Andrei. 1900–1946. He was captured by the Nazis in July 1942, while in command of an army attempting to relieve besieged Leningrad. Vlasov was allowed to form, from among Soviet prisoners of war, an army whose purpose was to fight against Stalin. Although the "army" was mainly a propaganda tool, historians have speculated that such a force might have been very effective during earlier stages of the war in winning popular support from those Soviet citizens who were willing to trade Stalin in for a new (albeit Nazi) government. At the end of the war, Vlasov was turned over by American and British forces to the Soviets, who promptly executed him. The name Vlasov was thereafter associated in the Soviet mind with the word *treason*, as is the name Benedict Arnold to an American.

Voroshilov, Kliment. 1881–1969. Early revolutionary and close ally of Stalin. Appointed marshal in 1935, he supported all of Stalin's purges in the military. President of the Presidium of the Supreme Soviet from 1953 to 1960, he was denounced in 1961 by Khrushchev, but subsequently rehabilitated in 1963.

Major Works of Vasily Shukshin

Novels and Short Stories

Sel'skie zhiteli (Country folk). Moscow: Molodaia gvardiia, 1963.

Zhivet takoi paren' (There lives this guy). Moscow: Iskusstvo, 1964.

Liubaviny (The Lyubavin family). Moscow: Sovetskii pisatel', 1965.

Tam, vdali (There, in the distance). Moscow: Sovetskii pisatel', 1968.

Zemliaki (Men of one soil). Moscow: Sovetskii pisatel', 1970.

Kharaktery (Types). Moscow: Sovremennik, 1973.

Ia prishel dat' vam voliu (I have come to give you freedom). Moscow: Sovetskii pisatel', 1974.

Besedy pri iasnoi lune (Conversations under a clear moon). Moscow: Sovetskaia Rossiia, 1974.

Brat moi (My brother). Moscow: Sovremennik, 1975.

Izbrannye proizvedeniia v dvukh tomakh (Selected works in two volumes). Moscow: Molodaia gvardiia, 1975.

Kinopovesti (Cine-novellas). Moscow: Iskusstvo, 1975.

Sobranie sochinenii v trekh tomakh (Collected works in three volumes). Moscow: Molodaia gvardiia, 1984–1985.

Liubaviny: roman (kniga pervaia i vtoraia) (The Lyubavin family: a novel [book one and two]). Moscow: Knizhnaia palata, 1988.

Sobranie sochinenii v shesti tomakh (Collected works in six volumes). Moscow: Molodaia gvardiia, 1992–.

English Translations

"Stories." Translated by Ralph Parker. *Soviet Literature* 5 (1964): 82–114.

"Inner Content." Translated by Avril Pyman. *Soviet Literature* 6 (1968): 138–45.

"Stories." Translated by Robert Daglish. *Soviet Literature* 12 (1971): 102–15.

I Want to Live: Short Stories. Translated by Robert Daglish. Moscow: Progress, 1973.

"The Obstinate One." Translated by Natasha Johnstone. *Soviet Literature* 10 (1974): 3–17.

"Short Stories." Translated by Hilda Perham, Robert Daglish, and Keith Hammond. *Soviet Literature* 9 (1975): 3–56.

"The Red Guelder Rose." Translated by Robert Daglish. *Soviet Literature* 9 (1975): 56–122.

"The Brother-in-Law." Translated by Donald M. Fiene and Boris N. Peskin. *Russian Literature Triquarterly* 12 (1975): 168–74.

"The Odd-Ball." Translated by Margaret Wettlin. *Soviet Literature* 10 (1976): 130–38.

Snowball Berry Red and Other Stories. Edited by Donald M. Fiene. Translated by Donald M. Fiene, Boris Peskin, Geoffrey A. Hosking, George Gutsche, George Kolodziej, and James Nelson. Ann Arbor: Ardis, 1979.

"Snowball Berry Red." Translated by Donald M. Fiene. In *Contemporary Russian Prose,* edited by Carl and Ellendea Proffer, 57–126. Ann Arbor: Ardis, 1982.

"Makar Zherebtsov." Translated by Marguerite Mabson. In *"The Barsukov Triangle," "The Two-Toned Blond," and Other Stories,* edited by Carl R. Proffer and Ellendea Proffer, 149–55. Ann Arbor: Ardis, 1984.

"Roubles in Words, Kopeks in Figures" and Other Stories. Translated by Natasha Ward and David Iliffe. London: Marian Boyars, 1985, 1994.

"Stories." Translated by Andrew Bromfield, Holly Smith, Robert Daglish, and Kate Cook. *Soviet Literature* 3 (1990): 3–106.

Short Stories. Translated by Andrew Bromfield, Robert Daglish, Holly Smith, and Kathleen Mary Cook. Moscow: Raduga, 1990.

Movies—Written and Directed

Iz Lebiazh'ego soobshchaiut (Lebyazhe calling). Moscow: Diploma Film at VGIK, 1961.

Zhivet takoi paren' (There lives this guy). Moscow: Gorky Film Studios, 1964.

Vash syn i brat (Your son and brother). Moscow: Gorky Film Studios, 1966.

Strannye liudi (Strange people). Moscow: Gorky Film Studios, 1971.

Pechki-lavochki (Stoves and benches). Moscow: Gorky Film Studios, 1973.

Kalina krasnaia (Red Kalina berry). Moscow: Mosfilm, 1974.